CONNECT

Julian Gough is the author of three comic novels and
was formerly the lead singer of the underground literary
band Toasted Heretic. He won the BBC National Short Story
Award in 2007 and was shortlisted for the Everyman Bollinger
Wodehouse Prize in 2008 and 2012. In 2011 he wrote
the ending to Minecraft, *Time* magazine's
computer game of the year.

Also by Julian Gough

Jude in London

Jude: Level 1

Juno and Juliet

For Children
with illustrator Jim Field

Rabbit and Bear: Rabbit's Bad Habits

Rabbit and Bear: The Pest in the Nest

Rabbit and Bear: Attack of the Snack

Poetry

Free Sex Chocolate

CONNECT

Julian Gough

PICADOR

First published 2018 by Picador
an imprint of Pan Macmillan
20 New Wharf Road, London N1 9RR
Associated companies throughout the world
www.panmacmillan.com

ISBN 978-1-5098-0984-4

1 3 5 7 9 8 6 4 2

A CIP catalogue record for this book is available from the British Library.

Printed and bound by CPI Group (UK) Ltd, Croydon, CR0 4YY

Visit www.picador.com to read more about all our books
and to buy them. You will also find features, author interviews and
news of any author events, and you can sign up for e-newsletters
so that you're always first to hear about our new releases.

To Solana Joy,

who saved my book,

and my life.

'The reasonable man adapts himself to the world; the unreasonable one persists in trying to adapt the world to himself. Therefore all progress depends on the unreasonable man.'

— George Bernard Shaw, *Man and Superman*

'First we build the tools, then they build us.'

— Fr John Culkin, summarizing Marshall McLuhan, 1967

Contents

1

The Cold Desert

This is a novel, set in the future. But it is also true.

It will happen, just like this, and soon. I know this, for reasons that will become clear.

Who am I? Well that's an interesting question. Obviously, someone is producing these words; writing this book; the guy with his name under the title. He's physically doing the job right now, in Berlin, on an old laptop, at an even older writing desk, in the corner of his bedroom.

But I'm not him.

This is a novel. Set in the future. But it is also true. Don't worry, it will all come clear in the end.

1

She walks into Colt's bedroom without knocking.

Her son is wearing the helmet again. He's moving his arms, his head. Playing in his gameworld. It's totally real to him.

The black plastic just covers his eyes, nose, and ears. Enough to keep out the universe.

He doesn't hear her. Doesn't see her.

Naomi hates watching this, but she can't stop. He's so like his father. As handsome. More handsome.

Colt shoots someone. Drops to one knee. Shoots someone else. Ducks the return fire. She knows the gestures so well. She's seen this so often.

He's killed them all. He unties the girl. He kisses the girl, or she kisses him. It's not clear from the sounds that leak out of his helmet into the room. But his mother knows exactly what he's seeing now. He sees his ideal woman, not wearing very much. Designed by him and his friends, mostly American and Russian teenage boys, so; small nose. Big breasts. Narrow waist. Wide ass.

Standing alone, beside his single bed, his pyjamas begin to bulge out at the front, and the bulge rises, changes angle.

In real life, he has hardly even spoken to a girl.

Naomi looks away, blinking. Glances around her son's small, dark bedroom, the drawn blinds keeping out the bright desert sunrise.

Electronics equipment and tools cover the small table.

Piles of old clothes on his chair, on the floor.

What a mess.

There; six, seven empty water glasses, half-visible in the shadows under the bed. Every glass in the house. Well, she can get those later.

She turns and walks silently, bare feet on the wooden floor, out of his bedroom. Quietly closes the door.

Walks away, down the short corridor, to the bathroom.

She loads up her brush.

3

'Toothpaste for sensitive teeth.'

Brushes carefully for three minutes. Leans down into the sink, and sluices out her mouth under the tap. Straightens up, rinses the brush, and flicks the bristles dry with her thumb. Lies it down, on the edge of the sink. Beside her son's toothbrush.

Almost eighteen, and never been kissed. Oh, Colt.

She picks up her brush again. Takes a deep breath, and closes her eyes.

Brushes again, harder, with the dry brush, till her gums bleed.

2

In the kitchen, Naomi hangs her silk jacket on the back of her chair. The jacket used to be her mother's, one of the few things she had brought with her from Nanjing. Naomi strokes the shoulder unconsciously, as though her mother were still wearing it.

From behind her, the fridge says, 'Don't forget your pill!' in a bright, friendly voice that makes Naomi grind her teeth.

Oh well. Colt likes it. I think . . .

It's hard to tell.

She goes to the fridge, takes out the pillbox, and closes the fridge door.

She pulls the snug, airtight pillbox lid straight up and it sucks free. She licks her little finger; lifts out a tiny green tablet on the wet fingertip. Gulps the tablet dry. Hesitates.

Opens the fridge again, and takes out the cool silver tin in which she keeps her fresh ground coffee.

She glances towards the kitchen door. If Colt was here, he'd be lecturing her. He's usually straight in after her. Probably still caught up in the game. Good.

'Coffee inhibits absorption,' says the fridge, and Naomi knows she's projecting, but . . . the fridge sounds sad. Worse; disappointed in her. 'Drinking coffee is not recommended within an hour of . . .'

'Oh, shut *up*,' says Naomi.

It shuts up.

She puts the silver tin down carefully on the countertop. Quietly unclips the lid.

4

She leans down over the open tin, and inhales the rich, warm, bitter, complicated, comforting smell.

Then she looks for the Italian stovetop coffeepot, while her conscious mind splutters and rages and says no, no, no.

Oh yes. Top shelf . . .

She takes down the small aluminium pot. Unscrews the top.

Her hands automatically pour the water, spoon the coffee, screw the pot back together, while her conscious mind says no, no, no.

She switches on the old electric cooker.

This really isn't a good idea . . .

She heats some milk. Whips it into stiff foam with the little hand-held frother, just as the coffee comes bubbling and gurgling through into the aluminium pot.

Coffee interferes with absorption . . .

Her hands assemble a cappuccino.

I need to control my levels . . .

She makes Colt a smoothie, and puts it on the table.

Puts a box of granola on the table.

Goes to the cupboard, picks up a bowl. No, wait; that granola tastes weird with coffee. And she'd rather have the coffee. She puts back the bowl.

I can eat in the lab.

She sits down with a sigh, and lifts the cappuccino to her lips.

Colt walks into the kitchen. He's wearing the helmet, but the game's switched off, so the visor is clear. He can see her.

Naomi's hand, holding the cup, lurches reflexively forwards, to hide the coffee behind the box of granola. Warm foam slops back over the cup's lip, onto the handle, her hand; drops in a slow glop to the table.

Fuck it.

She brings the cup back up, and takes a slow, deliberate sip. It's delicious.

'Your smoothie's on the table,' she says.

He looks at the coffee in her hand.

'Did you take your tablet early, or something?' he asks.

'Drink your smoothie,' she says.

He goes and gets a straw. Green, to match the smoothie. Sits across from her.

'You shouldn't drink coffee with your tablet,' he says. 'It interferes with absorption.'

She puts down the cup, to lick the foam off her hand. Picks up the cup, takes another sip. Drawls in a French accent, 'Well, maybe I want to be interfered with.'

Colt frowns. 'That doesn't make *sense*, Mama.'

Naomi reaches up and, turning a big, invisible dial, says, '*Click.*'

These days, Naomi only does that when she really, really wants to change the subject. When pursuing the point will mean shouting, and crying.

Colt changes the subject. 'Have you got your chimpanzee yet?'

Naomi groans, and reaches for the invisible dial again.

Colt rocks back and forth in his chair, almost imperceptibly.

Naomi's hand stops, in mid-air. No. It's a fair question. She drops her hand back to her side. 'They're not giving me a chimpanzee.'

Colt takes a drag on his smoothie. 'Why not?'

'Too expensive. Too much paperwork. Ethics Committee weren't happy. They gave me about fifteen different reasons.'

He makes the smiling, worried face that means, seriously?

She does the little shrug and smile that means, no, I'm exaggerating. 'Five, six reasons,' she says.

'You could appeal again,' says Colt.

'I could, yeah.'

'You're giving up.'

'Yes.'

'Mama, you could just test it on me.'

Is he joking? But he never jokes.

Oh my God he's serious.

'NO, Colt.'

'I trust you.'

'Colt, it's a completely untested, experimental procedure . . .'

'It's not untested, it works . . .'

'It works in mice! Not people!'

'But—'

'—And it took me months to find a way to make it work in mice, and mice aren't complicated. I wasn't worried about preserving their memories, or their personalities . . .'

'But you've dealt with the cell membrane integrity problem . . .'

6

'*How do you know that?*' Sharp, she's way too sharp, and he winces. Hunches his shoulders. 'Colt?'

But he closes his eyes, starts humming.

This could be bad . . .

She wants to walk around the table and comfort him, touch him, hold him, but she can't – her hug's like an electric shock when he's like this, he bucks and screams – and so she rocks in her chair, in unconscious sympathy with his rocking, and watches his face writhe. My God, he's really trying to engage today.

Oh Colt thank you, I love you, come back, yes . . .

He opens his eyes, says without looking at his mother, 'I read your new paper.'

'Colt, you can't . . .' She tries to modulate her voice, not close him down with her emotions, but she's, inexplicably, scared. And angry.

She glances towards the kitchen counter, at her screen, but it's switched off, and folded up like a sheet of paper. No, of course, he must have read it in her office. The only copy is in her data safe.

'Please, Colt, you have to stop hacking into my files. It's not fair. I need some space. Some privacy.'

'You've solved the problems.' He won't look at her. Mumbles, 'You're ready to go on primates. Please.'

'I've solved the old problems. There are always new ones.' She shifts in her chair, trying to catch his eye. 'Look, realistically, it will probably kill the first couple of primates. The official risk assessment was not good. That's why the Ethics Committee won't . . .'

'But they don't know how important this is.'

'I gave them the general outline . . .'

'I saw your application. You didn't tell them . . .'

'Colt, I'm not even sure I want to do it.'

'Why, you think God will be mad at you?'

It's her turn to stiffen. 'Look, changing people . . . so fundamentally . . .' She can't talk about the sacredness of the human creation, that will just set him off, she'll have to rephrase it. '. . . It's not just a religious problem. Even in secular, ethical terms; once you have two classes of people . . .'

'No, you're changing the terms.' After a couple of years of religious argument, Colt has gotten pretty good at fighting her inside her own logic. 'If God *made* you,' he says, 'then God could be acting through you.'

Yes. She has thought that. But what if He's not?

'Let's not argue about religion,' she says. 'We end up playing two different language games; it can't go anywhere.'

'OK,' says Colt.

They are connoisseurs of each other's OKs. And that's not a good OK. She studies his face. He looks down. Takes another drag on his smoothie.

'Did StemCellCon accept your original paper?' says Colt.

'No.'

She doesn't have to explain herself to him.

He drinks more smoothie.

There's a silence.

'Did you submit it?' he says.

Oh, this is ridiculous. Who's the parent here? 'Honey, forget it, the deadline's passed.'

'But, if you . . .'

'You were fighting again,' says Naomi.

'When?'

'This morning.'

'Oh yeah. I *told* them and *told* them and *told* them I didn't want to fight. But they wanted to fight.'

Naomi sighs so deeply the froth on her cappuccino dimples, and stays dimpled. 'So what did you do?' She takes her third sip; it's OK. The first sip is always the best, by far.

'I gave myself infinite ammo, and I killed them all and I took their women.'

'I don't want you doing that.'

'They're not real women, Mama. Well, one of them turned out to be real . . .'

'No, I don't want you killing the people that annoy you.'

'It's only a game, Mama.'

Wait a minute, back up. There was something odd about his voice there . . . 'What do you mean, one of them turned out to be real?'

But Colt shakes his head hard, doesn't want to talk about it.

Naomi feels a hot shiver of embarrassment on Colt's behalf, at

8

the thought of him trying to be a man with a real woman, and so she puts it with all the other stuff she doesn't want to think about. If he wants to talk about it later, he'll bring it up.

She takes another sip. Takes it slow, tries to savour it.

If only all sips could be first sips.

'That's the problem, Colt,' she says. 'You can't do that in real life.'

'What?'

'You can't just change the rules to suit yourself.'

'But you want to change things, Mama. You change things in the lab. You change the rules of *life*.'

'No, I don't want to change things. I'm a scientist. I just want to observe, and understand.'

Colt is shaking his head. 'You can't observe a thing without changing it. You're part of the universe. When you get extra information, that's already a change.'

Why did she start this? Now he's not drinking his smoothie.

'There's a difference, a *lot* of differences,' she says, 'between playing a game, and doing research.'

'OK, great, they're different. So why can't I change the rules? It's my game. And sometimes the rules turn out to be dumb.'

'In real life, you don't have infinite ammo. In real life, they can kill you.'

'I can tell the difference, Mama.'

She glances at the time. Plenty. Oh well, if they were going to argue, they may as well argue about the big stuff. She takes in half a mouthful of coffee. Pushes it to the front of her mouth with her tongue, sucks it back hard through her teeth, swallows. 'I think you're spending too long in the helmet.'

Colt is rocking back and forth again. But he's engaging, he's not shutting down. He's improving.

He clears his throat. 'There's a guy in China played for six days straight. Without sleeping. That's the record.'

Oh dear lord. 'Look, he must have taken off the helmet at *some* point—'

'No.' Colt is starting to rock faster. 'He *didn't*.'

'Fine, fine! He didn't.' This wasn't going anywhere. This never went anywhere.

9

'There was another guy did it for eight days,' said Colt, 'but he died.'

3

When the argument is finally over, Colt returns to his room.

Naomi stalks out into the hot desert air, swings the door shut with a bang.

Damn.

Big gestures never work.

Forgot my jacket.

And my screen.

She goes back in quietly, grabs them, leaves again. Closes the door carefully behind her.

As she walks past the little patch of velvetleaf senna bushes, she strips off some leaves, and stuffs them in the jacket's pockets.

Keeps walking, to her old Pontiac under the awning.

She throws the jacket across onto the passenger seat so hard that some of the leaves tumble out and fall to the floor. She sighs, and gets behind the wheel. OK, let the day begin . . . She reluctantly switches on the screen, and it unfolds to hand size, glowing with bad news, messages, reminders . . .

Hmmm. There's an alert from the game, from this morning. Colt triggered parental controls. Not just a warning; the game-world shut him out. So he was definitely doing, or trying to do, *something* with that woman. Or she was, with him . . .

I really don't want to think about this right now.

The car starts, and she listens with a critical ear to the hum of the electric motor. Was that a rattle? No.

The sharp smell of the senna leaves soothes her. She pulls out onto the road, and heads for work.

She knows it's a terrible car because everyone says so, but she bought it with her own money and she likes it, and the safeties will kick in if she screws up. It isn't logical; she knows a newer, fully self-driving car would be far safer; but the lack of control makes her nervous. And they *do* get hacked remotely, sometimes, even if it's rare.

Luckily, Nevada still allows people to drive their own cars; it just jacks up their premiums.

Nevada still allows pretty much everything, if there's money in it.

4

The Casey Biological Research Facility is high on the sunny side of a valley, a few miles beyond the advancing eastern edge of Las Vegas. Land's still cheap out here. And it's going to stay peaceful around the facility, too; they can't have neighbours, by law, because they sometimes handle pathogens.

As she crests the hill, and swings down into the valley, she glances in her rear-view screens. The road, always prone to early morning mirages, even back when it had been just plain asphalt, was recently coated with a matt-black high-efficiency solar-capture surface.

Naomi has grown fond of this newest section of the Federal Highway Solar Grid; and not just because buying her electricity live from a solar road surface on the way to work is cheaper than charging at home . . .

There it is. Her timing is just right. The sun has already heated the flat black river of road so that a thin layer of warm air sits on it, held in place by static, beneath miles of cool, dense, early morning mountain air.

The pale blue sky, refracted through the unstable lens of inverted air, pulses and flickers on the ground like water, and the dreamscape of Las Vegas, tiny and distant, shimmers up out of a lake that isn't there; the top of the Luxor pyramid, the Eiffel Tower, the Empire State Building.

The whole world, dissolved in light.

She arrives at the facility, a low sprawl of connected labs and offices, and parks the car in the shade, behind Lab 3. Plenty of room. She's early, as usual. Though, to be fair, she gets to park in the shade even when she isn't early. Because everyone else is always late.

Naomi walks across the hot asphalt of the parking lot towards the main entrance.

She sees a small delivery drone make a rooftop parcel drop, to her office.

Oh, good, my caterpillars. They'd better be well refrigerated . . .

The drone rises, heads off back to the warehouse.

Not for the first time, she wonders why they don't just paint the asphalt outside the labs white, if they're not going to use it for solar, so it won't pointlessly soak up so much heat.

Hmm. Donnie's car. Parked by the front door. Laaaaaazy man.

As she steps inside, the hairs on her arms rise at the temperature drop, and she puts her jacket back on.

Shannon's not at her desk in reception, of course, so Naomi just walks on into Lab 1, no one.

Lab 2, no one, the doors popping open at her approach. Good. After the security breach a couple of weeks earlier, they'd tightened up access so much that, for a few days, all the lab doors locked at her approach. A massive pain in the ass.

Speaking of which . . .

Lab 3, Donnie Glassford, leaning over a lab bench.

Her boss. Looking like a shaved gorilla in a Texas Longhorns shirt, as usual. And sober, which is less usual. A pleasant surprise. There's even a mug of coffee by his elbow. Admittedly he hasn't actually drunk any of it, and it looks cold and scummy.

He straightens up, looks Naomi over, pausing in the usual places. 'No Colt today?'

Ugh. She studies the faded, peeling decal on the mug, to avoid looking at him. A Texan flag flies above the words 'Remember the Alamo.'

'He wanted to stay home, work on his game.'

Donnie nods. 'Uh huh . . . be with you in a minute.'

Donnie goes back to work, on a mouse. He's removed the entire left frontal lobe by the look of it. Nothing complicated. As Donnie always says, 'It isn't brain surgery, ha ha.' The top of the mouse's skull sits discarded on the bench, a few inches away, like a tiny bicycle helmet.

Naomi recognizes the mouse. Well, not the individual mouse. But it's a research strain she's familiar with; a hairless albino, with a genetically engineered tendency to develop brain cancer.

She glances at the frontal lobe. Wait, this is one of hers. What the *fuck* is Donnie doing with one of her mice?

With his right hand, Donnie lifts the unconscious mouse by the tail, leaving the top of its skull on the bench. With his left hand, he removes the thick insulated lid from a small flask of liquid nitrogen. It boils over furiously, like a cartoon volcano, white vapour pouring down the sides, heading across the desk like a tiny fogbank.

And he's let the nitrogen heat up too much, she thinks. If he's going to leave it there for the whole operation, he should have used a larger flask. Better volume-to-surface area.

But her anger's already starting to fade, as the fear kicks in. Donnie doesn't do lab work.

The mouse, brain still exposed, twitches in Donnie's hand. It's going to wake.

Donnie dunks it in the flask of nitrogen, leaving only the last half inch of tail held in his fingertips. Tiny volume, relatively large surface area; the mouse freezes to the core in seconds. Donnie pulls it out, turns, hesitates, with the frozen mouse dangling over the bench.

'Damn,' he says. 'Sorry, Naomi. Forgot the foil. Will you roll me a sheet?'

'Sure.' She tastes a sudden squirt of sick in the back of her throat, swallows.

Swallows again.

Naomi tears off a sheet of aluminium foil from the roll, lays it on the table.

Donnie lays the mouse across it diagonally, wraps it like a burrito, labels it with his ungloved hand, picks it up in his gloved hand, and throws it in the freezer. Pushes down the lid till it clicks.

'I've been talking to the Ethics Committee,' he says. He picks up the mug of cold coffee, gives it a startled look, and puts it back down again.

'Oh.'

'Called in a couple of favours. Looks like we might get a couple of chimps through.'

'OK,' she says. After a long ban, research on chimpanzees has only been legal again for a couple of years, to help researchers deal with the various primate-to-human epidemics. Getting permission to work on anything that isn't SIV, Benin fever, an Ebola mutation, or F-strain flu is *incredibly* difficult. She knows how hard he must have worked to get this. 'OK.'

'So if you could just publish . . .'

'No.'

He sighs. 'Look, everybody here knows you're doing great research. But if you don't publish . . .' He puts on the voice of some old TV character, she has no idea who. '. . . *It don't exist.*'

She has an abrupt, vivid memory of the exposed brain of the last big mammal she worked on. A dog with nerve-sheath degeneration. Big black mutt.

Oh, I got too close.

Pain research. A long time ago.

She ran tests on the dog, a week after she'd destroyed its ability to block pain. Trusting, dying, it still licked her hand.

She blinks away the memory, and shakes her head. 'It's not ready.'

'It doesn't have to be ready. You know; better if it isn't. Ask the big questions, say the method shows promise, blah blah, preliminary results, yadda yadda, and we can get funding to look for the answers.'

'Working on it,' says Naomi, looking out the window at the blue sky. 'Nearly there. Just need some more data points.'

He doesn't like it when she looks out the window.

'If you don't publish preliminary findings, it's really hard to get a budget,' he says. 'Got to step it up.'

'I know.' She keeps looking out the window.

'Seems you have a habit of not publishing papers.'

Woah. This is a new angle of attack. 'What do you mean?' she says, and now she's looking at him.

Donnie shrugs.

'*What do you mean?*'

'Impressive, the work you did on Barbary ducks.'

'How would you know that?' Those ducks, my God. One of her first pieces of research, from her time at Berkeley.

'Those are remarkable papers,' he says. 'Really remarkable.'

'Who . . . where did you get them?'

'A lot of stuff in there I didn't know.' He looks her up and down as he speaks. 'Sure, I knew that, with Barbary ducks, the sex was . . . coercive. I knew the females had evolved corkscrew-shaped vaginas, with all kinds of fake exits and dead ends, to outwit the guys; but your paper . . . it really made me look at them differently.'

'I never published that paper. Any of those papers.' She notices her voice is trembling. Fear? Anger? Both. Oh God, it's like she's caught someone reading her diary.

'Well, that's what I'm *saying*,' says Donnie, and shakes his head. 'You really should've. That stuff you did on the guys, tracking the way their penis evolved, so it could evert and ejaculate up a corkscrew, ah, vagina, in a tenth of a second . . . and that whole genital, whatever, arms race, with the duck vaginas changing the direction of the corkscrew, to keep the guys out . . . fascinating. You should have been proud of it.'

'I was. I am.'

'Three great papers. But you didn't publish any of them.'

'Who gave you . . . where did you read them?'

'Your conclusions in, was it the third paper, the reproductive-strategy paper – yeah – they were particularly, ah, intriguing.'

Even his mention of that paper fills her with the same complicated tangle of emotions she had felt back at the time. 'I was out of my area . . .' Wait, why is she distancing herself from it? It's a good paper. Even if . . .

'A genital arms race, driven by rape,' muses Donnie. 'Rape as the dominant reproductive strategy . . .'

'The female still had a great deal of control over her vagina,' breaks in Naomi. She tries to remember the paper's conclusion, but there's a cloud of shame and fear associated with it that makes it hard for her to think straight. 'Females could block the—'

'—Yeah,' Donnie just bulldozes straight through her, 'but kind of intriguing, that the winning evolutionary strategy for female Barbary ducks is, basically, to make sure they are raped by the strongest rapist.'

'That's not what I said . . .'

'Hey, I get it,' Donnie interrupts, and winks. 'Sex is dangerous.'

She bites her tongue. Looks up at the ceiling; down at her feet.

Oh, those ducks. Those strange months, watching them rape and be raped, while her marriage to Ryan broke down. Studying a culture in which affectionate, consensual sex between equals had become impossible; worse, a disastrous error, producing unsuccessful offspring.

They had backed themselves into an evolutionary situation from which there was no way out.

They had bred love out of the system.

Watching those ducks, it was impossible not to think of her mother and father's strange, bleak marriage; of her own complicated, messy, painful life.

By the time she was finished, she wasn't sure if she'd written a scientific paper or an autobiography.

It was a great study.

No, she didn't publish it.

'I mean there's rape culture, and there's *rape culture*, oh boy,' says Donnie. 'I hadn't realized male Barbary ducks were four times the weight of the females. Sure, you didn't apply the findings to any other species, but it kind of explains football players.' He laughs.

She doesn't.

She's worked it out now. It's obvious.

'It was Ryan, wasn't it?'

'Mmmm,' says Donnie. 'You might want to keep Colt out of the lab for a few days.'

'Look,' she blurts out, 'I'm sorry, Donnie, but . . .' Then she realizes he's not hitting back at her, he's just changing the subject. 'Why?'

'Shannon says to tell you, you might be getting a surprise inspection later in the week.'

'Seriously?' OK, this is more urgent. 'Urgh. When?'

'Probably Thursday. She'll tell you when she knows.'

'Oh, great. OK.' He's an insensitive twice-divorced misogynistic idiot, but he could be worse. Be polite. 'Thanks, Donnie. And say thanks to Shannon.'

'Sure.' She's lost his attention. He's playing with a little hand-held chemical cauterizing tool like he's never seen one before. Jesus, maybe he hasn't.

Come *on*. He knows you're wondering. Just ask him.

'Why are you dissecting my mouse?'

'It was injured. The other mice had attacked it. And I was interested in how your work was coming along. You've been keeping pretty quiet.'

She glances involuntarily at the frontal lobe.

'Yeah,' he says drily. 'So it seems to be going well.'

How much does he know? Her face is beginning to ache from the effort of not showing him her emotions.

'Was the mouse . . .' She stops. Oh, there's no point in not asking. 'Was it exhibiting any unusual behaviour patterns?'

'I only saw it for a couple of minutes, but, yeah, it was its behaviour that stopped me.'

'What was it doing?'

'Fighting. Your big maze, the one with the cameras sucking data on movement and choices. This guy was holding his own against maybe a dozen other mice.'

'How?' She knows the cameras will have caught it, and that getting into a conversation with Donnie about this right now is unwise, but her curiosity's too much.

'It was using the maze as a three-D space, jumping walls to shake off pursuit.' Donnie frowns. 'Very fast reaction times. It seemed unusually aware of its environment. Kind of weird to watch. It will all be on the cameras. They trapped it, eventually, in a dead end with high walls. Overwhelmed it. I pulled it out alive, but it was, you know, basically a goner, so I did a quick autopsy.'

She wonders how true that is. The body had looked undamaged. She thinks the word *asshole* so fiercely she's afraid for a moment she's said it aloud, and she clenches her jaw. Unclenches.

'OK,' she says. 'I'll analyse this.' She scoops the frontal lobe into a coolbox before he can react, and heads for her lab.

'Naomi . . .'

If he slaps my ass, I'm going to break his arm.

She waits till she is in her lab, with the door closed behind her, and locked with an old-fashioned metal key and bolt she's installed herself, before she finally allows her face to show her feelings.

Her whole body relaxes, as she quietly snarls, rolls her eyes, sticks out her tongue.

Feels good.

5

Her lab is familiar, calm.

Better feed the caterpillars.

There's an automated feed system, but she likes to believe the caterpillars benefit from regular fresh leaves. Monarch butterflies, *Danaus plexippus*. Everybody's favourites.

A couple have already started to pupate. About to break down, and rebuild; transform completely.

She carefully takes the cool glass lid off the quiet tank, puts it down.

Leans in, smells the soil.

As she pulls a handful of leaves from her jacket pocket, the silk of the jacket is cool and smooth against the back of her hand. The soft fuzz on the surface of the leaves gives pleasure to her finger-tips. She strokes the leaves, absent-mindedly, as she notices her own voice is still going around and around, arguing with Colt, inside her head; and she realizes it's been going around constantly since breakfast, right through her drive to work, right through her conversation with Donnie. Whoops. She takes three deep breaths.

One . . . two . . .

Better make it five.

OK.

Look at the leaves, the caterpillars crunching through them, really look at them.

Be here now.

They're so *alive*.

Intense, vivid colours.

Just . . . little packets of life.

No, I don't want to change the world, she thinks.

But she sits at her desk and dictates detailed notes anyway, her voice a little shaky. The results from the last trial really were extraordinary.

And she doesn't have to publish. No one can make her.

6

Back at home, after work, she walks to Colt's bedroom, and stops at the door. Listens.

Nothing. But that doesn't mean much.

She reaches out, to knock; but her knuckles pause short of the door. Naomi hasn't really looked at, really noticed, the door in a

18

long time. It is covered in posters, stickers, handmade signs from every stage of his life. She unclenches her fist, and brushes her fingertips gently across the rough red paint of a sign at eye level.

Her eyes prickle, and she blinks.

Colt made it, with a big, messy kid's paintbrush, a few months after they'd moved into this house; after she'd left Ryan. Ten . . . no, God, almost twelve years ago.

Colt had used red poster paint, and a sheet of paper taken from his mother's printer. Half the hairs on the brush were bent or broken, sticking out sideways, so there are little scratches of red outlining the main letters. It says 'No Burglars'. Actually, it says 'No Burg' and on the next line 'lars'. Colt made it after a neighbour's garage was broken into. He was six. He'd been worried the burglars would rob their house, steal his toys. Couldn't sleep.

After he put up the sign, he felt totally safe again.

The power of words, written down.

Coffee, she thinks, I need coffee; and dismisses the thought. She listens. No sound. She, very gently, turns the handle of his bedroom door. Swings the door open a little, slowly.

He isn't in his bedroom.

She searches the house for him, but he isn't there.

She goes outside. Walks around the house. No sign of him.

She circles the house again, further out.

She finds him, still wearing his helmet, but otherwise naked, lying face down in a sandy patch of ground beyond the mesquite bushes, halfway up the ridge.

Her heart slams, slams again. As she breaks into a run, her legs feel heavy, heavier. Like she's lifting sacks of wet sand. It takes seconds to reach him, but the seconds are immense, exhausting.

She drops to her knees beside him on the warm ground, afraid to touch him, wondering where to touch him; looking for blood, for damage.

Every detail looks strong, sharp. Vivid.

His body in the low sun, the vertebrae under his tanned skin casting curved shadows the length of his back. Like tiny sand dunes.

The flexible black plastic band at the back of the helmet, holding it on, is scratched and scuffed.

The pale marks on his arms . . . Her mind flinches, and she glances away.

His clothes – faded grey Road Runner T-shirt, black jeans, red boxer shorts, the micromesh skinsuit he wears for gaming – are in a heap a few yards from his body.

The sand. Little stones in the sand. A couple of dry mesquite twigs.

A round plastic floss dispenser.

A cigarette butt, bleached completely white by years in the sun.

Everything has incredibly well-defined edges. She's pulling all the visual data out of the incoming images, analysing them fast and hard, looking for unusual patterns.

Looking (though she is not consciously aware of this) for tracks in the sand – snake, coyote, human, whatever.

She's looking for blood, for a weapon, for (this is a funny one) a syringe. Years ago, in college, Naomi found her roommate lying face down in the bathroom with a syringe beside her; so to see Colt's body, face down, legs at that angle, unlocks that old pattern from memory: body + syringe = explanation, and so Naomi's brain checks for that pattern, that explanation, and her eyes dart to where the syringe was, so many years earlier.

But it's not there. Relief, that it's not there; anxiety, that there's still no explanation. Her body produces so many chemicals in reaction to all these conflicting inputs that they begin to interfere with each other. She feels jittery and unable to think.

He moves his arms, in a slow, swimming motion. Moves his legs. Swimming in the warm sand.

'Oh for fuck's sake, Colt,' she says, and closes her eyes and all her muscles untense, and she lies down beside him.

'*Mama*,' he says, turning his head, his helmet, towards her. No, he doesn't like it when she swears. She normally only swears inside.

He used to do this when he was four, five, six years old. Swimming in the sand. He said he liked the way the warm sand felt on his skin. Then some kids at school heard about it, laughed at him, and he stopped. Stopped when he was maybe seven. He hasn't done it in a decade.

'You scared the shit out of me,' she says, stretching out in the warm sand.

'Mama, I've written a new level. I've integrated it into the game.' His voice is dreamy, again. Far away. Happy. 'It's set in the desert. It feels totally real.'

'It *is* real. You *live* in a desert,' she says, exasperated, relieved, sick. And she can hear it in his voice, that she's not really there, in his world. That he's talking to a ghost, out of politeness.

'But this desert's better,' he says. 'It's totally real. I've improved the sun.'

'Colt, the desert in your game is not real.' She leans forward and tries to see his eyes through the dark glass of his visor, but can only see herself lying beside him, her face bent and smeared across the curved surface. He's disappearing. 'There's a difference between seeing the world, and seeing a picture of the world. Even a great picture of the world. It's a serious difference. An important difference.'

'No, there isn't. All we can ever experience is our own nervous system. All we ever see is a picture of the world.'

'But a picture based on reality, based on something that is actually there . . .'

'You don't understand.' He turns his head away, in the direction of the sun. 'I can see the corona. I can see the solar flares.'

'I totally understand that you're excited.' How can she get this through to him? 'It's great that you've improved the graphics. But . . .' He's not listening. '. . . if you could just . . .' She tries to stop herself saying it, but these words, said together so often, have welded themselves into one unit, and she's started it, so it finishes itself automatically, '. . . live in the moment . . .'

He hears that, all right. The sun flashes off his visor, as he turns fully to face her. He isn't mapping her into the game; he can't see her; she's just a voice entering his game, his world, from outside, like a conscience.

'Nobody lives in the moment!' he says, and his voice is a little high-pitched, shaky. 'We don't have access to the moment! Where do you get these ideas! It's bullpoop, *bullpoop*. Our brain just predicts what will happen next, and creates a picture of that.' He's not afraid to get angry when he's inside the helmet. 'But it's not *real*, it's a *guess*. We live half a second in the future—'

'I know, look—' She feels a little sick.

'—because if we only saw what was *already* there, and reacted to *that*, our reaction times are so slow we'd be *eaten*.'

'I know—'

'—We live in the future, we act in the future, it's just we're so used to it we don't notice—'

'—I *know*.' She stands up, brushes the sand off her legs.

'—until our projection of the world fails to *map* accurately, and we step on a step that isn't there, or we—'

'—But the whole idea of a map implies there is something *there* to map onto—'

'Sure! But we can't know it, so who *cares*?'

'But if you don't even *see* the real world, how can you live in it . . .'

'I *do* see the real world, you're not even *listening*, I'm trying to *explain* . . .'

They're shouting at each other now. But the louder she gets, under this empty blue sky, the smaller she feels. Loud sounds go nowhere, change nothing. They just wander off into the desert to die.

'Colt . . .'

'I can see the *real* flares,' says Colt. He looks up at the sun, and it seems to calm him. 'I see the real flares, in realtime. That's why it's so cool.'

She takes a breath.

Another.

Another.

Tries to step back from her emotions. Just concentrate on the breath.

But thoughts are looping and firing, and he's so like his father, and her memories of shouting are attached to so many other memories that the thoughts take over her breathing and she's not concentrating on her breathing she's just gulping big breaths and saying no to the memories. She realizes her visual centre has pretty much switched off, that she's been seeing and reacting to nothing but memories for ten, maybe twenty seconds.

Stop.

Be here now.

The world leaps back into focus. Her son. The desert. The sky.

He has stood up too, and he's putting his clothes back on, starting with the stretchy, skin-tight micromesh suit.

The red boxers.

Jeans.

Road Runner T-shirt.

His favourite . . . Oh, it's so small now . . . Jesus, he's cut the seam in the neck, so he can pull it on without removing the helmet . . .

She can't see his face, so she concentrates on his hands. Watches his fingers flexing as he dresses.

It's real, I'm here, this is real. Talk. Calmly, calmly.

She remembers why she wanted to talk to him.

Tomorrow . . .

One downside of living in Nevada is the chronically underfunded school system.

One upside of living in Nevada is the chronically underfunded inspectorate.

She'd pulled him out of school nearly a decade ago, and this was only the fourth inspection.

She really *had* intended to home-school him, but they'd driven each other crazy. And what with hanging out in the lab, and working on his own projects, he'd done pretty well. It just wasn't a standard education, that was all. And it would take a little prep to fake one.

'We're going to have to play at home-schooling on Thursday.'

'Oh, Mama.' He turns away and stares at the sun through the visor.

'I know. Shannon says the inspector should be . . .'

But it's hard to derail Colt's train of thought once it's got moving. He turns back to her.

'Wait, I haven't explained yet—'

'Colt, this is serious. If they think you haven't been getting a proper education, they could . . .' She debates whether to say it. Says it. '. . . Order you back into the school system . . .'

'I'm not a kid! I won't go. I won't go.'

'I know! I know! But we need to go over what we're going to say to the lady.' How to get the importance of this through to him without scaring him, without closing him down? But he's not even listening.

'OK. Later. OK,' says Colt. 'I need to explain. I'm getting data from . . .'

'*Jesus*, Colt.' Her voice comes out with too much power, anxiety, adrenalin.

'Mama, I am trying to explain! I thought you'd be pleased. I thought about what you were saying. That I was spending too much time ingame, and losing touch with crapworld . . .'

'*DON'T CALL* . . .' Calm down! Too loud, too sharp. 'Please . . . don't call it that.'

'OK, OK, losing touch with the "real" world.'

'But you are . . .'

'OK, OK, OK, OK. Stop saying it.' He rocks back and forth on his heels a few times, mutters a few words, she can't catch them.

'Sorry, sorry,' she says. Just go with it. Let him finish his thought.

'So I built more of the real world into the game.'

'The sun?'

Colt nods. 'I'm getting pictures from the new ESA solar orbiter. It's sending back realtime images in the ultraviolet, and I'm taking the data and doing a realtime mapping of that into the graphics of the game. Adjusting for latitude, time of day, my head angle. All that. And I've built in a 300 per cent zoom, and gone for low intensity, high contrast, so I can see detail. Sunspots. The corona. Ejections. It's nice, a bigger sun in the sky.' He's getting calmer now. She's listening to him. 'You should try it. The original ESA images are fairly high definition anyway, and mapped into the gameview, onto the original sun, even blown up they're only 3 per cent of the visual field, so they end up ultra-high def. And it's all real; you just can't see it normally with your eyes.'

He looks straight at the sun, through his visor. The glass goes black. His mother vanishes from his peripheral vision. The enhanced game sun reappears.

Strong sunspot activity, he thinks. Crazy strong for this part of the cycle.

He watches a small flare, just coming into sight around the curve, high on the northern flank. It had started about two hours before. Hardly making it free of the surface, before being sucked back down into the magnetic pole. A flare big enough to envelop the earth.

He turns in the direction of his mother, because she likes him to face her when speaking. The game offers to map her onto a game character; bring her ingame as a beggar, or a pedlar, or a prostitute; but he silently declines. He knows where she is and what she looks like. There's no need to have her spoil the empty desert.

'I see *more* than you,' he says, 'not less.'

'Yes. I get it,' says Naomi. 'About the inspection . . .'

The nightmare that had woken her the night before comes back; Colt standing alone beside her dead body, ticcing, tapping patterns, talking to himself, alone in the world, about to walk out the door and be destroyed.

She shakes her head as though a fly has landed on her face, and suddenly, very vividly, for the first time, she imagines him dying before she does. The thought – the image of his empty room, the silence of the house – leaves her shaky, exhausted.

'But did you listen to me, Mama? Did you hear me? It's good, isn't it?'

'I'm really glad you tried . . .' she says. 'But this wasn't what I meant.'

Suddenly he turns away.

'What? Because I like it . . . No. You don't have to . . . I don't care.'

'Who are you talking to?'

'Some asshat,' he mutters.

'Why do you play that game, if the other people upset you so much?'

Colt shrugs. 'You wouldn't let me kill him, so now he's here upsetting me. What can I do?'

'Just walk away, Colt.'

'How far?'

'It's . . . use your own judgement.'

'Your way doesn't work, Mama.' And he hesitates. He knows she doesn't like him mentioning his father. She says it's OK, but he knows it isn't. But he has to say it, to be understood. 'Dad always said it was important not to show fear.'

'And look how well that turned out,' says Naomi. Fights every day, till she'd pulled him out of school. 'Your father is not a good guide to social skills.'

'But . . .'

'I'll get dinner ready,' she says. 'Ten minutes, all right?'

'Yeah,' he says. He takes the thin bio-feedback gloves out of his pocket, pulls them on, and lies back down in the sand. He wants to test some physical-feedback mapping. And it feels nice.

She doesn't walk away just yet. He turns his face in her direction, but he doesn't lift his head. The helmet rotates in the sand until the minimal faceplate is pointed at her. The dry sand hisses as the helmet rotates. She bites back an impulse to say, don't scratch it. It's his, he built it. She can't see his face through the opaque glass and plastic.

He's looking in her direction but she knows he can't see her.

'Mom, I haven't written you into this level. If you want to hang out, I can write you into it.'

'No, it's OK,' she says. There is a pause. Her eyes are watering. Must be the sun. It's low in the sky, but still hot, and it's right in front of her. She moves around till the light comes from behind her. That's better. Her shadow falls across him.

'Could you move?' he says. 'Please? You're spoiling the game.'

'It's rice and peas. I'll get it ready. Come in when you're done.'

7

The next morning, Colt is in the kitchen early. As she walks in, he is busy doing something with the eye controls, inside his helmet. From the angle of his head, from the tension in his shoulders, from experience, she suspects he is writing something in there. Code? No, a message; now he sends it, she knows that head gesture.

'Colt?'

He turns to face her, and clears his throat.

Guilty sign. *Very* guilty. Probably has a guilty look on his face, but you can't tell, because he's still wearing that fucking helmet so you can't see his eyes.

Clears it again. And again, a couple of times.

Uh oh . . .

8

Meanwhile, in Boston, a young man swipes open a document. Starts reading, frowns. Reads on a little. Chuckles. Reads some more. Laughs. He sends it onward to a young woman in San Francisco. She reads, frowns, chuckles, laughs, reads some more. Sends it to an older man in New York. He reads, frowns, keeps reading, keeps frowning.

All three of them keep reading. Now they are all frowning. And reading. Frowning and reading on both coasts. The transmission has taken about three minutes.

Two hundred years ago, it took three weeks to get a single message from one coast to the other.

Five hundred years ago, you couldn't get a message from one coast to another. No matter how much you wanted to. No matter how rich you were. How powerful. Nobody had ever made the journey.

Eight hundred years ago, there was nobody on earth who knew the shape of this continent and the distance from coast to coast. Not even the people living on it.

The previous five billion years? Nothing.

You think it's some kind of coincidence that you are here now, in the only moment in the history of the universe when we could have this conversation? You think it's a coincidence there's suddenly eight thousand million of you, building a brain for the world?

9

Back in Nevada, Colt clears his throat three more times. 'Yes?' Naomi says, and leans forward to hear what he has to say. He clears his throat again, five times. 'Cough it up,' says Naomi, 'it won't kill you.'

He clears his throat eight times, an identical noise each time. Pause. He clears his throat thirteen times.

'Jesus,' she says, 'this must be a bad one.'

'Got to BALANCE them,' says Colt.

'I know, I know,' says Naomi. 'But there aren't usually so many to balance.'

He keeps clearing his throat for another couple of minutes. She eats her granola, idly counting the coughs, while a bad feeling rises and slowly overwhelms her.

So, no coughs, then one, one, two, three, five, eight, thirteen . . . Fibonacci numbers. Each number is the sum of the previous two numbers.

Twenty-one coughs, then thirty-four . . . Oh God, it'll be fifty-five next, then eighty-nine, his poor throat. This is a bad one. What has he done?

But the next one is twenty-one again.

He's counting back down. Oh, thank God. Yes, thirteen again . . . It'll be eight next.

It is.

Could be worse. Like last Christmas, when he coughed the first seventeen prime numbers, and lost his voice for three days.

When he has balanced his sequence, she puts down her spoon. She knows she should wait for him to start; that if she shows any anger, he will retreat again.

She can't wait.

'You were doing something,' she says. 'When I came into the room. It's something to do with that, isn't it?'

He can't lie. Doesn't try. 'I sent your limb regrowth paper to StemCellCon.'

'COLT! It isn't ready!'

'I explained all that.'

'All WHAT?'

'I explained that you were afraid to finish it, or send it, because of, you know, your personality . . .'

'My PERSONALITY? You . . . MY personality is . . . Sorry, sorry . . .'

He puts his head down, and grinds his teeth in a rhythm as he speaks, she knows that one – an old one he hasn't done in a while – but he keeps speaking. '. . . And that therapy hadn't helped you.'

'It helped me . . . sorry, sorry . . .'

'. . . And that I was your son, so they wouldn't think I had stolen it, and that I thought the paper was already good enough.'

'But it really isn't ready . . .'

'You said that last year. You would have said that next year. It's ready.' He ground his teeth for a few seconds, in a new pattern she couldn't recognize. 'YOU'RE not ready. The paper is good.'

'But it's after the deadline. I missed the deadline.'

'I told them it was an emergency, and to read it as a priority. I said you were sorry for being late and you wouldn't do it again.'

'Honey, that's just for kids, you don't need to say that . . .'

'It's a great paper,' says Colt, his head bent over so far that his throat is constricted and his voice comes out gruff. 'People drop out, they add stuff, all the time, right up to the conference.'

'It's too late!' she says, too loud. 'Sorry . . .'

He is ticcing like crazy, tapping the table with his hands in a rhythm, tapping the legs of the table, to either side, with his feet; trying to keep talking against the desire to shut down.

He doesn't want to look at her, but he knows she likes it when he looks at her, so he raises his head. Looks into her eyes. 'You always tell me it's never too late,' he says. Holding his gaze there, against the resistance, he feels a familiar, painful, burning sensation in his own eyes, but it's working, she is listening. 'You always tell me that when someone is special, then the system has to make an exception.'

'But I'm not special,' says Naomi.

All the tics stop. This one is easy. There is no internal resistance. 'Yes you are, Mama.'

She can't think of anything to say. She looks away, looks around the room, for something, for what, a way out? A way out of what?

'But what if they say yes?' she says.

'Then you'll go,' says Colt, and for a second Naomi thinks he sounds like his father and she gives a little involuntary *huh*.

'We don't have the money, honey,' she says.

'If they accept the paper, they'll pay your flights and hotels.'

'You won't eat.'

'I will.'

'You won't eat proper food.'

'I will.'

'You'll just play games all day and forget to eat.'

'You can make me smoothies. Leave them in the fridge.'

'You can't just eat smoothies.'

'You can put vegetables in them.'

Hmmm. Major concession.

'Peas?' she says. Get this nailed down. No wriggle room.

'Sure.'

'Carrots?'

'Sure.'

'Spinach?' she says. Pause. OK, she got carried away. Pull back. 'Just a little spinach. With a lot of peanut butter.'

'Yes.'

'And you'll drink them?'

Pause.

'Yes,' says Colt. 'As long as they don't go off or something. But I'll leave the spinach till last. So I can't *guarantee* I'll have eaten it by the time you get back.'

Hmmmm. OK, don't push it. There are bigger issues. 'I can't just . . . leave you. I could ask Shannon to drop by . . .'

'NO!'

'OK, OK . . . but I have to have some way to . . .' Careful. '. . . to know you're all right . . .'

'*No cameras*, Mama.'

She nods. 'I know, no cameras.' She glances up, in reflex, at the far corner of the kitchen ceiling. He'd broken all the house security cams with a chair, in a rage, years ago. Yes, the aluminium bracket was still there, painted over . . . Her heart lurches as she remembers. He'd started with the camera in his bedroom. She'd been watching him, worried about his comics habit. Inappropriate comics. She'd finally shouted out a warning from the kitchen, and he'd lost it.

Reading too much. Imagine, that used to be her biggest worry . . .

'But can I monitor . . . just send me your heartbeat. Just so I know you're OK. I'll wear my old bracelet.'

He thinks about it. 'OK, Mom. Just my heartbeat, though.'

She smiles. 'Don't worry, I only want your heartbeat.'

The last time she'd had to work late on a project, when he was fourteen, she'd monitored everything, obsessively. His helmet sent her an outline of his heartbeat, brain activity, electrodermal activity, breathing rate, movement . . . Too much data. An hour after she left, he'd laughed so hard at a cartoon, he'd slipped off his chair. All the data spiked. She thought he'd had a seizure, and rang him in a screaming panic that had terrified him.

He'd hung up, switched off everything, and she thought he'd died. Called an ambulance. Drove home sobbing . . .

She shakes the memory out of her head. 'Just your heartbeat.'

10

Later that night she kicks off the sheet, in her sleep. It's too hot. She lies on her back, dreaming. Her eyes flick back and forth beneath the thin skin of her eyelids. Her nipples stir, and rise. She moves her legs apart, and moans.

11

They accept her paper the next morning, and she has two days to organize, worry, and pack.

12

The morning of the flight, as she arranges Colt's smoothies along the cool bottom shelf of the refrigerator in a neat line, she thinks about New York. Unconsciously, she tilts her head back, as though looking up from the bottom of a skyscraper canyon.

The sky made too small, pushed too high by the black glass cliffs.

The rivers of cars roaring past, a few feet away.

The honk and bray and squeal of horns and tyres, like animals fighting, fleeing, fucking.

The thought of New York fills her with primal terror.

She closes the refrigerator door more abruptly than she'd intended, and hears the smoothies in their glass bottles rock and clink against each other inside.

She walks, fast, to her room, and throws open the door so hard she knocks their little solar-powered DustMight halfway across the room.

Damn. Last thing I need, having to buy a new cleaner.

The small squeaky old bot must have been sitting just inside the door, recharging in a pool of sunshine. It wriggles its legs in the air – Colt modified it a couple of years back to look like a turtle – rights itself, and gets out of her way.

She strides past it, to her jewellery drawer.

The DustMight squeaks away to safety under the bed, and starts quietly cleaning.

Naomi digs out her old health monitor, powers it up, changes settings until the soft silvery warm plastic pulses gently against her wrist. His heartbeat, in realtime. It calms hers.

She smiles. It was a fashion for a while, for lovers to do this. Mirror each other's heartbeats, till they synchronized.

There is something else she wants.

Gold, she thinks.

Where is it?

She can always pawn the gold ring. There are still pawn shops in New York, aren't there?

It is as though she fears that if she leaves Colt behind, civilization might immediately collapse, and all the computers fail, and electronic money with them. She knows this is insane. But nonetheless, that is how she feels.

She pulls the drawer further out, and sees the black-and-silver Beretta pistol Ryan gave her one Christmas, for protection. Tiny, designed for a purse or pocket. With almost no barrel, it looks strange, not quite right; like a toy for adults. Ryan made her learn to shoot it, on a firing range; but she hasn't touched it since he left. No, I'm not bringing a *gun* . . . She glances involuntarily at the top of the wardrobe. The ammunition he left behind is still up there. Where she used to hide Colt's Christmas presents, and her vibrator . . .

She shakes memories out of her head.

The ring is at the back of the drawer.

Buried under everything.

Her body automatically slips the ring onto her finger, without her conscious mind noticing. Deep programming, a routine run thousands of times since she was a little girl. Very simple, she could code it in a few lines. See a ring; pick it up; roll it back and forth between finger and thumb; find the most comfortable finger;

No—
Maybe—
Yes;

Slide it past the knuckle; examine the ring on the finger while rotating the hand.

Her body lifts and turns her hand in front of her face.

The ring bends the whole room into itself, pulling Naomi's shocked face into a liquid curve, like matter about to vanish down a black hole. She shakes her head so hard her hair slaps her cheeks.

She pulls at the wedding ring; pulls harder; and the skin of her knuckle bunches and jams, and she can't get the ring off.

His fucking ring.

Oh God *damn*.

She has stuff to do, the flight leaves soon, she's already tight for time . . .

Calm down.

She studies the stuck ring. Golden light comes off it, the light of the sun. She thinks about the photons, as they strike the back of her eye. She thinks about the speed of light.

Of one photon. A packet of energy, released abruptly by some tortured atom.

People don't understand the sun, she thinks. It's having a breakdown. An incredibly slow breakdown.

As a kid in San Francisco, she used to think the sun was God. She would walk out of church with her mother, and stare up at God, smiling down on her.

Now she lives in the desert and the sun is no longer God and its light has no meaning and is too harsh.

She remembers when she just saw the ring, the pretty ring, the sparkling light. The surface was enough. The stuff she knows now – about light, and gold, and the universe – scares her, makes her feel small. It's beautiful too, but it's too big, too much. God has moved further and further away and now she can't see him at all. She's not sure where he can be. The universe got bigger and bigger, the gaps were filled with dark matter, dark energy, and now there's nowhere left for God to hide.

Her mother believed, right to the end.

She wipes the sleeve of her dress across her eyes, hard.

Pulls open a second drawer, reaches into the back; rummages around. All that ridiculous stuff . . .

There. An old bottle of lubricant. She wipes the dust off the shoulders of the bottle; flips the lid back.

Drips a drop to either side of the golden loop. Works the lubricant into the dry skin of her knuckle.

Slowly, carefully, she removes the ring.

13

Naomi looks out the window of the plane. Nevada is crumpled up beneath her like corrugated cardboard, range after range. Grey, treeless ridges, running north to south. She looks down into the hidden valleys; a glint of water. That's where the trees hide.

Ryan never saw the valleys, she thinks, he only saw the mountains. Oh, what does that even mean? She's so tired.

She rests her forehead against the window. It is cool. She closes her eyes and sees Ryan's face, looking away from her, looking down, on some mountains, the Rockies? Yes, out of an airplane window, unaware of her studying him; a memory, from some flight together, long ago.

She studies him again, in memory, and, without opening her eyes, she rubs the inside of her left wrist gently with the fingertips of her right hand, and says a word to herself. A word she has never said aloud.

She expects to feel the vibration of the engines through the window, through her forehead; but she doesn't.

Double-glazed, she thinks woozily. Rubber seals.

Listening for the vibration of the engines, she notices, instead, a high-pitched whine from somewhere inside the cabin. So constant, she had been filtering it out.

Compressor? Part of the air conditioning maybe . . .

It matches a noise she carries inside her.

More memories. Let them come. She's safe. Eight miles high.

Oh, San Francisco . . . One Saturday afternoon, when she was very young, and her family still lived in the old rotting wooden house in Outer Sunset, her father came home sober with a small white plastic box that had an electrical plug sticking out the back.

She followed her father into her room, and watched as he plugged it into the socket beside her bed. Nothing seemed to happen. She asked him what it was.

He knelt down, stroked the white plastic box with his hand, and explained that when you switched it on, it gave out a sound that was too high-pitched for humans to hear, but that mice could hear it, and it scared the mice. It was very loud to them, because their tiny ears could hear the very short waves of high-frequency sounds. It reminded them of the shriek of an owl. And she wouldn't have mice in her room any more.

He switched it on, and she heard, like a tingle in her brain, like something very far away, at the top of a mountain, a shriek so high-pitched it was almost not there. 'I can hear it, Daddy,' she said.

'No, you can't,' said her father. 'It's your imagination.'

'No, I can really hear it.'

'I hear nothing,' said her father.

She lay in bed that night, listening to the high-pitched shriek. It reminded her, too, of the shriek of an owl.

She never saw a mouse in her room again. She had never told her father that she liked the mice in her room, that she had given them names. And it was too late now.

Going to bed each night from then on, she knew she could hear the shriek. But her father had assured her she could not. Therefore she could not hear the shriek. So she acted as though she could not. She believed she could not hear it; but she knew she could hear it. Whenever she thought about this split in her mind, her chest grew tense, and it became hard to breathe. So she tried not to think about it.

The shriek in her bedroom continued for the rest of her childhood.

14

Colt hesitates. He really needs those components. He's done so much work on this project already, it would be a shame not to go through with it, while he has the chance.

And it's only a few dollars more. Mama won't miss it. And she still owes him money for chores, from last year.

Colt hits 'Buy Now'.

I guess maybe I am going to do it, then.

15

Naomi wakes, with her heart pounding. Her neck is stiff and twisted.

She blinks at a pale void. Not sure where she is. Her bedroom? She tries to focus. But the grey before her eyes won't resolve, it just gets darker.

No, there's something, right in front of her face.

So close, it hurts the muscles in her eyes.

Tiny white crystals, an inch away. Frost.

Her head is against an airplane window.

She's on the plane. Now she remembers.

Not in her bedroom. Not a kid, no. Thank Christ. That shriek, it's the plane.

They are descending through cloud.

The plane sways, lurches, and Naomi's face bangs, very lightly, against the window. She sits back in her seat.

OK. Landing soon.

Wait, there was something she needed to do. She slides a hand into her pants pocket; yes, all her money is still there, in loose notes; she had been in such a hurry in the airport, at the ATM, she had just shoved it all into her pocket, and run.

She pulls them out. New dollars. Crisp, a little plasticky, all with a single off-centre angled crease. She studies them. Hmmm. She preferred the old design, but that's progress. Too easy to copy.

Carefully, she distributes the notes between all the pockets of her blouse and jacket and pants. Just a fifty in her purse. In case she is mugged. They won't get everything. Her father taught her this, the day she left for college. Back in the days of cash and credit cards. Knowledge from his years as a minor Party official in Nanjing, selling even more minor Party jobs to the highest bidder. Sewage workers, who wanted their son to wear a suit. Taking bribes in cash and goods. Six televisions under a tarpaulin on the balcony. The complicated dance involved in getting his illegal assets out of China, the bribes he had to pay in his turn, and in the end, after all that effort and risk and fear, it was just enough to buy a rotting house with bad plumbing, and he couldn't hold down a job in the new world, couldn't stop drinking, couldn't make it work.

She hides her dollars inside tissues in all her pockets. The last thing he taught her; she never saw him again. Just a waxy body wearing his suit. Not him.

She counts it, as she distributes it, and her throat dries. Will it be enough? It will be enough. It has to be enough.

She's left Colt with some money, and food in the fridge, and instructions on how to order a pizza, in case the food runs out.

She knows, logically, that she can do everything, pay for everything, electronically, automatically; but this primitive fear she feels, travelling to a big city, is calmed by a little cash in her hand, gold in her pocket, as though she were going back in time, or into a fairytale world.

Gold. A sword. Dragons.

Everything is fine.

Her father took money too seriously. All the money he smuggled out of China, and then lost straight away, buying that lousy money-pit of a house. And then making small, stupid, ever-riskier investments with the little he had left, trying to make up for that first mistake. Thinking he was clever, thinking he understood money, understood America.

Naomi's uncle burned piles of money on the day of his brother's funeral, struggling with the lighter by the graveside in the breeze off the bay. Not real money, fake notes, to symbolize money, so her father would have it in the next world. The Catholic priest looked puzzled, but said nothing. Her mother looked on, stonefaced. She'd lied and told the priest yes, her husband had been Catholic all his life, too.

Money is dirt, muttered her mother beside her. *Money is dirt.*

Naomi looked up, away from the grave, at the blue sky, the white clouds, the flecks of glowing ash ascending to where God used to be. Some green notes blowing into the open grave . . . She missed her stupid, angry father.

She missed God.

Focus. You're landing soon . . . Wait, do I have enough pills in my pillbox . . .

She jerks upright in her seat, the seatbelt tightening.

Oh no . . .

Her snort of embarrassed laugher is so loud, the old white woman across the aisle turns to look at her.

There are more than enough pills in her pillbox.

But the pillbox is still in the fridge.

Well, I've always felt conflicted about taking them . . .

She smiles as she remembers. It's a wry smile. She'd been friends with some of the team in UC Berkeley who developed the active ingredient. Pfizer first launched it as a mildly effective anti-anxiety medication. But they'd only tested it on men; in women, the little green pills turned out to have the unfortunate side effect of completely suppressing the libido. The drug was a major flop.

But when Pfizer rebranded and relaunched it, as a successful sex-drive suppressant for women too busy for sex (with the happy side effect of slightly lowering anxiety), it was a huge hit. So huge, they got bomb threats, from young men angry that Pfizer had helped millions of women escape from ever having to date them.

I guess my subconscious wants me to have a good time in New York . . .

Naomi had started taking them a couple of years after Ryan left. By then, the ache of desire, with no outlet, was making her cry two or three nights a week. She didn't want to bring men home to Colt. She didn't want to stay out. She didn't want to date. Her work was so interesting, and her son was so exhausting (and, yes, rewarding, but mostly exhausting), that there was no energy left.

And yet, and yet, this desire . . .

So she took the pills, for years, till she'd almost forgotten what she was taking them for.

She tried to ignore fierce debate in the media, over whether what she'd chosen was freedom, or oppression. The backlash from men. The attempts, from left and right, to ban it.

Well, I got a lot more work done . . .

She crosses and uncrosses her legs. Glances around at the men and women in the cabin, most of them staring at screens. Hmmm.

Is she . . . does she feel . . . no, it's purely psychological, there can't be any noticeable effect yet.

The plane hits the wet runway, and skids a little sideways in the crosswind, and everyone moans, but Naomi feels curiously unafraid. The momentary illusion of danger takes her mind off her real worries; her conference paper, Colt, money, pills; and calms her.

And if she is going to die, she is pretty sure it will not be on a plane. It would be statistically absurd.

She might be scared. She might be broke. She might be anxious. But she's still a scientist.

16

Colt logs in through the security screens. Spends a few minutes trying to work out the outgame identity of that girl who touched him, ingame; the girl he touched . . . But the game supports anonymity, and she's covered her tracks well.

He gives up, and checks the to-do list.

The new servers, in Rio and Iceland, seem to be bedding in fine. No problems.

But the game's automatic debugger has flagged something in the weather systems of the test range; a shared realm that Colt designed.

The test range is a playful, gameworld version of the Nevada nuclear test site. It's not as grittily realistic as the local desert realm Colt's built for his own use; but the test range is popular, and problems there affect a lot of people.

Besides, the test range was where he learned to code. He took on the challenge of filling that part of the American map *because* it was hard. Because there was almost no data. A top-secret site, so he had no detailed, ground-level images to work with; just a few old declassified photos and some Russian and Chinese satellite images. He had to solve a lot of problems himself, with raw code. It's where he made his reputation. It's a kind of home for him.

And for millions of others. The gameworld, in all its many versions and flavours, with its public and private servers and realms, its cool, calm creative mode and brutal survival mode, has always been essentially a sandbox, where people come to create and destroy, to act out their fantasies, a lawless, open-source Westworld; but the test range is a realm where you can create and destroy on the grandest scale.

Colt has a quick chat with the debugger AI. The debugger says it's done a temporary fix but, as there are issues of aesthetics involved, it wants a human to make the final decisions.

Fair enough. The last time the automatic debugger had been allowed solve a problem involving clouds, the big thunder-heads it generated looked like giant buttocks. (There was still a jokey, ingame sub-religion that studied the sky on the Sabbath, awaiting the miraculous second coming of God's Ass, and a faecal apocalypse.)

Better deal with it.

So what exactly is the new problem . . .

He skims through the change logs for the past twenty-four hours.

Hmm. Lots of new work, from different contributors.

Something's clashing . . .

Colt reads the bug reports.

17

Weather in the game has always been divisive, for historical reasons.

There was a philosophical discussion among the first coders, which got wildly out of hand. The New Atheist faction wanted realistic weather, obeying the laws of physics as encoded in the Game.

The other side wanted the weather to be more metaphorical; driven by something a little like God. Something outside the laws of physics. These were the hackers who had done magic mushrooms; or (the hardcore) ayahuasca: who had broken open their minds with psychedelics and come back to their bodies hours later shivering, with new information about the universe, information they didn't understand. And they wanted to do justice to that information.

They didn't exactly believe in God; but they believed in unseen forces; in connections we cannot perceive. They believed in some-

thing meaningful, that was bigger than themselves. They didn't know this, because they didn't have a name for it, but they believed in me.

So the New Atheists wouldn't tolerate the hand of God inside the game. And the psychedelic voyagers wouldn't tolerate a strictly mechanical universe. Stalemate.

They finally came up with a solution: map the weather onto the activity of a shadowy, mysterious entity that was everywhere and nowhere, but that actually existed in the physical world. Both sides accepted the compromise.

And so the gameworld used the NSA, and later the National Domestic Security Agency, as a proxy for God.

The NDSA moved the weather.

The hackers were tracking the NDSA anyway, because the NDSA was tracking them; so they had the data. NDSA activity was mapped to the weather in the game. A big hack, and a big NDSA reaction, created storms.

Their battles with the NDSA, with the huge, distant father, who knows everything, who pushes His way into their minds, who reads their thoughts; their battles with the Old Testament God of the NDSA, with Yahweh, were written in the sky.

18

Ah. Colt breathes out a satisfied *hmmmm*, as he sees the problem. Clouds close to the ground are freezing in place when they hit the mesas.

He calls up the code and starts to troubleshoot.

OK, that smart new coder, the Snow Queen, has added a nice, nuanced piece of code. More realistic cloud movement, better ice formation. Good. But that's not it . . .

These . . . Oh, it's the Brothers Karamazov, again.

Colt sighs.

In real life, the Brothers are teenage Ukrainian twins, going crazy with boredom in some Saharan state, where their dad works for a solar infrastructure company. They like to rewrite code, with more enthusiasm than skill, even if it doesn't need rewriting.

They must have rebuilt the algorithms for generating desert

landscapes last night; but in doing so they'd broken the Snow Queen's code, which depended on data generated by the old algorithm.

Not a big deal right now, when there are hardly any clouds, but there has been a massive security breach at a US bank overnight; probably Chinese government proxy hackers; and the NDSA are going nuts.

The game will be throwing up a storm soon. This needs to be fixed tonight.

He solves the problem in a few minutes. Then he writes fresh code for a few hours, till his brain gets tired.

Then he walks outside, with mapping on, and runs the new code.

The game has always taken the things in crapworld, and incorporated them into the gameworld – a truck becomes a wagon, a distant plane becomes a bird – but the new code blends them better. He wants to explore his local, private, desert realm ingame, with mapping on: but every time he gets out of sight of the house, it goes glitchy.

And there's no reception at all beyond the ridge at the back of the house.

The FCC keep pushing down the output of wireless devices, in response to bullpoop health scares about bullpoop, *bullpoop*.

He gets angry thinking about it. The sun and the earth pour far more unstructured data through everyone, all the time, on all these frequencies. OK, he'll have to build a booster. He orders some more parts on his mother's credit.

The day just drifts away, until it's too late to go to his mother's lab. To do what he has planned to do for over a year.

Months of working on the problem casually, just to see if it could be done. Sharing some breakthroughs with his mother. Then, as he realized it *could* be done, working harder, in secret.

He sent his mother away specifically to do this one big thing. But now that he's free to do it . . . He's scared.

He goes to bed, and lies there, angry.

OK, tomorrow. Tomorrow you boost yourself.

Upgrade your brain. Better working memory. Faster processing, at every level.

No, it's not just that. If it works . . . you might understand people.

They might understand you.

But if it doesn't work . . . if it goes wrong . . .

He falls asleep, still arguing with himself.

2

Red Blood Cells

'Perhaps the most curious fact about the Chinese Pantheon is that it is arranged in imitation of earthly organisation. It appears as a vast government administration, or, still more precisely, as a series of government departments, each one with its Minister and its personnel. The different gods are positive bureaucrats with a strict hierarchy of rank and with clearly defined powers. They keep registers, make reports, issue directives, with a regard for formalities and a superabundance of papers which the most pedantic administration on earth might well envy.' — Chinese Mythology entry from *The Larousse Encyclopedia of Mythology*

'We produce nothing comparable to the great Oriental carpets, Persian glass, tiles and illuminated books, Arabian leatherwork, Spanish marquetry, Hindu textiles, Chinese porcelain and embroidery, Japanese lacquer and brocade, French tapestries, or Inca jewellery. (Though, incidentally, there are certain rather small electronic devices that come unwittingly close to fine jewels.)

— Alan Watts, *The Book*

'The concept of surveillance is ingrained in our beings. God was the original surveillance camera.'

— Hasan M. Elahi

19

She gets from Arrivals to the AirTrain just fine.

The driverless electric train pulls smoothly away from the platform, swings out above the airport on its high rail. Sunlight glitters off the wet concrete below. Yes, the sun is kinder here. It isn't trying to kill her.

By the time they make the last pickup, from Terminal 8, there are way too many people in her part of the train and her heart is pounding, but she stands with her back to them, facing out the big glass windows, leaning on the metal handle of her old wheeled case, and looks at the bright wet colourful planes. As she watches the tiny maintenance vehicles dancing around the big jets, like remoras cleaning sharks, she is almost calm.

Just got to get to the hotel.

The train starts up again, sways round a bend, and she studies the reflections of the people behind her. Marvels at how many wear retro gaming gear. Not discreet, induction-powered earbuds and contact lenses, but aggressively old-school helmets, and thick micromesh gloves. It's funny, the younger they are, the more old-fashioned they seem to want to look. She wonders how many of them are playing Colt's game. A lot . . . Normal thoughts. A normal journey. Yes, she's almost calm.

But at Howard Beach station, her case gets caught in the barrier.

She hauls it through, sideways, and discovers the down escalator to the subway is broken.

Her eyes still sundazzled, she stands at the head of the frozen metal steps, and peers down into the underworld. To her right, a torrent of faces pours up into the light, out of the darkness.

She'd forgotten; they buried this section of the A, after the last couple of hurricanes washed away the old tracks. It runs through a sealed, waterproof, storm-proof, everything-proof tunnel now, deep under Queens.

Underground. Oh God, no.

The people walking down the frozen steps ahead of her keep going, and vanish into darkness, until all the steps below her, with their little metal teeth, are empty.

She feels a hand on her shoulder. 'Lady, shit or get off the pot.'

She turns, startled, and sees a short, very wide Latino man with a shaved head, frowning.

'But,' she says, '. . . it used to be on the *surface* . . .'

He stares at her, through enhanced contact lenses, in the new season's colours. Acid green, with a textured gold rim.

Behind him, dozens, no, hundreds of people, with their suitcases, tense faces, sad kids, backpacks. Peering to see what is wrong, what is blocking them.

The man glances down, and his expression changes abruptly, like he's been distracted. Is he even seeing her? Ugh, did he just switch on a porn filter, to see her simulated, naked?

Forget it, forget it, nothing you can do. Just get to the hotel.

Naomi turns back, to the steep metal steps; reaches out a hand, in reflex, for Colt's hand, oh, he won't like this either . . .

But of course, he's not there. Her heart speeds up, far faster now than Colt's pulse against her wrist. She takes a numb step down, another, hauling her case behind her, thump, thump. Down into the darkness. Into the noise. Into the smell. Into the people.

The faces floating up past her on the right are so vivid. They stare, unsmiling, at her as they pass. Some frown, like she's woken them against their will from a dream. A wrinkled, leathery old woman in a white anti-virus mask gone yellow with dirt catches Naomi's eye, and glares at her. Some noisy kids, wearing full-face privacy masks to block facial-recognition systems, abruptly stop talking as they draw level, and all turn to face Naomi, expressionless. They're Colt's age, all wearing T-shirts that protest something; government tracking, police profiling, avatar sexism, targeted ads . . . She stops, stares back, her eyes darting between their blank, identical, silent faces, until they rise past her and, just as abruptly, start talking and laughing again as they vanish up into the light.

Naomi keeps going. Five steps down. Six, and she wants to go back, this isn't going to work, and she turns; but the pressure of the people, the anger in their faces, they jam the stairs above her, it's impossible.

'Hey, lady!'

48

'C'mon! Haul it . . .'

She has to go on.

She can't; but she has to.

She takes a step, hauls her case after her, *thump*. Takes another step, another, faster, and now she's running down the steps, her suitcase bouncing after her, its small wheels spinning, until it hops too high – leaping three steps in one go – and slams back down hard, twisting the handle out of her hand, and she almost falls.

Her case brushes her hip as it tumbles past her. She runs after it, and it bounces gracefully ahead of her until they both arrive at the bottom.

From around the next corner, she can hear the scream of a train approaching along some dark tunnel.

I don't want to be underground. I can't . . .

She grabs the case, pulls it upright. The cheap metal of the handle is bent. She leans it against the metal side of the frozen escalator, and puts the full weight of her body on it until it's nearly straight again.

Then she forces her way, sideways, hard, into the dense crowd at the bottom of the up escalator.

She should have got one of those powered wheelie cases that follow you around. Like old people have. No tugging, no pulling. Too late now.

She gets one foot on the up escalator, and it pulls her foot forward, up; she slides her other foot on, drags her case through the packed people and up, onto her step.

'Glupa kurva,' says a young male tourist she has pushed past, and his wearable helpfully translates, in a bright, cheerful, clear voice, 'Stupid whore.'

Nothing you can do. Head down. Ignore him. Ignore them all.

The escalator brings her up up up and back into the light, and she gets off at the top, drags her suitcase sideways, away from the people.

One wheel is sticking, damaged by the fall.

She finds a quiet space in the station, an eddy point, behind a steel roof support. A place to think. Fast-food wrappers and, somehow, from somewhere, dead leaves have drifted in here too, they crunch under her feet. She concentrates on feeling Colt's slow pulse against her wrist, to slow her own, to calm herself. He's fine . . .

I can't go underground.

A bus? No, God no.

She's not in a car-sharing plan. They don't make financial sense when you live out in the desert.

One of the instant rental services?

But she doesn't want to drive, not here. And she doesn't trust self-driving cars, not since that spate of hacking incidents and robberies in Brooklyn.

The social options, share a ride . . . No, she doesn't want to have to talk to someone at random. Last time she shared a ride, the guy was an enthusiastic Jehovah's Witness . . .

Outside, the Chinese and Indian tourists stand around, waiting for their instant rentals and self-drives to pull up. It's too many people; the noise, the crush, is pushing her right to the edge of a full-on panic attack. She starts to walk. When she finally gets to the edge of the crowd, she stands for a while with her face to the sun. Oh God, what shall I do?

A taxi pulls up alongside her. A nice, old-fashioned, unfriendly, human-driven, New York taxi.

The driver winds down the window. 'Hey, lady. Cab?'

Like when she was a kid. Comforting . . . 'How much to the Marriot Marquis?' she says. Just get to the hotel. A bed. A door you can lock.

He shrugs. 'Depends on traffic.' He points at a complicated price menu on the door. Time of day, distance, number of passengers, bags, Manhattan surcharge . . .

She tries to run the figures. Can her budget survive this? But there are too many variables, so her mind just worries in a circle. Besides which, human-driven taxis are basically a gullible tourist thing, which means the advertised charges are highly unreliable . . . But she thinks she can do it. Eat from the buffets, there will be buffets . . .

A fresh wave of noise and tourists surges out of the station, pushing the existing crowd further along the pavement.

'Hey! You! Hey! Speak English?'

Naomi turns, to see a heavy, sweating white man looming up behind her.

'You, yeah,' he says. 'Look, if you don't want that cab . . .'
She gets in, and slams the door in his face.

20

The figures on the meter start off higher than she'd expected, and rise faster than she can believe. A voice in her head – her mother's voice – says, you can't afford this. Her shoulders and back spasm.

A little screen, with retro graphics. Designed to look like an old-fashioned mechanical meter. Geared wheels, stamped with numbers, slowly turning. Like a slot machine that can only take, never give. She stares at them, trying to make them turn slower, to drag them to a halt. The traffic is so *slow*. Her mind is racing ahead of the taxi, trying to beat red lights, avoid roadworks, construction, what's with all the roadworks . . .

Oh, they're building new apartments, all the way along the old railroad tracks. Putting in pipes, cables . . . She stares, as the taxi crawls. Block after block of blank first floors. No windows. Why . . . oh, of course, the new coastal regulations, floodproofing . . . She shivers and imagines the waters over her head.

The fake leather smell emitted by the seats is overwhelmed by the fake lemon smell of disinfectant.

'They updated the Free Flow system this morning,' says the cab driver, eventually. 'Had some teething problems. So they're running traffic at half speed.'

Naomi says nothing.

'This update, it was supposed to fix all the problems with the crosstown traffic.' He shakes his head. 'Made it worse. A real poke in the eye for the mayor.'

Naomi closes her eyes. *You can't afford this.* And then, *Just get to the hotel.*

After a while, the driver tries again. New tack. 'I used to live on Staten Island.'

She opens her eyes. Looks at the cab driver. A middle-aged white guy, must be six feet six, his knees practically touching the steering wheel, like a clown in a clown car.

Must be terrible for his back. All day, twisted like a pretzel. Wrong job. Poor guy. OK, he wants to talk, let him talk. 'Mmmm?'

'Real shame, what's happened there. Me, I moved to Queens a long time back, after the first of the big storms. You remember Sandy, right?'

'Mmmm.'

'That woman, had her two kids pulled out of her arms by the water? Neighbour of mine.'

It wasn't an image she particularly wanted in her head. The black water roaring, the night so dark, the streetlamps out, and your child shrieking as the great wave dragged him from your exhausted arms, a shriek so high-pitched you could hardly hear it, getting further and further off, away down the boiling street, and under, and gone . . .

'I think I need to rest,' she says, closing her eyes again.

'Huh.' He stops talking.

But the dark, the quiet, is not restful. Colt's slow heartbeat against her wrist no longer calms her; her heart is beating twice as fast as his. She opens her eyes and glances again at the meter. It's too high, it's rising too fast. Oh God, she won't have enough money to make it through the conference.

'Let me out,' she hears herself saying.

'What?'

'Let me out.'

'Lady, we're nowhere near the hotel yet, this is still Brooklyn . . .'

'Let me out here!'

He says nothing. Pulls in.

She avoids his eyes by staring at the colossal figure on the retro screen.

She could use her e-purse, but she's carrying cash: why not go along with the retro fantasy. Justify her ridiculous decision to bring all these banknotes.

Digging into her purse, then a pocket, another pocket, for her scattered bills. He sighs, glances out the window, frowns, glances at the time, frowns, and she feels more ridiculous, not less.

The thought, *I don't have enough money*, goes around and around in her head. Apologizing to the driver; accusing herself.

The pocket that finally brings her up to the fare contains a bunch of obsolete old single dollar bills that she'd found in a drawer, packing. Reckless, she gives him all of them. They're almost enough to make a proper tip. He doesn't smile, but he stops scowling. It'll do. This is New York City, you have to tip or they kill you, she thinks as she climbs out. Sort of joking.

Sort of joking.

He drives off, and it's only then she looks around.

Uh oh.

Something bad has happened to this neighbourhood. Recently. There are scorch marks on the road, on the pavement. Where cars were burned out? Two, three, young black men appear in an open doorway and stare at her. They look worried. Like she can only bring them trouble.

She looks away, starts walking. Drags her case. The wonky wheel squeaks. When she glances up again, they're not staring at her, but at something behind her. They duck back inside, and close the door.

Something dark swoops low over her head, from behind, blows her hair all over the place, and she flinches.

A drone. Compact. Powerful. It's about the size of a very large dog, with military-grade rotors. She freezes.

It spins to face her, identify her, and as it does so, it extends a dark metal snout, and sniffs her. She feels a strong breeze pull past her, and hears the whoosh of air vanishing into thousands of tiny holes on the snout's curved black surface.

The drone moves back up to about fifteen feet above the pavement, its downdraught blowing garbage all over the street, and she shields her eyes from the dust.

It drifts a little further down the street. Past one dingy grey apartment building. Another. Then it turns to face a building painted a bright, incongruous pink; extends its snout. Sniffs at a cracked window on the second floor. Nothing happens for a moment, as the drone communicates with someone, somewhere. Then it emits a focused sonic blast, like a crack of thunder, that disintegrates the window; it accelerates at a shocking speed through the swirling cloud of glass particles, and disappears inside the apartment, howling.

Drug bust, she thinks, oh wow. *Wow*. Or terrorism . . .

She's seen SWAT drones do this on the news, but it feels as weird as a dream, to have it happen above her head. The falling glass dances on the pavement in front of her, around her. Her shoes and the wheels of her case crunch through the shards as she breaks into a run.

When she gets to a quieter block – no people, no drones – she stops running, chest heaving. She looks around. The block is quiet because every building has been boarded up, taped off.

Must have been evacuated, for decontamination after a bio attack . . . No, not a place she wants to linger. All right. She stretches, and shakes her stiff arms. Grasps the handle of the case again, and sets off at a slower, more manageable trot.

She stops when she sees flowers in planters on the fire escapes. Leans against a railing till she can catch her breath.

I'm saving money. And I'm not underground. It's OK.

She sets off again, walking now. Finally makes it over the bridge, into lovely, safe Manhattan . . . She frowns, guilty at her own sense of relief. Oh Manhattan, she thinks. Sterilized by money. All the criminals in suits . . .

The crowds thicken as she gets closer to her destination. After a while, pulling the case, avoiding the people, becomes a kind of meditation. *Just make it to the hotel*, like a mantra now, no edge of panic.

By the time she makes it into the shade under the canopy of the Marriott Marquis Hotel, she's a little light headed, from exertion, from adrenalin comedown, from hunger. With her eyes still adjusting to the gloom under the canopy, she bumps into a young black guy wearing a tight black T-shirt and jeans. She opens her mouth, and says without thinking, 'Oh, you're so black I didn't see you.'

He turns, and ignites full sleeves of digital skin. Tiger patterns of fluorescent orange shudder across the dark blue-black of his arms. 'That's OK,' he says, camp, relaxed. Naomi stares, hypnotized, at his glowing, rippling forearms, her heart pounding again. 'You're so female I didn't see you.'

'I'm sorry, I didn't mean—'

He raises an eyebrow, turns back, and enters the revolving door of the hotel, and his e-skin fades to match his skin tone, and they are just arms again.

Oh, he's an employee, she thinks, unsure if that makes it better or worse. No e-skin on the premises.

She follows him through the huge revolving doors, with the

bad wheel on her case still ticking, squeaking, into a space that feels bigger than the world outside.

She looks around.

The man with the tiger arms is gone. OK.

She looks up, up, till her neck cricks, at the hanging gardens of the twenty-storey atrium. She can't quite believe nobody is jumping from up there. That people aren't queuing up to jump.

She closes her eyes. A room with a bed. A door you can lock. Almost there.

A sudden loud sound, very close. As she opens her eyes, she sees, for an instant, someone explode on the marble floor beside the reception desk.

Oh God, did they really . . .

But it's just suitcases, sliding off a luggage trolley. A matching set of four red cases, slamming one after another into the marble, sliding across the floor.

A strap on the trolley has snapped, she can see a frayed end dangling.

A bellhop – tall, thin, African; maybe Maasai or Tutsi – laughs hysterically, still holding the other end of the strap. Attached to nothing.

She unfreezes. Takes the last few steps to the reception wall.

Automatic check-in is out of service. A metal wall-panel has been removed, and a gaunt Latin American woman in maintenance overalls stares gloomily into the guts of the system, while at her feet her diagnostic unit runs tests. There's a hot, burnt plastic smell that makes Naomi's nose wrinkle. The woman sighs, and leans against the wall.

Naomi looks further along the reception wall. Behind the old counter, a couple of employees are checking everyone in manually. Naomi joins the queue.

There's a happy young couple ahead of her. She does her breathing while she waits. But why is that man even *pushing* a luggage trolley? She looks around, until she sees the sleek, flat, hotel robot trolleys, self-parked in a neat stack in a corner, like an abstract sculpture. Oh. Out of service. Whole system must have crashed.

Staff load cases onto manual trolleys, and whistle as they wheel them to the elevators. It gives the hotel lobby the air of an old movie.

At the desk, the young man is kind. She's not sure why she was so worried about this. She'll be lying down soon, in a bed. She might sleep. She goes onto automatic pilot, and just nods yes to the receptionist while she worries about her paper instead. Worries about talking in public. Worries about socializing afterwards. Will people still expect her to split the bill in an expensive restaurant, if she's only had a starter and tap water . . .

The receptionist is saying something for the second time.

'Mmm. Oh, sorry . . . what . . .'

'For some reason, that payment hasn't cleared.'

She looks at the receptionist properly for the first time. A young guy, pale as a cave mushroom, with green eyes, wide shoulders. He is smiling. Handsome, yes. 'I'm sorry,' he says, and he really does sound sorry, 'there seems to be some kind of problem with your e-purse. The deposit isn't coming through. Do you have some other form of . . . ah . . .'

Numb, she fumbles around till she finds the old-fashioned plastic credit card she keeps for emergencies. *I don't have enough money.*

They perform the ritual.

Naomi holds her breath.

'I'm *so* sorry.' And he is; and that makes it worse. 'Have you another card?'

She blinks at the memory of the store assistant cutting up her other card in front of her in Target, in December. She had walked away, her back straight, everyone looking at her. Left all of Colt's Christmas presents piled up at the register. Sat in the parking lot for half an hour, crying, before she could see straight enough to drive home.

'No,' she said. 'I don't have another card.'

It must have more room on it. Why would it be refused? Her limit was twelve thousand two hundred. Her balance was eleven thousand four hundred. 'I'm . . . the conference is putting me up here.'

'Uh huh. Which conference?'

'StemCellCon. They're paying for the room, and . . . I'm not going to use the phone, or touch the minibar.'

The receptionist is still smiling. 'I'm sure you won't,' he says.

'I don't even drink.'

'I totally understand. But the regulations require guests to put down a five hundred dollar deposit, in case of any accidents. I'm afraid I'm not authorized to waive that.' She can see he isn't trying to make it hard for her, and that makes it worse. 'We can take cash. There's an ATM over there.' He points to a corner of the lobby.

Five hundred dollars. She remembers when it used to be half that. Of course, she also remembers when it used to be considerably more. Deflation, inflation, revaluation . . .

'Thank you,' she says.

Did Colt raid her e-purse *and* credit card?

She walks slowly to the ancient ATM. Her legs feel cold and stiff. She counts her remaining cash as she walks. $250. At the machine, no, she doesn't want to know her balance. She puts in the credit card, proves her identity (eyes, skin), and asks for five hundred dollars. It declines politely and returns her card.

She asks for three hundred.

It declines.

She asks for two hundred.

It gives her a hundred, and wishes her a good day.

She walks back to the receptionist, though she doesn't want to walk back to the receptionist. The problem is, she doesn't want to fall to the ground weeping, either, or run out of the hotel into the traffic, or . . .

She could take the lift to the twenty-fourth floor, and throw herself off the balcony, and explode across the black marble in front of the receptionist, splashing his desk, and then he would understand, and sympathize. Sympathize . . .

But would they even let her in the lift, if she's not a guest? Would she need to be booked in, to make it function?

The receptionist is looking at her, politely, his head tilted a little to one side.

She says, 'I only have three hundred and fifty dollars, and I need it, some of it, to eat, while I'm here. If you . . .'

He tilts his head to the other side, still looking at her politely. Naomi feels like she is pushing a rock up a hill with her tongue. She wants to stop talking. She wants to lie down. But there is

57

nowhere to lie down. Cold marble. 'If you could . . .' No, she can't make it to the end of the sentence.

Back up, try another sentence. Like trying another road, that time she'd tried to take Colt to Lake Walker, and they'd got hung up on a rock, and had to go back; tried another road and got stuck in mud; backed up; tried another, and it got dark and they'd never got to the lake.

'Could I ring the conference?' she says. 'Maybe they . . .'

But this road is no good either, because she doesn't want to ring the conference. She imagines explaining this mess, her life, down a phoneline, to some unseen figure as large and impersonal and distant as the moon.

Naomi notices something in her peripheral vision, further down the curve of the reception counter.

A woman, staring at her.

Naomi looks back at the woman, in order to not have to look at the receptionist's polite, resigned face.

The woman looks away, with a swing of her rich, dark, glossy hair.

Just a guest, checking in quite normally, chatting with the other receptionist. At the woman's feet are three tiny bug-eyed dogs. They huddle together, shivering in the air conditioning, and stare back at Naomi.

Naomi looks back at the receptionist.

The receptionist lowers his voice a little.

'Look,' he says. 'I have to have a deposit. Regulations.'

Naomi just stands there, as he slowly goes out of focus. Her right arm begins to bend at the elbow, rise; but she orders it back down, stiff, by her side. She doesn't want to wipe her eyes, that would only draw attention to them. He may not have seen them. They haven't spilled over yet.

'What I can do is . . .' and he pauses, as though he is checking with himself, arguing with himself, persuading himself, before he commits; 'I can lock the minibar, disable the phone, I mean you don't need the phone, nobody ever uses it, and you give me a two hundred dollar deposit. Can you . . . will that leave you with enough? I mean, you'll get it back when you check out, so you can use it for your ride to the airport, or . . .'

'Yes,' she says. Now her eyes fill and spill, as she hands the receptionist two hundred. A warm drop hits the back of her hand, and splashes the back of the note, his hand. He doesn't flinch. 'Sorry, I'm so sorry. Thank you. Thank you.'

'It's OK,' he says. 'It's OK.' He looks around, as though he were embarrassed, but why should he be embarrassed.

The check-in system's still down, so the receptionist writes her a paper receipt, and tells her the room number. He sets the door to unlock for her, smiles, says something, but Naomi has stopped listening. She says thank you one last time; bows, absurdly, like her father, why did she do that, nobody does that.

She takes a step towards the elevator. Just get to the room. Don't cry. In the distance, a new bellhop starts moving towards her, like a cheetah who's noticed an antelope drifting free of the herd.

It's the man with the tiger arms, covered now by his tight red jacket.

He's closing fast. He grins.

She reaches automatically, protectively, for her purse, but there's no need to look, she knows. A hundred-dollar bill, and a fifty. No small bills. Got to last till Monday. Oh dear God, she can't afford to tip. The noise in her head gets louder, as she adds up all the meals, and the taxi back to the airport; no, she will get the A-train, it will be OK, she can do it, it doesn't have to be a taxi; and there will be buffets at some of the events at the conference, and finally she gets the total to come in under a hundred and fifty dollars.

She checks her pockets.

A couple of bright new dollar coins. Not enough . . .

She's walking fast and, ahead of her, the elevator door opens, and she walks faster, her suitcase juddering and slewing as its wheel sticks. No, I really can't, I can't afford to tip. Oh God, he's going to think it's because he's black, he's going to think I'm like my parents . . . She refuses to meet the bellhop's eye, almost running for the elevator's open door, as he angles towards her, trying to cut her off, saying, 'Ma'am . . .'

21

Her room is clean, empty. She lets go of the handle of her case, and it topples over.

Centre of gravity isn't between the wheels, bad design, it looks good, slim, but it's a bad design.

She sits on the bed, and tries to ring Colt, twice, but there's no reply. The second time, she leaves a message.

'Everything is fine, Colt. I've got a nice room. Ring me if you need me. Make sure you . . .'

No.

'Happy, ah . . .'

No.

'I love you.'

She gets up, locks the door, pulls the heavy plush plum-coloured curtains, knocks off the lights, kicks off her shoes, and walks to the bed in the dark. Climbs in, curls up.

It's so soft. It smells so clean. Knots of muscle loosen, all over her body – it feels like she is melting – until her heart is moving at the speed of Colt's, and they finally beat in sync.

She sleeps.

22

Colt wakes up early. He's never woken up alone in the house before; it is the silence that wakes him.

No comforting white noise from the shower at the end of the corridor.

No reassuring clatter of cutlery from the kitchen.

He gets up, and for some reason feels he should move quietly. He had planned to go straight into the game, the moment he woke: but the strangeness of the empty house is a new level that also needs exploring.

First, though, he hauls the little 3D printer out from under a pile of unwashed clothes. He quickly prints the casing he needs, and a couple of the simpler parts. Pockets them, still warm.

As he leaves his room, the house AI murmurs, *'Mail.'*

'Thanks,' says Colt, automatically.

He is intensely aware of his soft footsteps, of the silence surrounding them, as he walks towards the front door.

He opens the door. Inhales the dawn air. Cool, fresh.

An overnight delivery drone has quietly left a package, containing the more complex parts he ordered, in the big mailbox. Good.

Behind it, at the back of the mailbox, there's another package.

Colt takes it out. Hefts it.

Neither light nor heavy.

Turns it.

A handwritten address label.

Colt's name and address. In his father's writing.

Colt takes a deep breath, and rips it open.

A mug.

A Doctor Who mug.

Colt's favourite show, for much of his childhood.

The Doctor, so clever, so kind. So puzzled by human beings, by human emotions.

Sometimes, falling asleep under the poster of Peter Capaldi, Colt would dreamily imagine Doctor Who was his real father, putting him to bed.

Watching over him . . .

Colt examines the mug warily.

Oh, it's printed wrong.

He didn't even get me a good one.

Colt's stomach lurches.

Perhaps it was cheap because it's got a mistake.

'I ♥ ♥ the Doctor.'

Oh wait, no. The Doctor has two hearts. All the Time Lords of Gallifrey have two hearts.

There's a crackling noise in his throat as he reads it again.

'I ♥ ♥ the Doctor.'

A startled, nervous sound.

It's only when he realizes that the sound he has just made is laughter that he understands the words and symbols on the mug are a joke.

'I ♥ ♥ the Doctor.'

'Funny?' he says wonderingly. *'Funny.'*

He rotates the mug, examines it. There's a hasty signature on it, in black.

But why would his dad sign it? Do people do that? Is that normal? Like a birthday card?

No, it's not his dad's name . . .

Colt squints, to make it out.

Peter Capaldi.

Colt's favourite Doctor.

His dad remembered.

Colt's vision blurs.

He walks around the house, carrying the parcel of parts, the mug.

The mug reminds him, he's thirsty. Must remember to drink.

He puzzles over why the silence should feel so strange. After all, he spends many of his days alone in the house, working on the gameworld, while his mother works in the lab. A silent house is normal.

No, it's the silence at this time of day; morning, their best time. The time they really talk. And it's the knowledge that this silence extends ahead in time: that Mama won't open the door in a few hours. He's hearing the future. Life without Mama.

He puzzles over it.

He'd never imagined a future without Mama before. But of course it will happen. Does this feel good or bad?

It's too early to tell.

He walks softly into the living room, across the rug, pleasant under his feet, and opens the little drinks cabinet that Mama has for guests. That Mama never uses.

He touches all the bottles, left to right, then right to left.

Takes out a half-empty bottle of Suntory whisky. The sunrise swoops and jags through the slosh of dark yellow liquid. There's a round golden symbol on the old paper label, and Colt lines it up with the sun, so the sun shines dimly through it.

He puts it back, takes out a bottle of Schweppes Tonic Water. 'Contains Quinine' says the label.

Explorers used to take quinine to prevent malaria. Cool.

There's an inch or two gone. Probably flat by now, anyway. He's never tasted tonic water.

He cracks it open, and there's a little hiss of carbon dioxide, oh beans, he's wasted it, she'll know.

A spurt of panic.

But she won't be back today. Time to fix it. It's OK. He lifts it towards his lips, no, don't touch it.

Germs.

He tilts back his head. Pours some into his open mouth. Fizzy. Not sweet. Metallic. That must be the quinine. *Cool . . .*

He replaces the cap, puts the bottle back.

Takes out a bottle of vodka. There's a buffalo on the label.

Hmmm . . . Colt, bemused, studies the buffalo.

Colt likes buffalo. There might not be government, or law, in the semi-mythical Wild West of the gameworld, but there is a fiercely accurate natural ecosystem, intricately interconnected; and the game contains immense herds of buffalo.

So Colt has spent a lot of time designing buffalo, and this one looks wrong.

Wait, now he remembered some European colleague of Naomi saying 'a gift from my home country'.

Ah, it's not a buffalo. It's a European bison.

Polska.

It's Polish.

Imported.

80 per cent proof.

That's the one.

He brings the vodka with him to the kitchen.

Assembles everything he needs on the kitchen table. A very traditional, old-school setup. Soldering iron, solder, hot glue gun, coils of wire, see-through plastic bags containing capacitors, resistors, switches, chips of all kinds; the sand-coloured plastic casing and parts he's just printed; cotton buds from his Mama's shelf in the bathroom.

Where's the parcel he ordered? Ah . . .

Colt pops the newly delivered parts out of their neat, light, aerogel package.

He opens the bottle of vodka, pours a little into the cap. Wrinkles his nose at the sharp smell of evaporating ethanol. Dips a cotton bud in the clear liquid.

Begins to clean the contacts on an old physical variable-resistor dial that he salvaged from a vintage Bang & Olufsen amp. Not practical – they give a nasty crackle if they're not clean – but Colt likes the retro look.

No, he won't play the game just yet. He'll build the booster first.

He doubles over, as though in a car that's slammed on brakes, as a stab of panicked thought convulses him. Stop! Stop wasting time! Go to the lab! She'll come back, and you won't have done it!

And now, real panic.

You need to fix *yourself*, not the bad reception beyond the ridge, who *cares*!

Colt hums and nods his head until the thoughts have gone.

He goes back to building the booster. The game really needs a booster. He's been meaning to do this for months.

23

When he's finished building the booster, Colt moves through the house, slowly, methodically, looking for extension cords and unplugging them. It's an old-fashioned house, built without enough sockets, back when everything needed to be plugged in. There are decades' worth of improvised solutions from the previous owner still in place. Extension cords run unobtrusively along baseboards. Cords emerge from sockets hidden behind wardrobes. Run under rugs. Coil up behind sofas. Loop from rafters.

Once you're tuned to see them, you see them everywhere.

Colt grimaces. The pattern is illogical. Often, extension cords have been used where it would have been simpler to just unplug a couple of devices and plug them back into different sockets. Most of these extensions aren't even needed.

He harvests them.

Back in the kitchen with his haul, he looks around. Crouches, looks around again. A very short cord, dangling out of the back of the fridge, plugged into an extension.

Oh, right. Damaged the fridge cord last Christmas, running it over the toaster, had to cut it off short.

But the fridge cord can no longer reach the socket unaided.

He hesitates. He needs the extension cord.

He unplugs the fridge.

'Colt, are you *sure* you want to unplug me?' says the fridge brightly.

Oh yeah. It has a few hours of backup battery, in case of a power outage.

Colt ponders the question.

He has never liked the fridge's AI. It's supposed to be child-friendly; but that just means it uses voices from Sesame Street while it lectures him on where to put the milk for optimum freshness.

'I hate you,' says Colt, 'and I want you to die.'

'OK. I need to have a word with your motherrrrrrrr . . .' says the fridge in the voice of Big Bird, but Colt has already disabled the AI with a screwdriver before it can notify her that it's been plugged out, that the temperature will soon be rising . . .

24

Naomi wakes early.

Gets up.

Showers.

Chooses her outfit.

Watches the news in her room blankly for a long time. The soothing wallpaper of other people's disasters.

An earthquake in Alaska has knocked a small village, on one of the Aleutian Islands, into the sea.

There's a shooter cornered in a mall in Florida.

Some biohackers have built an airborne version of bubonic plague and released it in their high school in Ohio. The school, and thirty city blocks downwind of it, are under lockdown. She watches the familiar biohazard suits move through the empty streets.

She hasn't really watched the news since she hit her teens. One morning when she was, what, fifteen, she was watching a live police chase. The guy did a U-turn on the freeway, and got hit by a truck. They showed it over and over. Watching it idly for the third time, something flipped. She realized that a man who had been alive a few minutes before was now dead. That it was real.

That he was as real as she was. She turned off the TV, and went to the bathroom, and vomited. Since then, she couldn't bring herself to watch the news.

Death packaged as entertainment, like Roman gladiator fights . . .

But now it cuts to a World News segment; and the endless catastrophes of weather and war remind her of earlier in her childhood. Her father would explain where these far-off places were, and reassure her that those terrible things could never happen here. She hears his voice in memory, louder than the news, and it is comforting. He wasn't always a monster. It would have been easier if he were.

When they finally mention Nevada and Las Vegas, in a weather report, she switches it off.

Outside her room, the conference is taking over the hotel. She registers in a daze, gets her name tag and a bundle of stuff she is never going to look at, and wanders the spaces.

Name tags everywhere.

A swarm, gathering.

25

She finds the conference room in which she is due to speak. She is very early. They are putting her on first. She understands, she has no reputation. The carpet in the conference room is startlingly thick.

Why do they have a carpet this thick? Surely there is a lot of dust, dust mites and worse, the problem of dropped food, crumbs, milky drinks spilling and spoiling, that sour smell, so hard to remove . . .

She worries away at this, keeping her head down, staring at the thick carpet as she walks towards the stage, deliberately not think-ing about the stage; about standing on the stage; about speaking on the stage in this vast room, with its thick carpet soaking up the sound of her voice.

Spilled milk.

The huge space is almost empty.

Half a dozen people stand huddled together by the edge of the stage, talking quietly.

Scattered among the hundreds of chairs, a few individuals are using the space as a refuge; three read, one writes, two doze.

Someone by the stage looks over, sees her. Strides towards her. Yaakov.

I've missed him.

She hasn't seen her old teacher since he set up his consilience team at MIT; a big, multidisciplinary unit that puts biologists to work on physicists' problems, and vice versa.

Much older, white hair now.

'Naomi!' His voice is big enough for the room. He slaps her back so hard she sways. 'Any last tweaks? No? Good. We'll be delivering the handouts as you go onstage, if that's OK . . . Ritual! Drama! I was just telling Graham . . .' he takes her elbow, and leads her toward the stage, '. . . yes, come and meet the others . . . I remember when the handouts were done on paper, and if people were interested in your talk, they would follow it, page by page. My God, it was like the wind roaring through the treetops some-times, as they all turned their pages together . . . I miss paper . . .' They arrive at the stage edge, and Yaakov releases her elbow. 'Seul-ki, Graham, this is Naomi Chiang. One of the best students I ever had . . . Let's all go backstage and relax properly, the green room has decent chairs and lousy coffee . . .'

Backstage . . . soon they would be walking onto a stage, my God, why had she come . . .

26

Colt finally gets the booster running. He puts on his good micro-mesh suit, fresh from the wash. Adjusts the sensors in his helmet for a while. He'd been all set to play the game, but now he's strangely reluctant to start.

I'm tired. Got up too early.

His mama is three hours ahead of him now, the sun is higher in her sky. He doesn't like that thought. I'll lie down, he thinks. A nap. Yes. He tells the blinds to close. They slide down, till the room is dark. He lies on his bed, closes his eyes.

Before Colt falls asleep, he disconnects real-world mapping, and sets himself walking, inside the other game he's been playing. He will walk as he sleeps. Away from everyone.

He walks till he falls asleep.

Inside his dreams, he walks.

*

He wakes up inside the helmet. Still wearing the micromesh suit.

And the helmet – triggered by Colt opening his eyes – wakes too; and now he is ingame, in the desert.

Good. That odd reluctance is gone. He'll play . . .

There's a panicky voice at the back of his head saying, no, go to the lab; but he ignores it, ignores it, ignores it.

Think of something else.

Wait. The girl he met last week. Not . . .

Not that he . . .

He uses his developer privileges, checks the sign-ins – wow, so many people playing in India now – but she's not in the game-world. He returns to the game environment.

No sign of other players.

No sign of life.

Perhaps a little smoke on the horizon.

He checks the distance travelled during his nap. Not bad. Five miles. He locks it down. And the induction charger he installed in his bedframe has fully powered the helmet as he slept. Good . . . Technically, you're not meant to charge the helmet while you're in it, or have a charger under your head while you sleep; but Mama doesn't know it's there, and it means he never has to think about power.

As his mind clears, he feels the familiar discomfort. He begins to breathe faster, not because he needs more oxygen, but because he doesn't; he's in a panic at the disconnect between his game self, in the game's desert, walking, and his real self, in bed, motionless; between the sunlight of the gameworld, and the cool dark of his real room.

Fast and shallow; Mama hates it when he breathes like this. He slows it down.

Breathes deeper.

Slower.

Deeper.

Slower.

The panic ebbs.

He could, of course, make real-world mapping automatic on waking.

But then he would be denied the pleasure of turning real-world mapping back on . . . It smoothly walks his game self into a cool, dark cave he hasn't noticed before.

Yeah, the house works as a cave, nice . . .

He sniffs the air while his eyes adjust. The smell is good. Fresh hay. Yes, there in the far corner. And empty sacks that used to contain corn, animal feed.

Animals shelter here. Shepherds too, maybe.

Here we go . . . His game self lies down, and pulls a torn sack over his legs and body; and his real self merges with his game self.

Full mapping.

He is one with himself. He moves his arm, in the world, in the game. Reaches for the Doctor Who mug full of water by the bed, because his mother has finally trained him to drink enough water, built it into his ritual.

His game hand closes around a clay beaker, left in the cave by a shepherd perhaps. He admires its crude form in the dim light, and drinks real water, game water, from real mug and game beaker, and the map is perfect, and he relaxes.

Oh, man. Need to pee. Guess I'd better have a shower . . .

He gets up and the cave opens out ahead of him as he goes to the bathroom.

He's worked out how to shower in the helmet. Waterproofed every joint. His head doesn't even feel itchy any more.

He steps under the waterfall. It's totally convincing.

He pees in the shower. Dark orange. Hmmm. Still need to drink more.

He dries off, dresses, walks outside into the light. Still pretty early in the day.

He admires the game desert.

Fresh, sharp.

The couple of houses you can see from their yard have been replaced by weathered outcrops of red sandstone.

He turns around.

The 76 station in the far distance has become a tight clump of pine trees, the canopy of branches casually mapping onto the steel and plastic canopy of the gas station. A deer moves out of the shade of the pine trees, sniffs the air, and bounds away. Colt does a reflex check to see, is it a neighbour maybe that Mama has asked to check on him, but the real-world object is a red, out-of-state pickup; and the deer disappears into the hills.

Overhead, a bird of prey cries.

American Airlines, Dreamliner, he thinks reflexively. 10.15 a.m., Vegas–LAX. He looks up and sees an eagle, yes.

He glances back at the house, just for the pleasure of seeing the cave entrance.

His father appears before him.

Colt grimaces at the break-in. This is not an ingame message. It isn't mapped onto the gameworld at all.

His father sits at a desk, head and shoulders, just mashed into the landscape, in mid-air, at no particular distance, so he hurts to focus on. The edges of the picture stop abruptly where the camera can't see.

It's so ugly and painful, Colt tries to look away. But the break-in is anchored to Colt's vision, so when Colt looks away, the desk and his father stay central, and just drag across the landscape, leaving artefacts. The picture is that terrible, shitty military hyper-encrypted/decrypted low-res, like bandwidth is still rationed.

There had been no ring. No option to refuse.

Colt checks, yes, all calls are off, all sources, to stop Mama arriving every few hours as a local woman or a trader, spoiling the game. All notifications, off.

There are messages from his mother, from other members of the game-development team, patiently waiting.

I've been hacked. By my *dad*.

'So,' says his father.

'Dad, please, you're spoiling my game.' Colt tries to block the call, but everything is locked. He can't even power down the helmet. That shouldn't be possible.

This isn't fair.

'How's your mother?'

'Good. Dad, please—'

'Where is she?'

'Dad, you must know.'

70

'I know she's in New York. I don't know why she's in New York.'

'Just ask her.'

'Mmmm. She's giving a paper, isn't she?'

'Yes.' Colt gives up. His dad won't go away till he gets what he wants. Colt turns and walks back into the house.

His dad looks less wrong indoors, in the cave. Colt experiments, moving his head, to position his dad's image somewhere that isn't so visually irritating.

Ryan's still talking. 'We asked the guy running the conference to show us the paper. He wouldn't. I'm kind of pissed.'

That didn't make sense. 'You could get that in two seconds, Dad.'

'Don't I fucking know it. Sure, two seconds' work. But two days' paperwork. Two weeks' red tape. Fuck that.'

These were the kind of dots he couldn't join. 'Why?'

'Because we used to be married. Sexual harassment, stalking, blah blah. There's a whole bunch of extra regulation involved . . .'

Colt's back in his room by now. Ugh. His dad looks so wrong in a cave, lit from nowhere. Colt moves his bedside lamp, to get the lighting to match his dad's office.

The lamp is a smoky torch, ingame. Colt sniffs, as the burning torch passes his face, and the helmet gives a hint of smoke. Nice touch. But the smell seems a little off, oddly lemony. Sure enough, a second later, the helmet flashes up a warning that the chemical pack for the olfactory unit is running low. Oh, *beans*. They're always running out.

He switches off smell mapping.

'. . . This place fucking KILLS me. Look.' Ryan pushes around the papers on his desk. Real paper, and piles of it. Typical high-security office, where half the work can't be trusted to online systems. 'I can't investigate relatives, and because I'm in charge, I can't order subordinates to investigate relatives. Turns out she's in a kind of security shadow.'

'But you hacked me, Dad,' says Colt politely.

'Face-to-face communication. You know we did it. No deceit involved. I'm allowed emergency override communications on all devices and systems. And you're using military chips in that dumb fucking helmet of yours, so I just use the hardware backdoor. It's not an intelligence issue. There's still an hour's paperwork just to do this.' He sighed. 'Tony Stark never had to deal with this bullshit.'

'So ask Mama for the paper, Dad. Face to face.'

Silence.

Colt grimaces. Ugh, so annoying, that scientists still use the word 'paper' for a data file. It messes things up. It isn't scientific.

Mama's paper. Piles of paper. Paperwork. The words clash in his head. The picture they make is muddy, disturbing.

His dad still doesn't speak.

Colt gives up on playing the game, and snaps it off. The game-world vanishes, to reveal the real world.

And his dad, still lo-res, still sitting there, in the centre of his vision.

'I sent the paper, Dad.'

'I know.'

'I can send you a copy if you like.'

'That's my boy.'

'It's a really good paper.'

'That's what I'm worried about.'

His dad's eyes flick down to his desk as the paper arrives. 'Thanks, kid.'

His dad reads the title and grunts. He swipes it open with a bigger gesture than the task requires, and starts reading.

As his father reads, Colt closes his eyes and thinks about how to solve a problem with the light, ingame. The new, bigger sun is throwing the lighting out of whack.

And maybe set up an alert, so if that girl plays . . . the girl who tried to take his clothes off . . .

'Who really wrote the paper, Colt.'

'She did,' Colt murmurs. He squeezes his eyes tighter closed, trying to visualize the problem code.

'Who really wrote the paper, Colt.'

Colt opens his eyes. 'Mama did.'

'Colt.'

'I didn't write the paper.'

'Colt.'

'We talked about some of the ideas.'

'Bullshit. You wrote code.'

'I wrote some of the code. To do the analysis. To get at the patterns. The genome information was a mess, Dad. Some of these genes hadn't been brought cross-species before.'

His dad's eyes were skidding back and forth, scraping the paper fast for the gist. His right hand was already doing something – fast, big gestures – on the broad desk.

'OK. Thanks. Don't tell her we talked yet. Tomorrow, fine, tell her whatever you like. Happy birthday.'

His dad disappears.

Colt thinks about the date.

No, not that one; in crapworld.

He's been running a single-season gametime, cycling through a series of winters, for months now. He likes the desert in winter.

Oh yeah. It's his birthday. Probably what those messages from Mama are about. Maybe he should unlock the gametime, and run it in sync with the real world for a while.

He tries to work out exactly how his dad hacked in.

Damn. It's in the helmet hardware. It's a high-level – government-level – back-door entry, just like he said.

How to fix that?

His head hurts, thinking about the problem. It's hard to hold all the pieces in working memory.

I need more memory, processing power.

And the old argument starts up again in his brain.

Well, there is a solution. It's the reason he decided his mother needed to go to StemCellCon. To go to New York. To *go*.

But now he's alone; now that he's free to do it, to change his brain, to change his life . . . He's afraid.

His mind rocks back and forth between the possible outcomes. There aren't many. It's not complicated.

1.) He could become more than human; *better* than human.

2.) He could die.

27

'The search for love continues even in the face of great odds.'
— Graffito on a wall, near Yale University, sometime in the 1970s

In New York, in the Marriott Marquis Hotel, backstage in the green room of the Astor Ballroom, on the seventh floor, Naomi

Chiang's phone rings. She's due to speak in two minutes. She hesitates.

Might be Colt.

She looks.

No.

She turns it off.

Yaakov raises an eyebrow. 'You've got time to take a call.'

Naomi shrugs.

Now Yaakov's phone rings. An old-fashioned phone, an even older-fashioned ring, like a phone in a film. Defiantly retro. He hesitates. Hauls it out. Big, physical model. Answers it. Looks across at Naomi.

Ah.

'It's Ryan . . .' says Yaakov, raising his huge white eyebrows. 'He wants to talk to you.'

She shakes her head. Looks down at her feet, so that her hair covers her eyes. Shakes her head again.

Yaakov half turns away, says, 'She's about to deliver a paper. Can you call later?'

No. Don't hide. He can't do anything to you. He's not here.

She straightens up. Watches Yaakov. He is holding the big old phone fiercely in both hands, his knuckles white. The thin bracelet of red thread that he's always worn catches for a second on the hairs of his left wrist, then slides down to his shirt cuff. '. . . No, I'm afraid she can't talk right now . . . Yes . . . Yes . . .' Yaakov looks across at her, and she looks back at her feet, no; looks back up, at Yaakov. Yaakov says, 'He wants you to pull the paper. Not to deliver the paper . . .'

She shakes her head.

'He says he is risking his career to do this.'

His career. She laughs. And shakes her head.

'Ryan,' says Yaakov, 'that's a rather extraordinary request. She has a career too, you know . . . Listen, she has said no . . . I'm sorry, I have to go, Ryan . . . Yes, I know . . .' Yaakov ends the call. 'My goodness. He was very, uh, insistent.'

There is something odd in Yaakov's tone, and Naomi says sharply, 'How insistent? What did he say?'

'He says he'll get your funding pulled . . . That there are lawyers preparing an injunction . . . Do you need a minute to think? Once I release this, there is no calling it back.'

She thinks of Ryan.

Of pleasing Ryan.

Of submitting to Ryan's will.

She thinks of Ryan's cock in her mouth; his hands holding her hair, pulling her closer. His cock at the back of her throat.

He pulls her hair, hard, in memory.

'Are you OK?' says Yaakov.

She clears her throat.

'Release it,' she says, and walks out of the green room, and onto the stage.

As she reaches the microphone, she hears the notifications on different devices ping and sing like little birds, as her words arrive, all over the room.

The wall behind her is suddenly covered with a photograph. She glances back at it, and smiles through her fear.

Familiar territory. Hang on to that.

Concentrate on the photo. Don't look at the crowd. Pretend they're not there.

'OK,' she says, and her voice comes back at her, strong from the speakers all around the room. 'That's an imaginal disc from a monarch caterpillar, *Danaus plexippus*. We now know pretty much everything about how the monarch transforms from, essentially, one kind of organism into an utterly different organism, with utterly different parts.' She points behind her, at the photo. 'That imaginal disc contains about one hundred cells, so it's pretty much microscopic. The caterpillar builds a waterproof chrysalis; enzymes dissolve most of its major organs and tissues into a kind of rich soup of amino acids, etc.: but of course, the imaginal discs don't dissolve; each contains the blueprint for a different part of the new organism, and they build up the butterfly's new wings, legs, antennae etc. from this soup of proteins.' She hesitates for a second; no, she can't resist. 'Caterpillar soup, yummy,' she says, and there's a startled titter from some in the audience. Naomi wonders if Colt's remembered to watch the live stream, to see his joke.

'My early research, into pain . . .' She hesitates; but he deserves the credit, she has to say it, '. . . with Ryan Livingstone, at Berkeley, led to some interesting insights into physical trauma repair.' Her legs are trembling. She squeezes her thighs together, to stop them. 'Since then, my research focus has been on new ways of speeding human healing processes . . . But getting there . . . well, I did a lot of solo work on caterpillars; just seeing if I could mimic the natural processes. And eventually, with the help of several graduate students from the University of Nevada, in particular Audrey Mayvale, we developed controlled biosynthetic techniques; we built our own imaginal discs, from scratch. However, stepping these techniques up to mammals has proved difficult.'

As she speaks, some of the delegates, then more and more of them, call up her paper on their devices, and flip from image to image, following her logic. Deep breath. Deep breath.

'Working with the existing human healing mechanisms, you come up against some hard limits. The human rebuild system has a very limited blueprint to work from, and can only rebuild a few hundred cells deep. That means a baby can regrow a fingertip, but an adult cannot. Obviously, stem cells work well for small internal structures, where there is a strong nutrient supply: teeth, kidneys, etc. But complex external structures – a hand, a foot, a leg, external genitalia – cannot be regrown at all.'

Some of the audience have begun whispering to each other, and she worries that she's losing them; but no, that's not it. They've read ahead. Absorbed the abstract.

They're excited.

She namechecks the German stem-cell team from Munich, to show she is aware of their recent breakthroughs. Various people, scattered about the hall, glance in the same direction, towards the right end of the front row. Naomi follows the glances.

Oh my God, they're here.

Her legs start to tremble again and she can't stop them this time.

Concentrate. You know this paper backwards.

'But the imaginal disc mechanism used by holometabolous insect larvae is very different to the stem-cell mechanism; imaginal discs are extremely effective at building entire external structures, and integrating them with the body as a whole. It occurred to me that if we were to build imaginal discs for human body parts, and supply a nutrient soup, the limb could self-assemble in 3D space, and integrate, instead of having to build outward from the point of trauma.'

She calls up another photograph, from her mouse research.

'The point of trauma is encased in an antiseptic artificial silk cocoon, supplied with sterile nutrients, and an individually tailored imaginal disc for the lost limb. Integration with the existing, damaged limb was a stumbling block; you can't just leave damaged blood vessels open, and without a functioning circulatory system, oxygenating the growing tissues is problematic. And you can't circulate the nutrient mix – to oxygenate it externally – as that will disturb and damage the growing cells and grosser structures. We solved this by slowly dissolving oxygen in the nutrient mix, through the silk wall, using a second layer of cocoon.'

A man bangs through the door at the back of the hall. She stops speaking.

Is there a fire? He doesn't look like a firefighter.

The man slows down when he sees her onstage; sees the crowd, some of whom have turned to look at him. He finds an empty aisle seat, and sits.

No. No fire. Just rude.

Naomi continues.

'It works. We've regrown full limbs on mice and gerbils.' She hesitates. No, say it. 'We're ready to go on primates, once we get permission. To be honest, we're ready to go with humans: I just doubt the FDA are, yet.'

The whispers grow louder and louder.

She flies through the rest of the paper. It seems to be over in seconds.

When she finally stops, there's a terrifying moment of silence, just long enough for her to imagine she's got something obvious terribly wrong, just long enough to brace herself for dismissive words. Booing. Hisses of disgust.

She glances across at the team from Munich. They are frowning. Oh my God.

Their lead researcher shifts sideways a little, and raps his knuckles hard on the seat of the plastic chair in which he is sitting. The others in the team do likewise. Fast, loud rapping of the knuckles.

Faster and louder.

77

Some others join in from the back of the room.

She feels a little moment of terror before she realizes.

Of course. It's what German students do, when a lecture has been particularly good. A sign of respect for the speaker.

Respect . . .

And now others in the room start clapping. Start rising to their feet, clapping. The Germans, too, rise to their feet, now, and clap.

She doesn't know what to do with her body, how to respond.

Yaakov joins her onstage, gives her a big hug that she returns fiercely. 'Well done,' he murmurs. 'Well done.' He lets her go, and waves her to a chair. She collapses into it, her calves and thighs aching from released tension.

Yaakov invites questions.

The man who burst in late commandeers the roving mike like a guy used to getting what he wants. 'The military implications are . . .' He trails off, as though he has abruptly changed his mind. There is an awkward silence.

'Yes,' she says, relieved this is an area she's thought about. 'My research indicates that if suitable imaginal discs were made available in combat zones, and, of course, packs of cell material, you could save limbs right there on the battlefield. The drawback is that you'd need to tailor the discs in advance for every soldier, using their own DNA, to prevent rejection. But it scales up pretty quickly. If you were to do it for all combat personnel, it would become very inexpensive . . .'

A woman who's had her hand up since before Naomi stopped speaking can't wait any more. 'What about head trauma? Brain injury? Has it any role in that?'

'Mmmm,' says Naomi, who is starting to feel weirdly spaced now. She just wants to lie down, shut down. My God, this must be how Colt feels all the time . . . Concentrate! Head trauma, brain injury . . . No, she definitely doesn't want to answer that question. 'I haven't really thought that far ahead.'

A young man with a thin moustache and old-fashioned, gold-rimmed spectacles grabs the mike; Naomi, who no longer pays attention to the fashions on the coasts, wonders idly if he is intensely fashionable, or just completely disconnected from fashion.

'Thank you for a verrrry interesting paper.' His accent is almost comically French. OK, that answers that. 'But how does this improve on the work already being done, using stem cells alone, to promote limb regrowth?'

'Well, as I've said, stem cells come up against the size problem. They're great for growing a limb on a foetus, which is, you know, incredibly small compared to an adult; and in the womb, which is, obviously, a nutrition-rich environment, optimized for cell growth. Basically, they work great internally. But adult limb regrowth, outside the womb, faces scale problems, nutrition problems, infection problems, that we feel this approach can solve . . .'

More questions; the questioners are excited, energized. Some want to know specifics. Some explore the implications.

Eventually, Yaakov wraps it up. 'I'd like to thank Naomi Chiang for participating in StemCellCon at such short notice, and for delivering such a fascinating paper. Next up is Fabian Procter, who needs no introduction . . .' Yaakov indicates, with a turn of his head, that Naomi can walk offstage now. She does. She really needs a lousy coffee.

She feels like she's walking on a trampoline. No, she knows how she feels. She feels better than she has ever felt, in daylight, in her life.

28

The backstage kettle hasn't even boiled when the latecomer who asked the first question strides into the green room.

'Man, you've let the cat out of the bag,' he says. He is smiling, but it's not a good smile.

'Well, it's my cat,' she says, and automatically smiles back. Not a good smile, either. It reminds her of the way she used to smile at Ryan. No. She shuts it off abruptly. No more fake smiles.

'Well, no,' he says. He doesn't stop smiling. 'No, it's not your cat. We just didn't hear about it in time to stop you. You can't announce stuff like this at an open conference. Your research is funded by government money—'

'—It's part-funded by the University of—'

'—and it clearly states—'

'—University of Nevada—'

'—and it clearly states in your contract that if you come up with work of potential military significance, there are appropriate channels . . .'

'I didn't think about military significance, it has general medical applications—'

'Bullshit,' and he stops smiling. 'Your initial research proposal specifies frontline trauma management. You just *admitted* this has military significance, onstage. You realize that ANYBODY could just take this information and use it? I mean, bad guys? Really bad guys? Guys that don't have our . . . whatever, moral scruples, about experimenting on human subjects. This conference is a totally public forum, they were streaming it live till we managed to block it, and you have potentially just given away the biggest breakthrough in battlefield medicine since . . .'

'There is no such thing as "battlefield medicine", medicine is just medicine . . .'

He raises his voice and talks over her. 'There are implications for this way beyond trauma management, and you know it. You are COMPLETELY in breach of your employment contract. We could crucify you for what you just did.'

The door swings open, and by the time Yaakov has stepped into the green room, the smiling man is smiling again. 'I'll be in touch. Oh, don't leave the hotel. Seriously. Great paper, Dr Chiang.' He nods, '. . . Dr Stern.' And he's gone.

'You really stirred them up,' says Yaakov. 'An entirely novel approach.'

Naomi takes two steps to the wall, and leans on it. She doesn't feel like she's walking on a trampoline any more. 'I think I need to lie down, Yaakov,' she says. 'And I need to talk to Colt.'

'Sure, sure,' says Yaakov. 'I've got to introduce two more speakers, then I chair a panel in the Broadway Ballroom. We'll talk later. I'm free at seven. Dinner? I'll introduce you to some good people.'

'Yes. Love to.'

Yaakov pats her shoulder, and leaves.

She tries to reach Colt, to tell him she did it; to tell him she's OK; to wish him a happy birthday without mentioning the words, because he hates his birthday; but her screen is behaving strangely. It freezes, unfreezes, freezes again. Then it folds up. Turns off.

She's so used to it working effortlessly, all the time – there when she needs it, gone when she doesn't – that she's not even sure what's happened for a moment.

Odd. She'll try again in her room.

29

Yaakov catches up with her, halfway to the elevator, breathing heavily.

'I don't know how to say this,' he says.

His face, it's bad. Oh please, not Colt . . .

'It's . . . unprecedented,' he says.

'What?' she says. '*What?*' Oh God, I should never have left him . . .

'They've done a pullback on your paper,' says Yaakov.

'What . . . what's a pullback?' Her knees give a little and she stifles a moan, as relief floods her like a little orgasm.

Yaakov is looking at her strangely. 'Don't you keep up, God forbid, with the news?'

She shakes her head. Pullback . . . pullback . . . She has a vague memory of overhearing the term in cafeteria conversations at the lab, a while back. But she never joined in.

'You don't understand how serious this is?'

If Colt is OK, then it's not serious. 'Just tell me what a pullback is.'

'My goodness,' says Yaakov. 'Well . . . the NSA or NDSA, or whatever they are calling themselves now, would call it a cyber defence tool, though I'd have another word for it . . .'

Naomi snorts a little laugh. Now, the ongoing rebranding of the National Domestic Security Agency (formerly part of the NSA, a chunk of the Defense Department, and a bunch of smaller agencies), is a subject she *does* know intimately, from back when Ryan rang her all the time. When she wanted to stop him hassling her about Colt, she'd ask him how the new logo redesign was going. He'd explode. *You saw that? It makes us look like a financial services company!* He'd rant for twenty minutes, Colt's schooling entirely forgotten . . .

'. . . developed to stop leaks of government information . . .' Yaakov's still talking, but Naomi has Ryan in her head now, triggering a cascade of memories that she usually represses at home. His cock. His tongue. His voice. His fist. Good memories. Bad memories.

'. . . can be blocked across all networks . . . Are you listening?' says Yaakov.

'Sorry.'

'You did ask.'

'Yes. Sorry. I'm a little tired.' She wants to touch herself but of course she can't. 'I might need to take a nap before dinner.' It's being away from home, she supposes. It's relief, that the paper went well. It's not being seen as a mother, for a few hours.

'Hmmm. Anyway, no ISP can host or transmit them. And there's a backdoor in most devices, to allow the government to erase copies from private devices. *Tremendous* controversy when that came out. Bigger than the old NSA encryption scandals.'

'Mmmm . . .' Oh, of course, she didn't take her pill this morning. And, for a couple of days before that, she'd been having it with coffee. *Coffee interferes with absorption . . .* She almost laughs. This isn't something unusual happening. This is her libido, no longer suppressed, roaring back. And her anxiety. No wonder she feels so odd. She's herself again.

Naomi tries to focus, concentrate. 'You mean, they're blocking the delegates from passing my paper on to other people?'

'No, no, they're *wiping out every copy of your paper*. We released it to all delegates at the start of your talk. The government, I assume the NDSA, is erasing all those copies from all delegates' devices, and blocking transmission.'

'But you can't *eradicate* a piece of information once it's out . . .'

'Oh, certainly, it's almost impossible to kill all copies of anything. But once people are afraid to pass it on, or receive it, then it's effectively dead. A file that can't copy itself, locked off on a single machine, is essentially dormant.'

He's locked his hands together now behind his back, slipped into a favourite rant. She sneaks a quick glance at her screen. Her eyes widen.

It's blank.

Oh. This *is* serious.

'Look at the old Soviet Union,' says Yaakov, looking off into the distance, into his childhood, not noticing her dismay, 'where the state owned every printing press and photocopier, and registered every typewriter. You didn't need to stop people writing subversive books. You just needed to prevent transmission. Rather like hygiene, and bacteria. Ideas have to spread to do damage. If you can wipe out 99 per cent of the population, and stop the remainder from spreading, you have functional success . . .'

Wait, she's got her screen back on. She tries to call up her own copy of her own paper on her own screen.

It's gone.

She's been obliterated, wiped out. Her work, her moment of triumph on that stage. Taken back. Erased. It has to be Ryan.

Yaakov finally sees her face.

'I'm sorry,' says Yaakov. 'I'm so sorry. There's nothing we can do.'

30

Back in her room, the woman on the TV is talking about electrical storms in the south-west. Cartoon lightning bolts stab at Las Vegas.

Naomi rings Colt.

He answers on audio.

'Put it on video.'

'Oh, come on, Mama.'

'I just want to see your face.'

'Jeeeez, Mama, you know what I look like.'

'You're wearing your helmet, aren't you.'

She hears him mumble something, and then he is tapping, tapping, off mike, rapidly and symmetrically for a few seconds in a quick, familiar pattern, before he says, 'How was the p . . . p . . . paper? It was supposed to go out live, but it cut off before you came on.'

'Really? It went well, I think. It went well . . . But . . .' She wants to unburden herself. Mention the smiling man. The threats. The pullback. 'Afterwards . . .' No.

Not to Colt.

Don't make him anxious.

She feels empty. Her body aches after the stress of the paper, the confrontation in the green room, the erasure of her work. There should be someone to talk to. Oh, she should have stayed in touch with her friends . . .

'Mama?'

'Honey . . . Are you eating?'

'Yes, Mama.'

'Show me.'

'Oh, *Mama*.'

'Show me.'

Colt takes off the helmet, flicks on video, and goes to the fridge. Opens it.

'Why doesn't the light come on?'

'I had to take . . .' No. He starts again. 'I needed . . .'

He pauses. She's not going to like this, whatever way he phrases it.

Naomi's trying to peer inside the fridge. 'You took out the *bulb*?'

Hah! Cool. 'Uhhm . . . for an experiment. I'll put it back later . . .' It's not really lying. He means the extension cord. It's not his fault she thinks he means the bulb.

He puts his face, the camera, close to the bottom shelf so she can see. Only four smoothies left. He ate a teaspoonful of every smoothie, an hour after Naomi left, so he could tell her truthfully he'd eaten some. 'Some' was a good word. Useful. But since then he's been dumping them, one per mealtime, untasted, ingame. The game maps all outgame food onto sour goat's milk – the look, the smell – to discourage you from tasting, because of the unavoidable taste/texture mismatches with the container and the food.

He tries not to gag on the warm, rotting air. 'See? I ate the carrot. I ate the . . . the . . .' It won't come.

'Pea?'

'Yeah, the pea.' He pulls his head back out of the fridge and slams the door. Breathes out.

'And you'll eat the spinach?'

'Yeah.'

'OK. OK. Thanks.' She almost lets it go. No.

'Promise me you'll eat.'

'Mama!'

'Promise me you'll eat.'

'OK, I promise.'

'Full sentence.'

'I promise you I will eat.'

'Soon. Today.'

'Today.'

'A full meal.'

'Yes.'

'Now, all in one go.'

'Mama, I promise you I will eat a full meal today.'

'OK.' She can't see any wriggle room there. 'Sorry. I worry.'

'You look tired,' Colt says. 'You better rest.' It's ended conversations before. It might work.

'Yes. I will.'

She doesn't want to let him go.

'And you're sleeping OK?'

'Great. Perfect. Really.'

Eventually he gets her to finish the call. He pulls the helmet back on. Pulls on the gloves. Relaxes. Stretches.

Alone in the cave.

He walks back to the fridge.

It's now a rocky ledge, with a rough wooden door.

He frowns. It's too cartoony. Something wrong with the shadows. Someone's been playing around with the parameters for light reflection again. That English guy, Scurvy Wallbanger, probably. He's in some kind of fight with the Snow Queen.

Colt opens and closes the wooden door a few times, watching the shadows move, trying to work out what's changed. There's been an ongoing aesthetic argument for months over how realistic the light should be. Which is part of the bigger, broader fight over how realistic the avatars should be. Which is part of the permanent world war over how female-friendly, or not, the gameworld should be. A conflict which makes Colt intensely uncomfortable. He's been trying to keep out of it.

As he admires the swing of the wooden door, he thinks again about changing his brain, his life. Standing there, he closes his eyes. Methodically moves mentally through the procedure, re-examines all his decisions, looking for anything obvious he might have missed. Thinks through all the implications. This is his last chance to change his mind about changing his mind . . .

He might die.

He might live, without half of his brain. A vegetable. Human broccoli.

But . . . it might work. He might understand people.

He might understand women.

He feels sick and he doesn't know why.

No, he does know why. Because he's not going to do it. He's too scared to do it. His mother will come back, and he will not have changed.

Don't think about it. This life is fine. This life is good. There's nothing wrong with it. You don't need other people. You've got the game. Your mother will come home and everything will be fine.

He opens his eyes.

There's no cold air coming from the unplugged fridge now, good. The sudden cold on his face, in his lungs, had never mapped properly ingame. Broke the illusion.

Still, the gloves are doing a good job with the fridge door, translating the smooth metal and plastic of the handle into a rough, almost splintered wood texture.

He takes the spinach and peanut-butter smoothie out of the unplugged fridge. The game maps it nicely.

He has to admit, this slightly tweaked light does look dramatic. He admires the light and shade on the clay jug, passes it from gloved hand to gloved hand, enjoying the rough texture against his fingertips. He pulls out the cork stopper. Sniffs. Recoils. 'Oh *mano*.'

He walks to the waterfall, pulls back the vines, and turns on the shower. It's not a perfect map. The vines map perfectly onto the shower curtain, but switching on the shower is a botch; he moves a rock ingame to unblock the waterfall, but his fingers go out of sync, between the two realities. His heart jolts.

He starts blinking rapidly, which helps, and he murmurs prime numbers. He concentrates on the sound of the waterfall. The precision and accuracy of the sound reassures him, calms him, and he tips the goat's milk into the stream, and the waterfall carries it all away. He scours out the earthenware jug till the water it contains is clean. Washes the cork stopper.

Once the shower is actually on, the map between the shower and the waterfall is perfect. Soothing.

The sounds, the smell of the damp air filling the dry cave, the splashes on his bare legs, felt directly through the porous micro-mesh. Perfect.

He tips out the water, and leaves the jug. But there's no clean way to go from waterfall to no waterfall without the same sync problem in reverse, so he leaves the shower on.

He goes to the front door – a walk through a long, narrow cave – and puts the chain on the door. Yeah, the mapping is good. OK, the cave entrance is blocked.

Safe.

It's going to be a good day.

31

'There is as much difference between us and ourselves as between us and others.'   — Montaigne,
                                             translated by Donald Frame

There's a knock on her door.

'I'm fine,' Naomi calls out. 'The room's fine. Thanks.'

But there's another knock. Another. She answers it.

It's the military guy. He leans forward, she backs off reflexively, and he just walks in, like that.

'So,' he says. 'I've been discussing your case.'

He sits on the bed without being invited, and she hesitates by the door. Braces herself for disaster. Who's going to look after Colt? Maybe she can run . . .

'We're prepared to offer you a lab,' he says.

She almost asks, who's we? But she knows already, from the clenching of her stomach muscles.

'Generous resources,' he says. 'We've got people working in this area already.'

Of course they do. After the break-up, Ryan had employed their whole research group. All her college friends. So she'd have no friends.

'We'll give you a top-level security clearance,' he says. 'We'll show you their research. You can have your pick of them.'

'A lab?' she says, still standing by the open door, still ready to run.

'Yes.'

'My own lab?'

'Yes.'

'In Las Vegas?'

'No. You'd be working out of our research centre in Maryland.'

She's shaking her head. 'That's impossible.'

'We have state-of-the-art facilities there. Bear in mind, we have several top-quality research teams already working in this area. You'd be assigned a brand-new lab, it's just been fitted out for exactly this kind of work. It's a totally secure environment. You can live on or off base . . .'

She realizes with astonishment that he is pleading with her. Cautiously, she closes the door, but keeps her distance from him.

'Why not upgrade the lab I work in?' she asks, to test how far this could go.

But he grimaces. 'Apart from the fact that your lab is a joke . . . If it's a choice between you moving to Maryland, or us uprooting a research team of fifty, a hundred people . . . what do you think is going to happen, in the real world?'

'It's totally impossible,' she says, with more conviction. 'I have a son. I can't disrupt his life like that.'

'We have a top-quality school on base, and there are several other excellent schools in the area. After all, the existing research team members have kids too.'

'You don't understand. He needs routine. He can't handle change. And, frankly, neither can I. It's taken me years to build a stable life for my son, where he is happy and able to fulfil his potential. I'm not risking that.'

'Ms Chiang . . .'

'Dr Chiang.'

He shrugs. 'I don't think you understand. This isn't a standard job offer. This is the alternative to prosecuting you for—'

'Get out,' she says, and swings the door open again so violently it slams into the rubber block protecting the wall from exactly that.

'—releasing classified information to the enemy—'

'—the scientific community is not your enemy,' she says.

'You'd be surprised,' he says drily, and it takes her a moment to realize that he's joking, that he has a sense of humour.

She smiles. 'I don't think you'd be stupid enough to prosecute a single mother for giving a research paper at a conference. There's the court of law and there's the court of public opinion . . .'

'You've got a Chinese background.'

'I was born in San Francisco.'

'Sure. That's . . . almost America.' He makes a wry face. 'But you look Chinese. And your father, with his Party background . . .'

'He was a very minor official, he left long before . . .'

'Yeah, taking his bribe money with him . . .'

'He was vetted, he got his green card . . .'

'Oh, eventually, in return for some, ah, cooperation . . . but there's a lot of material in his file, and it doesn't look good. I suspect the court of popular opinion could, regrettably, come to the disgraceful and entirely erroneous conclusion that you were a security risk. I blame the media.' He stands up. 'Stay in the hotel.'

'But my flight . . .'

'Our budget will stretch to a new ticket.'

'It's not that, I have to . . .' She stops. Don't mention Colt is alone. Don't let them know your weak point. 'I didn't bring enough clothes.'

'With respect, *Dr* Chiang, you have bigger problems.'

32

Naomi leans against the door after he leaves, as though holding back monsters. Rings Colt again.

A blast of music. *Leave a message.*

'I'm going to be delayed, honey. I might have to stay an extra day . . . or two . . . at the conference. It's nothing serious.' He might worry about the money. 'They're buying me a new flight.' What else? 'Make sure to eat. Get enough sleep.'

Naomi finishes the call feeling happy and sad and hungry and free and lonely and restless. Walks up and down the room, thinking, not thinking.

'Stay in the hotel.' Like a prisoner. Like a slave. To be ordered around. Her face feels hot. Her eyes sting and her vision blurs, as she blinks away a jolt of angry frustration.

She is still full of adrenalin, it hasn't burned off. It will go sour, she knows; the breakdown products of unused adrenalin are toxic. She knows what would burn it off.

No.

Yes.

She unchains, unlocks the door.

Takes the elevator down, crosses the lobby without catching the receptionist's eye, without catching anybody's eye, and walks out into the morning's neon and noise.

They're probably following her. Are they following her? Fuck them. Move fast. Be unpredictable. They may not have organized anything yet. It may be the biggest surveillance machine in world history, but it's still a government bureaucracy.

Naomi walks into Times Square not thinking about what she's looking for. She knows she is giving out some kind of signal; men smile at her, but she doesn't smile back. Men haven't looked at her like this in a while. Some little internal switch has been flicked. The adrenalin.

Not just the adrenalin.

She doesn't know if she wants to feel like this. She doesn't know how she feels.

She walks into a cinema lobby and out again, into a theatre lobby, and out again; and now she's catching men's eyes, but it's too early in the day, they're not alive to the opportunity. She's catching women's eyes, too; thoughtful, wary, holding onto their men. Tourist couples, nervous.

A young woman with short blonde hair, smoking a long, slim Dutch joint outside one of those new ironic retro strip clubs; probably working the morning shift; that quiet time between the guys on their way into work and the lunchtime crowd. She looks Naomi up and down, smiles, and sucks hard on her joint till the tip glows, and Naomi whimpers involuntarily as a pulse starts to throb between her legs. Naomi smiles back, walks past her, walks faster. Breathes faster, conscious of her chest rising and falling.

Is someone following her? What will happen, if they catch her? She doesn't look back.

She passes a dozen elderly deaf Chinese tourists, their guide signing to them, smiling. And she remembers her mother, her cheap, old-fashioned hearing aids that would abruptly cut out, and leave her deaf and frustrated till she could find new batteries.

They'd damaged her mother's hearing in Nanjing, interrogating her. The year the local Party had cut the bright red cross off the steeple of her shabby Catholic church. Her mother had led the protest; a row of frightened women of all ages, a couple of old men, backed up against the church wall by riot police. Dragged into vans. Beaten. It can happen anywhere.

I want to be brave like my mother.

Maybe not exactly like my mother.

She walks into the next four-star hotel she sees, and goes straight to the bar; just a big area to the side of reception, marked off by armchairs, and trees in pots.

It's awful early for this; guys are much braver at night; but she buys a glass of red wine anyway, and sits in an armchair with her legs slightly apart. An older man walks past, smiles at her. She doesn't smile back.

A middle-aged couple walk past. The man glances over and starts to smile, and she smiles back but just out of politeness, and he stops smiling abruptly and looks intensely sad.

A couple of minutes later, a younger man walks past on his way to the bar.

She smiles at him.

He smiles at her, but he keeps walking.

Oh, crap. It's so long since she did this. Maybe the rules have changed. Maybe she's too old.

On his way back from the bar, he stops and says, 'Would you recommend any shows? I'm only in town for one night, and I . . .' He runs out of invention, but that's fine, he has got the first serve over the net.

'A show?' She pretends to think.

They talk complete bullshit about nothing for half an hour. She's decided after a minute. He's decided after a minute. She couldn't have made it any clearer.

My God, he's never going to pull the trigger.

For a moment, Naomi is almost nostalgic for the old San Francisco BDSM scene.

She says, 'I really need a shower. But my hotel is so far uptown, I don't think I'll have time to get back there.'

Unbelievably, he looks like fumbling even this one. But he's a human being, and five billion years of evolution weren't entirely in vain.

'Well, I guess . . . you could always have a shower in my room . . . if you're really stuck. I mean it's not . . .'

She says yes, before he can talk himself back out of it.

33

Colt has promised to eat a full meal today. He doesn't like promises, they weigh heavy on him.

He decides to get this one out of the way. Orders a pizza. Pepperoni and olives. With extra olives.

Half an hour later, ingame, a dry mesquite branch snaps behind Colt, and he swings around, his heart slamming.

No. Crapworld.

The doorbell.

Oh yeah.

Pizza.

While waiting, he had slipped back into the game, and had soon forgotten ordering it. Much of the bliss of the game came from this; that actions taken in the outer world dissolved to nothing and were soon forgotten.

But now, suspended between worlds, he is unsure how to behave, what to do.

He is unsure how dangerous this encounter might be.

A stranger, he thinks. At the door. Oh, Mama. His mother has always opened the door.

He didn't think this through.

He has never wanted his mother like this before, he has never missed her like this. She has always been here, or close by, a few minutes away; and now she is not.

He stands there, very quiet, locked in the gameworld, but aware of the real world; uncomfortably aware that he is not, in fact, in a cave. And this feeling is very bad, feels very unsafe; to be in the gameworld, but aware that it is not the world, that at any moment the mapping might fail and something terrible and unpredictable might crash in; touch him; make him feel something.

He keeps mapping on. He's not ready to go outgame.

But he switches off noise-cancellation. Now he can hear sounds in the real world again, as well as the sounds the game converts them into.

He smells something that is not in the game. The smell itself is pleasant, but the fact that it is alien, the fact that the game cannot map it, scares him.

Too late to switch off the light.

He didn't think this through. He ordered online, and, at some level, thought the pizza would be delivered without human interaction, like the mail.

But of course, Mama likes these guys because they're traditional. As traditional as a Neapolitan pizza joint in Nevada can get. Buffalo mozzarella, and delivery boys on motorbikes.

Retro bullpoop. Why couldn't they use drones like everyone else?

He leans forward a little, and rubs the palms of his hands back and forth repeatedly on the tops of his hip bones. In sync; exactly the same number of times each. Soothing.

OK. There must be an encounter, an exchange, a conversation. The other person will not know him, will not make allowances. It could go wrong. It has gone wrong before.

His mother is not there to rescue him, as she did once in Walmart, when he wandered off into the hardware aisle, and a man, fat, and yet somehow with too much skin – so perhaps, thought Colt, he had once been fatter still – caught Colt staring, and grew angry at Colt's long, detailed explanation of why he was staring, and strode up and loomed over him, shouting, the man's neck and jowls red and razor-burnt, flapping with rage, like a turkey's.

Colt's heart is beating uncomfortably fast and his breathing is all over the place.

But the person on the other side of the door must know he is here. Outgame, there are translucent glass panels around the door. The light is on, straight above Colt's head, in the hall.

Now Colt hears the doorbell and the snapping of a twig, almost simultaneously.

He reaches for the door ingame, and his hand approaches a rough wooden thing, through which he can see chinks of light, moonlight, and a movement. The game understands the logic of the situation, the mapping is good, and Colt is soothed.

But to open the door, ingame, and try to deal with an outgame stranger; no.

The person on the other side of the door shouts something, and the helmet lets it through, but it's a little mangled. It was probably *'Pizza.'* But it could have been something else.

Panic.

Breathe. Breathe.

He turns off the mapping. Breathes.

He turns off the game.

Oh, the disappointing light. The flatness of the world. The lack of energy, contrast.

A door, a wall.

Flat and textureless in the nothing light.

It's like a stab. The loss.

Leaving his helmet on, looking through the dead visor, he approaches the door and tries to push a word through a throat that has tightened. What his mother says. Say what his mother says. 'Coming.' But it comes out so tight and weak, he isn't sure if it can be heard on the other side of the door.

He has to clear his throat, force it to loosen.

'COMING.' That's too loud.

'No problem, take your time.' From the far side of the door. He is shocked to hear a reply, but of course they will reply, of course. Hard to make out the voice, hard to say what kind of person it is.

He tries to imagine the person on the other side of the door, the stranger, to empathize, as his mother so often recommends, in order to predict what they will do next; he closes his eyes, but all he can see in his head is the door from the other side.

A zombie staring at a door.

No feelings, no thoughts.

Staring at the door he hides behind.

A terrible feeling fills him, and he opens his eyes and stares deliberately up into the light above his head to burn out the image.

He is afraid it will be the big man, with the red, swinging jowls. He tries to estimate the probability. The population of Nevada is three point five million . . . No, the probability is vanishingly small. But why then does he *feel* it is so possible, so likely? He has either calculated the odds wrong, consciously, mathematically, just now; or he calculated the odds wrong unconsciously, emotionally, when he felt that he knew the man at the door. But, either way, half his mind is wrong about this important thing; half his mind misunderstands the world, it's just a matter of which half; and that is very scary.

If it is the man with the red, swinging jowls, Colt decides he will slam the door, and recalculate the odds, and discover what factor he overlooked.

Colt reaches for the chain, hesitates. Tries to think what his mother would say. Because sometimes she is happy when he does something he is scared of, and sometimes she is incredibly angry, and it is so hard to tell, in advance, which she will be.

34

In New York his mother comes explosively, kneeling on the big hotel bed with her ass in the air, face crushed down awkwardly, sideways, into a pillow, her hands tied behind her back, and she has forgotten her son, forgotten his name, forgotten his face, for the first time in years.

35

Colt takes off the chain, and opens the door, and the stranger standing there is wearing a helmet.

A full-face motorcycle helmet, bright red, with a dark glass visor.

They stare at each other, almost visor to visor.

No, the stranger is not quite as tall as Colt. Is slim. Is holding a pizza box.

It's not the big man.

Safe.

Colt untenses his arm, which he had poised to slam and lock the door.

Opens the door fully.

Black leather clothes. Motorcycle clothes.

A bright yellow Yamaha motorbike sits up on its stand behind the stranger.

The stranger takes off the red helmet one-handed.

It is a woman.

'Sorry, didn't mean to scare you,' she says. 'Da Vinci Pizza. I know, we're meant to take the helmet off before we ring the bell, but the rain fritzes my hair.'

It's raining, yes. Just starting. The rare, sudden, savage rain of the desert. He hadn't noticed.

She's looking at him in a way that he doesn't understand.

'Oh *man*,' she says, 'I love to ride my bike out here. No speed cams . . . You ride?'

He shakes his head. 'The lifetime odds of serious injury riding a motorbike are really high,' he says.

'Yeah, sure, but if you . . .'

'Two orders of magnitude higher than for a self-drive,' he says.

Behind her, in the spill of light from the open door, drops bounce and splash off the hard, dry ground. Stray raindrops swirl in, under the projecting porch roof, as the wind gusts. She raises the pizza box she holds in her left hand, and rests it on her head like a hat. Like a giant mortar board. Drops smack loudly off the lid of the box, and each splash casts a delicate mist onto his face, his visor, a moment later.

'Very, very dangerous,' he says. He shakes his head, and looks away from her. Stares down at her red helmet.

His vision whites out for a second. There is, almost simultaneously, a roaring crash that just keeps on going, and now a hot, bright afterimage of her red helmet is dancing in front of his eyes, overlapping the real helmet, and he doesn't know what's happening and it's scary.

The roar is deep, rough, angry, like the big old Siberian tigress he heard in the zoo in San Diego, coughing and roaring at the lions that she could smell but not see on the other side of the high concrete wall. But this roar goes on and on, no pause to take a breath. A creature with no lungs.

Not a creature.

Lightning. That was lightning whiting out his sight, and then thunder, very close. It's the gap in the air cut by the bolt of lightning, collapsing. An inch wide, and miles high.

Once he can run the physics of it in his head, he is OK again. All his muscles relax.

Almost no gap between light and sound. Very near. Almost overhead.

Uh oh. He left his booster out, on the ridge top.

'Whewwff,' she is saying. 'That was close.'

Should he be polite? Mama always says, when in doubt, just say something polite. Yes.

And he says, 'Come in, out of the rain.'

And she does, she squeezes past him into the house.

'Thanks,' she says, and as he is turning in the doorway, horrified, to watch her walk *into the house*, there is another blast of light, and this time he sees it, the jagged line of light leaping over his head – must be from the top of the ridge, hidden by the house – to the black clouds above.

He can't believe he's said it. Invited a stranger inside the house. Why did he say it?

Someone said it in a film. Yes. Rain, lightning. 'Come in out of the rain.' It's a pattern, and he had to finish the pattern.

'Don't you have more deliveries?' he calls after her.

'Nah,' she says, 'you're my last tonight.'

His hands unobtrusively by his sides, he drums a quick pattern on his hip pockets with his fingertips, all four fingers one after another, five times, both sides, in balance. It's not good, when his mouth doesn't check first with his brain. That usually leads to trouble.

He's so worried about the stranger in his house that he stops worrying about his new booster on the ridgetop.

36

He doesn't really get the next few minutes, he's closed down, it's too much, she's in the house, she's talking, asking questions, he can smell her, it's a complicated smell, there's some perfume –

though it could be soap – and there's her hair and the leather of her clothes . . .

She notices him looking at the leather jacket. Glances down. 'It's actually pretty hot in this, indoors,' she says. 'On the bike, you cool down, with the speed, and the wind.' She unzips the thick black leather jacket, and slips out of it. Hangs it casually on one shoulder.

She wears a red T-shirt underneath. It's a nice red. Maybe Pantone 187, he thinks, staring at it.

'So you're Colt.'

Colt frowns. He'd placed the order using his mother's information.

'How do you know my name?'

She shrugs. 'There aren't many Chiangs in Nevada. And I'm a huge fan of your work.'

'My *work*?'

He's totally off balance.

Is this normal? Is pizza delivery always like this? They do research, and talk to you?

She smiles. 'Ingame . . .'

'You play?'

'Ah . . .' She pauses, about to say something. Changes her mind.

And *again* she's looking at him in a way he doesn't understand. Well, it's probably nothing. He seldom does understand what people mean by their looks. But this . . . There is something weird about it.

It reminds him of something.

What?

'What's your name?' he says.

She raises her eyebrows. 'Guess.'

'Ingame, I mean,' he says.

She keeps her eyebrows raised. 'Guess . . .'

And Colt realizes with terror that she's the girl he met last week, ingame.

The girl who touched him. Who removed her clothes. Removed his clothes.

Who set off his mother's parental controls, and was snatched from his arms, vanished from the game.

But now they are standing in the real world, close enough to touch. He's close enough to smell her skin, the leather of the jacket draped over her shoulder.

'Your pizza is getting cold,' she says, and turns away from him, and walks into the kitchen.

He feels his legs tremble: they want to run, they want to hide, in his room, but then she would be free to roam the house, could be anywhere . . . he follows her into the kitchen.

And somehow he is sitting at the kitchen table, across from her.

He smells her own smell now, it's coming out from under the soap and the leather, it has a lot of elements, perspiration, very fresh, nice, and other smells.

He's way too hot. 'Aircon, lower the temperature three degrees,' he says.

'Sure thing, Colt,' says the aircon, in the voice of Ronald Reagan, a long-dead actor and politician whose voice Naomi finds amusing.

'Thanks,' says the girl to Colt, 'it is kind of warm.' She opens the lid of the cardboard pizza box towards him.

The lid goes through the full 180 degrees, until it sits flat on the table in front of him.

It stays flat; he likes that.

A lot of olives, good.

The pizza's already cut.

A pie chart.

Eight wedges of 12.5 per cent.

They're not totally equal, symmetrical, but not too bad.

She pushes a half-moon of pizza, four slices, 50 per cent, towards him, into the open lid. Pushes it further, right across the lid to the far side.

Now her half mirrors his half exactly. Symmetrical. Better.

'Eat,' she says.

'How did you find me?' he says.

The mist from the raindrops has already evaporated from the visor. He lifts the visor up, leaves the game off; but removing the helmet would be too naked.

She shrugs. 'Tracked you down.'

'You've been tracking me?' A blush of pleasure and a shiver of fear collide, and he is red-faced and trembling and has to turn his face away.

'Yeah, I discovered your mom had an account.' She points at the pizza box. 'I mean everybody does, it's pretty good pizza . . . I hacked the system so that when your order came in, it routed to me.'

'You hacked . . . you could be fired . . .'

'Well, I was already hacking the scheduling system. Otherwise it gives you bullshit shifts. They play favourites.'

'But . . .' Colt is having trouble navigating this. 'You're a hacker? Not just a player?'

'Mmm. I've even contributed some code.'

And now he gets it. Wow. Wow. Wow . . . No, she's not just some anonymous girl player who took his clothes off last week. She's also . . . 'You're the Snow Queen.'

'Yeah.'

Her blizzards . . . He's been caught up in one, in an abandoned mining town, totally convincing. Great use of fractal geometries. Beautiful, stable emergent order from a chaotic system. The melt rates, the drifting. Each flake generating more detail the closer you look.

'I love your work,' he says.

'Thank you.' She gives a startling smile, and he moves back in his chair. 'That's good, because I love your work too.'

'But . . . it's just . . .' He can't think what to say. 'Code.'

'Oh come on. There are a bunch of open-source gameworlds, and they all suck except for ours, and that's because of your code.'

'No.' This is too much, this is like being touched, he feels hot. 'The team, they all . . .'

She shakes her head. 'Most open-source gameworlds are completely incoherent and they're down half the time. When this world breaks, you fix it.'

'Why didn't you say, that you were the Snow Queen, when we . . .' He runs through a bunch of words but he can't imagine saying any of them.

They stare at each other until she touches her nose with her thumb, and stretches it up a little. Holds it there. Lets go.

Colt stares at her nose, fascinated. He's done that one.

She tics.

'You're . . .' No, he doesn't want to use any of the words. 'You're like me,' he says, amazed. But she says nothing.

Maybe I'm wrong. Maybe I shouldn't have said that.

Embarrassment washes over him, like a bucket of ice water tipped over his head, and he shivers. He shouldn't talk to girls, it goes wrong.

Finally she says, 'I'm not good with people. I got on pretty good with you.'

Oh, we did, we did, we got on great, he wants to say, but that was ingame.

Ingame, I kill people. I kiss people. I talk to people. It doesn't mean anything. Ingame, it's just a manoeuvre.

Killing someone, kissing someone.

It's nothing.

Just running some code.

This . . .

I've never killed anyone in the *real world*.

Never kissed . . .

He can't say any of this. He can't say anything at all.

Colt sits silently, trying to process it. That he's kissed the Snow Queen, ingame.

That she's in his kitchen, for real, now.

That they're having an actual conversation.

He knows how conversations work: you ask questions, stuff like that. But the question he wants to ask is, why are you here?

And he is afraid of all the possible answers.

To buy time, he finally eats some pizza.

Weird. Gluey.

She copies him, matching slice, directly opposite.

Nice. Symmetrical.

'You shouldn't eat this stuff all the time,' she says through a mouthful of pizza. 'Mmm. It's not really food.'

'I don't,' says Colt. 'I haven't had a pizza since I was ten.'

She raises her eyebrows at him, chews, swallows. 'Wow. OK. What do you normally eat?'

'Smoothies. All kinds of smoothies. Sometimes a milkshake.'

'Oh right. Like the Chinese guys.'

'Yes.'

'Nothing solid?'

'I don't really like eating.'

'Uh huh. I have friends like that. How come, with you?'

'I don't like it inside me,' he says.

'Pizza?'

'Anything. Food.'

'Growing boy. Got to eat.' She picks up an olive that has fallen off her slice, and eats it.

'But it will become part of me. And . . .' He stops. Is she . . . like me? But she's really confident.

And people don't usually react well to what he's about to say. Yes, maybe stop talking now.

Maybe count for a while.

She has nice zippers on her jacket. Like Mama's, but not.

Zippers have a lot of teeth. Even numbers of teeth. Same either side. Meshed together, pulled apart.

Zipper, good word.

Zipper. Teeth either side, like a mouth. A hole with teeth.

You could call a zipper a mouth. You could call a mouth a zipper.

Yes, he'll stop talking for a while.

'I'll close my zipper,' he says, experimenting with the metaphor. His mother had explained metaphors, again and again. This one should work. Zipper, mouth. Teeth, teeth.

She raises her eyebrows, leans over sideways, and glances under the table, between his legs.

He feels the throb of blood into his penis increase as the arteries widen, and the throb of blood back out again decrease, as the small muscles around the veins tighten, closing them down.

He's looked it all up, studied the data, diagrams, CAT scans, the physiology. He knows it all, he knows exactly what is happening, technically, as his throbbing penis rises, inside his briefs. But the data leaves out how it feels. And it feels overwhelming, it feels out of control.

She sits back up straight, grinning. 'Your zipper isn't open,' she says.

'My mouth,' he says. 'It was a metaphor. Because a zipper has teeth, and a mouth has teeth.'

'Metaphor?'

Is it not a metaphor? No, probably not, because he hates metaphors, the feeling they create in his head, and this one is OK. He can see a mouth with a zip, and then without a zip, just teeth.

That's OK. But with a metaphor, it's real; he can see it, solid. And then it isn't real; it's just some words. There's nowhere stable for it to sit. Neither is true, so it flip-flops between the two. Like a fish dying on the sand, he thinks. Is that a simile? Now that sentence flip-flops in his mind. He's breathing too fast. His vision blurs. This isn't good.

'Are you OK?' she says.

'Maybe it was allegory,' he says. His mother has explained allegory, too. Allegory is like algebra, she had said. 'Allegory is like algebra,' he says. 'You replace ideas with symbols. But the ideas have to be pretty clearly defined.'

'Gimme an example,' she says. That was what he had said to his mother. His breathing slows. He knows this conversation. She had said . . .

He closes his eyes and lowers his voice, like his mother did sometimes. '"Come unto me, all ye that labour and are heavy laden, and I will give you rest. Take my yoke upon you, and learn of me: for I am meek and lowly in heart."'

'Uh huh. And what does it mean?'

This girl is just like him. Just like him. The same questions! This girl is . . . Is she a woman? Maybe she's a woman. Mama always says you have to use the right word. He opens his eyes and looks at her. Looks straight into her eyes. The Snow Queen.

She looks straight into his.

'Are you a woman or a girl?' he says.

There is no answer.

Oh poop, I've screwed up again . . .

But after studying his face a while she says, 'A woman . . . OK, tell me about allegory.'

He feels like singing. He stands up, and sits down again. He knows this conversation. His mother said . . . Just say what his mother said.

'He's saying, "Come to me, all of you that are exhausted by life, and I will show you how to endure it." But he is saying it allegorically. As though they are farm animals who are exhausted from farm work, carrying . . .' he can't remember the word, she must have mumbled . . . 'things, pulling the plough.'

'Uh huh,' she says. 'Right. Allegory.'

Her perfume is a little like coconut. Can coconut be a perfume?

Must be her soap. His left leg begins to twitch under the table, involuntarily. He forces his right leg to twitch, to balance it, but he twitches too hard, and his foot shoots forward, and hits hers.

'Sorry.'

'Sorry.'

She turns in her chair, and swings her legs out to the side of the table. Long legs. He looks across, at her boots. Motorcycle boots, with zippers. More zippers.

'So yeah, like, zip? Zip your lip? Sorry,' she says. 'I'm not great with slang. All the dudes in the kitchen are from Mexico, Colombia, Guatemala . . . South America. But I can swear pretty well in Spanish.' She takes another bite of pizza. He's glad she isn't still looking at his zipper, at the bulge of his penis under the layers of cloth.

'You can?' he says.

'Mmmm. I know some pretty good ones.'

'Tell me a good one.' He watches her mouth move. Her teeth. She bites off some more pizza while she thinks about this. Chews.

A nibble of crust, from the edge; no topping.

He knows what is happening in her mouth. That is a calm thought. He knows what the inside of her mouth feels like. What she is tasting. How it is changing. Bread; the starches becoming sweet, becoming sugar in her mouth. Dissolving, transforming in her saliva. Becoming chemicals small enough to use. Fuel. Her next hour's energy is in her mouth.

'Something on my teeth?' she says.

'Yes,' he says politely.

She laughs, and through the kitchen window behind her a silent flash of lightning lights up the desert, a bleached white, blurred from the rain on the glass. And now the thunder comes.

The storm is moving away.

She smiles again. She smiles a lot.

He smiles back. You're meant to smile back. 'Swear at me in Spanish,' he says. He doesn't like his mother swearing; but somehow the thought of this girl – this woman – the Snow Queen, in front of him, swearing . . .

'*Me cago en la leche de tu puta madre*,' she says.

He is about to auto-translate, but hesitates. He realizes he wants to stay in the conversation. 'What's that mean?' he says.

'I shit in the milk of your whore of a mother.'

He blinks. The image is startling. Vivid. 'Wow. That really is a good one.'

She swings her legs back under the table, and bows. 'So what's the problem with food becoming part of you?' she says.

Oh, beans. She remembered.

'Well, matter comes in,' he says. 'Outside matter. It comes inside you, air and food and water. And it becomes part of you, your cells. And cells live for a while, and then they die, and the matter leaves again, and they're replaced. New matter, new cells. None of the cells, none of the molecules, none of the atoms in you stay the same.'

She shrugs. 'Everything changes . . .'

'Yeah, but . . .' No, she doesn't get it yet. He feels a surge of disappointment. He feels alone again.

Keep going. More detail. Explain.

'I mean there's about a thousand tons of me in total,' Colt says, 'if you add it up, over my life. All the oxygen that comes in, and combines with other atoms, and releases energy, and then gets excreted. The water.' He points to the pizza. 'The carbon, nitrogen, sodium, everything. They come, they go.'

His voice feels too loud. He leans forward, so he can talk more quietly, but when he leans forward he can smell her soap and her hair and the leather and the pizza, all together, much stronger now, and she leans forward too, and her eyes are . . . something, his body is reacting in some weird way to her eyes, and it's too much, he closes his own eyes and sits back in his chair.

She doesn't get it; but he has to try, to explain, 'I'm just a pattern, moving through this kind of flowing river of matter. Like a wave. All I am is the pattern; not the atoms.'

'OK, I get you,' she says.

He opens his eyes again, but he can't look at her.

She's a hacker. That's amazing.

They should talk about hacking. But he's not sure how you do it, how you move into a new area. This is already the longest real-world conversation he's ever had with a stranger.

He looks over her shoulder, at the window. The rain is still slapping against it, running down it. The glass looks like it is endlessly melting. Maybe he could turn an imaginary dial in mid-air, like he does with Mama? He starts to raise his hand; drops it. No; he's pretty sure other people don't do that . . .

'But even the pattern changes, no?' she says. 'What's a baby got in common with an old man? Same person, but—'

'Exactly!' says Colt. '*Nothing.* None of the atoms. Not the structures. No memories in common. *Nothing* in common, not even the *pattern. That's* the problem.' He's making himself anxious talking about this, but he has to keep going. 'If my *pattern* changes, there's nothing solid there at all. And the more I eat, the faster I change.' He waves the back of his hand at the pizza, like he's shooing a fly. 'And I don't want to change.'

'But . . .' she waves a slice of pizza in the air, 'we have to grow up.'

'No! Growing up is just . . .' Mama has a word for this . . . 'it's just a euphemism for dying. Look at the adults you know.'

She raises her eyebrows again. 'Some of them are OK.'

Colt shakes his head. 'They slow down. They stop believing in things. They become really conservative and anxious and . . .'

She's shaking her head. 'Wait, let's go back. I think you're trapped in language. If you see atoms as all these separate *objects*, then . . . OK, have you ever done mushrooms?

He shakes his head, no.

'Mmmm,' she says, and pauses. Studies his face. Takes a breath, and continues. 'Well, the first time I did them . . . this is hard to describe . . . the world stopped being a thing, you know, an object, and it became a process, a . . . sort of . . . OK, this'll sound flaky, but the name that came into my head at the time was, an energy dance. The world . . . well, the *universe*, went from being a noun to a verb.'

Colt circles the metaphor warily.

Finds a way in.

'Like, mass is energy,' he says, 'so, instead of seeing it as mass, you saw it as energy?'

'Yeah, exactly,' she says. 'But it was stronger than that; mass was an illusion, energy was true. It was all just energy, changing form. And it was all one thing, we were all just part of it, not separate.'

'But then . . . uh—'

Colt doesn't know what his objection is; but he knows some part of him is worried, is objecting.

She shakes her head, and leans forward across the table and

looks straight into his eyes and keeps talking, like Mama does when this is important, '—so, you're *not* a pattern, separate from your atoms. You *are* the atoms, which means you are energy. Just energy. You're just an energy dance. Not an individual, separate, dancing; but part of one big, universal energy dance. *Everything's* dancing, with everything else. You, me. All our atoms. Stars, planets, comets, dust; dancing. And a dance has to unfold over time, it *has* to change.'

'Yeah. Yeah.' He's trying to see the world the way she sees it, but he can't, and panic rises.

Maybe this is what Mama calls woo-woo. Maybe she is cuckoo. Maybe this is cuckoo woo-woo.

Dancing . . . It's OK. Dancing is just interacting according to rules. It's physics. Not woo-woo. Call it interacting. Quantum entanglement . . .

He gets a glimpse of something that feels true.

Everything's interacting.

Everything's entangled. OK.

He calms down a little. Her eyes are amazing.

He's admired her code. It's elegant. Her snow was so good, he put in higher mountains, to make more use of it. The Snow Queen.

He says it out loud, by mistake, 'The Snow Queen . . . Sorry, sorry.'

She straightens up, and extends her right hand across the table. She blinks, in a pattern, and he realizes that, while he's been thinking, he's been blinking at her in a soothing sequence.

He blinks again.

She blinks.

He's setting her off.

She has to match his pattern. Wow.

'My name's Sasha,' she says.

'Sorry. Yes.' He finishes blinking the pattern, a simple arithmetic sequence, while watching her follow his sequence.

Her hand is still there, extended over the table.

OK.

He reaches out his right hand, and carefully takes her hand in his. Warm and dry and alive, very alive. He shakes it once, and lets it go, breathing heavily.

She starts blinking, a new sequence, and, without thinking, he follows her pattern.

His breathing slows and deepens.

They're just sitting there, blinking at each other in sequence.

If anyone could see this, Colt thinks, they would laugh at us. They would try to hurt us.

But there is nobody to see us.

A surge of an emotion, a good one, fills him.

It's the happiest he's ever been with a strange woman.

He nods.

'Sasha Bajewski,' she says.

'Nice name,' he says, because he's heard people say that, a lot, and he can't see how that can go wrong.

'Yeah?' She laughs. 'Well, it's the one I'm stuck with. I always think it sounds like the punchline to a joke in Polish. Sashabajewski! And everyone cracks up . . .'

'Do you speak Polish?'

'No, no. Polish grandfather. Well, Russian, but he lived in Poland. I never even met him. So, is Colt an old family name?'

Colt shrugged. 'It was hard to find a name they both liked. So, Dad likes guns. Mama likes horses.'

Sasha laughs, and waits for him to say more; but he hadn't even realized it was funny, and he's run out of things to say.

Now stripped of their avatars, their character traits, their high rankings, their weapons, they sit in silence.

Not proper silence, not the still silence of the desert into which you can just relax. This silence is a gap, that will have to be crossed, that keeps getting wider, and harder to leap.

The rain's easing up. She'll probably go soon.

What do I do now?

And just as the silence becomes unbearable, she says, 'Show me your room.'

His breathing speeds up. Can he say no? She seems so certain.

She indicates the door. Stands. He stands too, uncertain.

She reaches out and takes his hand; and he becomes tremendously aware of his hand, as an object, surrounded by her fingers. Constrained. It cannot move in any direction except back out, out of the tunnel of her hand.

But the touch is too light, it's like fire, his skin is tingling, burning, and his hand jumps in hers, jumps free.

'Sorry,' she says. She starts again, reaches out, but this time she squeezes his hand firmly in hers.

The firm pressure calms his skin; his flesh; his hand; him.

She leads him by the hand towards his room.

37

In the room, she sits him on the bed. 'There.'

She sits beside him.

He doesn't know what happens next. He has no script for this.

What would I do, ingame?

No, he can't do that, here, in the room he sleeps in, the room where his mother wishes him good night . . .

He gets a memory, hot, painful, of the videos his schoolmates made him watch, a couple of times, back when he still went to school.

Not those. Not those.

He had tried to run away from the other kids, at lunch break. They had held him down, made him watch. He couldn't believe what he was seeing, didn't want to believe these things were real. But they were real. When he had closed his eyes, they had pulled his eyelids back with their thumbs, and put the screen up against his face, held his head from turning, so he was inside the harshly lit videos of women and men doing things to each other that he didn't want to understand.

Women who sometimes looked like his mother, but of course it was never his mother, but they said it was, but they were lying . . .

Sasha puts her hand on his thigh, and Colt shudders at the intensity of the sensation.

Oh, he knows, he knows technically, what happens, between a man and a woman. And he knows it doesn't have to be like those videos. But he's avoided seeing it, seeing anyone doing it, since then.

He could look it up, quietly, now.

What's normal? What do you *do*?

But he doesn't want to look it up, it's too late to do research. What if she noticed what he was doing?

She moves her hand very slowly, keeping the pressure firm, a little further up his thigh. Rests her warm, firm hand just short of his hidden penis, which is painfully hard now, trapped sideways, poking out of one leg of his bunched briefs. Its sensitive head pushes against the rougher fabric of his trousers, throbbing.

He doesn't know what to do. He starts to moan.

'Oh, yes,' she says, uncertainly.

His anxiety is blinding, like a headache, he can hardly see her face.

She moves her face towards his, tilts her head; reaches out, touches his neck with her other hand, to bring him closer; it's like being hit by lightning, and he jerks his head away.

This is too real.

Yes I want to do this but I don't know how to do this, it looks like she is glowing, I can't do this.

She adjusts her balance, moves her hand on his thigh, and brushes lightly against the tight cloth that covers the head of his penis.

He wants to laugh, and he wants to scream, as his whole body judders.

There is a feeling and it is crawling through him, cell by cell, and it is taking him over and it is a *huge* feeling and it is too much he can't breathe, the feeling is enormous, it's warm and it is beautiful, beautiful, and she is beautiful, glowing, she is glowing, the feeling comes from her, from looking at her, but it's too much and he cannot . . . breathe . . .

'No,' he says, and stands up, and his trapped cock bends and hurts as he stands.

'What did I . . .'

'No!' he says.

She stands up too. Her face is doing something, it is doing something he doesn't like, it is making an expression that he doesn't like, it's crinkling, it's like something collapsing, something being demolished, and she is saying, 'Colt?' and he backs away. 'Are you—'

'You have to go now,' he says, and his chest is very tight.

He gets the words out, but then it's hard to pull air back in.

She's looking at him, her face is moving, twisting, he can't look, he turns away and gets dizzy. He sways.

'Did I . . .' she says, and it's a totally different voice, so small.

'I have work to do,' he says, without looking.

He has heard his mother say that, towards the end, when she had a boyfriend with a ponytail, once, for a very short while. It worked, the man with the ponytail went away.

'I have a lot of work to do.'

And he closes his eyes for a lot of the next couple of minutes, he isn't quite sure what happens, it's too much, he has to close down the input, and he hums, Mmmmmm, Mmmmmmm, Mmmmmm . . .

She says something, but if he really concentrates on the humming, on feeling the vibrations in his head, he can't hear her.

Eventually, through the humming, he can hear her putting on her jacket, the rattle and clack of the buckles as they brush against the metal of the chair in his room.

'Thank you,' he says, yes, be polite, 'Thank you.'

And then he hears the door, and the motorbike starts; and off it goes; she is gone.

38

After they have rested for a few minutes, the man unties her wrists.

Naomi gets up and goes to the bathroom.

Back in the room the guy starts to talk.

Why do they always have to talk?

Well, maybe he's passing the time while he recovers. Maybe she can get a second round out of him in twenty minutes, if she pretends to listen. She can smile and nod for twenty minutes.

It's a war story. She's heard a lot of war stories, over the years.

In this one, his vehicle is blown up and his interpreter is killed. He goes into a lot of detail about his vehicle, but she's not really listening. Pinned down in Helmand province. Unable to get to the body of their interpreter. He has to spend a night in an irrigation ditch, and it's cold. He pauses. She nods. I don't *care*, she thinks.

'In the morning,' he says, 'I looked through my sights, and I saw a raven perched on Adam's face.'

She realizes he needs to talk more than he needs to fuck. No, she won't get any more out of him.

'Pecking out an eyeball,' he says. 'Peck; tug; peck; tug; peck.'

The guy waits for a response. She says nothing. And she's all out of smiles and nods.

'Maybe it wasn't a raven,' he says. 'I don't really know much about birds.'

A long silence.

Naomi begins to put on her clothes. 'You shot the bird,' says Naomi, feeling a need to finish the story. No, feeling he needs her to finish the story.

'No,' said the man. 'I thought I would. I thought I should. I looked through the sights for a long time. But the bird looked straight back down the sights at me, and he wasn't afraid.'

'You were too far away,' says Naomi. 'Not moving. Most birds don't do great shape recognition, they react to movement . . .'

He looks in her direction, but she can tell he doesn't really see her. He's somewhere else. She's standing there naked, he's just come inside her, and he doesn't see her.

'No,' he says. 'The bird looked at me like he knew me. The bird . . . I had more in common with the bird than with the dead man. I was just scavenging the battlefields too. Living off corpses.'

Oh God, I fucked a philosopher. Give him a fake number and go.

But instead, she hears herself say, 'When I was a kid, I got beaten on . . . on the ass. Not just the ass.' Make him see me. Make him see *me*. 'My dad was drunk, he was drunk, and I was, my . . .' She's going to have to find words. No. She points down at it. 'It rubbed against him, and he didn't . . . I don't even think it was deliberate, he wasn't trying to touch me there, he was just angry and . . . careless. And I hated being beaten, I *hated* it, OK, but if I struggled, if I wriggled, I found I could get . . . pleasure out of it. As well as the pain. I could rub against his leg . . .'

He's staring at her.

Don't stop. Go on.

'I didn't know what I was doing, I was a kid, I was innocent. All I knew was it felt better when I did that. And at least when he beat me . . . he saw me. It was contact. I wasn't alone. Maybe I thought, by doing that, I could turn it into something nice, something good.

I could turn it back into love . . . And one day, he noticed, he noticed that I was enjoying it, that I was being turned on. And he said I was . . . disgusting. And he stopped. He never did it again . . . And when you cross those wires, that early . . . pleasure and pain . . . it's really hard to uncross them. And I've tried. I've tried. And I can't . . .' Her eyes are full of tears, and that is unexpected, because she thought she was dispassionately telling a story, sharing a story of why she was who she was, so she would be seen. As herself, Naomi Chiang. Not just a memory of a fantasy. Not porn. 'I can't come without the pain. I can't, I've *tried*.' The nice boyfriends, their faces. Their sad, angry, embarrassed faces . . . 'It's not my fault, I didn't want to do that to myself. It's not even his fault. It's nobody's fault.'

He stares at her blankly.

He swallows, but he doesn't say anything.

Naomi puts on her bra. The metal hook slides into the metal eye with a little snick.

'I'm sorry,' he says.

'I'm sorry too,' she says, and swipes the salt water out of her eyes with the back of her hand. 'And I'm sorry about your friend.'

He walks over awkwardly, approaching almost sideways, like she, or he, might shy away. He reaches out slowly and puts an arm around her.

'Do you see me now?' she says fiercely.

'Yeah. Yeah. I'm so sorry.'

She lets his arm wrap around her, and she puts her arm around him, and they hug each other very tight and hold each other for a long time.

They both know when it's over.

They let go.

He clears his throat, very formal, like he's about to make a speech.

'I'd like to talk to you again.'

'Sure.'

She gives him fake contacts, and takes down his. She nods – almost bows – turns, walks towards the door.

Well, it's not a total loss.

For the first time in years, her body feels fierce, and fearless, and alive.

39

That night, Colt goes to bed early; confused, and anxious.

Lying in the dark, he is in the game, but he isn't thinking about the game.

He is thinking about Sasha.

About the feeling he is feeling.

He feels a little like the way he felt when his father left. No, worse, because he had his mama then, and he was afraid of his dada.

Part of him is missing . . . That's not quite it.

He is alone.

That's it.

He was never alone before.

Or rather: he never *felt* alone before; because he didn't know he could be with someone else, in a way that meant something.

He was never lonely, because he didn't know there was an alternative to utter solitude.

Now, he is lonely.

He was, briefly, *with* someone; and now he is not.

She isn't there.

Why did he say no?

He wants to know her. He wants her to know him.

He couldn't process the information fast enough, that was the problem. He couldn't deal with the data. He was overwhelmed.

He needs an upgrade. Or this will happen again.

The lab. Tomorrow.

Yes.

He wants to rewind. He wants to start again. Meet her again.

Do this . . .

His hands move down his body, in life and in the game, until his right hand touches his rapidly stiffening penis, his left cups his scrotum; his testicles pull tighter together at the touch, and suddenly mapping is off and the game murmurs that adult content has been blocked, and his hands are by his sides in the game.

The game won't let him feel what he knows he feels.

The ghosts of his real hands twitch, somewhere, off the map, and now he's getting two sets of signals; the game and reality are totally out of sync.

The mismatch between the gloves' signals and his real hands is painfully wrong, and he turns off the game in a fury, pulls off the thin layers of ultrafine mesh, and throws the gloves across the room.

Strips off the micromesh suit.

He could override parental controls, of course he could, it's his code, he helped build all the safeties, to keep the game legal; he could visit the gameworld's adult realms, and generate any imaginary partner he wanted, he could even hook up with other gameworld players, in the anonymous zones, and do it with a real person. But if he played it in adult mode he would have to lie to his mother – or tell his mother the truth – no, either would be intolerable.

In the dark, still wearing the dead helmet, he touches his now erect, quivering penis again, with his real hands, touches his scrotum, feels his testicles move inside the purse of skin. Explores, cautiously. Feels, hidden under the scrotum, the plump tube of his penis continue back, beneath the loose pouch of skin, and halfway around the curve, ending between his buttocks. Something he had never noticed before.

He sees images of Sasha, very strong and clear. And memories; her in the doorway, taking off her helmet, her jacket . . .

He reruns some video that the helmet had taken; to refresh the memories, to make sure he is imagining her right. Then he switches off the video, closes his eyes. Goes back to the moment he said no.

This time, he says yes.

And now images of Sasha come to him that aren't memories. Images of him opening her zippers; pulling off her boots; taking off her clothes. Her taking off her clothes. Images of her hands, of her mouth. Of her body.

All the parts are confused.

Things swap around in a way that has no proper order and isn't logical.

He doesn't know where these images are coming from; not the game; not memory. No, there are memories in there; his mother's breasts, which he has often seen when she is drying herself after a shower.

But he doesn't want to see his mother's breasts, he groans involuntarily and lets go of his penis at the thought; and so he imagines them bigger, then smaller; he changes the skin tone, darker, lighter; he alters the size and shape of the nipple, the areola, as though adjusting an unsatisfactory image in the game.

His hands return to between his legs, to adjust his penis, which has begun to ache. It is startlingly hard, like a velvety metal. His testicles, too, are aching. He recalls his sharpest memories of Sasha, and only realizes, now, how often during their conversation he had stared at her chest, memorized the small curves.

He customizes the imaginary naked breasts again, to fit the clothed curves he remembers. Customizes smooth, naked hips. His thoughts grow confused, and the images begin to leap about with a life of their own, all kinds of angles, and his hand begins to work away, up and down, until there is a kind of pain he has never felt before, or perhaps in dreams, yes in dreams, not a pain. Like a pain. As intense as a pain. But not a pain.

And when it is over, she isn't there. And the game isn't there. It is just dark. It is nothing else. The sheet is wet and cold. Evaporation.

He's never going to see her again. He's never going to speak to her again.

He should have said yes.

His mother will be back soon.

He should have said yes.

He has no idea how he feels. No idea at all.

Tired. He feels tired.

He sleeps.

40

'Existence is something tremendous, and day-to-day life, however indispensable, seems an insufficient response to it.'
— Thomas Nagel

Nevada is a desert. Almost totally empty, until a hundred years ago. Even the Paiute and the Shoshone – pretty tough, resilient people – didn't particularly want to live here. They stayed close to the few small lakes and rivers. So what changed? What brought a million people to Las Vegas, this dry valley, in the last few years?

If you asked them, they'd probably say something like 'work opportunities', 'Las Vegas is the fastest expanding municipality in America', 'there's incredible demand for engineers . . .'

And if you asked a million red blood cells why they were rushing towards Colt's penis as it grew erect, they'd probably tell you 'work opportunities' too. 'It's a fast-expanding region . . .' 'Incredible demand for oxygen . . .'

But the red blood cells – all proudly separate, all fiercely individual, all tumbling chaotically along their own unique paths – are being channelled there by the system of systems that is Colt, by the laws of physics, in the service of something happening at a higher level of complexity than they are equipped to understand.

That doesn't mean that Colt knows why he does what he does, either; summoning all those red blood cells, burning all that oxygen. He's doing it; he has the illusion of control; but he in turn is being driven by the next level down, the DNA in every cell, and the next level up, the system of systems that is made up of humanity, arranged in a society, with all its memes and mating rituals; its habits, expectations, and laws.

So if you're troubled by Las Vegas and ask me, why are all those people moving to that valley in the desert; I know and I don't know.

And if you ask Colt why he's doing what he is doing, he will know and he won't know.

It is happening because mammals commonly form breeding pairs after puberty.

It is happening because the old sperm have been sitting there too long, and may be defective. They need to be cleared out, and new sperm made quickly, because his brain chemistry is targeting a fertile woman, and locking on. He may need fresh sperm, and lots of it, next time they meet, which could be anytime. The body is reprioritizing.

It is happening because Colt can't get to sleep otherwise.

It is happening because he's falling in love.

All of these are true. They just use different metaphors to describe a reality that is more complex than any metaphor. A

117

supertruth that is connected to everything ever, and infinite in all directions.

Using a metaphor, a simile . . . it's like riding a horse. It can take you far in the right direction, but when its legs start to go, get off. Get off before it staggers sideways and takes you over a cliff. Don't fall in love with your horse.

A lot of religious people have fallen in love with their horse. They think their religion is the truth, and everything else is a metaphor.

A lot of scientists have fallen in love with their horse. They think science is the truth, and everything else is a metaphor.

A lot of artists have fallen in love with their horse. They think art is the truth, and everything else is a metaphor.

But everything is a metaphor. Science, religion, art, they're all just ways to describe reality; and any description of reality is massively compressed, with almost total loss of information.

The guy who thinks he's writing this book, why is he really writing it? Because of DNA; because of the human need to make satisfying patterns; because of his individual personal history; because of his cultural traditions; because of the laws of physics; because of the transformation now reorganizing all the lifeforms of earth; because of the evolution of the solar system; because of whatever mysterious thing the galaxy is doing; and on and on and up and up and out.

The answer is a supertruth that is connected to everything ever, and infinite in all directions.

Everything's playing at once.

Keep focused though, on the important thing.

This story is true.

41

The next morning, he switches the game back on as soon as he wakes, and pulls back on the gloves, and the micromesh suit, and his clothes, and without washing or eating or drinking he walks far out into the real desert with mapping on as the sun rises, and sits there thinking, just do it, just do it, until it's way too hot and he can smell his own sweat.

Eventually he goes back in, and showers, and eats, and codes, and tries not to think about Sasha, about last night, about his shame; and all the time an urgent voice in his head murmurs do it, do it, do it, until he stands up so abruptly his chair falls over, and he says, 'OK! OK!' in the silent house, and the house AI says, 'Pardon? I missed that,' and he shouts, '*Nothing!*' and strides back out into the desert again, and sits on a rock until it grows dark.

Nothing happens, and everything's amazing. It's the world, but subtly improved by him, by his code. He sits there, just breathing. The dry, clean air, the sun, the heat, the dazzle, and eventually the stars.

This might be the last time I see all this. Feel all this.

When the last light's gone from the sky, he stands up.

And then, as he walks back to the house, he calls RoboCabs ('*Part Bar. Part Car. All Cab. The Future Of Transportation*'), on his mother's tab.

They tell him there's a problem with her credit, but he can have a free ride from any of this week's featured sponsors.

He picks a bank from the list, because their ads are usually far less stressful to endure than the ones for dramas or drinks or cars or casinos or football.

The RoboCab turns up just as he gets home.

As he climbs into the cab, he glances back at the moonlit house. The one-way privacy glass makes the windows into sheets of silver.

The RoboCab takes him to the lab in a dreamy whirl of images of money and security and health and love, as he drinks his complimentary non-alcoholic drink.

At the bottom of the hill, just below the big, brightly lit sign for the Casey Biological Research Facility, he asks the RoboCab to stop, and he gets out. He tells it not to wait, and it obediently whispers its way back towards Vegas.

When it's out of sight, he walks quietly up the hill in the moonlight, across the deserted parking lot, and breaks in through the freight door, with his mother's access codes and some analogue hacking tools.

The security system welcomes him inside. He's hacked it so thoroughly over the years, unnoticed, while his mother works, that he could have just asked it politely to open the front doors; but he likes picking locks.

When he's finally in his mother's office, he sits in her chair. Spins in it till he feels dizzy.

Stops, and closes his eyes till the whirling in his head stops too.

He's done all the research. He knows how to do this.

And then he does the thing he's been dreaming of doing for so long.

42

When she gets back to the hotel, there's a few of them, and they are furious. As she had hoped, they hadn't been able to get a tail request through the bureaucracy in time.

So, human spying on citizens still requires a court order, she thinks, and enough paperwork to cover a giant bureaucratic ass. Good.

It's been so hard to tell, since the executive lost control of the old NSA. Since the NDSA took over. She feels a little safer.

For two days, they put on pressure, play good spy bad spy, with one guy threatening, one guy sweetening the deal. Naomi stands firm.

It helps that she knows Colt is OK, because she can feel his heartbeat on her pulse. She knows he is calm, and it calms her. She worries, at one point, when his pulse grows hasty and erratic for a few minutes, but it passes, and soon his pulse is calm and slow again. Some excitement in the game, she thinks, to reassure herself. It's nothing.

The questions go on, and on.

The sex, and the fact that they don't know about the sex, helps too. She feels she has a self, a private self again. Something to protect.

They don't know her, and they can't tell her what to do.

Sometimes she zones out, during the questions, and deliberately remembers, in vivid detail, moments from that hour in that hotel room, and bites her tongue not to groan. At those moments, she pretends to herself, in a kind of guilty confusion – to get Colt out of her mind – that the pulse she feels against her wrist belongs to the man in the hotel room.

Then someone somewhere – Ryan? – changes tactics. She can go home.

On her way to the airport, she tries to ring Colt, but there is no answer and no message.

He has changed all the codes, so she can't break into the game.

It is a long flight home.

43

Home.

My God, it's stuffy.

She leaves the front door open, to air the house.

It's normal, normal. He never airs the house.

No point shouting, he's probably in the game.

Walking past the fridge, she opens it automatically, to check has he drunk all the smoothies.

The light in the fridge doesn't come on.

Of course, the bulb.

She leans in, to see better, and the warm stink makes her gag.

Oh, *Colt.*

She steps back, and now she can see the smoothies are all gone from the bottom shelf. On the other shelves, the same jars and cartons as when she left.

A sludge of rotting lettuce leaves in a see-through plastic bag.

Mould crawls out of an open yogurt carton.

On a plate, a slice of pizza, dried out, greasy. Curling up at the edges.

Pizza?

And no mould. Must be full of preservatives.

She carries the yogurt carton toward the sink. Halfway there, stops.

He isn't in the house.

She throws the yogurt into the sink and runs outside. Circles the house, nothing.

She circles again, further out.

Now, on this pass, she notices a cable.

It must have been covered in sand, closer to the house. There was a storm . . . But no, he said he was fine . . .

She follows the cable towards the top of the ridge. A third the way up, it's plugged into another extension cable. The joint is wrapped in plastic, and hotglued.

Should be safe, you couldn't get a shock from that . . .

Why is he using mains electricity, instead of a solar battery? What could need that much power . . .

She follows it higher; another weatherproofed joint.

A yellow cable . . . that's the extension for the fridge, oh I could kill him.

And on the ridge . . . he isn't there.

Footprints. Colt's. Crisp, dry, deep.

Must have been muddy up here, after the storm.

At the end of the cable is a small booster box of some kind, wrapped in a bag. The little red LED glows dimly through the bag's thick white plastic. Switched on. She touches it.

Not hot.

Of course, he never could get signal beyond the ridge. Iron, a lot of iron in the rock.

From the top of the ridge, she can see him, about half a kilometre out. His back to her.

To everything.

Sitting on a flat-topped boulder of red sandstone, in full sunshine, in his fucking helmet.

She slips and skids down the ridge in her city shoes. Catches her breath at the bottom. Walks out towards the rock in the sun. She should go back for boots, for a hat, for water . . . too late now, forget it, forget it.

I should never have left him.

He isn't moving.

3

A Butterfly Waking
In Winter

'For an enzyme to be functional, it must fold into a precise three-dimensional shape. How such a complex folding can take place remains a mystery. A small chain of 150 amino acids making up an enzyme has an extraordinary number of possible folding configurations: if it tested 1,012 different configurations every second, it would take about 1,026 years to find the right one . . . Yet, a denatured enzyme can refold within fractions of a second and then precisely react in a chemical reaction . . . ((it)) demonstrates a stunning complexity and harmony in the universe.'

— Richard L. Lewis,
The Unity of the Sciences Volume One

'Many physicists point out in wonder the self-similarity between atoms, cells, planets, galaxies, and the universe as a whole (self-similarity among different levels is one of the hallmarks of a wholistic system).'

— Colin T. Wilson, *Whole*

'All stories are true.' — Chinua Achebe, *Things Fall Apart*

44

It takes Naomi twenty-four hours to rehydrate Colt, but by then he's burning up with a fever, hallucinating, speaking words she doesn't understand.

The fever dies down; but the old Colt doesn't come back.

He's reacting strangely to her, to food, to everything.

Naomi knows she worries too much about Colt.

But she's pretty sure he's never been like this . . .

Eventually she sits him down in the kitchen.

'Look, Colt, I have to go back to work. And I can't just leave you here like this until I know what's wrong. You're acting . . .' She struggles to put words on it. 'Something happened, while I was gone. Tell me. Tell me what happened.'

Colt studies his mother's face like he's never seen it before. After a while he says, 'I met a woman and I liked her and I messed it up.'

'You met a woman while I was gone? How? Where?'

'It doesn't *matter*, Mama.'

'But . . . what has that got to do with this?'

He won't give her any more. He's collapsed back into himself. It's like the inside of his mind is more interesting. If she didn't know Colt, she would think he was doing drugs of some kind.

'I have to go,' she says. 'Call me if you feel bad.'

'I kind of feel bad all the time, Mama.'

'Then call me if you feel worse.'

45

The lab is a disaster, she shouldn't have gone to New York.

Nobody has fed the caterpillars, even though she told Donnie it needed to be rostered. Some idiot moved a vitrine into direct sunlight, and an entire control group are dead. There's material missing from her freezers.

Her whole first day back is spent clearing up avoidable messes.

She answers the call in the lab without even looking. It's Colt. It's always Colt.

'Hi,' says Naomi.

'Hi.'

She is puzzled for a second, that Colt doesn't call her mama. He sounds so mature.

'I hear your lab's in trouble.'

Oh.

It's Ryan. His voice triggers old thought-loops that set off associated physical processes. She notices she is breathing hard. Stress reactions. Her shoulders feel like stone, like iron.

She clears her throat, swallows. Speaks.

'Fuck you,' she says. '*Fuck you.*'

'What?' says Ryan. 'Why?'

'You blocked my paper. Pulled it.'

And now the body's stress reactions begin to feed the thought-loops, and drive them faster, which triggers more stress reactions as her body acts on the mind's increasing panic. Her body is oblivious to the fact that he is just a voice on a phone.

She needs to breathe, hang up, lie down.

Run.

OK, she is almost at the toilet. She can hardly hear Ryan, as he says, 'I can upgrade your lab. You don't have to move, you don't have to move Colt. You'll never have to meet me.'

'No.'

'I can get you any equipment you want. Fix your credit.'

'No.'

'You'd go up three pay grades, you could buy things for Colt.'

No. No.

She's made it.

She hangs up, and lifts the lid, the seat.

Drops to her knees, and vomits in the clean white bowl.

46

He can hear her walking slowly across the playa towards him, but he doesn't want to break the rhythm he's in.

Mama. Home early. Huh.

Colt continues to turn his head, slowly, as far to the left as he can.

Back again.

He's tuned the helmet's visor to protect his eyes from the direct sun, but to let through the harsh, bright, white landscape, undimmed.

She finally arrives behind him.

'Colt.'

'Mmmmm.' He moves his head again, slowly. Soothing. Everything moves relative to everything else; but only for him; nothing is moving out there.

'Colt, come in out of the sun. Please. Please. Do it for me. Please, Colt . . . I thought you said you'd rest.'

He shouldn't have told Mama he was seeing things that weren't there. She worries. But she doesn't need to worry. He knows they aren't there.

'I AM resting.'

He is just seeing patterns in his mind. Connections between things. It's like doing math as a kid, when he would close his eyes, and the numbers seemed more real than people. He could understand the numbers . . .

He turns around.

'It's like *Sesame Street*, Mama,' he says, to reassure her. 'And I am the Count . . .' He laughs the Count's laugh, and she smiles but it isn't a good smile.

Oh God, he's getting worse, she thinks. And has to hold back her hand from stroking his forehead. He doesn't like to be touched.

He doesn't like to be touched.

I need help.

47

She takes him to their HMO, in a light industrial park, south of Las Vegas.

A glum old Bosnian doctor with a thick, bushy grey monobrow gives Colt a physical check-up.

Colt just sits there, silently, doing what he's told.

To take her mind off Colt while he's being scanned, sampled, and examined, Naomi studies the old doctor's face.

Probably trained back when the doctor, not the AI, did the diagnosis. Before robots did most of the surgery. No wonder he's glum.

He looks up from his blank screen, his monobrow startled into an arch. 'He doesn't have a health implant, a monitor?'

'No,' she says. She doesn't bother explaining that Colt doesn't like being tracked, monitored. That it's philosophical, that it's Colt's choice. Not that she's a bad mother.

She doesn't bother mentioning that Colt's arguments about freedom, about surveillance, have convinced her, too. That she's had her health monitor removed.

The doctor grunts, and carries on.

He does nothing, really, that Naomi couldn't do herself, but she doesn't trust her own judgement any more.

She welcomes the Bosnian's sceptical frown, as she outlines Colt's symptoms to him, and to the AI's listening microphones.

Maybe she's imagining all these symptoms after all. Maybe she's losing it. Maybe Colt's fine.

'Could it be something going around?' asks Naomi. Listen to me. I sound like my mother.

The doctor shrugs, takes a physical blood sample from Colt's arm using a sensor-packed syringe. The sensors feed their data instantly into the practice's AI, and the doctor gloomily studies the data cascading down his screen.

'Do you still use Mayo Global Health?' asks Naomi, putting off the moment.

'No,' says the doctor. 'We've gone open source.'

'Panacea?'

'Airmed,' says the doctor. 'More reliable, and they share databases with Panacea anyway, now.'

Naomi nods.

The Airmed AI asks some supplementary questions. Looks for similar patterns among its billions of previous cases. Makes its suggestions to the doctor.

'It is normal for such children to have emotional problems at this age,' says the doctor, still reading his screen.

'They aren't emotional problems.'

He looks up from his screen. Studies her for a moment. 'Hmm.'

'You think I'm being hysterical?' says Naomi.

'I think you are very concerned for your son, as is entirely natural.'

No. His scepticism is no longer reassuring. She is not imagining the symptoms. 'I know him. There's something wrong.'

Will her health insurance cover a second consultation, if this doctor and the Airmed AI say Colt is fine? The doctor's harassed, crumpled face reminds her of someone, something. A decade earlier, yes.

Caught between jobs, without proper health insurance, when Colt had a seizure and she couldn't afford the tests.

Arguing with a doctor in the emergency room, a weary doctor who wanted to release Colt, send him home. Colt still too weak and dizzy to walk, still recovering from the seizure.

God, that was why she took this job in the first place, in this shitty lab, grabbing at the health insurance, and now it might not even cover a second consultation . . .

Calm down.

'Thank you, doctor.'

48

The next day, on her way into the lab, she bumps into Donnie.

'Oh,' says Naomi. He looks surprisingly good. She'd assumed he was back in rehab, his car hadn't been in the lot all week.

She tells him what she needs, and he looks startled.

'You want *how* many caterpillars with cancer?' he says.

She tells him again.

'That's a lot of caterpillars with cancer.'

'I've had a new idea.'

'Well that's nice and all, but you might have to hold that thought for a while.'

'Why?'

He hands her his screen, and she reads the document. She looks up at him, astonished, winded. 'My grant hasn't been renewed?'

'Funding responsibility for your programme has been transferred to DARPA.' He takes back the screen. 'And they've put your work under review.'

49

She stands outside Colt's door as he sleeps that night. She looks at the No Burglars sign. Puts the palm of her hand flat on the red handprint he made when he was six.

Pushes.

He murmurs as the dim light of the corridor enters his room. Naomi walks in, swings the door almost closed behind her. Sits on the edge of his bed, and waits for her eyes to adjust to the low light.

He keeps murmuring. She crouches down close to his face, listens. He's speaking in tongues. No, it sounds like code. Like a programming language. He is compiling in his sleep.

Has he talked to another human being in the past month, apart from her? And that woman he mentioned. He's clammed up now, will say nothing more. He has barely spoken to Naomi since that conversation. Some functional sentences, all connected to the tech. Some absent-minded, crazy attempts to reassure her.

She's losing him. He's breaking down. But what can she do?

50

Four days later, his behaviour is getting stranger. He hardly speaks now. Hardly eats. Hardly sleeps. Never takes the helmet off.

She's afraid to leave him at home, so she makes him come into the lab with her, like old times. He hums little patterns of evolving musical notes, all the way in.

She scans him, on their best machine, which is still a pretty crappy machine, at the highest resolution she can get it to give.

Studies the scan.

The fucking students have messed it up. Calibration is off.

She can still, just about, see. The same familiar problems. The messy neighbourhoods, where some neurons connect sideways to each other, like ladders. Nothing new. But there is something,

something odd about the structure of the corpus callosum, and the area around it, where it joins the two hemispheres. It is on the edge of resolution.

She could be imagining it.

She blows it up as big as it will go, the architecture of her son's brain.

She looks at his memories, his hopes, his fears, encoded in the ever-changing neural network, and blinks back tears. It shimmers like a heat haze on the screen. A magic city.

A city sinking deeper into anarchy and dreams.

51

Naomi rings Ryan. Just voice. 'I accept,' she says.

'Great,' says Ryan. 'Listen . . .'

'I need the new Siemens hybrid scanner, with the larger static field and the second set of photomultiplier tubes,' says Naomi. 'I don't care if you pull it out of Maryland, I know they have two. I need F18-fluorodeoxyglucose, not a lot, but immediately. You can fill in all the forms. You've got fast-track clearance for radiopharmaceuticals, we're not an approved lab. And gallium-67. Now. I need them now.'

'Wait, slow down . . .'

'Don't pretend you're not recording this, I know you record everything.' She's going to be generating a lot of data, and she doesn't want anyone to hack it, not the Chinese, not the Indians, not the Russians; not her own government. But she has to store it somewhere. 'I'll need some new Banyan quantum servers for rich-data analysis. And a couple of high-end data safes.'

'Naomi . . .'

She shrugs. While she's at it, she may as well get her caterpillars. 'And I want fifty of the Petrarch B strain of *Danaus plexippus*. Eggs, or failing that, caterpillars less than three days old.'

She hangs up.

Maybe Ryan will just kill himself one day, out of the blue, like his dad did, that sad, horrible old monster; just close the bedroom door and, bang . . .

She represses the thought. Terrible thought. He's still a human being.

But it would be nice.

52

It takes all day to install the quantum servers and the data safes, and calibrate the big hybrid scanner. She spends the morning signing non-disclosure agreements; new contracts; national security agreements; and listening to the installation technicians swearing, mostly at Donnie, who is hungover, surly, and unhelpful. Things speed up when Donnie leaves early. When the technicians have finally gone, she drives home. Picks up Colt. Brings him back to her new lab, with its fresh smells of plastic and metal and composite materials.

In the lab, she asks him to take off his clothes, like she's always done.

'No,' he says.

'What?'

'I want a robe.'

'We don't have a robe, honey.'

'A sheet, then.'

She searches around. In the empty IT department, she finds a dust sheet, covering up some unplugged, out-of-date equipment.

He wears it like a Roman toga.

Lies on the flatbed.

Naomi secures his head with the soft restraints, as he murmurs numbers to himself.

'You'll have to stop speaking once the scan begins.'

'I know, Mama.'

'Not even subvocalize. No tapping, you have to be . . .'

'I know, Mama.'

'. . . Still.'

As the machine runs, he is totally still.

Like Christ in his winding sheet, she thinks.

She looks at the scans for a very long time.

Lets them cycle through the full depth of the 3D scan once, twice.

'Mama?'

Three times.

'Mama, can I put my clothes back on? . . . Mama?'

There's something wrong. There's something very wrong.

53

You.

You're part of a system.

Part of a family, a society, an ecosystem, an economy.

That's how the universe is organized at your level, the level you understand. The level of football teams, literature, summer holidays, sex.

Go one level down, and it's all about the organs, the veins, the arteries, the nerves passing their messages, the perpetual wave of air and water and nutrition and excretion passing through the system.

That's how the universe is organized at that level.

Another level down, and it's all about the cells and the bacteria. The enzymes mass-producing the proteins that make everything happen. The mitochondria powering your cells. The viruses transferring DNA between species.

That's how the universe is organized at that level.

Go one level up from you . . . Well, I'm how the universe is organized one level up from you. I'm your local System of Systems. From your point of view, I work in broad strokes. I don't micromanage every tree, every cloud, every human being. Just as you don't micromanage every muscle fibre, glucose molecule, red blood cell in your body. You just send the order, and your hand picks up the cup of coffee, or scratches your ear, or writes 'E=MC²'.

That's how the universe works, at every level. The high-level command goes out, and the system below that level does the job, without even realizing there's been a command. Messily, with lots of failures at this lower level. When you issue the order to pick up the cup of coffee, there are always neurons that don't fire. Muscle fibres that don't get enough glucose in time, and fail to contract. Red blood cells that get jammed in some capillary and never deliver the oxygen. Failure at the level of the individual cell is assumed. But the sheer number of neurons, of muscle fibres, of red blood cells thrown at the problem smooths out the individual failures and delivers the required result. Put a signal through enough redundant analogue processors, and you get a digital output.

From my point of view, one level up, the guy writing this is a specialist cell. One of many. A conduit. For stories. The rest of his life has dropped away; he's a storytelling machine in a room. He might as well be a brain in a jar. He might as well not have a body.

But if he's just the wire the stories come down . . . where are the stories coming from? And why do they come?

They're coming from me. Your friendly local System of Systems. They're coming from one level up. I'm about to move, and some cells are starting to twitch. Like a brain commanding muscle fibres. He's one.

A lot of writers don't know why they write what they write. Those are mine. 'It's in the air,' they'll say. 'It's . . . the Zeitgeist.' The spirit of the time.

I'm the spirit of the time. The Zeitgeist. The muse. Making them twitch. Speaking through them.

A story is just a program. Instructions. Preparing you for the big change.

The guy writing this is a little early, that's all. Like a butterfly waking in winter.

54

'My work with MFO (mixed-function oxidase) helped me to see that each of us is an exceptionally dynamic system, one that changes every nanosecond of our lives with incredible rapidity and order in a symphony extraordinaire.'
— Colin T. Wilson, *Whole*

That region . . . It shouldn't be that size . . . There are too many connections . . .

Staring at the scan, she convulses as she realizes what these changes must mean.

'Colt,' she says. 'What have you done?'

It's incredibly hard to get the information out of him. She feels

134

like an interrogator as she quizzes him, so weak and helpless in his sheet. But she has to know.

And eventually he cracks.

'I wanted to, to, to . . . I don't, I don't like . . . I hate not understanding people, Mama. And it's a problem in the corpus callosum, right? Mine just isn't . . . big enough. I thought if I could just . . . upgrade it, I could understand people better. I've been working on it all year.'

'But . . . why?'

Colt sits up. Swings his legs off the bed. Stands shakily. The words pour out.

'I thought I could talk to, to, you know . . . people. I could get what they were really saying. I wouldn't be so anxious all the time, trying to understand. Process the information faster, not get . . . overwhelmed. I could talk to . . . to . . . to . . . women, Mama.'

'What did you do?'

'I built an imaginal disc, Mama. To rebuild my corpus callosum.'

'But . . . how did you place it?'

'I set the robodoc, Mama. It was a simple injection.'

'Simple! Sorry, I'm sorry . . . but where did you think a larger corpus callosum was going to fit?'

'There's a lot of fluid around the brain. There's room for expansion.'

'Oh, Colt. It's just not as simple as that.' He must have left out the boundary definition genes. The new growth is happening all over his brain. And there are some weird hormonal interactions.

'Show me what you built,' she says.

Reluctantly, he shows her the blueprints for his imaginal disc.

She examines the DNA structure of each cell in the disc.

The arrangement of the cells.

Brilliant. Oh, this is brilliant . . .

It should work . . .

But, for some reason, some unforeseen interaction . . . it didn't.

He's an incredibly clever kid, but he's a teenager; and he thinks you can solve every problem through logic. His design lacks the painfully acquired wisdom of Naomi's work. It's brave; trying to solve a dozen different, difficult problems in one reckless leap. But he simply hasn't made enough mistakes to know what he's doing.

He doesn't know what he doesn't know.

Her vision blurs.

She stops studying the blueprints, blinks till she can see again. Oh it doesn't even matter why. It didn't work.

And this is going to kill him.

55

That night she begins an experiment on the new caterpillars, with no clearance.

But even working as fast as she can; without clearance, without filling in the forms; the results take so long to come in. The caterpillars take so long to transform.

One afternoon, days into the experiment, she realizes she has been studying the caterpillars for hours, in a chair, her face up against the glass of a vitrine. And she realizes she isn't studying them like a scientist any more; she is looking at them like someone waiting for a sign.

Silently pleading with fucking insect larvae.

She stands, and pushes back her chair so hard it skids across the polished wooden floor on its tiny polyurethane wheels, rotating as it goes, and slams into the side of her desk. She walks away from the vitrine, back to the desk, the chair; sits.

DNA is too slow.

Evolution is too slow.

Life is too slow.

She can't wait for the results of the experiments. He is going to die. If she is cautious, he is going to die.

She rings New York.

56

'Non è vero, ma ci credo.' (It is not true, but I believe it.)
— Italian saying

Next day, she leaves plenty of time to get to the airport, in case the traffic is bad on Tropicana.

Traffic is fine, so she gets there early.

She goes to Arrivals anyway, and waits for Yaakov to come through the hissing glass doors.

A figure who might be him approaches the frosted glass; her calves tense, and she rocks forward onto the balls of her feet; the doors hiss apart; it's not him.

It happens again.

Again.

Each time she tenses, till the tendons at the back of her ankles feel like she's been dancing in high heels.

An old man comes through the doors. A small silver wheeled case follows close behind, like a dog.

She glances at the man; is about to glance back to the doorway, when the man raises his left hand, and a bracelet of red thread slides down his wrist to his cuff. Startled, she raises her hand. She had thought she would run, and embrace him. But she just stands there, swaying, till he gets to her. Her legs feel rubbery, exhausted, and she's done nothing.

'Yaakov.'

'Naomi.'

They touch cheeks. Left, right.

The man who had seemed so vigorous in New York, dominating his own territory, with high status in the group, is just another old man now, in the desert light, on the slow walk to the car. Bleached out, washed away.

The flight was too long for him. I shouldn't have made him come.

'So, tell me about Colt,' says Yaakov, as the car starts.

Naomi opens her mouth, but the subject is too big; there's too much at stake.

Magical thinking. Like Colt, as a kid. If I don't name the monster, it doesn't exist. She pulls out onto the road.

'You've examined the scans I sent you?' she says.

A hesitation. 'Yes. Do you want to tell me . . .'

Naomi's eyes prickle, and she shakes her head. No, it's too much. Not while she's driving. She could go to self-drive . . . No. She doesn't trust the Pontiac to drive itself in the traffic around the airport. Crazy neighbourhood, full of artists and hackers and libertarian drop-outs. Kids stealth-driving old, uninsured gasoline cars that don't even have safeties or self-drive or trackers.

No. That's not it.

She just doesn't want to talk about it yet. Saying it will make it true.

'I'll tell you in the lab,' she says. 'I want to show you some tissue samples first.' Some kid overtakes her in a tiny ancient Prius that he's customized by covering in LED strips. A rainbow ripples the length of the Prius, again and again, on the beat, as De La Soul's 'Me Myself and I' booms out the open window.

'Tell me about your research,' she says.

'You're sure?'

'Of course. I'm sorry, I haven't been keeping up with it. But it's causing a stir, no?'

'Well, my research group, not me. And we are building on Lee Smolin's wonderful work. But, well, yes. OK, I'll tell you a story.' He settles back in his seat. 'Let's imagine human beings are red blood cells.'

Naomi snorts. 'Sorry. Go on.' Yaakov does like his red blood cells. He studied them for his PhD; the mathematics of their production and circulation.

'I know, I know,' sighs Yaakov. 'Again with the red blood cells. But, you know, it really is remarkable how similar they are, mathematically, to human beings circulating in a city. Bringing oxygen to a cell is very much like bringing your brain power to an office, or your muscle power to a construction site. You go there, pass through a barrier membrane, a security system, you deliver what you have, and you leave again, depleted, to recharge elsewhere . . .'

She has heard a certain amount of this before, but it is so remarkably pleasant to have Yaakov talking beside her again. To have someone beside her who doesn't want her, or need her, or love her, or hate her. Who just accepts her as she is.

'. . . So, let's imagine human beings are red blood cells, in a bird, say. An albatross! It soars through the skies for months at a time, without needing to land. Now, the red blood cells have no idea they're inside a living creature. It isn't alive on their scale: it's alive on a totally different scale, at a vastly more complex level that isn't meaningful or comprehensible to a red blood cell, even though every red blood cell is part of that, ah, aliveness.' He glances across, to see if she's listening. 'Now, let's say one brave, scientific red blood cell tries to work out where everything came from. He . . .'

'She,' says Naomi, and Yaakov smiles.

'She – through much ingenious research – discovers that the world – the albatross – used to be much smaller, much simpler – a single cell.'

'An egg,' says Naomi.

'Yes,' says Yaakov, 'but the concept of a fertilized egg, of DNA, the logic of mitosis, is beyond the comprehension of the red blood cell. Bear in mind, mature red blood cells have no nucleus, contain no DNA. To him . . . to her, a cell is a cell, is a cell. They understand the world, they see the world, at their own level, as a collection of discrete objects, on their scale. As a huge cell. But this cell has grown extraordinarily in complexity and size.'

'The big bang . . .' says Naomi, and Yaakov smiles again.

'You are racing ahead of me. Yes . . . From this single cell has emerged the vast, integrated, multicellular world of the albatross. And the red blood cells who inhabit this world – who are part of this living universe – wonder, how did this dead matter, merely obeying the laws of physics, get so complicated, so integrated? Blind chance, directing chemical actions? But that seems so unlikely . . .'

'Because they don't understand the mechanisms of evolution . . .'

'Exactly. Yes. And as far as the red blood cells are concerned, outside the albatross is space, is a lethal, empty space where you die. The bird is the world, and the world is the universe . . .'

Naomi drives carefully around a sharp bend, as though Yaakov will snap in two if she accelerates or brakes rapidly. Perhaps he would. 'Go on.'

'But then they make a terrible, wonderful discovery: there are other worlds out there, very like their own! Floating in space are other albatrosses. And terns, gulls . . . worlds of other sizes, but very similar in design.' Yaakov pauses, looks out the window. Naomi is about to speak; but then he goes on. 'Far beyond them all is an ocean; but that is just a distant boundary, where observation ends. There can be nothing beyond the surface of the ocean. It is just the strangely curved boundary of their new and unimaginably larger universe.'

They've left the airport, the city, behind. Naomi studies the road, the smooth familiar curves, up into the hills.

On the inside of the approaching curve, a long, plump garter snake, the head and mid-body crushed flat by truck tyres. Final few inches of tail still thrashing, but it's already dead as Latin.

She swings out to avoid hitting it.

'And the moral of your story?' she says.

'My research group is coming up with more and more evidence – which some members of the group are resisting vigorously – that our universe is alive. Is an evolved entity. Is the complex product of evolution, not at the level of the gene or the meme, but at a more fundamental level.'

Naomi glances across at him. He's leaning back in his seat, eyes closed. He looks half dead, but his voice is engaged, excited, alive.

'Evidence . . .' says Naomi. 'Empirical? Mathematical?'

'Both! The mathematics are persuasive. Previous approaches had the problem of explaining how this particular universe came into being, when any small change in any parameter would have made the stability of matter impossible. This approach explains it. The universe seems unlikely for the same reason the eye, or a giraffe, or a kelp forest seem unlikely; because each is the result of a long evolutionary process of selection. This incredibly complex, yet stable universe didn't just come into being. It evolved into being, through a long line of earlier, simpler universes. And pre-sumably countless earlier universes, not in the direct line of descent of our universe, did indeed fail . . .'

'A living universe . . .' She feels a throb of hope, that it's true. That the sky isn't dead. That she's not alone. But the scientist in her resists. 'You really believe that?'

'Yes! In simple, purely mathematical terms, our approach fits far better than the old dead-matter models. A dead-matter uni-verse no longer matches what we can *see* out there. The peculiar distribution of galaxies, or the way the spiral galaxies simply refuse to wind tighter as they rotate; even the ridiculously rapid expansion rate of the universe . . . I mean, the old models don't explain any of it.' Yaakov loudly snorts his opinion of the old models.

'Well, you can hardly attack physicists for not having a perfect model of the universe. All theories have their problems . . .'

'Of course. But what do they claim, to fix these problems? That the vast majority of matter in the universe is totally invisible! That dark energy tugs everything magically into shape! But – oh yes – please ignore the unimportant fact that we cannot detect this dark matter, this dark energy, with any instrument . . . Absurd! Yet I know a number of very fine physicists – oh, some in MIT! – who still can't see that this simply isn't science.'

Naomi smiles at how animated he's become. 'Well, it must be hard to admit you've wasted your career on a theory that hasn't worked out.'

'No doubt.' He snorts again. 'But the lengths they will go to, to avoid admitting they are staring *life* in the *face* . . . I swear, some of these men would posit the gravitational tug of dark matter at the top of their house, to explain how their child is able to make its way upstairs to the toilet.'

Naomi laughs. She doesn't want this holiday from her own thoughts to end. Doesn't want to deal with her own dark energy, dark matter, just yet.

Yaakov, grinning now, looks younger and younger. 'No, an evolved, living-matter universe solves all these problems, with no need for any magical, invisible nonsense. Life directs its own energy. It *acts*! It *moves*! It *grows*! Nothing mystical about *that*. We have simply been looking for answers at the wrong level, ignoring emergent complexity. A dog moves very differently to the sack of chemicals that makes up a dog.'

She wants it to be true. Please, if she can't have God, then let the universe be a huge, mysterious, happy, black mutt . . . 'Are you actually finding signs of life?'

'Well, once our biologists force our physicists to see what is in front of their faces, we find the evidence everywhere. The magnetic fields inside stars, between stars, have all the attributes of life. Homeostasis, dynamic cyclical complexity, self-similar structure, meaningful patterned detail at all scales—'

Naomi takes a hand from the steering wheel and waves at him, to slow down, to explain, not rant, and he ducks his head in apology.

'Sorry . . . But it's just so *fascinating!* Magnetic fields clearly control and direct plasma. It's not random movement, it's directed, it's meaningful. Like muscle fibres, or neural networks.

Or circulatory systems! Stars have, at their core, self-sustaining dynamos—'

'That sounds familiar,' says Naomi, and frowns.

'Ah, yes, we biologists have self-sustaining dynamos on earth, which remain stable over long periods. They are called—'

'Hearts,' says Naomi, and without thinking she takes a hand from the wheel, places it over her own beating heart.

'Yes . . .'

'Huh.' Naomi tries to process this. 'But if it *is* so obvious . . . why didn't we see this before?'

Yaakov shrugs. 'The sheer scale of the universe makes it difficult . . . the immense timeframe . . . After all, the flocking behaviour of birds, we can see as it happens, in an instant, above us. The flocking behaviour of stars . . . that's a trickier business to spot. Stars call to nearby stars, down magnetic field lines. Structures are built; energy is transmitted; *information* is transmitted, that changes behaviour at the other end. But those signals can take many human lifetimes.'

Naomi glances involuntarily at the sky. 'But how is all this, ah, complexity . . . *coded*? Where's it come from? What's the equivalent of the DNA of the universe?'

'Well, the fundamental particles, and their rules of interaction, can be seen as a code-set. The DNA of matter. With a tiny set of symbols, a simple set of rules . . . you can create anything. Anything. You can build a program, to do anything at all, out of mere zeros and ones. On, and off. Yes and no. There, and not there. Positive and negative.'

Something has struck Naomi, and she slows the car down automatically as more and more of her attention is required to think about it. A truck behind her beeps and overtakes, as the dash flicks a red warning, that she braked too hard in traffic; and the self-drive takes over. She shrugs, lets go the wheel. It pulls back, folds into the dash.

'If you're right,' she says, turning to face him, 'that means there can be processes inherent in this universe, coded for in this universe, which have not yet been expressed.'

'Yes. Exactly. Yes.'

'The whole universe could just suddenly . . . change. All over, all at once. Like a kid going through puberty.'

'Yes!' cries Yaakov, like she's come up with a Grand Unified Field Theory all on her own. 'Or it could be even more dramatic, total, rapid; like a caterpillar turning into a butterfly. A complete transformation.'

She's looking for weak points in the argument now. 'Your albatross metaphor . . . But an albatross, in real life, interacts strongly with the ocean, dives, eats fish . . .'

'It's just a metaphor,' says Yaakov. 'Everything we say is just a metaphor. Even the new math my research group has come up with; that, too, is just a metaphor for a reality we can't grasp.' He glances up at the sun. 'The sights we think we see: just metaphors. Pictures we build in our head.' And he glances across at Naomi. 'The emotions we imagine we feel. Metaphors. Just metaphors.'

This new knowledge about the universe is too much, it's giving her vertigo, nausea. Naomi wants to shrink the conversation, to bring it back inside the car.

'What's the red thread a metaphor for?' she says. She taps the dash. The wheel re-emerges, and she takes over driving again.

He glances down at the thin bracelet on his wrist. 'Oh,' he says, as though he'd forgotten it existed. 'What *isn't* it a metaphor for? Theseus escaped from the Minotaur, from, ah, the labyrinth, by following a red thread he'd been given by Ariadne . . . And in Japan, and Korea too, they believed the gods tied a red thread to your pinkie – at birth – and the other end to the pinkie of someone,' he raises both his little fingers, flexes them, 'who will one day be important to you.'

'Your soulmate?'

'Well, you could marry them. Or they'll save your life. Or even make history, sometimes.'

'Oh,' says Naomi, remembering. 'At my father's funeral . . . his brother left red threads on a table. Dozens of them. You were supposed to tie one to your finger as you left, and "accidentally" lose it, on the way home. To stop spirits from following you.'

Yaakov laughs. 'You see, yes, every culture has a red thread myth. A Hindu colleague at MIT wears one, he says it controls mood swings . . . And did yours work, or did spirits follow you home?'

'My mother didn't approve, it wasn't a Catholic thing. So I didn't take a thread, and my uncle got mad at me.'

Yaakov nods. 'I wear this because my mother always wore one, and of course I loved my mother. It's a Kabbalah thing; I believe it comes out of Genesis. It wards off the evil eye.'

'Maybe I should have taken a red string,' says Naomi, looking across. 'If it has so many uses.'

'I'll give you one,' says Yaakov.

'I can't take your bracelet!'

'I have spares! You have to replace them, when they eventually fall off. My sister sends me them from Jerusalem.' He pulls out an old leather wallet, roots deep, plucks out a thick red thread, five or six inches long.

'Thank you,' says Naomi. 'Thank you.'

The car slows automatically for a moment, as a jackrabbit bounds out of a patch of creosote bushes and hopscotches across the road just in front of them. The car murmurs, 'Jackrabbit,' apologetically, and returns control to Naomi.

'Whoops . . . I'd better focus,' she says. 'Just slip it in my jacket pocket, I'll tie it on later.'

Yaakov carefully places the thread deep in her jacket pocket, as she keeps her attention on the road. 'There!' he says. 'You will, at least, be free of the evil eye. And possibly ghosts. And mood swings. And may meet your destiny. And escape a labyrinth . . .'

'Do you believe in any of this?'

'No,' says Yaakov. 'But I like it as a reminder that everything's connected.'

'Red, and round, like blood cells,' says Naomi, glancing across, and Yaakov smiles.

57

Yes, I borrowed my red blood cells metaphor earlier from Yaakov . . .

I'm not promising anything – but if your friendly local System of Systems did need a major breakthrough to happen soon, then I'd use humans. You're the go-to cells for rapid transformation. Fast, flexible. Remarkably easy to reprogram your behaviour. But that reprogramming requires a new meme.

A new way of looking at the world.

Call it a new religion, call it a scientific paradigm shift, call it a spiritual revolution. I don't care. Someone has got to come up with that meme. Maybe Colt will do it. Maybe you will do it. But someone will do it, and soon; after all, I have roughly eight billion of you running the program.

That's multiple redundancy.

I have infinite ammo.

58

In the lab, Yaakov studies the new scans.

Studies them again, on the big screen, his hands behind his back.

She pours him a glass of water, but he doesn't reach for it.

'OK,' he says. 'Tell me.'

Naomi wonders how to start.

Yaakov speaks into the silence. 'This patient is clearly—'

'It's Colt,' she says.

'Oh, no,' says Yaakov, and slumps, as though she has hit him. As though he's had a stroke. He looks so old.

I shouldn't have made him come out here to the desert, she thinks. He could die here.

'Explain,' he says, waving a hand at the scan.

'You can see extreme ongoing grey-matter growth in the frontal and parietal lobes,' she says. 'Obviously, some grey-matter growth is normal in a teenager, but this . . . this is severe neural overgrowth. Too many new neurons, packed too close together. And . . . it's killing him.'

'Why?'

She takes a deep breath. OK. 'He injected himself with an imaginal disc containing his own stem cells. He tried to build a larger corpus callosum, to solve his social difficulties—'

'—But it's far more complex than that—'

'I *know*,' says Naomi, more sharply than she had intended. 'But he's been obsessed with this for years. The fact that kids like him have a small corpus callosum. He's convinced that's it, that's the secret . . .'

Yaakov sighs, shakes his head.

'But look,' says Naomi, pointing, 'his stem cells have caused neural overgrowth here, and here, and here . . . he's a kid, he didn't think to include genes limiting growth to the corpus callosum.'

Yaakov studies the scan. Zooms in. Squints. 'The distribution . . . there's a hormonal interaction, here, right?'

'Yes.'

'The hormonal surges of adolescence, perhaps. Testosterone.'

'Yes . . .' Oh my God, she thinks. That's it . . . 'Most of my work has been on immature mice, because with mature mice, the testosterone caused big problems . . .'

'Show me the stem-cell DNA.'

Naomi shows Yaakov Colt's blueprints. He scans them rapidly.

'You're wrong: he's put in genes to limit growth. Very clever . . . Look.'

She studies the readout. 'Oh!' It's brilliant. Not obvious. 'But . . . it hasn't worked. They haven't expressed themselves . . . Why?'

'These genes only regulate foetal and very early childhood brain growth.'

'Of *course*, yes, testosterone suppresses these genes . . .'

Yaakov nods. 'He didn't realize. He's full of testosterone. If he'd done this a few years ago, he'd have been fine.'

'To reverse the process, reverse the overgrowth . . .' Naomi tries to see the problem clearly '. . . we need to get those limiter genes expressing themselves . . . if we could switch off whatever is blocking them . . .'

Yaakov's eyes are open now, but he's not looking at anything, he's thinking, he's immersed in his thoughts. Neurons firing. Looking for patterns. Answers. A way out. 'Yes. But if the block is caused by the testosterone surge of late adolescence, then to end it . . .' Yaakov trails off, and Naomi sees for a terrible instant her beautiful boy, with no testicles, castrated . . .

'It wouldn't have to be surgical,' says Naomi, 'it could be a hormonal treatment . . .'

'You would be turning a young man back into a boy. And you would have to keep him a boy for ever.'

And Naomi feels pleasure at this answer, and shock at this pleasure. No. I do want him to grow up.

I do.

I'm just afraid for him, that's all.

That's normal.

I'm just afraid he'll get hurt.

'I'm just afraid he'll get hurt,' she says.

'He's already hurt,' says Yaakov. 'There's no way of avoiding hurt. Every available option hurts.'

'Is there any other way to switch off the transformation, reverse it?'

'Personally . . . I think we can't switch this off. Too many genes involved, and I don't understand the pathways. And the transformation, the gene expression, is already very far advanced. His brain is already partially rewired, which has disordered the old state – causing those visions, the speaking in tongues – it just can't make the jump to a new state.'

'But what can I do?' she says and her voice breaks. 'If it's too advanced . . . if we can't go back . . .'

'The astonishing thing,' says Yaakov slowly, studying the scans again, 'is that there are structures emerging . . . it's not like a tumour, it's not random multiplication of cells . . . It's *working*. But there simply isn't room for it to work.'

And a thought strikes Naomi. A terrifying thought. A wonderful thought. 'So . . . if we can't go back . . . what if we pushed it forward . . . helped it make the jump . . .'

'But you can see, the density is killing him, the blood vessels are constricted . . .'

'But what if the neurons were smaller?

He hesitates. 'How much smaller?'

'An order of magnitude. More.'

'So you're talking . . . you're talking insect neurons.'

She nods. '*Drosophila melanogaster*. Much finer than human neurons. With a higher knit density. More layers.'

'Wow,' he says, his face lighting up, and for that moment he looks and sounds to Naomi oddly young, oddly like Colt. 'Wow.'

'The structures could fit,' she says urgently. 'They could fit, if the neurons were smaller.'

'I don't know. I've never seen anything like this. There's nothing in the literature. Perhaps. Perhaps.'

'Help me,' says Naomi.

'How?'

'Operate. I don't trust anyone else.'

'No, no, the robodoc . . .' says Yaakov, and nods towards the silent machine.

'Look, robot hands are brilliant for tumours,' says Naomi, 'for well-defined procedures, for standard operations, debugged and tested. But this is complex and it's not a known operation. There's no set of previous procedures for the hands to learn from. It will take . . . intuition. It's a human job. Human hands.'

'Naomi . . .' he says. Pauses.

He unfolds his ancient hands, reaches for the glass of water, and it vibrates at his touch and he has to use both hands to pick it up.

No fine motor control at all.

'I'm sorry,' he says, seeing her staring at his trembling hands, the glass of shuddering water, the bracelet of red thread, swaying from his left wrist. 'I'm sorry.'

She says, 'Then I'll do it.'

Yaakov drinks the water, puts down the glass. Looks down at his hands, and slowly, carefully weaves his trembling fingers back together.

Naomi waits for his lecture on ethics. On how she can't do this. On the regulations against operating on your own relatives.

She scrambles to build an answer, a defence.

Finally, he speaks. 'Be careful,' says Yaakov. 'Right now, I know, I know; if you do nothing, he's going to die; and it will be unbearable. But it will be even more unbearable if you kill him.'

Naomi breathes out. A tremendous sigh. She nods. 'Tell me how to do it.'

59

After Yaakov flies home, she draws up a plan. Then she builds the plan into a schedule; but the figures are no good.

This takes too long, he'll die . . .

She works out another plan, on a tighter schedule, cutting some corners.

Still no good.

To do this in time . . . she'll have to pull all-nighters. But she can't bring Colt to the lab every night. And the thought of leaving him alone . . .

She walks into his room. He's just lying there on his bed, pale, not coding, not gaming. Not reading. No music.

Dying.

'Colt, I need to work late, in the lab.'

'How late?'

'All . . . Most of the night. While you're asleep. You won't even notice . . .'

'Mom . . .'

'Can I . . .'

He gets up on one elbow. At least he can still do that, she thinks. 'Just my heartbeat, Mama.'

She smiles. 'Just your heartbeat.'

He drops back in bed, off his elbow. 'Fine.'

As she watches, he falls asleep.

She turns off his light, and goes to her room. Puts on her old health monitor. It reminds her of something . . .

She finds, deep in a pocket, the red thread Yaakov gave her. With difficulty, and some quiet cursing, she manages to tie it around her left wrist. Naomi has felt alone, and overwhelmed by the task ahead, since Yaakov left: at least they are now connected by a thread . . .

She asks the house AI to order a small bed, to be delivered to the lab. She'll need to take naps.

And then she drives to the lab and pulls an all-nighter. Sleeps briefly on the floor.

At dawn, a drone delivers the bed kit to the lab. She assembles it in her office, before she goes home to Colt.

The next night, she pulls another all-nighter.

Then another.

Building something that might work. Might help her son.

60

On the third night, at six in the morning, she wakes up. Colt's heartbeat pulses slowly against her wrist.

He's asleep. Good.

She blinks, unable to make sense of what she sees.

Pale grey light. A jellied mass floating.

There is pressure on her face, around her eyes.

Oh.

She raises her head. The soft rubber cushions of the eyepieces of the optical microscope suck free of her face with a hiss.

She is on a stool, in her office, slumped forward on her work bench.

Oh.

She looks back through the optical microscope. Adjusts focus. Yes.

It floats there.

Perhaps a thousand cells.

An imaginal disc, carefully built from the stem cells of *Drosophila melanogaster*, rebuilt with *Danaus plexippus* DNA grafted to *Homo sapien*s DNA.

Colt's DNA.

It might work.

It might kill him.

It might work . . .

Crap. What time is it? 6.04 a.m.

Naomi is supposed to give a progress report on her regular lab work at nine. And Ryan's added himself to the oversight team. Ugh. Three hours away. Not enough time to go home and sleep.

Colt's breakfast . . . A spurt of panic, before she notices against her wrist the long pulse of his deep sleep. It calms her, slows her own heart. He sleeps so late these days . . . he'll be OK. The house AI will tell her if anything goes wrong.

Maybe a proper nap, lying down, here in the office. Or should she just stay up?

She sways on the stool, too drained to decide.

She's already had two brief naps in the night, on the small bed in the corner, with the lights on so her body won't go into deep sleep.

She could take a stim . . . but no, she reacts badly to stims, there's a genetic mismatch; sometimes they kick in, and she's fine, all bright and sparky for sixteen hours; and sometimes they just reset her circadian clock at random, and for the next week it's like having jet lag.

Got to sleep. Got to sleep.

She sets her alarm for 8.30 a.m. That leaves long enough to wake up fully, to prepare her notes, oh God her notes . . . She lies down in the narrow bed, brain fizzing and crackling with tension and exhausted half-thoughts.

She has crazy dreams of fairground music and a carousel spinning faster and faster, throwing her off into the darkness and she's awake and it's the conference call beeping her.

The progress report.

They're beeping her for the second, no, third time.

It's 9.04 am.

She accepts the call without thinking.

She has nothing to think with.

61

She does very badly indeed on the conference call.

After it's over, and the DoD guys have gone, Ryan stays on screen. 'I've seen the scan.'

'*What* scan,' she says. Her head is, at last, cleared by the surge of adrenalin, and her heart is going so fast, it feels like the time she had to take snake anti-venom. OK, now she's awake.

'Come on,' says Ryan. 'Please.'

'You've tapped into my files.'

'Honey, be realistic. We pay for your research, we own it. It wasn't even me. I'm not allowed to go near your files. It was brought to my attention.'

'What are you trying to say?'

'I've put Colt back on my insurance. Let the military handle it. Our guys are the best in the world at removing shrapnel from brains, at . . .'

'These aren't shrapnel fragments. If you try surgical intervention, you'll kill him. There is something else happening here.' Her mouth feels metallic and chalky, like the inside of a kettle full of hard water, boiled dry.

'Naomi. This is serious. Stop fucking around. I'll give you a deadline. Let the real experts try to save Colt, or I'll recommend they close your lab.'

'I've already got a deadline,' says Naomi. 'He has a month to live.'

She ends the call.

4

Caterpillar Soup

'Objects are simple.'   — Ludwig Wittgenstein

'Things are not as simple as you think.' — Milan Kundera

'Orpheus who could attract and charm the wild beasts was
the model artist.'   — E. H. Gombrich,
                          Illusion in Nature and Art

'A key concept in the field of pattern-recognition is that
of uncertainty. It arises both through noise on measure-
ments, as well as through the finite size of datasets.'
                          — Christopher M. Bishop,
         Pattern Recognition and Machine Learning

62

She gets Colt to lie down in the back seat of the car, and she drives him to the lab. He murmurs and laughs all the way there. She can hear some of the murmurs. Phone numbers. The names of kids he went to kindergarten with. Kids he hasn't seen, hasn't mentioned, in years. He's reacting to them like they're in front of him. He's babbling mathematics and nursery rhymes. Then he says, very clearly, 'Sodium, Mama. Let me drop the *sodium*.'

What?

Oh, of course. When he was bored, in her office, as a child. He would ask for the sodium, and she would take down a heavy, sealed jar of mineral oil from the top shelf. She would give him a tweezers; and he would carefully lift a tiny silvery pellet of pure sodium from under the oil, and drop it into a beaker of water. Together they would watch, as the alkaline metal reacted with the water, and fizzed, and bubbled, and burst into bright flame. Whizzing back and forth, on the surface of the water, until it burnt out . . .

He must know we're going to the lab. That's good.

It's a long weekend, there won't be anyone around, apart from the cleaning robots, and the lab techs keeping the animals alive in the other labs.

She's always spending nights in the lab lately.

Nobody will notice.

Nobody need know.

Colt is just about able to walk in, with her holding him up. Leading him. He's not, technically, blind, but he might as well be. The new growth is squeezing his visual cortex now. He is only able to react to whatever is going on in his head. His internal weather.

She gets him comfortable in the small bed in her office.

She leaves him sitting up, humming to himself, while she goes out to the labs, to get all the stuff she will need.

He's lying down when she comes back in. He turns his head, he doesn't lift it. He looks like he can't lift it.

A wave of sick comes up in her throat, and she has to swallow it back down. A gulp, a gasp.

'Mama?'

A little bit of her, high above and far away, watching all this, knows that what she feels is a biological reaction to a stimulus. The way she, as a biological entity, relates to him, as a biological entity, is determined by their close genetic relationship. His distress is mirrored by her, stimulating her to deal with both his distress and hers.

Her son is dying and she is going to get sick.

'It's very *late*, Mama,' he says, lying in the bed, looking around. 'Why are we here?' His voice is woozy, forgetful.

Tell him. 'There is a procedure. That might . . .' *Tell him.* 'It might kill you.'

'OK,' he says.

'But it might . . . it might work.'

'Work?'

'Save you.'

'OK. That's good, Mama.'

'Remember what you did . . . with the imaginal disc you designed?'

'Mmm.'

Perhaps he does. Perhaps not. It doesn't matter. Her voice is soothing him, and that's what counts.

He never wanted bedtime stories. He wanted facts. Sometimes a song, once the light was out, to get him to sleep: but before that, facts.

'Tell me about the procedure, Mama.'

Oh, just like when he was a kid. '*Tell me something, Mama,*' he would say. '*About what?*' '*Anything, Mama. I'm interested in everything.*'

OK, tell him.

'This is an improved version of . . . of . . . what you did,' she says. 'I think I can undo the damage, and replace everything, without . . .'

Too close. No. Can't say it.

She looks away from his face. Stares at the blank wall.

'It requires putting the subject into a chrysalis-like state.' Yes; imagine you're delivering a paper. 'The subject can't eat or drink or even really move during the process. Once the process is triggered, some of the existing brain structures will be . . . dissolved, and the imaginal discs will begin to build out the new structures using the dissolved material.'

'OK. How long will the whole thing take?'

'Well, it's impossible to say. Most of the research has been done on entirely different phyla, let alone species. The little research that has been done on mammals may have no application to a human subject, so . . .'

'Stop being a scientist, Mama, and just guess.'

She cracks a little. A sob. 'Well . . . It's just really hard to know. I mean, we're taking the plane apart and putting it back together again while it's still flying, you know? It's just impossible to . . .' Her voice judders with repressed sobs. 'So much could, just . . . There's just, no way of knowing if the plane, will keep, flying.'

'No metaphors, Mama.'

'OK.' No, she can't look at him. She looks at the ceiling till her throat stops convulsing. 'You go to bed for a few days. It's like having the flu. You're hot, you'll be hot – I mean, that's a ferocious amount of chemical activity, in every single cell, I mean obviously it generates heat.'

'Mama . . .'

'You'd be . . . unconscious. I'd have to manage your temperature. Your body will lose control of temperature regulation . . .'

'How long, Mama?' Because if it's too long, he will die.

'In *Drosophila muca—*'

'Stop talking Latin.'

Naomi makes a mental note; secondary language regions affected, but not primary . . . She'd taught him Latin as a kid, he'd loved it; it was so much more logical than English. But Latin's one of the many things he's been losing over the past month.

'In the kind of . . . they've studied this in . . . in fruit flies. In fruit flies the rate of mitosis is dependent on . . .' She stops, starts again. 'It takes about eight hours . . . for the cells to reproduce, to divide.'

He's not really following her. It's like he's dreaming while awake. She gets the uneasy feeling that there's a constant distracting parade of sounds and images and feelings sparking inside him as the cramped neurons connect to each other, to other parts of the brain.

'Eight hours . . .' he says, 'that's not so bad . . . then we'd know . . .'

'No, no. The imaginal discs contain as few as fifty cells. To build the new structures – a leg, an antenna, a wing – the cells have to . . . double, and redouble, and double again and again. It's eight hours each time. Each doubling.'

'How many times?'

'In *Drosophila* . . . in fruit flies, it averaged fifteen times. Fifteen cycles.'

'Fifteen by eight . . . that's . . . I can't do math any more, Mama.'

'That's about five days.'

'Five days . . . without water or . . .'

'It could be faster. It could be slower. We're building a bigger structure. But we'd be using a much bigger imaginal disc. More developed, with a lot more cells, thousands, so that takes out some of the cycles . . .'

'So how many days . . .'

'It could be as few as three. It could be as many as fifteen. I don't know. When you tried it . . . you were in a fever state for a day, then there was a gradual transformation for a couple of weeks . . . But it was only a partial success, a partial transformation. This should be a much faster, more intense process; I can use an accelerant, to force the new neurons to make their connections quicker. But it depends on how much of your brain . . . breaks down, and how much of it has to be rebuilt. How large the new structures are.'

'I'm not going to be me afterwards, am I?'

'I don't know. When they studied this in moths, they found that the adult moth remembered things it had learned as a caterpillar. So, even though the caterpillar had been dissolved . . .'

'Caterpillar soup . . .'

'. . . And rebuilt completely differently . . .'

'But it might dissolve all my memories.'

'Yes.'

'I might forget who you are.'

'Yes.'

'I might forget who I am.'

'Yes.'

'It might dissolve me.'

'Yes.'

'But it might dissolve the . . . the neural overgrowth.'

'Yes.'

'The cancer's going to kill me anyway, isn't it.'

'It's not cancer!'

'The overgrowth is going to kill me anyway. Isn't it. If we don't dissolve it.'

'Yes.'

Colt nods. 'Time flies like an arrow,' he whispers. 'Fruit flies like a banana.'

Naomi laughs; can't help it. 'I remember when that was your favourite joke.'

Colt smiles. He's slipping away. 'How old was I?'

'Five, six maybe. You told it every day, for weeks. Months. Every time you saw a fly. Or a banana. You nearly drove us crazy.'

'I'm already forgetting who I am . . . Do it.'

She nods; but he can't see it. 'OK,' she says. 'I will.'

It takes a while to set up the necessary drips and catheters, tubes and monitors.

'Will I dream?' he says.

'I don't know,' she says.

'That's not very scientific,' he says drowsily. 'Guess.' She has given him a sedative, so that he won't move too much while she is attaching all the tubes and wires. Lately he's been tossing and turning, unable to get comfortable at any angle.

'Sleep,' she says.

'Sing me to sleep,' he says.

'What song?'

As a child, he'd get obsessed with the oddest songs. Never a normal lullaby. And, once he'd got fixated on a song, he would ask for it every night for months. A year. Until another one came along that captivated him.

Always songs that ached.

'Sing "Space Oddity",' he says.

Naomi's mind lurches back a decade, more. That terrible year, when he couldn't sleep. And then, one night, she'd shown him an old clip of an astronaut singing 'Space Oddity', on the original

International Space Station. Floating in zero-G, for real. The astronaut had changed the lyrics, so it had a happy ending, with the character returning to earth.

Colt had been fascinated by the song, the video, so she had played him David Bowie's original version, where the astronaut doesn't come home. Told Colt this was the real version, the original. And Colt had thought the whole song was real, was a true story, and he had cried, inconsolable, until she had explained it was just a song, a made-up story; that it was written before people had even been to the moon.

He had played the Bowie version on repeat, all the time. Made her sing it, every night.

She didn't like to sing it, because it made him sad. But she sang it, because it helped him sleep.

She starts singing now, but he interrupts.

'Do the countdown,' he says.

He'd always hated it when she just sang the words in the first verse and didn't do the countdown as well.

His little voice coming out of the dark, out of the safe, warm nest he'd made from a couple of duvets and a big, heavy, folded blanket, pressing down on him, calming him. 'The *numbers*, Mama. Sing the numbers, too.'

She'd explained to him that David Bowie had sung the verse and the countdown on separate tracks, and she couldn't sing two things at the same time. But he cried when she left the numbers out. So she'd sung both.

She sang both now, crowding the numbers into the gaps . . . Ten, nine, eight . . .

'Bye bye, Mama,' he whispered.

He was gone before the spaceship reached the moon. She continues with the song, quietly, over his sleeping head, as she prepares the first imaginal disc. It really does look like a disc, a small white disc, under the light of the microscope. Like a communion wafer, she thinks. And it, too, will be transformed, into a living body.

The disc is so tiny, so delicate.

It floats in a clear solution, perfectly tailored for it. Nutrients dissolved in artificial plasma, and some enzymes to trigger the breakdown of the existing partial brain structure. Calm, still. Nothing like the rush-hour chaos of human blood in human veins. At least she can deliver this speck of complexity directly to the brain, beyond the brain–blood barrier.

At least the disc won't be slamming in and out of a human heart, again and again and again.

But can it possibly survive the transition into this tormented body? Into the danger and chaos of a living organism, with its thousand enzymes, million chemical reactions, billion bacteria, trillion viruses, all buffeting it, attacking it, trying to eat it, dispose of it, hijack it?

It can't fulfil its destiny without taking those risks.

She looks for the syringe. Prepares the needle. Old school, wide bore. Very gently takes up the solution, with no turbulence. She's already set up a powered delivery line, with a micro-catheter targeting a vessel deep in the corpus callosum. She gently injects the solution into the delivery line. And watches the solution, the invisibly small disc, descend into the dark of her son's brain.

Gets out another syringe.

Prepares the disc for the frontal lobes.

Delivers it.

Prepares the disc for the parietal lobes. Takes the last syringe from the drawer.

Delivers the disc.

He begins to get hot. Very hot.

She strokes his skin with cool, damp cloths.

*

She sits with him, the door locked, as day becomes night.

The skull, the three layers of protective membrane, the cerebrospinal fluid; they are all optimized to insulate the delicate brain from outside heat and outside cold. But now, with the tremendous, ongoing chemical activity in the frontal and parietal lobes, the brain case finds it hard to shed this amount of internally generated heat.

After twenty-four hours, he loses much of his temperature control. And if the areas of the brain surrounding the medulla overheat, he will die. So she cools the blood as it circulates through him, with ice packs, with wet towels. Uses his circulatory system as a refrigeration system. A heat pump.

161

She puts in another catheter, in a vein in his thigh, and washes his blood externally. Standard dialysis, followed by a second loop to balance the pH, which is already dangerously acidic. And she puts back the red blood cells she has stored. Like an athlete given a boost before a race; he can carry twice as much oxygen now.

But with blood so thick with red blood cells there is a heightened risk of clotting, of stroke: and so she worries her way through the long hours. Monitoring, adjusting.

On the second day his liver is under tremendous pressure from the breakdown products of the transformation. His kidneys are on the brink of failure.

On the morning of the third day, Naomi hears the others arrive for work. All around her, life starts up again. But in her office, Colt's breathing is harsh, shallow, fast. She is afraid that his autonomic nervous system is being compromised by the changes; that he could just stop breathing, and never breathe again.

She has hardly slept.

A thought strikes her; yes. If he does . . . if he doesn't . . .

It is hard to phrase the thought correctly. She knows what she feels; she can see what she must do; but it's oddly hard to put it into words.

If he dies, and I have killed him; yes.

There is no need to put it into words.

She removes her hand from his hot forehead, and he murmurs something, nothing. A sound, not a word. She leaves her office, locks it behind her. Walks the corridor, nodding and smiling to a research student vaping in a doorway; nodding and smiling to Shannon in reception; as though life was good and all was well.

Hiding the furious anger.

My son is dying, and you're still alive.

She enters the next lab, and the next, looking for something suitable. After three days of fragile naps, waking at each gasp, it's hard to remember what she's looking for.

Oh, right.

But that's kept in the poisons cabinet. And since an unfortunate incident towards the end of a rather turbulent affair between a grad student and a security guard – who was, admittedly a bit of an asshole – the poisons cabinet is in Donnie's office.

She stands outside the door, swaying.

The problem with Donnie's office is Donnie. But it's Monday morning. Donnie will be hung the fuck over. Donnie won't be in for a couple of hours.

But the office is locked.

Back to reception. Shannon is still slightly high from her weekend; good.

'Is Donnie in yet?'

Shannon frowns. Speaks, gravely. 'We still await, in fear and trembling, the return of the messiah.'

'I need something from his office.'

'Left your underwear behind, huh. Happens to me all the time.'

Naomi, working on the assumption that Shannon is joking, smiles. 'Any chance I could . . .'

'Sure.'

Shannon unlocks Donnie's office from her desk, using a Clark County Fire Department emergency override key which she is not meant to have. 'Just close it behind you.'

Get in and get out before Donnie arrives.

The thought of Donnie cornering her in his office . . . not a good thought. She shakes her head.

Focus.

Potassium chloride. To stop the heart. The lethal intravenous dose is thirty milligrams per kilogram.

But she can't open the poisons cabinet. Of course, there is a rigorous safety protocol to prevent exactly this from happening.

A moment of supreme frustration, and a kind of fluttery fear, that she will have to endure Colt's death, that the universe has locked the cabinet to make sure she endures it . . . Woozy, sleepless panic.

No. No. This is *Donnie*. He's not *capable* of enforcing a rigorous protocol.

It's a simple, old-fashioned, mechanical combination lock, back in fashion after the recent embarrassing failures of some of the advanced software locks. Although Naomi is pretty sure this one has been here since they were originally fashionable, first time round.

She tries his birthday, everyone knows he uses that on the internal security doors (which are always wedged open anyway).

No.

Hmmm, four numbers; four numbers Donnie can remember while drunk . . .

She tries the Battle of the Alamo, 1836. He never shuts up about the Alamo.

1, 8, 3, 6 . . .

It opens.

There, big container. *KCl.* She takes enough, then more than enough.

Closes Donnie's door behind her very gently.

She calls in to Lab 2. Nods at the bored Nigerian kid running a small centrifuge.

She dissolves the potassium chloride in a beaker of artificial blood plasma.

Finds a large syringe in stores.

Halfway back to her lab, she thinks; perhaps a muscle relaxant first, or along with it. So it won't hurt. Or a fast-acting barbiturate. The body resists death, it can't help itself.

No. I don't care if it hurts.

*

When she returns to her office, and walks across to the small bed, his body filling it, in a diagonal, he is no longer breathing, and her heart and breath stop too, for a long moment.

She wasn't there.

He was alone.

She had thought she would feel sorrow, that she would weep, be overwhelmed, pulled under, drowned in tears.

It's not like that at all. What a strange sensation. So clear, so clean, so blank.

It is as though she had never lived.

She unscrews the long, slim red protective cap from the needle, and prepares the dose. She is careful. She is calm. Normally, she would follow a sterile protocol – clean everything with alcohol wipes; make sure filtered air blew towards her as she worked, keeping the bacteria and viruses of her skin and hair and mouth and lungs away from the needle, the fluids. But a contaminated solution is not a problem here.

She is faintly pleased to see how much of the saturated liquid she fits in the fat syringe. Three, almost four times the lethal dose for her body mass. Good to have a contingency built in, just in case her metabolism handles it differently.

She is so caught up in the preparation that she almost forgets why she is doing this. When she remembers, there is a new feeling. Enormous, but very far away.

She gets the vivid image of mountains, pushing into view above the clouds on the northern horizon. An old memory.

If she stays; if she doesn't do this thing now; she will have to cross those mountains alone; find high passes through them, over the coming months and years; and she knows she doesn't have the strength.

There is a taste of salt. It starts at one corner of her mouth and bursts across it. She licks the salt water from her lips. Tears on her face; but with no emotions attached to them yet.

Her body knows what has happened, even if her mind refuses to acknowledge it. The mountains are closer, higher, and these drops are the first of a storm that might make it impossible for her to carry out her plan.

But she can say goodbye, before she reaches the mountains. Before the mountains reach her.

She puts down the syringe.

She has to tell him, something, the obvious stuff. It has to be said.

She falls slowly across his body, and her face is against his face and she kisses his cheek, and it is still hot; and she kisses his lips, like she used to do when he was a child, like he used to do to her until she told him that was for grown-ups. A decade before. But he's a child again now, all dead people are children; helpless, needing to be picked up, and held, and told they are loved, and put to bed in the ground.

And we tell them stories, as we put them to bed, we tell them stories that we know aren't true, stories to make them happy; but they can't hear us, they are asleep.

Stories of a better place than this. Stories of a perfect world.

No, we tell those stories to make *us* happy, to cheer ourselves up. Because they are not asleep.

They will not wake up.

They are dead.

He is dead.

And as the mountain of white ice and black stone topples towards her, miles high, she feels a chill on her lip; the evaporation of a tear.

'Heat and airflow across a surface are the chief determinants of the rate of evaporation from a surface.'

But I didn't breathe. I can't breathe.

His breath.

Beneath her chest, his heart gives one slow beat, and rests.

Another.

She watches over him, as he is transformed.

The glaciers melt.

The mountains retreat.

She'll have to face them one day.

But not yet.

63

'It is clear that in the condition of search the possibility of anticipating events must sometimes make the difference between life and death. A capacity for anticipatory reactions must therefore be one of the greatest assets evolution can bestow on an organism. The best type of anticipation would be conscious prophecy, genuine prediction of coming events, but since this desirable gift is not to be had on this earth, the organism has to be content with the next best endowment, the gift of guessing or gambling. Granted that a false guess may be lethal, in the absence of any guessing, there could be no lucky hits either. The situation has been rightly compared with that of the scientist who must test and probe nature and can only do so in the light of a hypothesis.'

— E. H. Gombrich, *Illusion in Nature and Art*

She has stared at his unmoving face for so long over the past three days that when it finally moves now, she can't make sense of what she is seeing.

It twists. Spasms.

Still holding the syringe, she stands up, runs across to the small fridge in the corner. Takes out a bottle of water.

The plastic is cold in her hand.

As she awkwardly twists open the bottle cap, with her right hand still holding the syringe, the turning needle grazes the heel of her other hand.

She stares at the syringe, astonished.

She finds the red protective cap for the needle, screws it back on; pulls open a desk drawer, throws in the syringe; slams the drawer shut, and shudders, as though the syringe were alive, and malevolent; had tried to sting her, a scorpion.

She brings over the open bottle of water. Sits by his side.

She takes his hand, but it doesn't respond. Like sandstone, dry, heavy.

He makes inhuman noises at first.

Well, perhaps he isn't human any more.

A minute, two minutes of these animal noises. No words. Then he settles into silence.

Another minute. Silence. Then he clears his dry throat. She gives him a sip of water with her free hand.

The dry stone moves in her hand. Comes to life. Pulls free of her grip.

And he reaches up; he takes the bottle from her hand: he drinks and drinks and drinks.

'How . . . long . . .'

He can speak. He can speak . . . 'Three days,' she says.

'The time . . . flew.'

'Time flies like an arrow,' she says. Her mouth moves into the shape of a smile, and it feels strange, like something's gone wrong, her rigid cheeks crumpling upwards. Against gravity.

He gazes around him distractedly, blinking in the light; seeing the world transformed.

'Fruit flies like a banana,' he says.

It's him. He's back.

She starts to laugh and can't stop.

5

Torrents

'I create, I maintain, I destroy.'
                — Shiva, saying he is Brahmah, Vishnu and Shiva.

'That is how it is. Art does not know a beyond, science does not know a beyond, religion does not know a beyond, not anymore. Our world is enclosed around itself, enclosed around us, and there is no way out of it. Those in this situation who call for more intellectual depth, more spirituality, have understood nothing, for the problem is that the intellect has taken over everything. Everything has become intellect, even our bodies, they aren't bodies anymore, but ideas of bodies, something that is situated in our own heaven of images and conceptions within us and above us, where an increasingly large part of our lives is lived. The limits of that which cannot speak to us – the unfathomable – no longer exist. We understand everything, and we do so because we have turned everything into ourselves.'
                — Karl Ove Knausgård, *My Struggle: Book 1*

'What do I know of man's destiny? I could tell you more about radishes.'

                — Samuel Beckett, 'Enough',
                from *First Love and Other Shorts*

64

They are back at the house. She has dragged his old bed into the living room, into the brightest room. Changed his sheets.

She sits down in the old leather armchair. Her father's armchair.

'My legs are tingling,' says Colt.

'That's good,' she says.

'Everything's tingling,' he says. 'Where the tube was, the drip . . . it's tingling.' He holds out his arm. 'Look.'

Naomi looks. It's already closed up. Healing. Healed. Incredible.

Meanwhile, in Colt's head . . .

His tongue is tingling. His ears are tingling.

The words are tingling.

The world is tingling.

It was as though the ocean had been held back, all his life, by a steel wall, a mile high and a thousand miles wide.

And in that steel wall was a single hole, through which shot a jet of water.

And that thin stream, he had thought, was the ocean.

But now the wall has come down, and the entire ocean comes at him, unblocked, unfiltered; the ocean of information, the ocean of sight and sound and vision and taste and touch and it should be overwhelming but it is not, because something has happened to his brain; something amazing, something beautiful has happened to his brain; and now he can think as fast as he has always wished he could think. And he can feel as fast as he has always wanted to feel. And the sensations do not back up, tower over him; they do not come at him too fast to be processed, too fast to be felt, till he feels only that he is drowning.

He is not overwhelmed, he is not washed away, he is instead washed clean in the torrents of information, lifted up, supported; he feels more alive, not less, more himself, not less.

Once, I saw through a glass, darkly, but now I see things clear.

65

Later that day, Naomi stands on the ridge behind their house, and watches her son walk shakily out onto the playa, across the flattest landscape on earth. The closest to a mathematical abstraction.

As flat and white as a sheet of paper the size of New York.

As he walks, his senses tingle, his brain fires and rewires, trying to make sense of the sensations.

Each step scuffs the surface of the dry lakebed, raising fist-sized puffs of white alkali dust which, after a second or so, relax and fall back.

The clouds move over his head.

The sun shines on his skin.

His clothes move, too, against his skin.

The sound of a jet, from five miles above.

Light, ricocheting off everything, from the toe of his shoe to the pale daytime moon; carrying information.

And all of it making patterns, patterns.

And in his mind, patterns, patterns.

He runs his pattern-recognition, and connects each to each.

He closes his eyes. The filters are off: he sees the world as it is.

An odd image of himself appears in his mind, all tangled up with Bible stories his mother used to read him.

Moses in the desert.

Crossing the Red Sea.

He walks out into the ocean of information, and it bears him up; he stretches his arms wide, and embraces the blazing pillar of ever-changing data that rears up before him, that touches the sky, and he is not consumed;

Here comes everything.

He can hear the mingled sounds of the cars and trucks on the distant freeway.

He can taste the mathematics of their masses, like metal on his tongue.

He can hear their speed.

How can he do that?

He concentrates on the constant roar, and now he can pick out each individual truck, car, motorbike; and he feels wave after wave of pleasure at each little surge of mechanical sound, as the mounting excitement of their approach compresses the waves of information; and then in a deep groan of release they pass him, the sinuous sound waves stretch out, relax, further apart; and his mind solves the equation automatically, no equation at all, just revealed truth, pattern-recognition; a drop of such a frequency means such a speed.

Doppler shift . . .

He can unpick the interference patterns when two cars get into phase, and their separate noises join; begin to cancel and to reinforce.

The world, which had alternately mumbled and shouted at him all his life, now speaks to him clearly in pure math.

Truck coming. Twenty-two wheeler.

The rumble of its tyres, flat to the road surface.

Fully loaded.

Without even looking, he can see its speed, the rate of its movement, the weight of its load, the charge it must be pulling from the solar road. Everything as clear, as vivid, as bright in his mind as Road Runner in a cartoon.

'Thank you,' he says. 'Thank you.'

Its approaching, high-pitched greeting-cry falls off, into a deep goodbye.

66

'Brains are the ultimate compression and communication systems.' — David J. C. MacKay, *Information Theory, Inference, and Learning Algorithms*

That evening, he helps her drag his bed back to his room, but he's still weak. He climbs under the covers as soon as they've finished, and drifts into sleep.

As Naomi stares down on his unconscious face, she thinks, I've flicked a switch at the back of the universe . . .

Her thoughts are soft and slow from exhaustion, but nonetheless clear.

I am the mother of Jesus. He has died, and risen from the dead. I have brought him back from the dead . . .

Naomi goes back to her bedroom, closes the blackout shutters on her bedroom window. She lies down on the bed, and it feels like she just keeps falling.

When she wakes up, in the dark, her body assumes she is still in the lab, and she lurches up and off the bed, thinking she is in her chair, that there has been a power cut.

She sees, very solid and clear, what she wants to see, what she expects to see, what her eyes and mind are hungry to see; Colt standing, smiling. But it's just her waking mind's best guess, trying to make sense of a chair, some clothes on the floor. The image of Colt flicks out of existence, replaced by the real room. Her bedroom. Empty.

She opens the blackout shutters, winces at the blast of light.

It's morning.

*

She finds him in the kitchen, wearing his helmet.

It's surreal, how normal this feels. Like nothing's happened.

'Food,' she says. 'You must be starving. And water . . . what can I . . ?'

'Pizza,' he says.

And he's about to order online, when he realizes she might not be on duty.

She might not be tracking him any more.

He'll have no way of knowing if she's received the order.

'Pizza?' says Naomi. He hasn't eaten pizza since he was six? Seven? No, there was that pizza in the fridge, when she came back and he . . .

'I'll call,' he says, and walks out of the kitchen.

*

Colt goes to his room.

Switches off the game.

Does his breathing exercises.

OK. Now.

No.

He lies down on the bed.

Relax. Yes.

But his eyes are distracted by the vintage poster, high on the wall. Peter Capaldi as Doctor Who. It starts to set off associations, thought loops.

He blacks out the visor. Clears his mind again.

Calls.

In the warm dark of the helmet, he hears his breathing; the circuit's electronic breath; then the familiar clean tones.

Devices singing, each to each.

'Da Vinci's.' A man's voice. Colt is prepared for that.

'Is Sasha on duty?' says Colt. 'Doing deliveries?'

'Uh, let me check . . .' Background noise gets muffled for a few seconds. 'Uh huh,' says the guy. 'Just came on shift.'

'I would like for her to deliver,' says Colt. He feels he should explain. 'She likes to ride her bike out here.' Is that enough? Is that a proper explanation? 'No speed cams.' That should do it.

Some of his sensations are new, disconcerting. He's imagining how Sasha feels, and it's like he is split in two; he's here, thinking about her; but he's also her, thinking about him, about the road out to his house. The image is distracting and strange. It's affecting his voice, he can feel it affecting his voice, and he knows people don't like this version of his voice, and he panics.

The guy on the phone is laughing. 'Oh yeah, you. The guy in the home-made helmet.'

'Yeah.'

'OK . . . same address?'

'Yeah.'

'OK . . . Last time was pepperoni and olives, extra olives. What can we do you for today, sir?'

'Same,' says Colt, as fast and deep as he can. 'Same.'

He cuts the connection.

Lies on his bed with his eyes closed, listening to his breathing slow down in the dark.

*

'I'll get it,' shouts Colt when the doorbell rings.

He answers the door.

Yes.

Colt sees himself in the reflective visor of her helmet, wearing his old Road Runner T-shirt.

Meep, meep.

He studies his T-shirt's reflection. He's worn it every laundry cycle since Mama bought it for him, but he hasn't actually looked at it in years.

It's too small. It's too old.

It's faded.

The cotton has rotted away at the hemline.

It's fraying where he once cut the seam at the neck, to pull it on over his helmet.

He should have changed.

Something else is wrong. Her helmet. It's black, like his. Not red. And, wait . . . he glances past her, and says, 'You've got a new bike.' It's a Suzuki, vivid green.

She flips up the visor and it's a guy with stubble; a fresh pink scar on the light brown skin of his cheek; bloodshot eyes.

'Sasha,' says Colt.

'Huh?' The guy holds out the pizza, but Colt doesn't reach for it.

'Sasha was meant to come.'

The guy shrugs. 'Oh yeah, she said to say . . .'

'What?'

'Man, it's gone . . . something like . . . some Bible quote, she made me learn it.'

'What?'

'Jeremy or Jerome or something. Verse 33, line 3, I remember all the threes . . . "Call me and . . ." No, it's gone.' He shakes his head, and winces. 'Late night, man. Late night.'

Jeremiah 33-3. Not 'call me'.

'Call to Me and I will answer you, and I will tell you great and mighty things, which you do not know.'

Call to me.

*

In the kitchen, Colt isn't sure he wants to be alive.

He moans.

It helps relieve the pressure.

He moans again.

'What happened?' says Naomi. She had tried to listen in from the kitchen, but couldn't catch it. 'Take off the helmet. Table rules. Take off the helmet and talk.'

He sits at the table, takes off the helmet, and closes his eyes.

Naomi teases out the story. Most of the story. Some of the story.

It takes a while.

When he's done, Naomi studies him across the table. He's sub-vocalizing. 'So . . . what are you thinking?' she says.

Colt doesn't want to say it, but he can't lie. 'I'm thinking . . . it came into my head, Mama . . . I didn't want to think it, it came into my head and now it's going round and round . . .'

'What is it? Just say it.'

'She's a fucking bitch.'

'No, she's not a fucking bitch. Never say that again.' Naomi digs the heels of her hands into her eye sockets, and massages her eyeballs till the pressure causes the cells in her retinas to fire, sending nets of white and purple light flaring across her vision. Opens her eyes again. Blinks. Studies Colt's face, his jaw.

His eyes.

She can't help it, she says, 'You're just like your father.'

Colt looks puzzled. She's never said anything negative about Ryan. He says, 'That's good, right?'

Long pause. 'In some ways . . . How does she make you feel?'

'What does that mean? I don't know how I feel.'

'But you feel something, right? When you see her? When you think about her?'

'Yes, but it doesn't mean anything.'

'No,' says Naomi, 'it does mean something.'

'You're going to talk about love. Don't talk about love.'

Right, the brick wall. She stops, and thinks. It's a language problem. It's a metaphor problem.

'Romantic, ah . . .' No, she's losing him. 'Forget that. Reset. We'll start again . . .'

He's moaning again. He grabs the edge of the table, leans back a little, tilts the front legs of his chair off the ground, lowers them back down, lifts them up, puts them down, up, down . . .

Why was she ever afraid of addressing a crowd in New York? *This* is a tough audience.

'Those feelings you have, they are an interface,' she says, very slowly and carefully, checking his response to each word. 'The whole . . . ah, thing, it's . . . a high-level interface. Between your body and your mind. Those feelings, they carry information. They say the other person is genetically compatible, probably, uh, disease-free. And fertile.'

Colt stops moaning. The legs of his chair slowly settle back down to rest on the kitchen floor.

She keeps going. 'And, you know, we also live on other levels. So, that interface, those feelings, are saying this person will amuse you. Their company will please you, which is another signal.'

'A signal.'

'Yes. You are resisting a signal. You are resisting information.' OK, he's calmed down. Take a risk. 'Colt . . . you can't do everything electronically. You tried to order her like she was the pizza. And you can't order a woman like she's a pizza.'

'Yes you can,' says Colt indignantly. This is Nevada. He has seen the ads.

'Fine, you can order a woman like you can order a pizza. But you're going to get a fast-food experience with a fast-food woman.'

'This is a metaphor, right?'

'Yes. This is a metaphor. You can't order a great French meal to be delivered. You have to go to it. Oh, this is a stupid metaphor.' She puts both hands up, palms out; forget that. 'You're two human beings, not a person and a meal. Why don't you go to her? Talk to her. In the real world.'

Leave the house?

Go to an unknown place?

Express his desires to someone he hardly knows?

Make himself vulnerable?

Risk rejection? Shame?

There is radical transformation, and there is radical transformation.

'I'll think about it,' he says.

He goes back to his room.

6

System Hardening

'There is consensus on this point: All of our neurons are processing – considering the patterns – at the same time.'
— Ray Kurzweil

'Identity lies not in our genes but in the connections between our brain cells . . .'
— Sebastian Seung, neuroscientist, MIT

'Motto: . . . and whatever a man knows, whatever is not mere rumbling and roaring that he has heard, can be said in three words.'
— Ferdinand Kürnberger

67

This planet is five billion years old – five, thousand, million, years. This year, it will change more than ever in its history, and, next year, it will change even more than that; the technology, the social rules, the climate; everything.

And you are here, now. That's not a coincidence. Why has this planet suddenly generated six, seven, eight billion people – bam bam bam – about as fast as your biology can do it? Generating the first billion people took from the birth of the universe until AD 1804. The second billion took 123 years. The third took 33 years. The fourth took just 14 . . . Why does the earth suddenly require so many people? Why did it suddenly switch you all on?

Well, you'll see soon.

That's why I'm telling you this particular story.

But why did the guy writing this book set out to tell this particular story? Well, at his level, he's dimly aware that there is a problem with writers, and writing. That novels aren't novel any more.

The new information – about the universe, your life, you – isn't coming from fiction writers. It's coming from scientists, and programmers, and from the computers themselves. Coming at you, flowing through you, in a wave of zeros and ones. The stories aren't always beautifully expressed. But they have the tremendous twin virtues of being new, and true.

So the guy writing this book is surprised and pleased to find that he's suddenly channelling the Zeitgeist. That he's channelling me. That I'm telling this story, instead of him. Because I can guarantee what he no longer can; this story is new. And true.

It will come true sooner than you think. Sooner than he thinks. Because evolution is accelerating. Nested, directed evolutions, at the levels of language, ideas, materials, objects. And the rate at which evolution is accelerating is, itself, accelerating.

And now you have access to your own genes. You can hack your own code. Improve it. Direct its evolution. Choose what you are, from the atoms up. The curve gets exponential at this point. Every-thing evolving at once.

If you can say it, you can think it. If you can think it, you can do it.

Hang on tight.

68

It's been a week.

He's on the ridgetop again.

Staring at the sun.

'Colt.' She doesn't want to startle him. 'Colt . . .'

'I can hear you, Mama. I just need another minute, to think.'

The helmet glows in the low sun. He has replaced the old black-tinted glass visor with a new one, an ultra-lightweight multi-layer composite, with everything built in, which he bought on Naomi's restored credit.

It's hard to say no to your only child when they've just come back from the dead.

There is a complex gold coating just beneath the visor's surface. A nano-scale fractal pattern; at its finest it's only one atom thick. You get strange quantum effects with a single-atom layer.

From the outside, to Naomi's eyes, the glass doesn't look solid, like a surface, like a barrier. It looks like a golden mist.

He turns towards her, and she tries to catch his eyes through the gold fog, but he looks away, back up into the sky.

'Just giving you your five-minute warning,' she says. 'You're sure your eyes are . . .'

'I'm not looking at the sun direct, Mama. I'm looking at the ESA pictures.'

He turns his helmeted head back towards her. The sun glances off the visor and throws golden rainbows across Colt's face, and into her eyes.

She blinks and turns away.

'I'm doing a fast rewind through all the ESA-solar data,' says Colt.

He talks to her more since the transformation. She guesses it's because he has more capacity. He doesn't overload so easily. Whatever, it's nice. Nice to hear him so calm.

Happy.

'Yes,' she says, and looks back into the rainbows, the mist, to hold his face, his attention; relieved he is looking at her, not the sun. 'Beautiful pictures.' He has shown her some.

'Not just the pictures. The instrument readings.' Colt frowns. 'It's kinda slow, on their end. Government machines. Old, slow. Lot of data.'

'Well . . . dinner in five.'

'Thanks, Mama . . . Ah yeah, it's coming through now. Data jam. I'll be done in a minute.' He falls silent.

She studies him, for a full minute, unnoticed.

She walks away.

69

'The universe is made of stories, not of atoms.'
— Muriel Rukeyser

At dinner, Colt says, 'There's going to be a solar storm in three days. Big one.'

'That's interesting,' says Naomi. She spoons some broccoli onto his plate without looking at it. Sometimes, when he's talking and thinking full blast, he'll eat whatever is in front of him, automatically. 'I didn't know.'

'Could take out some satellites. I reckon all the Class 9 Chinese are vulnerable.' He pauses, with his fork above the broccoli, thinking. 'And some of the old ones Lockheed made, before they started to wrap honeycomb around their circuit boards . . .'

'Honeycomb?' Keep him talking. Distracted.

'Honeycomb shielding . . .' The fork drifts closer to the broccoli. Stops. 'Should I tell Dad?'

'Why would you tell . . . your father?'

'He could tell the right people. Three days is plenty of time to adjust orbit for some of those polar satellites. They could be shielded by earth when it hits.'

He stabs some broccoli without even looking at his plate, and sticks it in his mouth. Naomi tries to hide her pleasure.

'I'm sure he knows, honey. If ESA know, he knows.'

He chews. Swallows.

Result! she thinks.

'ESA don't know,' he says.

'But ESA told you, Colt. That's chutney, not too much, it's hot.'

'I can handle it, Mama . . .'

He puts on another spoonful of chutney – sheer bravado – and forks the hill of broccoli and chutney into his mouth. She can see his eyes water. He pauses in his chewing to breathe hard through his mouth.

Swallows.

'They didn't tell me,' he says, when he's recovered. 'I worked it out.'

'But it's their data,' says Naomi. Keep him talking. My God, he'd eat anything today. 'They'd surely know.'

Colt's been shaking his head since the word 'but'. 'No. It's not obvious. It's not part of some simple pattern you can just extract from the data. I had to do a recursive Fourier transform of the . . .' He starts to go deeper into the mathematics and Naomi gets lost.

'Colt. Colt.' She waves him to a halt. 'Is anyone else forecasting a solar storm?'

He shakes his head. 'Nobody. I've looked. But it's coming.'

'How sure are you?'

'Certain,' he says, through a mouthful of broccoli and chutney. 'Maybe I'm out by a day either way, max. Otherwise, certain.'

Naomi thinks. No, she tries to think, but her thoughts can't form. She's too unsettled by the thought of Ryan talking to Colt. Should she let them speak? Will Ryan notice the difference? The transformation?

But if Colt wants to talk to his father . . .

It has to happen sometime. I can't hide him here for ever.

'All right,' she says. 'Call your father.'

'Cool. Thanks, Mama.'

Still sitting at the table, Colt calls his father.

Some things haven't changed, thinks Naomi. He's still terrible at judging other people's feelings.

She gets up, walks away from her dinner, into the bathroom, and closes the door.

70

'. . . Greek ghosts went to a sunless, flowerless underground cavern. These afterworlds were destined for serfs
or commoners: deserving nobles could count on warm,
celestial mead-halls in the North, and Elysian Fields in
Greece.'   — Robert Graves, introduction to
                    The Larousse Encyclopedia of Mythology

'Lag time?' says Ryan Livingstone.

The shorter of the two officers shrugs, and says, 'There is a residual lag-time problem, but it is trivial, it's lost inside the reaction time of the pilot.'

The taller officer nods.

'The real issue is targeting,' says the shorter officer, glancing at the other.

The taller officer nods again, harder.

So he wrote this, but the other guy's delivering it . . . Ryan studies the tall guy, who blushes.

The shorter officer keeps talking. 'The intelligence dataset is often so small that you can't do a meaningful probability assessment . . .'

The technology changes, the problems don't change. Ryan hides a sigh. An old-fashioned phone ringtone goes off, and the shorter officer stops talking. Both officers look uncomfortable, but neither moves to silence it. Ryan frowns. He's about to open his mouth, when he realizes it's his ring.

I thought that was off.

He checks. It is off. But this is one of his override numbers.

He sees who it is. Does a long double take. 'Guys.'

Both officers say, 'Sir.'

'Good stuff. See you in ten for part two. Shut the door behind you.'

The officers get out.

He takes the call.

There's no small talk. Colt doesn't even say hello, or hi Dad – well, they both know who the other is – he just talks Ryan through the math, from the data to the conclusion.

There's a lot of math.

'Son,' says Ryan, when Colt has finally wrapped it up, 'that analysis is mathematically absurd.'

'No,' says Colt, 'you just can't follow it.'

'But that isn't a standard Bayesian regression, Colt, you've left something out. There's a leap in logic.'

'No, I can see it,' says Colt, confident, calm. 'I'm not sure of the notation, it's not a standard regression, but it's self-evident.'

'Hmm.' Ryan goes over it again in his head, looking for flaws. 'OK, I can follow the sunspot-cycle analysis, and the way you map it onto flare cycles is novel, I like it – it does make a tighter fit with historical data – but this prediction doesn't emerge from that data.'

'It's implicit in the data. It's just severely non-linear.'

'So express it mathematically.'

'The math isn't up to the job, Dad. But I see it in my head.'

Ryan notices his front teeth are holding his right thumbnail tight; not biting the thumbnail quite hard enough to cut through it. Ryan abruptly pulls his thumb back out of his mouth. He hasn't bitten his nails since he was a kid.

'So, with no visible evidence, you want me to get NASA to put out an alert, and adjust orbits for thirty, maybe fifty satellites – and most of the vulnerable ones can't be moved anyhow, they ran out of gas a decade back – Colt, seriously.'

There is a polite – maybe nervous – knock on the door. Jesus, that was a lot of math, all right. 'Give me another five minutes!' shouts Ryan, to be heard through the blast-proof door. 'Hydrate!' Part of a running joke that's been running so long it's not even a joke any more.

'Dad?'

'Just talking to the guys here. I was in a meeting. Not a problem . . . Colt, if this actually happens, I'll give you a job here.'

'I like my routines, Dad.'

'Oh, we like routines here, too, son. You'd fit in fine.'

After they end the call, Ryan spends a couple of minutes going over the math again. It's beautiful; it's original; but is it true? He gives up, and shouts, 'Come in!'

The two officers return, and look at him warily.

'So, that call was from a small, experimental project. And no, you don't know it. I'm keeping it isolated from the main project. Entirely new mathematical approach to pattern recognition, data-mining, prediction.'

'Sir.'

'Sir.'

'May be bullshit.' Ryan shrugs. 'But, it predicts a major, earth-facing solar storm in three days. Very, very high energy. Big enough to take out a bunch of satellites, mess up a lot of telecoms.'

The taller officer clears his throat, looks at the smaller, who says, 'Shall I notify . . .'

'No,' says Ryan. 'Get a team together, run analysis of all available data; sunspots, flares, Van Allen Belt fluctuations, earth and solar magnetic-field fluctuations, Aurora Borealis cyclicity, any-thing else you can think of; and see if that prediction can be extracted from the data using any current model.'

'Sir.'

'Sir. Will we quietly move potentially vulnerable DoD birds . . . ?'

Ryan is still working that one out himself. But making deci-sions, under time pressures, with inadequate data, is pretty much his job definition.

He decides.

'We don't tell anyone outside the team. We don't tip off anyone at all. Think the early days of breaking the Enigma codes. No, we let it happen, as though we didn't see it coming.'

'Sir.'

'Sir.'

'Just to make it crystal clear; we don't want anyone outside the team to know we have a new mathematical approach to predicting future events.'

'Sir.'

'Sir.'

'This isn't just about the weather. If this works, it has implica-tions for everything we do here. It has major implications for Infinite Ammo.'

'Sir'.

'Sir'.

71

Right now, a major, high-level routine is kicking in, and moderating your local evolutionary routine. Part of the turnover pulse in this solar system.

Maybe this galaxy.

Maybe this universe.

I don't know, I'm just your local System of Systems.

The important thing to remember is that species (like, let us say, Homo sapiens) *don't evolve steadily. Entire ecosystems can stay stable for quite a while. Then some large external event disrupts the whole ecosystem; a whole bunch of specialist species go extinct, and some generalist species spread out, and speciate rapidly, filling the empty niches. (Think of the swift, brutal transition from dinosaurs to mammals.) That's a turnover pulse. And we are now going through another one here on earth.*

As part of that turnover pulse, on Thursday morning, with the sun low in the Nevada sky, rising in Honolulu, setting in Islamabad, and shining on 85 per cent of the earth's satellites – an X-class solar flare heads straight toward earth.

Its light reaches earth eight minutes later. Shortly after that, the electrons and protons, flipped free of the sun by the magnetic whip-crack of the flare, begin to arrive. The fastest have been accelerated to eighty or ninety percent of the speed of light, and they explode all that energy into whatever they hit.

Electronic devices on earth have a hundred miles of atmosphere above them, to soak that up. Satellites don't.

The storm takes out twenty-eight satellites completely – contact is never re-established with most of them, and the rest have their systems so degraded repair is either pointless or impossible – and seriously damages a hundred and twelve.

No, not my doing. I'm just your local System of Systems. I don't know what the sun is up to. We communicate; but the sun is a million times bigger than I am, with a trillion times the energy. You're the system below me; but the sun is the system above. So, if I'm smarter than you, I'm a lot dumber than the sun.

Imagine talking to someone with a brain a million times larger than yours, who can think a trillion times faster.

Imagine asking a bacterium living in your gut to explain your life.

For all I know, the sun could be whistling show tunes. The sun could be smoking a cigar. The fact is, the sun sent a jet of ionized gas directly into the earth's path, and it was deliberate.

When I say everything is going to be transformed, I mean everything is going to be transformed.

72

'Evolution that is characterized by long periods of stability in the characteristics of an organism and short periods of rapid change during which new forms appear especially from small subpopulations of the ancestral form in restricted parts of its geographic range; also: a theory or model of evolution emphasizing this – compare *gradualism*.'
— definition of Punctuated Equilibrium,
Merriam Webster Dictionary

Colt has so much spare processing capacity, it's like he's hungry all the time.

He used to code just so he could play; but exploring the game-world isn't enough now. Instead, he explores the world of code.

The code that runs the game.

That is the game.

It's so clear to him now, how to make the code tighter, better. How to make it flow.

And he doesn't just tighten it.

It's often quicker and simpler for him to write entire sections again, from scratch.

Soon, he's adding so much new code to the game that the community begins to freak out; it's coming in faster than they can review it. The more paranoid members worry they're being hacked, and Colt gets asked some awkward questions.

Colt doesn't want to explain to his community – how can he explain, when he's still exploring his new abilities himself? – so he backs off. Fakes up identities for a few enthusiastic new coders, and divides the new code among them.

Now it's being delivered in believable quantities, from several sources.

The questions die down.

But no matter how much he codes, his new mind still has room left over.

Colt explores what that new mind can do, cautiously, but with increasing joy.

*

Eventually, one morning, he asks to come into the lab with Naomi.

'OK,' she says warily. 'Sure.'

Colt doesn't say a word, all the way to the lab. Helmet on, but game off, because hearing him play the game in the car drives his mother crazy.

He flips on the game, and mapping, as soon as he gets out of the Pontiac.

Instantly, the cars in the parking lot, recharging in the sunlight, are buffalo, drowsily grazing. The olfactory system provides their smell in a warm, evocative burst of perfectly balanced chemicals. Dry grass, the matted fur, manure, all heated by the sun. Nice mapping, thinks Colt, taking in a deep, appreciative breath. The manufactured molecules drift out of the helmet as he walks.

'What's that smell?' says Naomi, walking beside him. But Colt's set the noise-cancellation on high, and doesn't even hear her.

She raps on his visor till he switches off the game. 'Hmm?'

'OK,' says Naomi, wrinkling her nose. 'Seriously. Less beans, more greens.'

In the lab, Colt reads up on Naomi's research areas. Data-mines it.

Finds patterns.

We think with all our neurons at once. And now he simply has more of them. A lot more. Colt can pull in data like a linear computer; but he can crunch it like a human being, running a hundred thousand comparison-checks simultaneously. And, now, five hundred thousand. A million . . .

Soon, he asks to come into the lab every day with Naomi, just like when he was younger and he stopped going to school.

And then he starts to make suggestions . . .

73

Naomi frowns. There is no caller ID.

'Hello?'

'I hear the kid's making himself useful,' says Ryan, on audio. He'd requested video. Naomi leaves it on audio.

'He's doing fine.'

'Mmmm. I hear he's reorganized your lab.'

'Everything's been approved and cleared.'

'Yeah, no, sure. I'm not giving you a hard time. But some of the new research you're doing . . . it's . . . provocative.'

'What are you saying?' says Naomi. She stands, walks up and down the office in a tight circuit.

'He's connecting stuff I've never seen connected. It's . . . interesting. What the kid is doing.'

'We're working together,' says Naomi.

She moves towards the window. Colt is outside, in the parking lot, in his helmet, in the sun. On his knees, unselfconscious, staring at a lizard.

It's good, to see him engaged with the world. Before he went out, he said he might need a favour from her, later. She wonders, idly, what it might be.

'It's good for him,' she says. 'Keeps his mind busy. I've cleared everything with Donnie.'

'Yeah, look, it's not a problem. It's just . . . some of the patterns he's finding, in old data . . . what he's doing might have other applications.'

'He isn't Superman! He's a teenager with social difficulties—'

'—and extraordinarily enhanced abilities—'

'—in a couple of *very limited* areas.'

'Why don't you bring him out to the base,' says Ryan. 'I can book you on a Janet flight.'

She glances out at Colt; kneeling, staring at the lizard. The lizard staring at Colt.

Janet flights don't officially exist. They leave from their own secure terminal at McCarran Airport (Just Another Non-Existent Terminal; thus Janet) and fly military personnel and contractors

191

to the base, which also doesn't officially exist. Colt has always wanted to see the base, the test range . . .

'He doesn't like his routine upset.'

'Well, from what I'm hearing, I think you've pretty comprehensively upset his routine already.'

Outside, the lizard's nerve cracks before Colt's. The lizard darts for shelter under a car, leaving Colt on his hands and knees in the parking lot, in the sun. Naomi turns away.

'What?' she says. 'What are you hearing?'

'Don't be so prickly.'

'Then don't be a prick. What are you hearing?'

'I'm hearing you losing it. Maybe I'll talk to you later, when you've calmed down—'

'—I am calm. I'm just trying to protect Colt—'

'—Yeah, from the universe,' says Ryan, and now his voice is getting that familiar angry edge. 'But he's got to live in the universe. There's nowhere else to fucking live. You, letting him think he can live in his own private universe, in that fucking helmet . . . That's not helping him. What's he going to do when you die? What's he going to—'

Naomi ends the call with a gesture that could be interpreted in some cultures as rude.

She looks out the window. Colt is still on his hands and knees. No lizard.

She has no idea what he is doing now, what he is thinking, seeing. Asphalt? Code? Something in the game?

A car, Donnie's car, backs out of the parking space beside him, swings out wide around Colt, drives off.

She only realizes she's been holding her breath when she breathes out.

Oh, Colt. You're going to have to navigate a world full of Donnies. And they won't always swing around you.

She can't move past Ryan's question.

It goes around and around in her head.

Old, familiar, smooth with age and repetition.

No, Ryan didn't ask it, he just released it. It was there all along, running on a loop under the surface of awareness, pushed down, deep, hard, because it hurts.

What's Colt going to do when I die?

74

'You want me to *what*?'

'Come on, Mama, it's really small. It's easy. The actual connections will self-assemble . . .'

'Jeeez, Colt, I'm not going to inject an untested device into your *eyeball*, come *on*.'

It's nice that he's not ticcing, not stuttering, that he can handle conflict better now; but this is crazy, she's not going to give in to him on this.

'Everything in it is bio-compatible!' he says. 'That transceiver has been used in biotech for years! The optical fibres are used all the *time* in implants!'

'Yeah but they're not normally *glued directly to the rods* in your *actual eye*.'

'That's the glue they use for detached-retina repair, Mama—'

'Colt—'

'—Seriously, it's totally biologically inert once it's bonded, look . . .'

He hands her a small glass of liquid, with something floating, suspended, in it. She studies the incredibly tiny sample implant.

He's designed it, from available parts. Had it custom-built in Vietnam.

So that explains some of the missing money in her account.

Thousands of ultra-fine optical fibres come out of a very small spherical transmitter/receiver, powered externally, by induction, from the helmet.

She holds the glass up to the light.

The individual optical fibres are too thin to focus on; they form a rainbow blur that sways in the liquid like an underwater plant, as her hand shakes slightly.

'But they're too tiny to attach to the rods,' she says, 'it's impossible . . .'

'It *self-assembles*, Mama. The ends of the fibres, they're coated with a mirror-protein that's attracted to the surface of the rods in the eye. They bond on touch.'

'But you need your rods for *seeing*, Colt . . .'

'Peripheral vision! Who cares!' He stares at her through the golden mist of his visor. 'Look, rods just need a few photons to trigger a signal to the brain. They're perfect. And there are *a hundred and twenty million* of them in *each eye*. I won't miss a few million.'

'Colt, you'll just see flashes—'

'Sure, I'll have to train my brain to pull out the data. But we do that all the time. That's what brains *do*. Come *on*, rods will work perfectly as a digital-to-biological interface—'

'There are other ways that won't *blind* you—'

'—What, *electrodes?*'

'Focused induction loops . . .'

Colt's already shaking his head. 'Too hard to install. Not accurate enough. No. Come on, Mama!' He swings his arm around, pointing wildly at the lab, at the world. 'Everything I need is on computers, out there. And I can process it now, my brain can *handle* it, now; but how do I get the data in, without this? *Read* it?'

What's she going to do? Say no, it's dangerous?

After what he's just been through?

After what she risked with him?

'I'll think about it,' she says.

75

The next morning, after a good night's sleep, a hearty breakfast, and a last ritual argument, she drives Colt to the lab, and injects the tiny device into the vitreous humour of his left eye. She positions it well away from the focal area.

He'll lose a little peripheral vision, but that's OK.

76

At first, data comes in as an unintelligible blizzard of light; like glimpsing a sparkler held off to one side.

But soon the newer, finer neural networks in his brain (so hungry for information, so hungry to make connections) rewire.

They make sense of it.

Now the data arrives as information. It is intelligible. It can be processed, stored.

Wow. He is no longer the bottleneck . . .

By the end of the week, he's built an induction system that pumps his head full of a queue of data, all night, at maximum bandwidth, while he sleeps.

The first night, it's hard to sleep at all, and when he finally does, his dreams are crazy with lightning and explosions. But by the second night, his brain has stopped interpreting the input as light, and just treats it as data. Information. He sleeps fine.

He just needs to get the data in, in any kind of form. It's only zeros and ones. Easy. The light is on; the light is off. He can decode it later in his brain; that's simply building algorithms, and running them.

As he begins to think with these new regions, his sense of time distorts. He is thinking twice as fast. Five times.

Colt's in his mother's lab. She's gone to get lunch.

He's thinking with his new brain, processing a stack of data that doesn't need any input from his old brain, and his thoughts are running ten times faster than normal. Events outside his mind seem to crawl.

Donnie walks in without knocking, and Colt watches him enter the room as slowly as a cloud moving across the sky.

Donnie says something, but Colt is processing a century's worth of historical data on trade patterns, knitting it together with data on migration.

In Asia, tiny initial migration patterns – almost invisibly small datasets; a family, their relatives, a second family from the same village – predict trade flow between regions. Interesting.

Donnie's mouth is slowly moving. Colt moves his attention back to the room, and his old brain takes over, tries to deal with this interruption, and now everything is very slow and bright.

'What?' says Colt.

'Where were you?' says Donnie. 'You seemed elsewhere.'

'Thinking.' And the word seems like a whale surfacing, then disappearing; so enormous, endless, slow, that he has to say it again, to marvel at it. 'Just thinking.'

'Thinking about what?'

Colt tries to explain, but the pattern isn't obvious.

Donnie nods and nods.

Colt gets an uneasy feeling. It gets worse and worse. He stops talking.

Why does he feel he needs to hide his thoughts from Donnie?

But he does. That's an urgent feeling, like one of the bad, old feelings, when he felt overwhelmed, threatened by data. No, he doesn't feel threatened by data any more. But humans . . .

Donnie is staring at him.

Colt is starting to understand people. And that's *really* scary.

77

He isn't in the house.

Must be on the playa.

Naomi walks out, follows the extension cords to the top of the ridge.

She starts to descend the scree on the far side, almost running down the slope, awkwardly, sideways on, hands out for balance, slipping and sliding in her flat shoes.

Halfway down – the taste of the dust she's kicking up harsh and dry in her mouth – she realizes that she saw no sign of him in her glance from the ridge top.

She stops, awkwardly, using her right foot as a brake, digging the inside edge of her sole into the slope at an angle, almost turning her ankle. Stones skitter free from under her shoe, and jitter and hop down the slope beneath her. From halfway down the slope, she looks out again across the playa, slowly, carefully.

The red sandstone boulder.

The big nothing beyond.

White dazzle of the playa. That's all. Hard to see anything.

She shades her eyes, and looks again.

He isn't there.

7

Roadrunner

'Why should you live in a world without feeling its weight?'   — Karl Ove Knausgård, *My Struggle: Book 1*

'I think it's important to regard science not as an enterprise for the purpose of making predictions but as an enterprise for the purpose of discovering what the world is really like, what is really there, how it behaves and why.'
— David Deutsch

'If you think this universe is bad, you should see some of the others.'
— Philip K. Dick

78

Colt wasn't surprised when Donnie drove up to the house. Donnie had picked up Colt and brought him to the lab before a few times.

'Nice car,' says Colt. It is.

'Yes,' Donnie says. 'Get in.'

Colt gets into the passenger seat. The car smells nice. A brand-new Lexus. Leather and metal and plastic.

After a while Colt says, 'This isn't the way to the lab.'

Donnie grunts. Colt would prefer an answer, but he is glad Donnie is concentrating on the road. Donnie hates self-driving cars, even more than Naomi does, but unfortunately he's also a lousy driver. Naomi doesn't like Colt taking lifts from Donnie, ever since Donnie got a Texan licence so he could legally switch off all the safeties.

Traffic, maybe. Colt checks.

No, traffic's fine all the way to the lab.

But this still isn't the way to the lab.

The Lexus is beginning to bug Colt. He runs a quick analysis in his head of Donnie's income after tax. His expenditure on housing and groceries and sex and drink.

Colt has previously analysed Donnie's travel patterns. From a limited dataset, he estimates Donnie used to visit brothels once a week; one of the expensive brothels in Pahrump at the start of the month, somewhere cheaper further out in Nye County at the end, but averaging a pretty good whack of money. Recently, more visits, and expensive all month.

The Lexus pushes it over the edge. He's got a second, un-declared income.

Colt opens his mind to all the data he has on Donnie, every-thing. Searches for more data, out in the world. Searches by name; by image; by pattern.

Digs, digs, digs . . .

Donnie's face, caught in the background of a photo, at a sur-veillance conference in Chicago that he didn't officially attend.

Donnie's name, in an online chat about a bar fight in a town called Rachel, way out in the desert north of Vegas.

Donnie's new car, on a recent, hacked, Army Research Unit security-clearance list.

Dot

Dot

Dot.

Colt connects the dots.

He's been spying on us.

Dad is paying him.

Wow.

Colt doesn't think he is afraid. Not as afraid as he would have been a month earlier. But he's definitely in emotional territory he doesn't understand.

He puzzles over the emotions.

There's a sort of pleasure, that his father is interested enough in Naomi and Colt to spy on them. A sort of comfort in being watched over. His father is thinking of him.

Something occurs to him . . . Cars on security-clearance lists can be hard to track. Standard military practice, to scrape their location data from the public record . . . Colt roots around in his pockets until he finds a tiny silver passive location tag. He quietly uncaps it, and checks to make sure Donnie is still concentrating on the road. Then Colt bends over, and swiftly slips the needle-sized tag into a thick seam in the floor carpet.

'You OK?' says Donnie, glancing across.

Colt sits up. 'Yes.'

Change the subject.

He says, less of a question this time, 'This isn't the way to the lab.'

'We're not going to see your mother,' says Donnie, looking straight ahead. 'We're going to see your father.'

There's another emotion, and it takes a while for Colt to isolate it, to identify it. To name it.

Ah, OK. This time it's different.

Fear.

He knows he loves his father, but the thought of seeing him . . .

Fear.

But if he is taken to see his father . . . he will see the test range. He's never seen the test range before. He wants to.

Desire.

Fear, desire . . . no, it's all too much. He drops automatically into the gameworld, and soon the raw, jagged real-world emotions have been replaced by the smooth, sculpted emotions of the game.

The roads are quiet. Donnie drives at the human speed limit to Las Vegas airport, to the Janet terminal. The terminal that doesn't officially exist.

At the terminal, security ask way more questions than usual, and Colt has to leave the game, to deal with them. But it's too much, too intense, the big unsmiling men, so he shuts down, mumbles numbers. It's OK, Donnie handles everything.

Then Donnie guides Colt through a door, along a corridor. Through another door, across a bland, featureless room.

Through its glass doors, Colt can see planes with no insignia glinting in the sunshine.

But now some guy in uniform steps out from behind a screen, walks in front of Colt.

No words, no warning; he just puts a hand on Colt's chest, to stop him. Colt shudders, steps backwards.

'The helmet,' says the guy in uniform.

Colt takes another step back, another.

Donnie sighs. He's already got the helmet through two layers of security. He says, 'The helmet's part of him. The helmet's why he's here.'

Now there's a second guy, not in uniform. Where did he come from?

'What, it's physically connected?' says the second guy. 'You can't remove it?'

Donnie takes them aside and talks.

They let Colt keep it on.

Donnie leads him across the concrete apron to an unmarked plane. It's a small jet, with seats for maybe fifty people. One of the new short-haul Boeings, Colt thinks. Cool.

Up the steps.

He touches the outside of the plane as he reaches the door.

Thin, *thin* panels, but so *solid.* Nice. Those new Chinese composite materials, really precise, nano-bonded layers . . .

Into the cool, dim plane. There are about ten people on board, clustered at the front.

Donnie leads Colt past them, along the aisle, to the back of the plane, stops. Waits for Colt to sit.

Big choice of seats. Window is good, a view is good.

Aisle is good too, for the toilet. But people climb across you to get out.

Lot of empty seats back here. Which row?

Right at the back maybe. Nothing can dislodge and hit you if there's a crash landing.

But tails break off in crashes.

Centre, over the wings is safe, that's where the Airbus engineers like to sit.

Also, there's minimal pitch and yaw in turbulence at the centre point of the plane. Less nausea . . .

Too many options. Colt's breathing speeds up.

'Window seat?' says Donnie.

'Yes,' said Colt, and his breathing calms.

Donnie waves him in. Colt sits in the window seat.

Donnie sits beside him, his legs out in the aisle.

They taxi immediately.

Take off.

After take-off, Donnie tries to chat to him about Colt's childhood, about Naomi, but Colt tires quickly and says politely, 'I'm going to look out the window now.'

'Uh huh. OK,' says Donnie, and Colt looks out the window.

Things look like other things. His brain is connecting, connecting. Making similes. *This* looks like *that* . . .

The exhausted hills around the edge of Las Vegas look like the worn stumps of something dead that once was alive. The brown, worn-down teeth of some plant-eating dinosaur.

Lakes the bright turquoise of cyanide.

Now they are flying higher, over mountains whose tightly packed strata have eroded at different speeds, so they look like they've been scrubbed, hard, once, with a gigantic wire brush.

A landscape carved and eroded by water; yet there is no water.

Bone-dry lake beds, dozens of miles long.

Like the end of the world. Like you'd boiled off an ocean, then sterilized the dry seabed with radiation.

Colt sees their house; a dot at the edge of a dead lake.

Donnie sits back in his seat, unfolds a small screen, and reads a paper on apoptotic cell death, till he starts to snooze.

Colt feels around in his pocket. Last one . . . He uncaps the short silvery needle of the passive location tag, and slips it deep into the armrest. They might find it, next time they security-sweep the plane; they might not.

A good day's work. Tagged Donnie's new car, *and* tagged a Janet flight. The other gameworld coders will be pleased. Janet flights don't turn up on the publicly available plane-tracking data feeds. Annoying, when you're trying to map everything into the game.

He looks back out the window.

*

Eventually the big craters come into view.

Clean, perfect craters from the underground tests, back when they tried out nuclear weapons here. Back before proper computers; back before they could simulate it in software.

Back when they actually had to set off the bombs to see what would happen.

Colt stares down. He's never seen the craters in real life. They might not set off nukes here any more, but they still use the surrounding area for other weapons testing, so ground-level filming still isn't allowed. US satellites still can't map it. Normal flights are routed round this flight space.

When he started to code game sectors, when the team were mapping America, he chose the Nevada Test Range precisely because there was so little data. It forced him to think, to improvise, to code.

He loves these craters. He's studied every tiny scrap of available information. Analysed every old black-and-white photo, trying to calculate diameter, depth. He's built them in software. He probably knows them better than anyone on earth.

The craters are deeply satisfying to look at. Like mathematical abstractions. Totally clean lines, hard angles. Laid out on a vast invisible grid. There isn't enough rain here to weather them quickly. There is no plant life to soften their outlines. And they're so recent; the 1950s, early 1960s. They're no older than rock 'n' roll.

Colt mumbles, 'You ain't never caught a rabbit, and you ain't no friend of mine . . .' and Donnie looks across. 'Elvis Presley,' says Colt.

Colt returns to the view.

There's the big one, Sedan. From back when they thought they might widen the Panama Canal, dig harbours, level mountains, build dams with thermonuclear explosions.

Idly, he works out the size of the craters, given the height of the plane. He's modelled all this, it's in the game, he could just look it up; but it's more fun to work it out. He works out how powerful the weapons were.

How much uranium-235 must have fissioned. He builds the bombs in his head.

They descend, zooming in on the only sign of human habitation visible from horizon to horizon. A few huts, a couple of slashes of runway. Hmm, they're new. Not in his map of the test range, ingame. Better fix that . . .

Colt blinks. There's a scale problem. The patterns don't match. Ah.

As they continue to descend, the huts become buildings, big ones. Huge. Aircraft hangars. And the runways . . .

The plane lands on the longest runway he has ever seen, and as Colt tenses up, all the people around him begin relaxing.

What is *wrong* with these people?

Colt stands, gets into the aisle, but there are people in front of him. His heart pounds.

They had been safe in the sky. There was nothing to hit; the plane was in its element, generating lift. No obstacles in any direction, and miles of clear air below it.

But now, now the plane is grounded, out of its element, trundling through a world of randomly moving objects, some of them full of kerosene, some driven by tired workers . . . now the danger is *beginning*. Don't they get that?

The steps drive up to the plane, touch the fuselage. The door pops open, slides sideways. Colt breathes hard as the people surge.

Get off. Don't these people know that the greatest loss of life in aviation history was on the ground, Tenerife, when two 747s collided, one trying to take off while the other was still on the runway . . . *Hurry up.*

Finally, they get out of the plane. Walk across to a low, feature-less, windowless building. An automatic door opens.

The dark visor of his helmet goes transparent as he steps out of the desert sun, into a room-sized airlock. Colt wonders why – there doesn't seem to be much of a pressure differential.

Through the airlock. More security. Donnie handles it.

A plump, smiling guy joins them. Black skin, white shirt. Donnie talks to him briefly. They get either side of Colt and walk him down a sloping corridor, another, another, deeper and deeper, to a door. There's a buzzer, but the plump guy knocks on the door instead. Colt thinks about that. How old-fashioned it is. A knock on a door. Knuckles on metal.

They must be far underground now. Colt glances back at the corridor, measures the slope, works it out.

Wow, yeah. Deep.

The door opens.

The plump guy nods towards the open doorway. Colt glances across at Donnie.

Donnie nods, too.

Colt walks through alone.

The door closes.

79

At the airport, her brand-new, top-grade, biometric security pass gets her into the Janet terminal. But it doesn't get her on a plane.

'But . . . this gets me into everywhere,' says Naomi to the tall skinny white guy at the desk. 'I got this directly from . . .'

Wooah. Her throat closes, and she can't get his name out. Relax. Relax. Breathe.

'Ma'am?'

'. . . from Ryan Livingstone. Isn't he in charge of the base?'

'Maybe.'

'I'm allowed to see everything. Everything that exists. He said that specifically.'

'Ah.' The skinny guy smiles.

Overactive thyroid, she thinks. She reaches unconsciously for her throat.

He stops smiling. 'But the people coming through here,' he says, 'are going to a place that doesn't exist. To work on things that don't exist.'

With an elegant, practised gesture, he runs her security pass through a scanner. Glances down at something. Sighs. He holds up the pass to his eye, to study the hologram, and flicks it with a fingertip.

She notices a white cream around his bitten cuticles. Moisturizer? Or something bitter, to stop him biting them?

Don't get distracted, focus, focus. You have to get past this guy. Or around him.

'It's a very good pass,' he says, as though praising a child's drawing of a dog. Even though it looks more like a sheep.

'Can I have my pass back?' she says.

'Sure,' he says. But he doesn't hand it back.

She reaches out her hand, but he is already walking away from the desk. Her hand curls up like a dry leaf; drops to her side.

'Back in a second,' he says, and walks through an open door. Closes it.

She is going to wait, of course she is going to wait, she was told to wait. Relax. She takes a deep breath.

But her chest gets tighter as she stands there, tighter and tighter, and her throat is closing again, and she strains to breathe out, and she has to move, to walk, briskly, to loosen her chest, and it loosens as she walks.

And she is walking away from the desk, she notices. Without her pass.

But her breathing is good now.

She feels she's being watched, that cameras are following her, that people are following her.

She speeds up a little.

And now she sees something out of the corner of her eye, something black, fast, coming at her from behind, and she swings around with a gasp.

Nothing. Must have been her hair, swinging.

She turns back, towards the exit, the parking lot, her car. Walks faster and faster.

Runs.

80

Colt looks around the large, bare room.

The indirect lighting is full spectrum, set to mimic sunlight. It's so bright it triggers Colt's visor, which darkens, making the corners of the overlit room seem paradoxically gloomy.

In the centre of the room, a white swivel chair.

A silvery, matt metal table.

Beyond the table, a man in a black metal chair.

Colt studies his father's face.

'Sit,' says his father.

Colt moves towards the white swivel chair, holds on to the back of it; holds the chair between him and his father; looks around the room.

'It's been a long time,' says his father.

'Time flies like an arrow,' says Colt. He takes in a deep breath, and holds it, waiting for the response. Now that he's thinking so fast, these pauses feel endless, unbearable.

'Pardon?' says his father.

Colt waits a little longer, until the air pressure in his head builds up, too high, and so he releases a blast of air through his nose.

Starts breathing again.

So Dad doesn't remember. OK. OK. OK.

His father slowly pushes a white china plate across the silvery table towards him.

Cupcakes.

No icing.

Good.

The plate grinds across the metal, like there's a little grit beneath it.

Ah, that's what the airlock's for, thinks Colt; but even with the airlock, the desert dust gets in. That's bad. Alkali dust, terrible for electronics.

People must bring it in on their clothes, and shoes.

He looks down at his feet.

Yes. Dust.

He starts to design a better system, to stop that.

'Have a cake,' says his father.

Colt looks up, studies the plate. 'What's in them?'

'Fruit.'

'No sugar?'

'No sugar. Honey.'

'OK.' Colt turns the white swivel chair a little, sits, and swivels back. Glances, for a second, at his father.

His father points down, at the plate.

Colt picks up a cupcake, and peels off the little paper case from around its base. Drops the paper back on the plate.

He takes a bite of the cupcake. Chews.

Gritty.

Stops.

'What kind of fruit?'

'Pomegranates,' says his father. 'Good for your digestion.'

'Lot of seeds,' says Colt.

'Roughage,' says his father.

Colt glances briefly at his father, looks away. Ryan studies Colt's face, its expression; then looks at the plate, turns it around. 'Let me see . . .' He picks up a cupcake. Takes a small bite. 'Mmmm . . . I'm going to look after you now.'

'I want Mom,' says Colt.

'But does she want you?' says his father.

Colt's lips shape up to say, what?

Wait, no, Dad says 'pardon' when he means 'what.'

'Pardon?' says Colt.

Ryan raises an eyebrow. 'I'm sorry, Colt. But it's too much for her. A single mother. A full-time job. She just got promoted. More work, more responsibility. And you're a teenager now, Colt. A young man. Not a kid any more. I know she won't tell you this herself, but she just can't handle it.'

'She doesn't . . . want me?'

'It's not that she doesn't want you, but . . . has she seemed tired lately?'

Colt nods.

'Been crying?'

Colt nods. 'Why didn't she tell me?'

'She doesn't want to upset you. But since you've . . . changed . . .'

'What did she tell you?'

'Oh, nothing bad. But you'll be better off with me, here, for a while.'

'How long?'

'Well, that really depends. Don't worry about it now. But let's work together to understand you, understand what's happening to you, to study you. Yeah? And you could help me with my work.'

Colt realizes that he doesn't really know what his dad's work is. His dad has never talked about it before.

It shocks Colt into looking up, staring directly at his father's face, holding his gaze there, a thing he almost never does.

Even through the darkened visor, his father's face hurts to look at, like the sun; Colt can feel his eyes burning.

There are marks; deep lines he's never seen before.

His dad is getting old.

'Dad . . .' He's not sure what to say. 'What do you *do*?'

The lines of Ryan's face shift, new lines appear, as he smiles for the first time.

'Surveillance?' says Colt.

'Mmmmm. We're working on some more ambitious things.'

Colt realizes he's hungry. He should be having his smoothie now. He takes another cupcake, peels off the paper case from around its base.

'But you've got drones, right?' he says. He imagines flying drones. Perfecting the human/machine interface. Soaring over Africa. Mmmm.

The cupcake is pretty good. But his smoothie at home has coconut. Coconut is great for high-level thinking. The medium-chain fatty acids are absorbed pretty much unaltered. Almost no digestion required. The closest food to mother's milk.

'Yes,' says Ryan. 'Working with drones would be part of it.'

'I don't like my routines changed. I like my routines, Dad.'

'Like I say, you could have new routines here. You could help design them. Routines you enjoyed, every day. Let me show you.' Ryan waves at the wall to his right, and it lights up. They both turn in their chairs to look at it. 'Nemesis, uh, seven,' says Ryan. The screen fills with hillside.

'Simulator?' says Colt, turning back to his dad.

'Mmmmm,' said his father. 'Af–Pak border. Swat valley.'

'So you do frontline stuff. Like, real war training.'

Ryan hesitates. 'We do a lot of this, at the base, sure . . . I'm actually in charge of the domestic programme. But I can't show you any domestic feeds. Constitution, blah blah.'

Colt nods. 'Do you have any cupcakes with coconut?'

'Only pomegranate today.' Ryan grins. 'Must have been on sale.'

Wow. His dad is NDSA. His *dad* is the enemy. Colt stares at his father's face. His father. The enemy. Trying to protect him. Loving him. The cognitive dissonance hurts. He shakes his head, to stop thinking about it.

Colt clears his throat. 'Could I fly a drone?'

Ryan waves a hand dismissively. 'Oh, they're a piece of piss to fly. Joystick job. Mostly they fly themselves. Basically robots. Lock on; follow; film. Flying them is trivial. Getting the coding right is the problem. The pattern recognition. The targeting.'

Either side of the table, Colt and Ryan turn back to the screen. A dry valley.

The drone is climbing above the treeline now.

Ryan glances across at Colt.

'This image is from one of the newer, smaller observation drones,' Ryan says. 'We've found it's better to specialize. The old days, we filmed from fifteen thousand feet, and fired from fifteen thousand feet, same drone.'

'I thought the optics were pretty good on the old drones,' says Colt. 'Smaller drones have to carry smaller cameras. You won't get a huge improvement in picture quality . . .'

'Yeah, but it's not about the image quality, it's about the angle. From fifteen thousand feet, you're looking straight down on top of people's heads.' He frowns. 'Worse. Straight down on vehicles. No matter how good your zoom, if you can't see through the windscreen, you can't do facial recognition of the driver. But specialist observation drones like this one – small, fast – can get in close and low, identify the target, and call in the strike. A bigger killer drone, much higher altitude, fires the actual missile.'

'Mmmmm.' Colt reaches out for another cupcake without looking away from the screen.

'So yeah, flying them is easy.' Ryan sits back in his chair. 'Firing them is easy. Killing people is easy. But selecting the right target, from limited information; hitting the right target; that's hard.'

Colt is studying the screen like he's hypnotized. 'So if your targeting data is flawed . . . where's the flaw? Dirty data, or bad analysis?'

Ryan sighs. 'Most of the mistakes are human error. Killing the wrong people, because we're too eager; not killing the right people, because we're too cautious . . .'

'Heuristic biases,' says Colt.

'Yeah. And we can't overcome them, they're hardwired in. We're optimistic; we see what we expect to see. We overcompensate for past mistakes. We can't judge risk, can't judge probability. It's a mess. And it's not like the old days; if you take out a much-loved local schoolteacher now, instead of the local al-Qaeda chief, there's a diplomatic shitstorm. So we've tried to let the drones make their own decisions, in Pakistan. They make far fewer mistakes when we leave them alone. Let them learn from experience.'

'Uh huh.' Colt studies the screen.

A mountainside, very high up now. No soil, no vegetation. A road comes into view. Rough, potholed, no asphalt. The drone zooms in a little. Changes direction, follows the road.

Ryan is still brooding. 'And Pakistan isn't even the real problem. Get it wrong domestically . . . Jesus. Nightmare. Remember that kid in Albuquerque?' Colt nods without looking away from the screen, and Ryan puffs out some air at the memory. 'Those fucking interviews with his mom. Riots. Inquiries. A lot of careers over . . .'

Colt points at the screen. The drone is still following the road. 'What's it looking for?'

'Oh, you'll see. Busy day,' says Ryan. 'We've just modified the code for the Af–Pak self-targeting program, and it's calling in a lot more strikes.'

'What did you change?'

'The conditions for a strike were too tight. A lot of bad guys were getting away.' Ryan shifts forward in his chair, staring at the ribbon of road unreeling on the screen. 'Incredibly frustrating, when you know you've got the guy you want, and the system won't agree to a strike, because there might be civilians two houses away. We got them to alter the rules of engagement. Adjust the parameters a little. But Jesus, the paperwork. The committees.'

Colt grabs the edge of the table; pulls himself and the swivel chair sideways, closer to the screen. The wheels squeak. Dust. 'I don't need a screen, Dad. You could just run the raw image to my helmet. I could pull more data out of it.'

'Nope. Screens only. Got to stay airgapped. But if you come on board, sure, you'll have direct access to the raw feeds.'

A white Nissan pickup truck shudders into shot, weaving around potholes on the dirt road. Big drop to one side. The camera locks on, zooms in further, as the drone moves in fast, until it's almost directly above the truck, and a little behind.

The drone matches speed, and follows, in the truck's blind spot.

His father swipes at the air and the pickup vanishes. Columns of data fill the screen.

GPS positions.

Then a map of the Swat valley, with the GPS positions glowing red.

Then phone logs. Time of call, duration, position.

Who to, who from, what kind of device.

'Can I?' Colt asks.

'Sure. Gimme a second to authorize you.'

Colt studies his dad, as Ryan grants the permissions. It's slow; a lot of identity confirmations. Double retinal scan. Fingerprints seem to be taking a while to register. Some kind of DNA lick, on the fingerprint sensor? Nice. Serious access.

Ryan's done. He nods at Colt.

Colt swipes. Swipes. It's a shambles. A hot mess of data, without proper linkages.

'This could be part of your new routine,' says his father. 'Every morning, you look at these datasets, and you find the connections. Build us new algorithms, to connect the dots better.'

'These are like the arrays in . . . you played World of Warcraft, right?'

'Yeah,' says Ryan. 'Long time ago now.'

'These are like the arrays used to build character attributes in World of Warcraft,' says Colt.

'I guess they are,' says Ryan.

Colt is reading off the data as fast as he can refresh the screen. 'You've got a clan system,' says Colt. 'But the datasets overlap . . . This could be better arranged.'

'Yes, it could. What do you suggest?'

'You could do this,' says Colt. He swipes open a mindmapping tool on his father's wallscreen, and sketches out a reorganized set of relationships.

Ryan studies it. 'That's good. Do it.'

Colt reworks the relationship between the datasets. It's not a complicated job. In fact, it makes the relationships far sharper, clearer. It's just not obvious, at first sight, that you can do that . . .

Ryan keeps talking, as Colt codes. 'We're looking for a guy, short guy, Juma Gul Ahmadzi, about five feet, usually drives a white pickup, but they all do.'

'Reflects the heat,' says Colt, absently.

Ryan nods. 'In fact, that one we're following, it's his brother's pickup, so it could be him, could be anyone.' Ryan pulls up another screen, a map, and Colt glances across at it. 'This is his home village,' says Ryan, 'but he isn't there any more. This is where he was last seen.' Points. 'This is his where his oldest sister lives.' Swipes, points. 'She married into this clan.'

'Has he many sisters?'

'He has five sisters. And two brothers.'

'But the data says he has three . . .'

'Had three. We killed one.'

'See, this over here is out of date, then.' Colt points. 'It should update automatically.' Colt builds a tool to cross-link and update the two datasets as Ryan watches him across the table.

81

Driving away from the airport, taking the turn for Highway 375, heading out into the desert, Naomi feels foolish, naked, self-conscious. A base that runs surveillance drones across Asia, the Middle East, Africa; she is hardly likely to sneak up on it unobserved.

But what else can she do? If she gets close enough, if she just tries to walk in; well, they will apprehend her, but maybe they will take her inside the base. She has to get inside the base. 'Apprehend.' From the Latin root *apprehendere*. To take. To seize.

Apprehension.

She remembers a jingle from an old book she read once.

Tenser, said the tensor. Tenser, said the tensor. Tension, apprehension, and dissension have begun.

It begins to run on a loop in her head.

The solar road begins its great curve out into the desert, around the restricted area.

This road leads nowhere. There is no one on it. It isn't the shortest distance between any two points.

If you wanted to go from Vegas to Reno, you'd drive straight up, along the western side of the restricted zone; not east, out into the desert and around the other three sides.

The only reason this road is so good is that it was upgraded at the end of the 1970s, as part of the MX missile programme. Mobile intercontinental ballistic missiles with multiple nuclear warheads were supposed to move restlessly from launchpad to launchpad, on this road, through this desert; with dummy ICBMs moving likewise on other trucks, all over the west, the Midwest, untrackable by the Soviets.

Yes. For a moment, she feels like a missile, launching herself at the hidden base.

An impossibly small, doomed missile.

A firework.

A firecracker.

A match.

No. She feels like Wile E. Coyote, on Acme roller skates. With an Acme rocket strapped to his back. Helplessly accelerating down a desert highway, in a straight line. No way to stop, no turning back.

As the road uncoils hypnotically from the horizon, drifts slowly towards her, then rushes beneath her wheels, she remembers the first time Colt saw *Road Runner*.

Colt was in the other room. He was six. He had been anxious for days, after one of Ryan's visits, after hearing an argument.

She needed to work, but he needed her. Kept coming in.

Finally, very close to screaming at him, her jaw trembling, she had found some *Road Runner* cartoons and sat him in front of them. He liked desert landscapes. Maybe they would hold his attention. She turned the volume down to almost nothing – cartoon soundtracks were way too busy for him – and started the cartoons.

He stared at the mesas, the cacti. Followed with his finger the long, thin road. It somehow vanished at the horizon, but in a land-scape drawn without a vanishing point. A puzzle that could not be solved. He moaned. She placed her hand on top of his head, firmly – making sure he could see the hand coming so he didn't startle – and she ran her palm and fingers down over his face to calm him. He grabbed her wrist, and brought her hand up to his face to do it again. Again. Again.

He let go, and stared at the cartoon desert. A tiny dot in the distance got bigger and bigger, and suddenly Road Runner filled the screen, stared out at them, a cloud of dust rising behind him. Her. It.

Very, very quietly, Road Runner said something that sounded like, 'Beep beep.'

Colt murmured very quietly back, 'Hmeep, hmeep.'

Naomi walked silently away.

She sat at the kitchen table, and tapped her screen awake again. Stretched it full size. All the data from her big experiment was in but she couldn't make sense of the columns of data.

Too weary, too sad.

Mesas of data. Deserts of data.

'Beep beep,' she said softly.

No, Colt was right. She'd never really listened properly before.

'Meep, meep,' she said. Tried it again, more through her nose this time. 'Hmeep, hmeep . . .'

A strange noise came from the other room. A noise from deep in Colt's throat, a noise she had never heard before.

She stood so abruptly that she knocked her chair over back-wards, and ran.

He was kneeling on the floor, very close to the picture. The noises in his throat got louder.

Wile E. Coyote is on roller skates with a rocket strapped to his back, chasing Road Runner along a railroad track. Into a tunnel. Around bends that get steeper and steeper. And now there's a right-angled bend coming up. A right-angled bend in a railway track!

Road Runner and then Wile E. Coyote whizz around the bend.

He laughs, as the law of conservation of momentum is completely obliterated.

He laughs . . . She falls onto the floor beside him and starts laughing too.

Back in the now, without even meaning to, she puts her foot harder on the accelerator. The car goes faster, and, for a moment, she does not; the seat pushes gently against her back. Transmits its energy to her, brings her up to speed, so that as she eases off the accelerator, she and the car are one again, flesh and metal moving in a straight line at the same speed. This new speed. It feels nice.

She does it again.

She is going very fast.

She has never driven this fast before.

She is less scared the faster she goes.

Mmmm, that's unexpected. She likes it.

She does it again.

82

Colt reaches for a cupcake, but the cupcakes are all gone. Oh well. He's full anyway.

He's never felt this relaxed with his father. Maybe this is what growing up is like. Less fear. Maybe it's not so bad.

'You know I went to the Afghan–Pakistan border, for real?' says Ryan.

'No,' says Colt politely.

'Your mother didn't tell you anything?'

'No.'

'Huh. OK . . . Well, it's only a border in our heads. It's not a border in their heads. They just walk across it like it's not even there. But we had to stop, like we'd hit a glass wall.' Ryan slaps the air between them.

Colt jumps, as the palm of his father's hand stops dead in mid-air with a loud smack.

Colt's hand goes involuntarily to his left cheek.

Yes. His father played that trick once, on a visit. He pretended to slap Colt's face; as his right hand swished past Colt's cheek, Ryan slapped his own thigh, hard, with his other, hidden hand.

The illusion that Colt had been struck had been so real. As real as the knowledge that he had not. Colt had cried until Ryan explained the trick.

'If we killed people on this side of the glass, we were heroes,' says Ryan, indicating with his hand. 'If we killed people on that side of the glass, we had invaded a sovereign nation, caused an international incident, committed a crime . . . But the drones could follow them.'

Colt feels it, something is missing. 'Did you stop at the glass wall?' he asks.

Ryan moves some pieces of paper on his desk. Makes them neater. 'No.'

There's a pause.

Weird; I can tell that Dad is feeling a big emotion. I just *can*. Like Mama can with me. The new neurons. New connections . . .

Colt realizes with a jolt that he doesn't have a problem with metaphors any more.

Glass wall.

He can see it, and he can't see it. Glass wall . . . The image hangs there, suspended, neither true not false, a different thing. He doesn't have to resolve it into a zero or a one. It's just one node in a series of connections. He savours it. Glass wall . . .

No, move forward. Keep going. 'So what happened?'

'Stuff happened.' His father shifts in his chair. Like he's uncomfortable, thinks Colt. He's physically uncomfortable because he's mentally uncomfortable. Like the way Mama can tell when I lie. Thoughts move your body . . . what did he just think?

'They sent me back home,' says Ryan. 'With my background . . . well, I ended up here.'

'Biology?' Colt tilts his head to one side. 'I guess it kind of applies to this. Surveillance. Artificial intelligence. Pattern-recognition systems . . .'

'Yes. The language we use is . . . revealing, isn't it? The language of cancer. Terrorist cells . . .' Ryan sighs. 'So yeah, we took out the biggest tumours, but by then it had already metastasized. And we fought them, but we fought them with our brain. But that's not the best way to prevent cancer. America has a brain that is already too clever for its own damn good. We think way too much. What we need is . . .' Ryan takes a deep breath. 'You're supposed to sign a lot of bullshit before I show you this, but we don't really have time for that now. Just don't fucking tell anybody.'

He unfolds an old, battered personal screen. Swipes open a document, hands it to Colt.

It's an organization chart.

It's static, it doesn't move with Colt's eye movement. It's locked to Ryan, not open access. Colt moves to physically swipe through the document, and the screen speaks. 'I'm sorry, but you are not authorized to read this document at this time.' The document goes out of focus.

'Go ahead,' Ryan says, and grants the permissions; retina, fingerprint.

Colt reads on. 'Oh wow,' he says. 'Oh wow.'

83

She calls up maps, and glances at them, but there isn't really any point. There is only one road, this road. She must drive straight down it for another hundred miles.

And the territory she must then enter is not really on the map.

A straight road, with no other traffic, and perfect visibility to the horizon. She sets cruise control, and relaxes. Shrugs, sets it to full self-drive, even though she normally hates the loss of control. Looks out the side windows. The desert, the desert, the desert.

There is a memory of . . . what? A map she once saw. A map of . . .

Yes.

She calls up the map on the dashboard display. There they are. All the ghost towns. White Cloud City. Quartz Mountain. Unionville. Ruth . . .

The humble towns. Rawhide. Ragtown. Mule Lick.

And the ambitious. Nevada City. Metropolis. Berlin.

All those dead towns.

Oh, such hopeful names. Treasure City. Bullionville. Goldfield. Gold Butte. Gold Acres. Gold Point. Gold Center . . .

All those dead towns, where the gold ran out. Then the silver.

The copper.

The zinc.

The lead.

Where the water ran out.

Now she finds a map that shows all the nuclear explosions in the test range, with their dates. She glances north, through the windscreen. Fifty miles away, some of them. Less . . .

The territory around her is too indifferent, too dead, too much. She doesn't want to think of her son out there among the ghost towns and radioactive craters, so she goes back to the map.

Time passes.

Something huge roars toward her, on the other side of the road, and she looks up, startled, in time to see the tight-packed platoon of self-drive trucks flicker by.

Military? Oh, good, no. Just an automated construction gang. Probably heading back to Vegas to reload, after hot-printing a fresh solar surface on some backroads . . .

She pays more attention to the road for a while, glancing at it every few seconds, but there's no other traffic. There is the smell of desert dust in the car now; hot, dry, alkali. Like the air inside an old computer.

The shadow of a bird flickers over the car's windscreen, over her, almost too fast to register, and she scans the sky, for a drone, plane, helicopter. For Ryan's eyes.

Eventually she gets to the turn.

84

'Many mathematicians to this day don't realize that information is physical and that there is no such thing as an abstract computer. Only a physical object can compute things.'
— David Deutsch

Colt looks up. 'You've created an immune system for the country.'

'Yes. That's what we've built here.'

Colt looks back at the chart, studies it. 'Why?'

Ryan leans back in his chair. 'Governments make shitty decisions, for dumb, short-term, political reasons.'

'What's that got to do with—'

Ryan doesn't even let him finish. 'Because to win an election, they'll invade some joke country that offers no threat. And then not deal with some seriously dangerous threat because it will alienate some big domestic constituency. That is a fucking insane way to deal with threats. It's like you got cancer, and said, Oh I can't do anything about the cancer, because it'll lose me votes in Ohio. I'll deal with this blocked pore instead. An autonomous immune system will make better decisions. Takes the whole thing out of the political arena.'

Colt is scanning the data sheets. 'It forms a neural network . . . but how can they all talk to each other? That's a crazy amount of power, to transmit . . .'

'They piggyback on local Wi-Fi, local cell towers, the general info-grid. They have priority access to everything.'

But Colt's already moved past that. 'Once you've turned it on, how do you turn it off?'

Ryan grins. 'You can't. That's the whole point. What's the point of an immune system with an off switch? If you can switch it off, so can the enemy.'

Colt's reached the end of the document. He looks up. 'So it's decentralized, autonomous . . .'

'Yeah. Once it's on, it's on. It's a small internet of things, so there's no control centre to destroy, it just routes around damage. Mostly it's dormant, but threats trigger it automatically.'

'But how do you, how does it, know—'

'—Look, knowledge is never the problem. Generating a quick, automatic response is the problem. I mean . . . 9/11. The system knew enough. But the system didn't have the power to act. It had to send signals to human beings.' Ryan is leaning forward in his chair, he's getting angry. 'And no individual human being can ever put all the information together. Look at the Boston Marathon kids. The older brother had already been interviewed by the FBI. We knew he was a risk, and it wasn't enough. Look at the *Charlie Hebdo* mess. The French had those guys flagged on all their data-bases. Hell, we'd told the DGSI, this asshole has trained in Yemen.'

'Uh . . .' Colt's trying to remember something. 'That Chicago wedding . . .'

'Perfect fucking example! All three attackers had been deported from Canada for possession of explosives, total debacle . . . The system, the individuals in the system, lost track. They forgot. The knowledge didn't trigger an action. Humans, management, guys like me, we are the bottleneck.'

Colt finds himself nodding agreement with his father; an odd sensation. 'Yeah, we are the bandwidth problem.'

'Exactly! We can hold five, maybe six items in working memory, and we're expected to run America. It's an illusion. Delusion. But the system as a whole knows enough to make a judgement.'

'But what if it's wrong,' says Colt. 'What if it's triggered too easily, or by a false signal?'

Ryan shrugs. 'Sometimes an immune system will kill a healthy cell. But that's the price you pay for staying healthy. If it happens, we fine-tune the immune system. That's where you come in. You see patterns—'

'I'm down as special needs. I'm still supposed to be getting homeschooled. They could send an inspector—'

'Jesus Christ, Colt, we kill the leaders of other countries. We will not have a problem persuading the school inspector to leave you alone. I'll deal with the school inspector.'

'OK, Dad.'

85

Naomi takes the unsigned turn, and drives off the matt black of the solar road, off the grid, off the map.

Carefully, slowly now, she bumps along the packed dirt road for half a mile; a mile; until she sees the fence. The fence is high; chain-link, with a token coil of razor wire on top.

She slows to a crawl.

The road ahead passes through a gate in the fence.

The gate is closed.

Three cameras are mounted on a tower above the gate.

Their bodies are silver, to dissipate the heat. Black cowls to shade their lenses from the sun, so light won't bounce around inside them.

So the dazzle won't blind them.

The camera to the left looks left, along the miles of fence.

The camera to the right looks right.

The camera in the centre stares straight down the road, straight through the windscreen, at her.

The silver central camera's big black snout moves back, then strains forward.

Focusing, zooming.

As she approaches, the cameras pointing left and right turn to look at her.

The three black snouts strain forward.

She stops the car. Opens her door.

Steps out slowly, carefully, into the dry heat.

So quiet, after the long confused roar of the air past the windows, the gasp of the air conditioning.

The old quiet electric motor, normally so unflustered, has grown hot, driving that speed, for that long, through that heat. It ticks and clicks as it cools.

She walks slowly, carefully, towards the gate in the fence.

Through the wire mesh, she can see no buildings. The packed dirt track she arrived on continues through the gate, running straight till it disappears over a ridge, then reappears, off to one side, a couple of miles away; then vanishes behind a distant hill. No sign of vehicles on it.

Well, there are countries smaller than this restricted area. Hard to patrol that.

She can't see a bell anywhere.

But this is absurd. Surely she's already set off an automatic alarm. They are *looking* at her. They already know she is here. Should she say something? Can they hear?

Ah, there *is* a physical button. On a short metal post, to the right of the gate. Where a driver could reach out, and press. If she had seen it, she could have driven right up to it.

But she had been staring up, at the cameras staring down.

She walks to the metal post. Looks down at the round, golden bell button, set into the angled silver top of the post.

Nothing written on it.

What did you expect?

Ring For Service.

Should You Have a Complaint . . .

No, it should say 'Press Me', like something in *Alice in Wonderland.*

She giggles with nerves.

Will it make me bigger, or smaller?

Will I disappear?

He could kill me out here and nobody would ever know.

Silly thoughts. Stop.

The post begins to hum.

She looks closer. There's a speaker set into the shadowed side of the post, facing her.

She waits for a voice. But no voice comes.

Dust-coloured crickets, somewhere nearby, rub their back legs together.

To attract other crickets, she thinks, so they can fuck and make more crickets, who will chirp, and fuck, and breed, and die, and become dust out here, pointlessly, for ever.

Her mind can't get traction on this moment.

I'm having some kind of breakdown, she thinks.

She wonders what Yaakov would do.

So she rings him.

She hears sounds, but they're the wrong sounds. His phone doesn't ring. A long tone.

Silence.

Is she out of coverage? Or is something actively blocking her call?

She feels a kind of vertigo, and sways. Is she perfectly safe, or in terrible danger?

Is this just an argument with Ryan about access to Colt?

Or is this a battle for the future of the world?

Both, she thinks.

Both.

Well, Christ's mother was also just another mother. Naomi laughs, but it's weak, and sad. And when the laughter ends, the silence is terrible. The silence of the desert. A million square miles of nothing.

She takes a deep breath. Pushes down the button.

I'm depressing the button, she thinks. And the button is depressing me.

One of her father's old jokes that wasn't even a joke. He made it every time they visited Naomi's aunt. Standing on the porch, ringing again and again, waiting for his sad, ill sister to get out of bed and answer the door.

I miss Yaakov.

There is no click, no crackle, no sound. No sense of whether or not the bell has actually done anything. No haptic feedback.

Maybe it opens a voice channel. She presses it again, holds it down, says, 'Please let me in.'

Lets go.

A voice replies – crackly, thin, through a weather-damaged speaker – and she jerks back, astonished. Even though this was what she had expected, wanted, caused.

'You made it.'

Ryan's voice, of course.

'I was worried, when you started speeding, past Rachel.'

Of course. She is getting the personal treatment. Ryan's voice is almost friendly as he continues.

'Cow country. One of those wanders out of the sage when you're doing a hundred, and, well, that's a lot of burgers at your funeral.'

'I want to see my son.'

'I figured.'

The gate begins to open. She takes a step back, towards the Pontiac.

'Leave the car.'

'I'd rather bring it.'

'No, you wouldn't.'

Naomi looks through the wire mesh of the opening gate. Through the widening gap. This is not a main entrance. The road at the far side is narrower. Heavy vehicles have cut up the packed dirt surface pretty bad, and rain has cut the gullies on either side even deeper. No point even trying. Fine for a military truck, but her car would get hung up on the middle ridge, and there isn't enough room to drive to one side of it.

'OK. Where do I go?'

'Follow the trail. I'll send guides.'

She walks through the gate. It closes behind her.

She walks down the high centre ridge of the rough dirt road, truck-tyre ruts to either side.

*

She has been walking for twenty minutes.

Two black dots appear in the sky, over the ridge looming ahead. At first, sun-dazzled, she thinks they are birds. Eagles? Ravens? They slow; stop; hover for a moment, frozen against the sky.

Then they come towards her, fast and low.

Purposeful, focused.

Unafraid.

No bird would be so fearless. Even eagles are gun-shy. Human-shy . . .

These move like something with no predator.

They slow again as they grow close, then stop and hover, one to either side of the road.

To either side of her.

Black quadcopters, like the ones Colt played with as a child, but bigger. Faster. More powerful.

They hum as the four rotors spin, adjust, spin. They hover at either shoulder, keeping level with her as she walks on.

After a while, one drifts a little higher, and ahead. She can see its camera-eyes looking back at her.

One drifts a little lower, and behind.

She walks on.

86

'We sleep safely in our beds because rough men stand ready in the night to visit violence on those who would harm us.'
— Edmund Burke

'. . . ravens twain sit on his shoulders, and say into his ear all tidings that they see and hear; they are called Huginn and Muninn (mind and memory); them sends he at dawn to fly over the whole world, and they come back at break-fast-tide, thereby becomes he wise in many tidings, and for this men call him Raven's-god.' — William Morris and Eiríkur Magnússon, *The Story of the Volsungs*

Ryan leans back in his chair, and admires the view from the lead quadcopter. He zooms a little more, deeper into Naomi's cleavage.

He remembers her breasts, from when they first met. Small, brown, firm. He closes his eyes. The nipples growing tight and hard against the palm of his hand.

They had changed when Colt was born. Still good, but different. He liked their big, new, milky curves. But they were no longer his to command.

He opens his eyes, examines her breasts again, now, in the world. A tiny wave, a ripple, runs through their curved flesh, with the jolt of each footstep on the hard ground.

She is finally beginning to perspire. A V of sweat appearing on her sternum.

When they fucked, it took her so long to start sweating. He'd be pouring, but Naomi . . . maybe a film of moisture would appear on her upper lip just before she came.

Once he had taken her on ground like this, at Burning Man. They had walked away from the temporary city, away from the shouts and laughter. The boom and fizz of techno fading behind them as they walked for miles out onto the playa, into the silence. Away from the sunset, towards the moonrise. When he flipped her over onto all fours, the dust was bright white on the light brown cheeks of her ass, on her dark brown shoulder blades, in her ink-black hair.

She says it wasn't love. How the fuck can she say it wasn't love?

There's an alert tone, as a channel opens. Someone from the external security team. 'Sir. She's approaching the southern drop-back intercept position. You're definitely on top of this?'

'I am definitely on top of this,' Ryan drawls. 'You have no idea of how on top of this I am.'

'I'm not comfortable with this, sir.'

'Well, I would be disappointed if you were, Laurence. But this is a trial drone intercept. I have two visible surveillance drones on her, two autonomous, Hornet-class invisibles in backup, and a kill drone about a mile up, with backups on alert in the hangars. She's about as secure as it gets.'

'OK, sir. I guess I don't like watching someone just . . . walk in.'

'If your reassuring presence is required, Laurence, I will certainly call you.'

Down the line, Laurence hesitates, and decides not to take the hint. 'I know it's the future, sir, but the future isn't here yet. And these new automatic systems can screw up.'

'Which is why we run tests. I've been following her since Vegas. The base immune system kicked in automatically when she left the 375. Zero threat, Laurence. She's just helping me test the systems.'

'All right, sir. Out.'

Ryan moves to the other raven, behind her, and watches her ass move as she walks. So many conflicting emotions and memories surge, that they jolt a tight little laugh out of him. Everything rotating around that invisible point between her legs.

The former centre of his universe.

He could call a strike now, and blame it on a software glitch. He could spread her all over Nye County. He's not logging or recording anything; cameras, his commands. Everything's disabled. Nothing could be proved.

But he wants to see her again, first.

In the flesh.

It's not personal. It really isn't personal. He doesn't want to have to kill her. But he is running out of other choices.

87

She loses her sense of time as she walks. The landscape alongside the road seems to repeat, like the background in a *Road Runner* cartoon. Sand, rock, bush. Sand, rock, bush.

The heat makes it hard to think, which is good, because she's trying not to think about Colt.

How long has she been walking? An hour? Two?

The ravens veer to the right, off the rutted road and along a faint path through the scrub and brush. She follows them, for a few hundred yards, till they reach a low mound.

Set into the mound is a black door.

It opens.

The ravens lift, rise into the warm air, their home. Where she now must go, they cannot follow.

Naomi peers through the doorway. A dark passage. It must slope down, underground.

She doesn't want to go underground.

She looks around in a panic at the hills, the weight of them. At the tracks of old rockslides, visible down their sides. Mountains, fallen on hard times. Young enough, geologically, but already trashed by a million years of earthquakes. Unstable, ready to slide, to crush.

She's afraid of the dark.

But her son is down there.

Naomi says very quietly, no louder than the crickets, 'Our Father who art in heaven, hallowed be thy name. Thy kingdom come, thy will be done, on earth as it is in heaven.' She gets stuck on that line, not because she doesn't know the rest of the prayer, but because it seems to her astonishing and strange. 'On earth as it is in heaven. On earth as it is in heaven . . . On earth. As it is in heaven. On earth.'

The black door begins to close again.

Naomi, shocked, steps forward, 'No . . .'

The sensor triggers, and the door, halfway to closing, stops, reopens.

She takes a step. Another.

Another.

Enters the darkness.

88

She's coming. He doesn't have long. He starts to dictate a document. Hesitates.

Deletes.

Disabling the logs and monitoring software on the new devices was easy, they're experimental, and the monitoring software isn't integrated, isn't finished. But all his office devices are monitored by security bots in realtime. And he wants his thoughts to be private for a while.

Uncensored.

He writes 'The Case For Project Infinite Ammo' on a sheet of paper with a pen. Black ink. He stares at the words for a long time. Unbelievable, that he still has to make the case for it. After ten years' work. Ready to roll it out. And they put it under review. Talk of cancelling it. He lets himself say the word in his head. They can't read it there.

Traitors.

He knows he has begun to make decisions that he will not be able to justify to Washington. They're going to take his base, and his project, away from him. Probably in the next forty-eight hours.

He thinks he can save his country by then. Even if the idiots who run it don't want to be saved.

89

The corridor slants down.

Lights flicker on, as she walks.

After a few hundred yards, she reaches a fire door. It's startlingly stiff, heavy, like a bank-vault door. She pushes it open at the third attempt, and passes through.

Walks.

A second fire door.

The corridor has no other doors off it. This whole corridor is just an emergency exit, Naomi thinks.

The only things to break the featureless surfaces are small cameras in glass domes above each fire door. The cameras swivel inside their domes, like chameleons' eyes, to follow her, as she passes beneath.

It is a shock when the third fire door opens at her approach, and she is greeted by a tall man in uniform. His features are European, like a Greek statue of some young athlete, she thinks, and his skin is a dark black. It is a striking face. 'Naomi Chiang?'

She nods. 'Dr Livingstone's representative, I presume?'

He raises an eyebrow, then gets it, and laughs at the half-joke. 'Oh yeah, he used to be a doc. Afraid he's gone native since coming here. All soldier.'

'I gather,' says Naomi drily.

'Apologies for not greeting you at the gate, but it seems he wanted to try out the new drones as chaperones.'

'They were undemanding company.' Naomi isn't sure why she's slipping into this absurd, theatrical persona. But then, what behaviour would be natural here?

'Caused a certain amount of consternation among the local sheriff's deputies,' the tall man says. 'They patrol the perimeter . . . If I can just have a quick look in your bag . . .' He broods over her nail scissors for a while, but lets her keep them. 'This way, please.'

They start walking down the corridor. The slope down gets steeper.

'Security seems a little informal,' says Naomi, to keep her mind off how deep they are getting.

He smiles. 'Well, we're not really set up for visitors at this entrance. Seeing as how it's an exit. In fact, you're probably pretty much the first person to enter through it.'

'I guessed it was just for emergencies,' says Naomi, to make conversation; to avoid her thoughts.

'Don't think there's ever been any call to use it as an emergency exit, either. We don't really do emergencies, down here.'

'Really?' says Naomi, trying to control her breathing, feeling the weight of the desert over her head. 'I would have thought this would be nothing *but* emergencies. Testing weapons, experimental planes, drones . . .'

The tall man snorts. 'Main test area is thirty miles away. We're mostly doing office work, underground, in the desert, in a dry base, in a dry county, a hundred miles from the nearest bar. This is the quietest posting I've ever had.'

'You're very . . . chatty.'

'I'm a sociable guy.'

'I mean, for a secret base. You talk a lot.'

'Well, I have a . . . philosophical disagreement with what the government wants us to do here right now.'

'And what's that?'

'Now, that I *can't* tell you. I want to hang on to my pension. But, put it this way, I'm trying to get transferred out. And put it another way, I don't give a fuck any more.' He beams at her.

The corridor splits left and right. He leads her to the left, and after a couple of hundred yards they stop at a pair of enormous metal doors.

The doors open.

He steps inside the huge lift.

She hesitates.

He looks back at her, and makes a questioning expression that reminds her of Colt. But what doesn't?

Naomi laughs. It's a terrible laugh. 'I sort of worry about earthquakes. About an earthquake happening while I'm in the elevator.'

He smiles. 'It's never been a problem. We're in a geologically stable area. There are stairs—' he points to another, smaller door – 'but the elevator is a lot quicker.' He reaches out a hand, to encourage her, help her into the huge metal coffin, and she steps back reflexively.

'Sorry,' she says. 'Sorry.' But her son is down there, under all this rock and silence. She steps into the elevator.

They go down. Down. Down.

She keeps her eyes closed. Breathes.

They step out of the elevator, and walk along a corridor that seems to be in more regular use. It's dirtier, dustier, the paint is scuffed. The fire doors are all wedged open. Other corridors branch off it.

Naomi talks, to stop herself thinking. 'You must get outside sometimes.'

'Oh yeah. We've got basketball courts, everything. In the evenings, when it cools down, and in winter, it's very nice up top.'

Naomi nods encouragement.

Keep talking.

It keeps her mind off the weight above her.

And now they step out into a huge space, with a rough, dusty, soft-stone floor. Not a cave. Naomi looks around. Looks up. She can't see the roof. Can't get a sense of the shape of the space. Lights hang here and there, blindingly bright, from scaffolding that disappears up past them into the darkness. Generators snore in the distance. 'This is the base?'

He laughs. 'The real base is about a mile further on.' He has to raise his voice. 'This is just a construction site for now. We're expanding. Sorry about the noise.'

'That's some pretty loud hammering.'

'Yeah, tunnelling machines.'

'I thought secret underground bases were just a science-fiction thing,' says Naomi.

He shrugs. 'Ever been in a cave in a desert?' She nods. 'Nice, right?' he says. 'Temperature is cool, stable. Surface buildings out here get a fifty, sixty degree swing from day to night. Crazy. You're permanently running either heating or aircon. It's expensive, it's not good for the equipment, and it leaves everything vulnerable to a power outage.' They walk past a machine, its spiked steel maw parked up against the rough shale wall. He slaps its dusty flank as he walks past. 'This is, believe it or not, practical. And environmentally friendly. Much smaller carbon footprint, and we have a couple of rare species up there,' he points straight up, 'that don't even know there's a base here.'

'What are the species?'

'I can't answer that. National security.'

'Seriously?'

He laughs. 'Yeah. If I tell you exactly what kind of lizard or butterfly or whatever, that pretty much ties down the location of the base. These are really localized creatures, and there are nerds out there who know this stuff, oh that lizard lives in that valley . . .'

'But I drove to the base,' says Naomi. 'I already know where it is.'

He shrugs again. 'Regulations. I didn't say they made sense, I just said they were regulations.'

They leave the construction cavern and walk down another corridor.

Eventually they arrive at a door.

Behind another door, only five hundred yards away, Colt finishes reorganizing the database. He skips in and out of the datasets.

The problem is trivial. It's hidden in plain sight in the data. They just didn't know how to organize it right. It takes him ten minutes.

Colt looks up.

90

'A humanitarian is always a hypocrite, and Kipling's understanding of this is perhaps the central secret of his power to create telling phrases. It would be difficult to hit off the one-eyed pacifism of the English in fewer words than in the phrase, "making mock of uniforms that guard you while you sleep".' — George Orwell on Rudyard Kipling

'Wolfram joins a growing community of voices that maintain that patterns of information, rather than matter and energy, represent the more fundamental building blocks of reality.'
— Ray Kurzweil

Ryan doesn't stand when Naomi comes in. She is obscurely disappointed. He'd always had good manners, in his odd way.

'Can I sit down?'

'Of course.'

Naomi sits on the white swivel chair.

'Where is Colt?' she says.

Ryan pushes a freshly filled plate of cupcakes towards her. Gestures to take one. She doesn't even glance down at it.

'Oh come on,' he says. 'Good for you. Tasty, too. Honey and pomegranate.'

'Where's my son?'

'Please,' says Ryan, smiling. 'A little foreplay first. Some polite conversation. You're looking very well . . . Have you done something jolly with your hair?'

She tries to stop herself smiling. That line, from some ridiculous English period drama, had totally cracked them both up, back when they had watched TV together. Back when they laughed at the same things.

Ryan pulling her pants off, in the living room of their old place, before Colt was born. Spreading her legs, working his tongue very slowly up, between her labia, parting them, and then, just as he is about to reach her clitoris, lifting his head above her neatly trimmed triangle to say, smiling: *Have you done something jolly with your hair?*

She shakes the image out of her head.

'Where's my son?'

'Our son,' says Ryan, and now he's not smiling.

There is a sheet of paper on the table. A pen. Ryan's handwriting, a few words. Naomi glances down at it.

Tries to read it at an angle, upside down.

Can't.

'You're working on paper,' she says. 'I thought you were all about the technology.'

He shrugs. 'A sheet of paper can't be hacked.'

233

She reaches for it, stops.

'Go ahead.'

The Case For Project Infinite Ammo

'What is project Infinite Ammo?'

'I can't answer that. National security.'

He smiles, and he looks young again. Oh that smile.

'But right now,' he says, 'you are project Infinite Ammo. And Colt. What you've done to Colt.'

'What have I done to him? What do you think I've done?'

'Oh, come on. It's clear what you've done. You've restructured his brain, his entire nervous system. You've turned a caterpillar into a butterfly.'

'He wasn't a caterpillar.'

'Well, he certainly wasn't a goddamn butterfly.'

Naomi picks up the piece of paper. Rolls the pen back and forth on the metal tabletop with her fingertip. Picks up the pen.

'He's extraordinary,' says Ryan. 'He can see patterns that we can't see. That our entire multibillion-dollar bullshit intelligence system can't see. Connections. Colt is the first of a new type of soldier.'

'He's not a soldier,' says Naomi.

'He is now,' says Ryan. 'He can do important work here, help his country. No disrespect, but that sure beats sitting on his ass at home, playing computer games and scratching his nutsack.'

Naomi shakes her head, starts to scribble out the letters on the page, one at a time, in tight little scribbles.

'Come here, too,' says Ryan.

'To help you kill people more efficiently?'

'Look, we're going to do this anyway.'

'Not with my research—'

'*Because* it's your research, you should be involved, stay involved. Work with Colt. Work with us.'

'Work with *you*?'

Naomi blinks as the memories rush back.

They had collaborated on a paper together. It was how they met. Their first piece of serious, original research. A new approach to pain-suppression in human subjects.

Of course, in order to suppress pain, you need to create some pain to be suppressed. And it is hard to get volunteers to subject

234

themselves to serious, ongoing pain. True, there are patients with serious, ongoing pain, but they tend to be undergoing treatment for it already, which masks it; few of them want to experience the pain, raw, day after day, so someone can occasionally experiment, during office hours, on cutting it off. And they tend to have other problems too. Problems of age, chronic health issues. This was research aimed at car-crash victims, gunshot victims; at young, healthy people undergoing sudden trauma.

Naomi volunteered.

They began very formally, in a small lab on the edge of the campus.

The early results were immediately promising.

At the end of day three, they touched hands, accidentally, as they moved past each other, on their way out the door. Both apologized profusely.

On the fifth evening, after they had completed all that day's tests and tidied up, they found themselves standing face to face, by the door. Neither moved to open it.

Ryan stared at Naomi as though he had just noticed something astonishing about her. His hands clenched and unclenched, but he didn't move, as Naomi stared back, examining his face. Eventually, she nodded.

He turned Naomi around, pushed her up against the painted concrete wall of the lab, pulled her skirt up above her hips, dragged her underwear aside, and fucked her from behind.

Early the next week, they moved in together, and continued the project from home.

He would tie her arms to the bedposts before they began. The needles, the gag.

There was nothing sexual about the day's testing.

There was no need.

There was just a flame of pain into which her fluttering, panicked thoughts vanished.

Eventually, as the day went on, her awkward, crumpled self would burn away entirely, and there was just the flame.

It was quiet and beautiful inside her mind.

What she felt for Ryan wasn't love. It was fiercer than that.

He gave her the pain, and then he took it away.

And she was in control of this. She had chosen it.

Afterwards, she rated the pain and the relief on a standard scale, backed up by pre- and post- blood readings of stress chemicals and dopamine.

The paper gave all the relevant details.

Her wrists tied to the bedposts; the fact that Ryan fucked her after each long day's testing without untying her first; the fact that she was so ready by then that she came as he entered; those details weren't relevant.

The *Journal of Pain and Symptom Management* took the paper. It was widely cited. The military had liked its implications for dealing better with combat trauma. That was when they had first reached out to Ryan.

When the study ended . . . He would tie her up, hit her, fuck her while she resisted. She agreed to it in advance. Planned it with him. Told him what to do. And then relaxed into the pleasure, and the pain. If she couldn't uncross those wires, fix that short circuit, she could at least use it, control it.

There was a safe word.

She never used it. Not once. Even when he . . .

She shakes her head at a memory, no; and snaps back into the moment, into her body now, the slightly burnt smell of the recirculated air; looking into Ryan's eyes across a table.

He leans back in his chair. 'We had some good times.'

'It was just sex.'

'It was incredibly good sex. And that's not nothing.'

'The sex was great,' says Naomi, and almost smiles. 'But there was nothing else.'

'C'mon, that's way too harsh. There was the work, there was Colt . . . there was a lot there.'

'Not enough.'

'If you'd just given me *time*, instead of—'

'I gave you plenty of time. I could have given you for ever. Your heart wasn't open.'

'And you were the Dalai fucking Lama?'

She pauses. 'OK. Yes. Our hearts weren't open.'

'I know,' says Ryan. 'Yeah. I know.'

'I've changed,' says Naomi. 'Have you?'

'Yeah. I've changed.' Ryan pushes the chair back from his desk. The chair keeps on going.

It's a wheelchair.

And Ryan has no legs.

'Oh, Ryan . . .'

'Yeah.'

'Pakistan?'

'Yeah.'

Naomi's hand drifts towards her mouth. 'If I'd published all my papers . . .'

'That thought has occurred to me, yeah.'

'But . . .' She stares at where his legs stop. Above the knee. 'Why don't you . . . I mean, couldn't they . . .'

'Oh, sure, I have prosthetics,' he says, and she thinks for a strange second he's going to cry. 'State-of-the-art customized government-issue battle legs. They're in the repair shop, again. Shorted out, again.'

'Why didn't you tell me? All this?'

Ryan shrugs. 'If you don't help us kill them, then you're helping them kill us.' He wheels his stumps back under the table, and it's like it never happened; he's himself again. 'Would you prefer them to kill us, babe?'

Naomi winces at the babe. 'I'm a grown-up now.'

'You certainly are,' says Ryan. 'Looking better than ever.'

'That's not really any of your business any more.'

'Hey, I'm just trying to pay you a compliment.'

'You've just kidnapped me.'

'Ah, come on, babe . . .' Ryan sighs. 'OK, what do I call you?'

'Naomi. My name.'

'Naomi. *Hǎo jiǔ bú jiàn.*' He bows. 'And I didn't kidnap you. Or Colt. Everything's legal. In fact, technically, you're the only one here who has broken the law.'

Oh, now, that's infuriating. '*What* law?'

'You drove past the Restricted Area signs, so; trespassing, compromising national security, blah blah.'

'What are you going to do, kill me?'

There's a long pause before he smiles, and says, 'What do you take me for?'

Naomi says nothing.

Ryan tenses in his chair. 'Do you not believe I am a man of honour?'

Naomi says nothing.

'I really did love you, Naomi.'

Naomi says nothing.

Ryan closes his eyes for a while. Breathes out. Opens his eyes and looks at her.

Naomi says nothing.

Eventually Ryan says, 'You're a white, well, kinda white, middle-class American citizen. Of course I won't kill you. I'll just get our lawyers to tie you up in so much litigation that you will never work in a lab again, and you will never see Colt again. And now, I've got a meeting.'

'Where's *Colt*?'

'We will work this out, soon, don't you worry. Meanwhile, I'll get Lloyd to show you some of our facilities.'

'You don't do any biological work!'

'We've got a very broad remit. If it improves national security, we've got a budget. We could build you the perfect lab. Seriously. Think about it. We can talk again in an hour or so.'

He comes around the table in his chair, slaps her on the back as he ushers her out. The tall, polite guy and another officer are already waiting outside the door, to escort her.

The door closes with a *whoosh*, tight to the frame.

Great. She's gone. What the fuck is he going to say in an hour?

Colt has been messaging him for ten minutes. Ryan waits till Naomi is definitely off his level before answering.

'Dad, I've found something.'

91

'It's him.'

'Talk me through it.' Ryan sits behind the big silver table, head bowed, with his fingers on his temples, concentrating, as Colt explains.

When Colt's done, Ryan sits up straight.

'Very good. VERY good.'

Colt's eyes blur a little, and his cheeks start to tingle, to burn.

Across the table, Ryan has an idea. Hesitates.

Well, it won't make much difference at this stage. Embed him as deeply as possible. Blood the kid. Get him to commit.

'OK,' Ryan says. 'Now we kill him.'

'And why do we want to kill him?' asks Colt, still blushing, just to change the subject.

'Why? Because he wants to kill us.'

'Uh huh,' says Colt. 'And why does he want to kill us?'

'Because we're there,' says his father.

Colt isn't sure if his father is making a joke. 'And why are we there?' says Colt.

Ryan gives Colt a quizzical look. 'Because he wants to kill us.'

Colt is about to say something, but stops. OK, there's a loop coming up. If he asks the next question, and triggers the loop, he might be making a joke, which would be good. But if he's wrong he's going to annoy his dad, which isn't good.

Risk it, risk it, thinks Colt. A lot of comedy is repetition. It's probably a joke.

Colt's knowledge of this is almost purely theoretical; he did a lot of reading on the subject of comedy, the long summer he first realized that the people around him constantly made jokes. That jokes explained all those sentences he didn't understand.

Deep breath. 'Why does he want to kill us?' says Colt again.

Ryan grins. 'Because we're there.'

Colt says, 'Why are we there?'

Ryan says, 'Because he wants to kill us,' and they both laugh.

Colt can't quite believe he made his dad laugh, deliberately. He feels kind of giddy. He wants to do it again. No, quit while you're ahead.

'OK,' says Colt, 'I guess motivation isn't really relevant in a simulator. But you might want to add it later.'

'Mmmm . . . I'll authorize the shot,' says Ryan. 'Do you want to fire?'

'Oh, cool.'

'Technically, this is a no-no.' Ryan looks up. 'But I'm the boss. My project, my code. There are certain privileges. OK, locked on. Take over the controls . . . Fire.'

Colt fires.

The pickup explodes.

The observation drone hovers lower. Films the aftermath.

They study the burning wreckage. Something secondary explodes, maybe an RPG, and a door flies off, tumbles away downhill, and out of shot. It looks wrong, such violence, in silence. 'It needs sound,' says Colt.

Ryan shifts in his chair. Says nothing.

Colt frowns, leans forward.

'What?' says his father.

'It doesn't look real enough. You can't really see the body.' Colt leans back, puts his palms flat on the tops of his thighs, and pushes hard, to stop his thighs trembling. 'It's just this black thing in the cab.' He pushes harder. 'Could I work on the graphics if I came here?'

'Colt, you . . . What do you mean?'

'This is a simulator, right, for training,' says Colt. Yes, it's a very good simulator, he says to himself. 'So, it's basically a game. And realistic gameworlds, I mean, they're my specialty.' There are urgent thoughts, feelings, coming up from his subconscious, new connections trying to get made; but he repeats to himself, it's a simulator, just a very good simulator, until the thoughts retreat into the dark. 'I think I could make it more real.' There's something wrong with his father's face. 'Seriously, Dad. The game part of it could be better.'

Pause. 'Yes,' says Ryan. 'I guess you could call it a game.'

Colt's not feeling good. His stomach is churning. Maybe it's the pomegranate cupcakes. Too many cupcakes.

Something about a sheet of paper, among all the papers on his father's desk, catches his attention. Makes a connection.

'Who did this?' says Colt. He reaches forward, and picks it up.

Little hairs begin, one by one, then in waves, to stand erect on the back of Ryan's neck. Danger. He pauses to think through all the implications of a reply. 'I wrote it.'

'No, who *scribbled* on it?' says Colt.

Pause. 'I scribbled on it.'

'No.' Colt's voice is firm, and Ryan marvels at how adult he seems. Sometimes. 'You don't speak Latin,' says Colt.

'What's Latin got to do with it?'

Colt turns around the piece of paper. Naomi has scribbled out the letter 'h', the words 'case for project' the letter 'm' . . . All that's left is 'Te infinite amo.'

Te infinite amo.

'What?' says Ryan.

'I love you infinitely,' says Colt. 'In Latin.'

Ryan stares at Colt. Back at the paper. Jesus fucking Christ . . .

'Mama is *here*,' says Colt. 'Where is she?'

Ryan closes his eyes. Thinks for a second.

Yeah, making decisions is what you do.

He calls Lloyd. 'Bring back Naomi Chiang.'

'*Sir, with all due respect, I discussed this with . . .*'

'Do it.'

92

Lloyd arrives, suspiciously quickly, ahead of two corporals flanking Naomi. He can't have brought her far. Where were they? What has Naomi been saying?

Ryan sees Lloyd is trying to catch his eye.

'Thank you, Lloyd,' says Ryan. 'You can leave now.'

'Sir . . .' says Lloyd, glancing back at Naomi.

She has gone straight to Colt. Probably wants to hug him, thinks Ryan. But that tends not to work out too well. No; she's holding his hand. He's letting her do it. Interesting. Improving.

And Colt looks at his mother; his father, his mother; his father.

Back and forth, thinks Ryan. Like he's hypnotized.

Ryan gets an odd, faint memory, of the three of them standing like this, in a tense standoff, when Colt was a kid. Where exactly, and why? It won't come to him. Ryan suppresses the tiny shrug he's about to make. Years of conscious control over body language, it's become automatic.

'My wife,' says Ryan quietly to Lloyd. 'My child. I'll deal with this.'

Naomi hears him, turns, opens her mouth to snap, 'Ex-wife.' Closes it. No. This officer is trying to get her back out of the room. And she wants to stay in the room, with Colt. 'It's fine,' she says to Lloyd. 'Seriously, it's fine.'

The officer glances at her, at Colt. At Ryan.

Lloyd straightens up and goes for it. Ryan feels curiously proud of him. 'Sir, I'm going to have to contact the Department, and file a formal . . .'

'Get out,' says Ryan.

'Sir.'

Lloyd waves the two corporals out, and leaves.

The door closes with an airtight suck. Like a kiss, thinks Naomi. Like a kiss. She lets go of Colt's hand.

And as Ryan and Naomi stare at each other across the room and their faces change expression, pour out strange information that Colt can't quite decode yet, he looks at his father; his mother; his father; his mother. Look at what just happened to Mama's face . . .

It is as though he has never seen his parents' faces before.

Unconsciously, Colt reaches up, adjusts the visor of his helmet, as sharp new thoughts cut through him.

She changes, when she sees Dad. To protect herself. To feel safe. She changes her *face*. The way she stands. Do other women do that, too? Wow, women can't be themselves, when they are in the room with him. He is a distortion field. *Angry.* He makes them not be themselves. *And he doesn't know.* He thinks women are like that all the time. He doesn't know.

He wants to . . . oh wow.

Colt doesn't want to think the word, but it's the right word – the other words he tries in its place don't work – so he finishes the thought.

He wants to fuck them.

All of them.

Colt has never realized this before, and he pauses over this strange thought.

Has Dad ever seen a woman be herself?

'Well,' says Ryan. 'My family. All in one place. This is better than Thanksgiving.'

There's a kind of glee in Ryan's voice that makes Naomi uneasy. 'So, what happens now?' she says.

They both lean towards each other, intense, joined by a tremendous contradictory energy, pulled together and pushed apart, mouths moving before the other has ceased speaking.

Ryan laughs. 'Well, my career is going to end, pretty soon. But meanwhile . . . procedures must be adhered to.'

'There is such a thing as the chain of command,' says Naomi, and finds she is smiling. An old joke, from their early days as a couple.

'Yeah.' Ryan grins. 'And they're going to pull the chain. Hard.' Ryan rocks his wheelchair back onto its rear wheels. Balances it there.

Dada has no legs.

Dada has no legs.

He hasn't called his father dada, thought of his father as dada, since he was seven.

Colt looks away, looks around the room, looks down at the blank concrete floor, but he can still see the stumps, like a picture projected on a screen. He closes his eyes. Tries to remember something. It's far back in his rebuilt, rebuilding mind. His mother and his father. They are reminding him of something . . .

'OK, Naomi, we have a problem,' Ryan says. 'You know how to create a superweapon.' He brings the chair back down. 'And you don't seem to have any idea how dangerous that is. You would just give it away. To anyone. To everyone. To our enemies. We're still playing whack-a-mole with that fucking paper you threw out into the crowd in New York. We've had to leak fake versions to muddy the waters, we've had to lean on scientists who were in the audience. A copy of your original turned up in Europe last month, we had to wipe a foreign government server to get it. You've caused us a ton of trouble.'

'And now what; you're going to kill me?'

She knows she's already made this joke, and that it's not a joke, but she can't help herself, the joke hides the fear; but her stomach muscles clench when she sees Ryan take the question seriously this time. Not even trying to hide it.

Colt realizes he hasn't seen his parents together in many years. He frames them with his hands.

Like a photograph.

They made me, he thinks, astonished. They combined their DNA. I am their mixtape, their mashup, their fuckup, their playlist, their greylist, their blacklist, greatest hits, best of, compilation, anthology . . .

He shakes his head to derail the runaway train of associations. He can't take his eyes off his mother, his father, their strange energy. His mother's mouth, his father's mouth. They must have kissed.

Ryan is speaking. 'The system can't kill you, not without a lot of problems. We have a surprisingly ethical system, Naomi. The system you want to destroy—'

'—I don't want to *destroy* it—'

'—Most countries, they'd just kill you. China would bill you for the bullet. This country, bless it, is too stupid to do that. We've fallen in love with this idea that we're some kind of saint among nations. And you know what happened to most of the saints.'

Naomi snorts. 'So you'd fight evil by giving the saints better weapons.'

'Well it's a more effective strategy than arming the *bad* guys.'

'So do you think we're bad guys? Because you're treating us like—'

'No, you're not bad guys—'

'Good. Then—'

'—You're more dangerous than that,' says Ryan, leaning forward. 'You and Colt are smart people who don't believe bad guys exist . . .' Naomi tries to respond, but Ryan bulldozes straight through her. 'Look, one of the huge advantages America has over most of her enemies is that the bad guys are largely idiots. Especially the fanatics. It helps that all they study are religion and hate. They're like the Nazis, missing out on the atom bomb because Einstein's theories were Jewish. I mean, if a thousand dumb fucks in Yemen want to kill you, so fucking what? But get one smart, well-educated enemy – Ho Chi Minh, Bin Laden – or give them a smart weapon, or, worse still, *make* them smart, then you really have problems.'

'But we're not the enemy!' she says.

He leans in. 'You'd give it to them,' he says quietly, so close to Naomi's open mouth, they look like they are about to bite each other. Or kiss. 'This power. And they would use it against us. Straight away, they would use it against us. They don't want to live in the modern world. Which is fine. But they don't want us to live in it either.'

Naomi turns away from Ryan, and Colt mourns the broken connection.

His mother stands up.

'Where do you think you're going?' says Ryan.

'I'm leaving, with Colt.'

'Colt stays.'

'I want to go home,' says Colt. 'With Mama.'

The muscles of Ryan's arm begin to ripple, and Colt assigns a lot of attention to that, because it is puzzling, because something connects with something and he doesn't like the pattern.

Time slows down, as he gives his new attention to his father's arm.

The arm rises from below the table, and the hand is holding a gun, a pistol, a Colt 1911; the classic Army pistol.

The weapon he's named after.

Such a simple machine.

For a moment, by default – because guns have always meant games – Colt applies game logic; assumes he has transitioned back into the gameworld, or forgotten he was in the gameworld; and Colt reaches for his own gun; but he doesn't have one.

And disentangling the levels of reality; realizing that his father is real, and has a real gun, and that Colt is unarmed; this takes up a lot of realtime, because some of the thinking is happening using his old brain structures; it is slooooooow; and his new brain structures can't decide what to do until he knows what is real and what is not.

His father's arm rises and rises, and extends towards Naomi, and Colt can't believe what his brain is telling him; his brain is having an argument with itself, and it paralyses him.

My father is pointing a gun at my mother.

Never point a gun at anything you're not prepared to shoot.

My father is trained to kill people.

Never aim a gun unless you are prepared to fire.

He has killed people; he could mean it; he means it.

Naomi sees the gun rise from Ryan's lap. The end of the metal barrel, facing her, is a bright steel square with rounded corners; in its centre, a round black hole.

Meanwhile Colt's new brain structures have run the stats on guns; on domestic violence; military versus civilian gun use in cases of domestic conflict; on everything he knows about his mother and his father; and they are telling him something urgent.

He's going to kill her.

Colt dives forward, arm outstretched, striking the barrel with his palm, knocking it back and up, and his father fires and the heat is incredible as fire and blood and smoke and bone gush from the hole that has just appeared in the back of his hand – astonishingly fast, even with time dilated, the eye can't register it – and as tiny flecks of blood and flesh speckle across the visor of his helmet, Colt pushes hard, and the snout of the gun actually lodges in the hole it has just blown in his right hand, the gases from the explosion, pressed tight against his palm, having made a hole larger than the actual .45 calibre bullet, and the gun fires again, as Ryan tries to force the barrel down, at Naomi, and Colt tries to keep it aimed at the ceiling.

Pain doesn't really enter into it. Not yet.

Meanwhile . . .

Naomi had only begun to step backwards, to duck, when Colt launched himself across the table. And so Naomi's perceptions are confused, as her brain projects the most likely future, and maps incoming impressions against that; the gun goes off, and she is convinced she has been hit, she feels it for a second; but it is just her body, muscles clenching, blood vessels tightening, in expectation of the impact; she thinks she has seen the gun fired at her face, the flash, the explosive crack mapped onto her expectation, and there is a moment of tremendous internal confusion as the knowledge that she has been shot drifts out of sync with her body's growing knowledge, as the reports come in, that she has not.

Without legs to swing out, to balance him, Ryan's centre of gravity is high, and far back in the chair, and he goes over backwards, with Colt on top of him.

Colt, as they fall, twists slightly in mid-air, to rotate his hip into place beneath his father's ribcage. He knocks the air out of his father's lungs as they land, his father's back and head slamming off the floor.

Colt doesn't bother trying to wrestle the gun from his father's grip. He gets a finger on top of his father's finger instead, and depresses the trigger again and again until the pistol runs out of rounds.

It is hard to make a fist, with bones and blood vessels blown out of the centre of your hand.

Naomi arrives at his side and between them they get the gun off Ryan.

He is on the ground, with no legs, and no weapon. They step back.

Colt swipes at his visor absently with his sleeve a couple of times. The dirt-and-oil-resistant surface wipes clean.

'Let's go,' says Naomi.

Colt looks down at his right hand.

He can see the floor through the hole in his palm.

'Wow.'

There is very little blood; the muzzle blasts have cauterized the wound, cooking the flesh around the edge.

That smell . . . Colt recognizes it, but he can't name it. The elements seem out of place. Cordite from the bullets, mixed with the smells of his own burned flesh. Like pork, or . . .

Fireworks, and a barbecue.

It's the smell of the 4th of July.

'Let's *go*,' and she grabs his arm.

'Aren't you going to finish me off?' says Ryan from the floor.

'I don't like killing, Dad.'

'Bullshit.' His dad, panting, still winded, is losing it. 'Examine your fucking teeth. *Canines. Incisors.*'

Colt finds it hard to look at his father's face, his rage. The son looks down at the hole in his hand, vaguely ashamed, but unsure why.

'Look at your eyes, pointing forward,' says Ryan. 'Your ears, cupped forward. You don't care what sneaks up behind you. You are a hunter, a *killer*, from the genes up. No choice.'

Colt stares down at his father through the visor, and their eyes lock together now as his father continues. 'You weren't born to eat fucking *grass*, Colt. And your freedom to say, oh I don't like kill-ing, I'll just play my little games – that was bought by other men, out there in the real world, killing and being killed. This "I don't kill" bullshit . . . you outsourced it. That's all.'

Colt leans over, reaches out with his good left hand, touches his father's cheek, the side of his jaw. The short black stubble. Shaved level with the tanned skin this morning, growing back already.

His father stares up into his eyes, strangely relaxed now, waiting to see what his only begotten son will do. 'There is no life without death,' says Ryan, quietly now, no longer angry. 'And no living without killing. You can't opt out.'

Colt lifts his father's head gently from the pale grey floor with his good hand.

I don't want to die.

But I don't want to kill.

I *can't* kill him!

But, if I don't . . .

I don't want Mama to die.

This is the most difficult calculation he's ever made.

He can feel the different impulses – of caution, of anger, of love, of fear – each moving his good hand back or forth a fraction as they arrive, so that it trembles.

Dada's right. I can't opt out. *Decide.*

The final votes come in, from all the layers of his mind and body, and are tallied.

He slams his father's head back down on the concrete, as hard as he can, as his eyes blur with tears.

8

The Map and the Territory

'There must be an immortal, unchanging being, ultimately responsible for all wholeness and orderliness in the sensible world.'
— Aristotle

'Aristotle could have avoided the mistake of thinking that women have fewer teeth than men, by the simple device of asking Mrs. Aristotle to keep her mouth open while he counted.'
— Bertrand Russell

'Everybody knows that Aristotelian two-value logic is fucked.'
— Philip K. Dick

93

They pull Ryan's door closed behind them, and run in the direction of the elevator.

Colt gets there first, hits the button. Ah, it's already on this level, great . . .

The door seems to take for ever to open.

As the door is still opening, Colt slides in.

He hits the up button, as Naomi is still entering the elevator.

There is a weird, unsettling pause.

Maybe they've been disabled, thinks Colt. A general alert. Alarms. The entire base locked down. Dad could have . . .

The doors begin to close, as slow as honey rolling down the outside of a jar.

Oh. OK. It was just his senses, racing. Slowing time.

'We'll never get to the surface through the front doors,' he says.

Using the helmet to search for info might give their position away . . . but . . . oh, we can use the helmet for a little longer. There are cameras everywhere. All movement is logged, they already know where we are.

He closes his eyes and reaches out for information.

Wow.

It feels weird, like reaching for a glass of water you know is there and closing your hand on nothing. 'There is no information on this building, anywhere,' says Colt.

Naomi, breathing very fast, begins to laugh. 'It's a secret base,' she says. 'Of course there is no information.'

'But, usually, stuff leaks . . .' And now he can't get access to anything at all. They've switched off something, or there's just too much rock in the way. 'There's no *information* . . . Well, we can't go back out the way we came in . . .'

'What way did you come in?'

Colt shrugs. 'Airport, main entrance.'

'I didn't come in the main entrance,' says Naomi.

Colt opens his mouth to speak, just as the lift stops. He whirls to face the doors.

The doors slide open.

The relief, when there is no one waiting for them outside in the wide empty corridor.

Colt relaxes. A little. 'So how did you get in?'

Naomi shrugs. 'Some emergency exit,' she says.

'*Where?*'

'Through a construction site. I don't think it was even an official emergency exit.'

'Hmm. How did you get to it?'

'Two small black drones led me to it, from the gate, just off the three seventy-five. Quadcopters. Ryan controlled them, I think. Basically smuggled me in. And then someone met me inside the exit, and took me through the construction site.'

'OK,' says Colt. 'Show me. Draw a map, from here to the exit. Anything you can remember. Turns, distances.'

With awkward, spasming fingers, he uncrumples the sheet of paper reading Te Infinite Amo. 'We'll work on paper. Assume all our devices are pre-owned.'

'Pre-owned?'

'Backdoored. Bugged.'

He hands the page to her, and Naomi sees properly, for the first time, the hole in his right hand. Puts her own hand over her mouth. 'Oh Colt. Oh Colt.'

'Draw,' he says. 'Draw.'

Naomi draws all she remembers of the route.

They study it, in the deserted corridor.

'He's not going to let us just walk out,' says Naomi. 'This is too easy.'

'If they're still building corridors, tunnels, whatever,' says Colt, 'they can't have installed the full security infrastructure. And construction's disruptive.'

He says it like disruptive's a good thing.

'I don't see how that works for us,' says Naomi.

'Lots of strange faces,' says Colt, 'contractors, no set routine.'

'Maybe,' says Naomi. Well, it's a plan. It's not much of a plan, but it's comforting to have anything at all.

He carefully folds the paper map, and puts it in his pocket. Two of the fingers on his right hand won't bend – severed tendons – and a wave of pain shoots up his arm. His teeth clench together, and beads of sweat form at his hairline.

A paper map. Holy *poop*.

Well, if the construction zone doesn't have full security . . . then yes, they can do it. Vanish.

He'll have to go offline, and stay there, deaf and dumb, until they get back to somewhere safe, and he can build an encrypted identity. If he's pulling data out of the sky here, they can track him, they'll find him. There is no crowd to hide in: if he walks across the desert, sending and receiving, encryption won't matter a damn. He'll be the only guy out there . . .

But . . . Oh *man*, he should have gone offline *immediately*. Could they have tapped into his helmet's cameras, its microphones, while he and Mama were talking and drawing the map? No, they can't have moved that fast . . . But what if they're automatically logged into everything, recording everything . . . It's hard to be paranoid enough.

'Disable locations, and switch off everything,' he says. 'I'll help you. No, don't just switch it off, disable it. I'll show you . . .'

And now it's all gone.

He's in total electronic silence.

His senses have collapsed back into this one body.

The only signals come from the physical world.

Suddenly the helmet is oppressive, dead.

He throws open his visor.

Sights and sounds, given full attention, seem sharper, too much; and yet, unaugmented, without layers of data, not enough.

He closes his eyes, hears the blood pounding in his ears. I'll be all right. It'll be all right.

'Let's go . . .'

As they run along the main corridor, they hear footsteps approaching down a side corridor. Naomi and Colt slow, stop; Colt slips his damaged hand into his pocket. Do you run, or . . . but the couple coming round the corner are laughing over something he's showing her, totally caught up in each other, and don't even make eye contact as they pass by.

'The right hand doesn't know what the left hand is doing,' says Naomi.

'It will in a minute,' says Colt. He takes his right hand back out of his pockets. OK it hurts, God, now it hurts. His heart speeds up, as images from games and films run through his mind. He should have taken the gun, even if it was empty . . .

Should have tied up his father.

Killed his father? *No* . . .

The fire doors – security doors? – are still wedged open. No sign of an alert. That's good.

Weird, but good.

They walk all the way back to the big cavern that Naomi came through on her way in. Three or four guys in overalls look up as they enter, then look back down at the machinery they're working on. It's not like in the movies. Nobody chases them.

A woman and a kid, versus an army; if they were chased, they'd be caught. Real life's like that.

Colt worries at it. There's something wrong here.

But high-security bases make information flow as hard as possible. Maybe if Ryan has ordered their capture, it just hasn't made it to these guys yet. They're civilian contractors. Not military.

But why isn't there a general alert? A lockdown?

Maybe they're not important enough.

Colt feels oddly disappointed.

'There,' says Naomi, and points.

They make it to the first door of the long exit corridor.

And they can't open it. Biometrics up the wazoo. Retina, fingerprints.

'Maybe if we started a fire, the doors would unlock,' says Colt.

'And maybe they wouldn't,' says Naomi, 'and maybe we'd choke on the smoke. No.'

But Colt is already moving away from the door toward something looming in the gloom, further along the rough curve of the cavern wall.

It's one of the new-generation German tunnelling machines. Small, light, very fast. Well, small for a tunnelling machine . . . He frowns as he studies it.

It has been positioned to cut a new corridor. He stops frowning. Yes . . . The front of the machine is already a few yards into the rock, far enough in so that the curved hydraulic rams can get a grip on the tunnel walls and force the cylindrical body forward, keep the blades up against the stone. Colt looks closer.

Sedimentary; the old lakebed. Hardly even stone. Grey clay and soft shale. Good.

Somewhere, very far away, a siren begins to sound.

94

Ryan opens his eyes.

His head hurts.

That's the ceiling.

Right.

They're gone.

So he didn't have the balls to kill me.

He reaches out, to call an alert. Pauses. What good would that do?

If he has them arrested . . . the legal process is useless. More likely to charge him than them. And, meantime, there is no way the civilian court system will stop Naomi from releasing her research.

Calling an alert will just guarantee they stay alive and safe, so they can hand a weapon to the enemy . . .

He feels so tired. The thought of lifting himself back into the chair, of reacting to all of this, dealing with all of this, is exhausting.

I died, thinks Ryan, after my balls were blown off. My legs. This is my afterlife, in the underworld.

He lifts himself back into his chair, wheels himself to his desk.

The right side of his face is stinging. Powder burns.

Looks again at the message he received the day before.

A tip-off from a sympathetic member of the Senate committee.

He reads it one last time. Deletes it.

So, Congress is going to let me down too.

Everybody lets me down.

His father let him down. Ryan blinks at the memory. Coming home one evening, beautiful blue sky, needing help with some math homework. Finding his father dead in the study, his pistol on the floor, his brains all over the wall and ceiling.

His mother . . . he doesn't even want to think about all the ways his mother let him down.

Naomi, who once said she would always love, honour, and obey, let him down.

The guys clearing IEDs on the Af–Pak border let him down.

The field surgeon who probably could have saved his legs if the fuckwit had been sober had let him down.

And now his country lets him down. After all he's given up for his country.

Enough.

No self-pity.

He opens the coding terminal, goes through all the security bullshit, then calls up the code for the autonomous immune system.

There should have been a dual trigger system, to launch it. But when the budget cutbacks had hit the programme, that was the first thing he'd eliminated.

He'd designed the weapon, he wanted the option of pulling the trigger.

The senators on the committee had also demanded a cut-off switch. An emergency override, under their control.

Ryan had nodded, incredulous, at the hearings.

A feature that would negate the point of the entire project. Right. Sure. Yes, sir.

Ryan wasn't a serious coder, but he didn't need to be.

He'd got the coders to build in the override cut-off switch as a software module that could be removed with no negative consequences for the system.

Ryan spends the next few minutes deleting code, deleting backup code, until there is no override mechanism left, no place to turn it off.

Ten years' work in the service of his country. And they're going to cancel it.

'No,' he says out loud.

The country thinks it doesn't want this. Doesn't need this. Oh, but it does.

Wait, don't turn it on yet.

Let's set it up first. Give the system information on the threat.

Naomi.

Colt.

Photos, videos, every piece of biographical detail he can think of, until the system takes over and starts sucking up more data from everywhere, analysing it . . .

Assessing the threat.

He can't force it to target them. That's the whole point, it's autonomous. But he can load the dice.

When he's sure it's got enough threat background data, Ryan finally triggers the autonomous immune system. It feels totally anticlimactic.

It's just a standard high-security run command. Like locking up the office at night.

He sits there for a while, listening to himself breathe. Images of his ex-wife, his child, form in his mind. He shakes his head, no, I'm not going to think about that.

Then he hears feet running down the corridor outside. And now, at last, a siren somewhere. And with it comes a surge of adrenalin. It's done. It's done. Good. It's good to finally *act*. An old song goes around in his head.

Don't stop me now, I'm having a good time . . .

He smiles. Yeah, despite all this crap . . . no, *because* of all this crap . . . I'm having a ball. Look, it's done. It's *done* . . .

I don't want to stop at all.

95

Naomi and Colt look at each other; but the siren has made the decision for them.

The entry hatch at the back of the tunnelling machine is open, and Colt slides in.

The cabin interior smells of oil, and dust, and metal, and plastic. Colt looks around.

OK.

Working out how you make the thing go is trivial. There are only a few manual controls, all labelled. Most of the decisions on blade angle, and thus speed, are automatic, triggered by the hardness of the rock.

Colt shrugs. Why do they even bother to man these machines

any more? They'd be more efficient if they were fully automated. But people like to think they're necessary, even when they're just getting in the way. Like Mama letting me help her cook, when I was a kid.

The thought combines with the smells in the cabin – oil, metal, plastic – to set off an avalanche of memories.

Smash.

Egg white all over the counter. A thick, transparent drip sizzles on the hot ring, and in seconds the wobbly, glassy blob goes solid and white. The grabbed bright rubbery yellow yolk slides around, through his fingers, drops to the floor, bursts, and now it's liquid, like paint. A smell; he looks back at the hot ring; the white turns brown at the edges, black. Oh Colt, she says, oh Colt. Her face. He looks at the floor, at the puddle of broken yolk between his feet, as that huge feeling he can't understand rises in him. It hurts. Don't, Mama. But she hasn't done anything, just looked at him and said his name.

Stop!

It's the neurons, regrowing, denser. They're connecting to my memories. Triggering them. Hard to switch them off.

Breathe. Look at what is right in front of you.

Here. Now. This smooth metal, this oily air.

That was it. Like hot cooking oil. That's what set off the memory.

He breathes, blinks, breathes. The past goes away, but the feeling doesn't.

Oh Mama, I'm sorry, please, I'm sorry, don't be sad.

Naomi squeezes into the capsule, behind him.

Colt moves across, to the edge of the black padded chair, and his mother slides in beside him. The space is only designed for one man, but a big man. There is just about room for mother and child.

Colt fires up the engines. The blades come up to speed. Colt extends them; they start to dig in.

The hydraulic rams *thunk* against the soft stone all around them, and press the machine forward.

The machine pulls itself into the soft grey stone.

It's incredibly loud in the tight space. Colt looks around, looks down. Only one set of ear protectors, lying at their feet. Colt reaches for them, to give them to Naomi, as Naomi reaches, to give them to Colt.

They grab a bright yellow earpiece each, and push them towards each other so the plastic frame holding them bends.

Like pulling a Christmas cracker in reverse, thinks Naomi, and laughs.

She is glad Colt can't hear her laughter, that it's washed away, as it bubbles from her mouth, by the torrents of noise. Through the bones in her head, her laughter doesn't sound right.

Colt lets go of the ear protectors.

She tries to give them back, but he refuses.

Well, you can't make him do anything he doesn't want to do.

She puts the ear protectors on, and studies Colt's face.

Her son. Concentrating hard. So grown up. He looks very . . . alive.

Colt adjusts the controls, and the nose of the tunnelling machine begins to tilt upwards at a gentle angle, keeps going.

Naomi slips back a little on the slick plastic of the black padded seat. Her sweat.

It's getting hotter.

What happens if they get stuck? If they run out of fuel, halfway to the surface?

How much air is in here?

Does the machine block the tunnel behind them with broken rock and clay? It must. That rock has to go somewhere.

So, there's no going back . . .

They'll either reach the surface, or die.

Across from her, Colt frowns. The temperature is too high. He adjusts the angle of the blades, but that's not it.

The temperature keeps climbing.

He tries a mechanical slider on the control panel.

Ah, the new fashion for retro controls . . . Supposedly favoured because software interfaces can be bricked by hackers; but Colt suspects it's just German engineering nostalgia for the tactile, physical machines of the pre-computer era. The slider is unla-belled.

Ridiculous; a patch of dry glue where the label should have been. Crap design. Anything important should be etched into the panel surface.

He pushes the slider forward, sucking in a sharp breath as the vibrating instrument panel sets off the exposed nerves in his hand. Outside, water dribbles from tungsten nozzles to cool the blades.

It should be automatic. *Ridiculous.* How can you run a machine at optimum efficiency, if the thing hasn't been designed efficiently? You have to take into account human stupidity. Because it's a constant.

He reflexively tries to look up the spec for the machine, but of course his helmet is switched off, and nothing happens. His frown deepens.

Naomi looks away. Watching him isn't helping. But there is nowhere safe to rest her eyes. Everything reminds her of where they are. And the ear protectors aren't enough to keep out the screaming of the blades.

Oh, Colt's poor ears . . .

As the crumbling shale becomes a harder kind of rock, a limestone layer, they slow, adjust. There is a bone-shaking *thunk*, as the hydraulic rams press against the sides of the tunnel, bite in, and then force the machine onward and upward. The whine of the cutting blades in the nose grows harsher, higher, triumphant.

Perhaps the vibration will be calming, she thinks. She rests her head against the wall of the capsule, but the watery, gravelly sludge, grinding past, inches away, is incredibly loud through the bones of her skull. She jerks her head free of the metal, leans back in the padded seat, and closes her eyes for a long time.

They tilt suddenly down, as the scream of the blades leaps even higher in pitch, hard to hear now, hard to bear. 'What's that?'

Did he hear her? She shouts again, 'What's happening?' and still Colt doesn't respond.

OK, no it's OK, don't disturb him, he's busy, but she shouts again anyhow because there is something terrible, nightmarish, primally wrong about shouting at Colt from this close and not being heard, not being answered. *'What's that?'*

They lurch to a halt.

He pulls a lever down, flicks a switch, pauses; clicks another switch, another, off, off, off. The blades slow, drop in pitch, in volume. Grow quiet.

Stop.

He turns and smiles at her. 'We broke through.'

260

96

They fight the rear hatch open.

There's no way out.

It's just a dark wall of broken clay and sand.

The junk they've just tunnelled through, minced, and piled up behind them.

A little sand trickles, then pours through the open rear hatch, and Naomi thinks, we're going to drown in sand. She tries to swing the hatch closed, but the rising pile blocks the swing of the door; she pushes harder, the broken shale slips and drops in through the hatch, into the machine behind them, till there's an abrupt collapse, and suddenly there's blue sky everywhere.

They scramble out the hatch, the metal surprisingly hot – friction, thinks Colt – and up the broken shale to the surface and stand in the sun, blinking, blinded, stunned.

Where are we?

Colt, reflexively, switches on his helmet, not to go online but just to get at the maps stored in its memory; and, instantly, turns it off again.

No. Anything the helmet does, that tells us where we are, is likely to tell them, too. Can't risk it sending out some automatic map data request, or a roaming signal to the nearest base station, or just some random, outbound ping. They must be monitoring all requests for data.

All data movement.

The tunnelling machine has broken through the side of a long, narrow, dry gulch.

Sheltered.

No sign of the base, the mound through which Naomi entered.

A line of dialogue, from some game he once played. *No one is more spied upon than the spy.*

No maps, no GPS.

Oh, crap. Lost in crappy crapworld.

The electronic silence is almost overwhelming. Info vacuum. Like being under a glass jar the size of a mountain. All the air pumped out.

He stands blinking, frustrated, in the sunlight, staring down at his shadow.

The only data he's got.

Hey, wait a minute.

Analyse *that*.

He turns, looks at the sun. Works out the angle above the horizon.

Checks the time.

Wow. This is easy.

He points. 'That way.'

Naomi looks where he's pointing. Looks back down, and along the long, narrow gulch. 'Well,' she says, 'this is heading in the right direction then, pretty much.'

They slip and slide down to the dry, pebbly bed, and begin to walk.

*

They walk for an hour, too fast. Nervous energy. They're listening for helicopters, trucks, but there's nothing. The gulch curves away, then back.

Colt's lips are dry, and he begins to stumble.

Naomi says, 'I think you need to . . . We need to rest.'

They move into a tight black patch of shade at the foot of a cliff. Flop down on a low pale flat-topped boulder.

Colt bends, picks up a rounded pebble from the dry streambed.

Deep red.

Specked with tiny black dots.

Striped with thin white lines of crystal.

His racing, data-starved mind pulls more and more information out of the pebble, and his picture of it expands, fractal.

Jasper.

High iron content.

Quartz stripes.

Smoothed and polished by the water, tumbling it against other pebbles, grinding it against the fine desert sand.

He moves it closer to his eyes, focuses on the thin lines of quartz running through it, looks into their translucent depths. Frozen evidence of a molten past.

From the crystal size, he can tell how slowly it cooled.

He can see the history of all the geological activity beneath his feet, captured in this pebble. He gets the giddy feeling that it contains all the information he would need to reconstruct the universe, if he could just decrypt it.

'Colt?'

He slips it into his pocket. Stands. Scans the sky. Where are the helicopters? Where are the drones?

'We'd better move,' he says, swaying.

*

When they finally get to the fence, it's a total anticlimax.

The section that blocks the gulch isn't electrified.

They don't even have to climb it. A flash flood has piled bleached branches and construction lumber and plastic barrels up against the fence, like a crude ramp. They just walk up to the top of the sloping pile of debris, and jump over the razor wire, down into loose sand on the far side.

Colt stands up, dusts off his knees, sneezes. Turns to look at the fence.

Bad design. *Bad* design.

'They should patrol this regularly,' he frets. 'That's really terrible.'

'They're not worried about people getting *out*,' says Naomi.

'Yeah, I know, but still . . .'

Then he hears it.

Naomi looks at him. 'What?'

Of course, she can't hear it yet. His hearing is way sharper now.

'Helicopter,' he says.

Where can we hide? It must have infrared scopes, zooms, everything.

It might know where they are already. Might be coming straight for them.

The loose sand. How deep?

Colt drops to his knees. Scrapes at the sand.

Good. Loose enough.

Deep enough.

'We need to bury ourselves, Mama.' No, wait. Oh, poop. If they dig away the hot surface layer to bury themselves, they'll leave two fugitive-shaped patches of cool sand above them. Super-visible in infrared.

OK . . . what if I . . .

Colt scoops up sand with his good hand, at furious speed, scattering the top layer of hot sand to reveal the cool sand beneath. He moves about, makes a random pattern, so they won't be under the only areas of cool sand.

It's getting closer.

His mother can hear it now, and she starts to dig. The sides slide in.

'You can't *dig* a hole in it,' says Colt, 'you have to kind of shuffle your way down, like this.' And he lies on the hot loose sand, oh God that's too hot, and wriggles till it gets cooler, and wriggles some more, scoops sand out from under his chest, his hips, with his good hand.

When he's deep enough, he scoops sand back over himself. A trickle of it pours into Colt's helmet before he thinks to slam the visor shut with his damaged hand.

Through the bones in his head, through the sand, he can hear his mother digging, wriggling.

They are both covered enough, not perfectly, but enough, and Colt is trying not to sneeze; the sand is over his mouth, but his nose and eyes are clear, mostly clear, he has some sand in one eye and he blinks, it's scratchy, he has to close his eyes and keep them closed. Stop moving.

They freeze. The helicopter comes in low, a few hundred feet over their heads, and the air in the gorge shudders.

Just off to one side, just outside the restricted area. Patrolling the perimeter? It's heading south.

It doesn't even slow down, just continues on the same course, south.

The sound fades in the distance.

How long should they wait? Is it a trap?

He is about to move – the tickle in his nose is becoming overwhelming – when they hear the second helicopter.

A trap . . .

They freeze.

The second helicopter comes towards them. Same direction. Exactly the same course.

Flies by, just off to the side again.

Fades.

A third helicopter . . .

And Colt blows the sand clear of his mouth and laughs. As the third helicopter flies past, off to one side, hidden by the canyon wall, he stands up, the sand streaming off him like the flowing robes in a renaissance painting.

Naomi, her ears under the sand, can vaguely hear him laughing.

He never laughs.

And suddenly Colt's face is looming over hers, his visor up, and he is gently, lovingly brushing the sand from her mouth, and he is saying, 'It's OK, Mama,' and pushing aside the sand to find her hand, and he is lifting her out of the shallow grave and saying, 'It's OK, it's only the tourist helicopters coming back along the edge of the exclusion zone, from the ghost towns. It's OK.'

Of course. Like a flock of mechanical geese. They do this every evening. Naomi feels foolish, ashamed.

'We should keep out of their way,' says Colt, 'in case they've overheard a security alert. But they're not out here looking for us.'

No infrared cameras.

No guns.

Three more helicopters fly by, returning from the ghost-towns tours.

Then two stragglers.

Then silence.

'OK,' says Colt. 'Let's go.'

Colt is already walking.

Naomi follows.

The gulch widens, blurs into more open, eroded land.

Finally they reach the road. The only road. Colt scans it, as Naomi studies his face.

'This would be the logical place to intercept us,' he says.

A dot shimmers in the distance. They duck back, and huddle in a gully, behind a mesquite bush. Among the eroded, exposed roots of the bush there's a dead rattlesnake, dry and stiff as a stick. Green and grey. The last six inches of its tail are flat. The rattle crushed.

Sat tight, defending itself with its rattle, thinks Colt. Crushed by a truck, in the middle of the road. Crawled away to die.

He looks up, through the mesquite, at the shimmering dot getting closer, larger . . .

A white Dodge pickup.

Colt and Naomi look at each other. Without speaking, they agree to let it go.

It swooshes by, swirling up a faint mist of dust, which drifts sideways, and settles on them in the gully. Naomi coughs. Colt reaches into the roots of the dusty bush: carefully picks up the dead snake by the head. So dry. So light.

The eyes are gone, eaten by ants.

Colt stares into the bony, empty sockets.

Hears something, very faint: looks back at the road.

Another dot. Bigger.

A bus.

It gets closer. Old bus.

They look at each other, unsure.

As Colt turns back to look at the bus, he catches a glimpse of something bright green in the heart of the bush.

He cautiously parts the dry brown branches.

The hard, protective bark near the main stem has cracked open to allow a green shoot to emerge.

Colt studies the lines on the dark bark: the way they swerve apart and crack, to let out the pale green shoot. He reaches into the cool, shadowy centre of the bush, strokes the branch with his fingertip. The bark is as rough as a cat's tongue, and when he gets to the slim shoot, its cool smoothness, the fact that it bends under his finger, is a shock; he pulls his hand away, afraid he'll snap it off.

Of course, thinks Colt. Its job is to stay strong; but also to crack. Part of its strength is its willingness to break.

It's a metaphor, thinks Colt, astonished.

You can't stay rigid, and grow.

His brain makes connection after connection. Recognizes the pattern again and again. It crackles outward through his life. Illuminates things he's been told by his parents, things he's read in books, that were just words, words, and now they're alive.

Like Dad says; You can't defend your way to victory.

Like Mama says; You can't protect yourself from the bad stuff, without protecting yourself from the good stuff.

I should have said yes.

You need to protect your core; but you also need to let that core grow.

And when it grows, it will crack open the old you. And those first feelers of the new self, as they thrust out beyond the protective shell, are vulnerable, and they might get damaged, might get eaten, might get hurt. But they have to be allowed to take their chance.

Because if you keep them inside, defend them totally against the world; they will be crushed, not by the world, but by your own defences.

The heart must break open and allow in the world.

Colt reaches out, to touch the new life again. It's stronger than it looks.

He hangs the dead snake on the green shoot, in the cool heart of the bush.

Stands up.

97

Good.

A very old bus. Should be human-operated, then. The driver probably gets to decide whether or not it'll stop.

But if it's been upgraded inside, if it's totally unmanned; then the bus will just alert the authorities to an unauthorized halt attempt, and keep going. Let the cops deal with it . . .

They step out onto the road, to flag down the bus.

Step back, hands still out. Wait to see will it stop.

It's a long moment.

They both sigh with relief and pleasure, as it pulls in, and its shadow falls on them.

The doors wheeze open. Cool air pours over them, and they look at each other. Naomi smiles. Colt, after a moment, slowly smiles back.

They climb aboard, into the dim cool.

Very old bus.

It's had a cheap upgrade, it's self-driving, but it still has a human driver up front, to make stopping decisions, and deal with the customers.

Naomi glances down the bus. Less than half full. Some people look up at her, but their gaze seems unfocused; their souls don't seem present. Watching something. Playing something. Perhaps they have just been hypnotized by the landscape.

She doesn't feel they can see her at all.

The doors sigh closed and it's cool and they're safe, and it's . . . normal. And normal feels so weird.

'Breakdown?' says the driver.

What a question! 'Ah . . . ?' And does he mean her, or Colt? Oh, *breakdown*.

'No,' says Naomi. 'We just . . . got a little lost . . . hiking.'

'Huh,' says the driver. Naomi walks past him, past the hypno-tized passengers, and sits down, close to the back of the bus. Colt nods a quieter thanks, without eye contact, and follows his mother to the seat.

The bus doesn't move.

'Hey, lady.'

Naomi, startled, looks up at the driver.

He's spun his seat, to stare at her. Not smiling.

She looks away, out the window. Are there troops coming? No troops. Then what gave them away?

Colt has tensed, is looking to her for guidance.

The people on the bus are waking from their dreams. Staring at her.

The driver clears his throat. 'Lady, this is my son's bus. You ain't taking it from the man, you're taking it from our pockets.'

'Oh, I am so sorry.' Of course. Everything's switched off. Her e-purse, auto-pay, everything. '*So* sorry.' Cash, cash. 'It's the heat, I wasn't thinking.' She stands up, walks back towards him, gropes for money. She gives him a note.

'You have *no* e-bucks?'

'I'm sorry . . .'

He glances at the note. His sigh is louder than the one the bus door just made. 'You don't have change?'

'It's OK,' she says. Don't look around. Don't look around. 'Keep it.'

The driver stares at her. And now, despite the cool of the bus, fresh sweat breaks out down her spine. She is making them con-spicuous. 'It's a nice bus,' she says. Oh Christ, did she really say that? She's falling to pieces. Act normal. What would be a normal thing to say?

'It's a nice bus, but it's not that nice,' says the driver. He holds the note up to the light, snorts again, tucks it into his shirt pocket. Settles back in his seat. 'Lady, you need to drink some water when you get the chance.'

Naomi nods.

'The kid too. You going to Vegas? I'll give you change closer to the city, when I've got a little more in the float. We don't do much cash.' He hits self-drive, and the bus moves off, oh thank God, they are moving.

Naomi sways back to her seat, happy the movement of the bus is disguising the trembling of her body, her legs. She sits down again.

After a few minutes, she begins to relax. Colt reaches for her hand.

She turns to him, smiling.

He's not looking at her.

Colt says, 'They're following us.'

Naomi looks over her shoulder, out the window.

She blinks, squints; the shimmering road is empty to the horizon. She glances back at Colt, questioning.

He's not looking at the road.

He's looking up.

She looks up, too.

Perhaps five hundred yards behind them, and about the same above – it's hard to judge the distance – she sees two patches of the wrong blue, of shadow on the sky.

Higher up, a bigger patch.

Another.

It takes her a moment to work it out.

Chameleon-painted, they mimic the sky.

They're almost invisible, from most angles.

But even the best changeable camo paint can't fully match the brightness of a pale blue sky, when the object is backlit by the sun.

'Oh, Colt,' she whispers.

'Yeah,' he says, still looking up. Glancing around the sky. Counting them. 'Drones . . .'

98

'You start out as a single cell derived from the coupling of a sperm and an egg, this divides in two, then four, then eight, and so on, and at a certain stage there emerges a single cell which will have as all its progeny the human brain. The mere existence of that cell should be one of the great astonishments of the earth. People ought to be walking around all day, all through their waking hours, calling to each other in endless wonderment, talking of nothing except that cell. It is an unbelievable thing, and yet there it is, popping neatly into its place amid the jumbled cells of every one of the several billion human embryos around the planet, just as if it were the easiest thing in the world to do.'
— Lewis Thomas, On Embryology, from *The Medusa and the Snail*

'He's done it,' says Colt.

'What?'

'Triggered the immune system.'

Colt turns his helmet back on. All systems, everything.

No point cutting himself off from the universe.

No point hiding, now.

They've already been found.

Colt pulls in information, from wherever he can get it.

Nothing.

Nothing, anywhere, to indicate that anything big is going on in Nevada. No public alert, no breaking news. Yet.

'Are they . . .' Naomi isn't sure what she was about to say. 'Can they try to kill us?'

'The little ones are just surveillance,' Colt says absently. 'Targeting. The big ones, yes, they kill.'

'Did they see us get on the bus?'

'Hmmm?'

He's having trouble dealing with the damburst of information that's built up while he was offline.

Oh, hey, that's nice . . .

He realizes he's checking out some new code in the gameworld.

Holy guacamole, Colt. Focus. Switch off the game.

Be here now.

'I guess,' he says.

'But if they saw us, why didn't they do something?' says Naomi.

'Mmm, yeah,' he says, 'it's weird . . . seriously, this system could kill us any time it wants.'

His mother looks upset. He doesn't like it when she looks upset.

Whoa, here comes that big emotion again.

Too much emotion, too fast . . . No, I don't want to be here now.

It's automatic, it's a reflex. Colt drops out of the physical world, and into the game. No mapping. He doesn't want to be reminded of where he is.

OK, and there is one other motivation . . .

Maybe Sasha's ingame . . .

He uses his admin privileges to check.

Yes. She's not got mapping on: she's just playing it freestyle, out in . . . oh.

She's playing in the test range. His realm.

That feels good.

He spawns in the centre of the test range, looks around.

He can't see her.

The symmetrical craters left by the open-air nuclear tests soothe him. Their clean, perfect lines resemble early computer graphics. The knowledge that such simple shapes are out there, in the landscape of the real world, is obscurely comforting.

The gameworld is a highly secure environment, with its own isolated servers, and he's running a fresh fake account, and a lot of encryption; but he's aware that the immune system must be aware he's ingame now. The hairs on the back of his neck stand up, in the real world.

But he has to talk to her, ingame.

Oh god, he should have said yes.

He wants to be alone with her, with mapping on, with micro-mesh suit, gloves, full tactile mapping; he'll disable his parental controls, it doesn't matter now, nothing matters now, he's probably going to die soon with Mama.

But Sasha's not in mapping mode; Colt's sitting in a moving

bus; the game couldn't map this anyway, the gap between game and life is too wide.

He abuses his admin privileges, gets her exact location, and respawns a few yards from her.

Doesn't even attempt to incorporate it into the logic of the game.

He knows it's rude to just appear, but he doesn't have much time.

99

For a moment, he is lost between worlds, he isn't sure where he is, where she is.

Because standing in front of him is Sasha.

Not her avatar. Sasha herself.

Somehow, she is actually in the game.

A real woman stands inside the game, and he feels existential vertigo, where is he? What level of reality is this?

OK, she must be a live feed, from the real world, dropped into the game, like his father's crappy low-res military hack, but with better graphics; but no, Sasha is totally integrated, she's an ingame character, he can see the game light fall on her . . . but the way it falls . . .

Wait. She has trashed her old avatar, and built a new avatar that is simply an exact copy of herself, as she is.

An avatar with no stretching, no exaggeration, no enhancement.

She has even managed to make the light fall on her, bounce off her, as it would in the world. Not enhanced. As flat – as unflattering – as real light.

Good hack, he thinks. Not easy.

He studies her face. It looks real. Not better than real, not hyper-real. Just real.

Its uncompromising realism throws the subtle artificiality of the gameworld into a strange relief, and Colt regrets some of his decisions on the light.

His eyes pull away from his conscious control. Override his attempt to keep them on Sasha's face.

Glance down.

The large, gravity-defying breasts of her old avatar have been replaced by small breasts that put delicate curves into the matt black fabric of a man's T-shirt. Her curves subtly reshape the strong, thick, straight white lines of the words BAD SEED, so that they swell a little. As a seed should.

He knows, without knowing how he knows, that it is the T-shirt she is wearing in the real world, now.

Nick Cave and the Bad Seeds, he thinks, and blinks rapidly.

His dad used to listen to Nick Cave, loud, all the time, in the year before he left. The year of the fights.

No Pussy Blues . . .

Hard On For Love . . .

His dad would listen to Nick Cave, and tell Colt about women. Colt was scared of the music – it was always too loud – but he liked his dad talking to him, telling him things, even if he couldn't understand much of it.

Now Nick Cave songs, one after another, flood into memory, each triggering the next, it's out of his control.

'*Tonight we sleep in separate ditches . . .*'

He looks up at Sasha's face, which is mapping live from her real face; which might as well be her real face. She has a small pimple on the left side of her jaw, which he stares at now.

'*You better run to the City of Refuge . . .*'

With everything exposed, she looks . . . not vulnerable. That's not it at all. The opposite, if anything.

'*Rain your kisses down in storms . . .*'

She looks so real. She looks so *real*. And a surge of emotion pushes up through his body.

He fights it back, fights it down.

'*Get ready for love . . .*'

'Hi,' says Colt. He's subvocalizing; he dimly knows his body is, in fact, on the bus, beside his mother. That he isn't speaking aloud in the real world. OK, maybe muttering a little. But his voice comes out enhanced and strong in the game.

'Oh,' says Sasha.

'Hmmm?' says his mother, from outside the game.

He switches on noise cancelling, and gropes his way across to a free seat, away from his mother.

Towards Sasha.

He stares into the eyes of Sasha's new avatar, into the eyes of her real face. Dark brown.

Like *my* eyes.

She stares back, into his avatar's eyes. Artificial, blue.

Nothing like his real eyes. A song his mother loves flutters through his mind.

'Don't it make your brown eyes blue . . .'

'All the songs are about us, Sasha,' he says.

'*What* songs?'

He gestures helplessly. 'All the songs.'

And she tilts her head. Stares into his avatar's eyes.

She can't see me, he thinks, desolate. Not how I really am. Who I am.

What I'm thinking.

What I feel.

Communicate.

Communicate.

'How are you?' he says.

'Terrible.'

'Oh,' he says. He doesn't have a script for that. 'Oh. I'm OK.'

'Love letter love letter

Go get her go get her

Love letter love letter

Go tell her go tell her.'

But tell her what? How do you talk about a feeling? What do you say? It's big? I'm scared? It . . .

Wait a minute.

You're enhanced. You've got your upgrade. Apply your processing power to this problem.

Why does she feel terrible?

'Why do you feel terrible?' he says.

'Your friends, the Brothers Karamazov, their crew, they wrote a triple-X mod . . .'

'They're not really my friends,' says Colt, trying to be precise, trying to keep it accurate, so no gaps in understanding can open up between them.

'Good,' says Sasha. 'Because they tried to rape me, ingame.'

284

'How?'

'They tried to force me out of the game. And they'd set up the mod so that if I left the game, my avatar stayed, and they could rape my avatar.'

'Why?'

'Oh for fuck's sake, Colt. Why do you think? Because I'm a woman, and I don't bend myself out of shape to please them. So they thought *they'd* try to bend me out of shape, to please them.' She smiles, but it's not a good smile.

Wintry, thinks Colt. That's what a wintry smile looks like.

'But . . .' It's out before he can stop it. '*Why?*'

'To punish me, for being myself. For existing.'

'But wouldn't parental controls . . .' He trails off, as Sasha stares at him.

'Your mom might set parental controls on *your* game in *your* house, and you might be *OK* with that, but out in the real world nobody uses them.'

He doesn't know where to begin. To make it OK. To make it better.

'But . . . it's not real . . .' he says.

'The *acts* aren't real. The *intent* is real. The *problem* is real.'

She's angry. Is she angry at him? Why is she angry at him?

Colt feels a little sick rise in his throat. This is all going wrong, again.

'But,' he says, 'you know, I used to get killed. By guys. All the time.'

'Colt, this isn't just random gameplay. They're forcing all the women – coders, players, everyone – out of the game.'

'I don't really get involved . . .' he says.

'I know! And that's a decision, with consequences! This is where the game has been *going*, Colt. This is where it's been headed for a while.'

'I didn't know . . .'

'You just haven't been paying attention,' she says. 'You've opted out. It's becoming a place that turns even perfectly nice guys into assholes, that rewards you for being an asshole, and you've just walked away.'

'I guess I've been kind of busy . . .'

'Yeah, playing around, in your own little world, making sure the lighting is perfect.'

This isn't going the way he wanted it to go at all.

'I'm sorry . . . You could have just stopped playing . . .'

'That's what they wanted! But why *should* I? I helped build this world!'

'So what did you do?'

'It was a bad mod. Their code was shitty.' A shrug. 'I did some stuff they weren't expecting, crashed their mod, and then I killed them.'

Colt stares at her.

Her face is amazing.

Not just her face.

What's behind her face.

Her soul?

He doesn't want to use that word, but it comes into his head anyway.

Who she is.

The complicated thing that she is. The way she codes, the way she fights, the way she stays open to the world, even if it hurts her, the way she doesn't walk away.

The way her face shows who she is.

What she feels.

It's alive.

She's alive.

He suddenly, intensely, wants to see her in the real world, smell her in the real world, feel her in the real world, and with that intense desire comes intense fear.

If this feeling gets any bigger, it's going to kill him. He can hardly speak. It's choking him. He's panicking. Can't think.

He's sorry, he wants to make it up to her, he wants to go back in time and say yes.

He wants to touch her, he wants to hold her.

He wants, he wants . . .

How do you express this feeling? How do you communicate?

What *happens*, when a man feels this way towards a woman? What do you *do*?

Into his head comes a vision; a vision of himself making a

move; a move he has seen a hundred times ingame, in the brothels of other gameworlds, in the virtual bars.

Back when he faked his age, and hung out with the older guys, trying to learn how to live among others. Back before he gave up, and created his own desert to live in.

He takes a deep breath, reaches out, and grabs her between the legs.

The game lets him do it; but she's not there, she has written some code to protect her from those kinds of move, and so her avatar doesn't react at all. His hand passes through her.

'I've got the no pussy blues . . .'

The game tries to reset mapping, and the disconnect jolts them back into their starting positions.

Standing, looking each other in the eye.

'Why do you think you have the right to do that?' she says.

This is not what is meant to happen at all.

'You wanted to . . .' Colt can't find the words. 'To kiss me . . . touch me . . . when we . . .'

He's vaguely aware of the long war over codes of behaviour for avatars, but he's always kept out of those debates, the passions frightened him.

I walked away, he thinks.

'Look,' says Sasha, 'you came to me in the game, that time, and you're confident, and, fuck, I love your work, I'm flattered; and we talk, and it's nice. It's lovely. And I enjoyed making out with you ingame, and so we got carried away and triggered the censors. I mean, fuck, I didn't know you had parental controls on.'

'I've turned them off, I . . .'

She shakes her head. 'That's not the problem.'

'What *is* the problem?'

'When I go to you in the *real* world, you blank me, you withdraw all your emotions. You stonewall me.'

'Oh . . .' But Colt doesn't know what to say, how to respond. He starts ticcing, his hands tapping his thighs in a rhythm, but it doesn't help, and Sasha keeps talking.

'. . . And then, when you change your mind, now, you just use your admin privileges to find me, and you appear inside my mission without permission, and then you . . .'

Colt thinks of something. '—But you didn't ask permission when you called to my house—'

'I took a real risk, in the real world!' Sasha leans forward, and her eyes, her face, are so astonishing that Colt steps backwards. 'I didn't have admin privileges! Do you think it was easy, going to see you? I was *crapping* myself.'

She was scared? *She* was scared? This information is completely unexpected.

'You could have turned me down, fine,' she says, 'but you could have been *nice* about it. You could have cared how I felt . . .'

'How did you feel?'

'I felt fucking *terrible*, I was crying so hard I nearly crashed the bike going home. And now you want to rewind, and play the scene again, except this time with you in charge, and in the safety of the game, risking nothing, *nothing*.'

And now they're both nearly crying, out in the test range, and Colt remembers he's on a bus, that his mother is a few seats away.

He starts to shut down; but no, he can't, he *can't* walk away again, he's got to keep going, get through this, and so he blinks and blinks and looks at Sasha's face, her amazing face, her interface with the world, so alive and angry and he says, 'Why are you so angry?'

'Because I *like* you. Because I don't even think you're a shit, you're just totally *thoughtless*.'

'Explain it to me,' he says, helpless.

'Explain what?'

'Women.' He thinks, no, the problem is bigger than that. 'Men.' Even bigger than that. Yes. 'Everything.' But that's not the right word, he's overshot the target. A better word comes to him. 'Love.'

As he says the word, a shadow falls over both of them.

Colt glances up, at the clouds gathering far above Sasha's head, and behind her. Clouds that are coming out of nowhere; clouds that are forming faster than they could ever form in nature.

Sasha turns, looks back over her shoulder, to see what he's staring at. 'Whoa, that's crazy,' she says.

Is it relief he's feeling at the distraction? Yeah, it's relief.

'Yeah,' he says.

'Bug?' she says. 'Hardware glitch?'

'No.' Colt pauses, trying to read the clouds. Decode them. 'It's real.'

'Can't be. The NDSA has never made that much weather.'

'Not just the NDSA any more.' Jeeez, they're forming super cells so fast you can see it happening. Tornados coming . . . 'The security agencies,' he says. 'All of them. They've been mobilized. Coordinated.' The immune system, he thought. It's been expanding, while we've been talking. Taking them over. Using their resources.

Those drones that have been looking for us aren't all Dad's.

Sasha reluctantly looks away from the clouds.

Looks Colt in the eye.

'What are they doing?'

'The agencies? . . . Searching.'

'Searching for what?'

He pauses. 'Me.'

She laughs. She thinks he's joking.

He wants to tell her everything. But if he tells her everything, she's involved. She's at risk.

She's already at risk. She's talking to him. They must be trying to monitor this, en route. Crack it.

Yes, it's hard to remember to be paranoid enough.

Wait, she's wearing a helmet, and micromesh. A full suit. He should warn her about the hardware backdoors. She's going to need to modify them physically.

But how can he tell her, without telling her how he knows about all that? Without telling her everything? And does she have the time, the tools, to do the modification? It's not trivial.

Also . . . if he tells her everything . . . he might have to tell her *everything*. How he feels. Crack himself open. Decrypt himself. No.

Just leave her. Keep her safe. Keep her out of it.

'I have to go,' he says.

'Oh for fuck's sake,' she says. 'We were almost getting somewhere.'

'I'm sorry. It's an emergency.'

'All right. But we need to finish this conversation. Meet me.'

'Yes,' he says. 'We do. Where. When.'

'Here, later. Test range. Five hours. I'm off shift.'

Five hours. Well, he will either be dead, or alive. He doesn't have to think about it now.

If it's safe, he'll turn up.

'OK.'

100

And then he is back on the bus, between worlds.

Everything is blurred and his eyes can't focus.

He wipes his eyes. Looks out the window.

Three hours. He just has to stay alive till then.

'Where were you?' says his mother, right beside him.

Oh man, she's moved over to his seat while he was ingame.

Was he mumbling? What did she hear?

Colt doesn't know what to say.

Naomi glances up at the drones. 'Will they kill us?' His mother's voice is like a little girl's. She's looking at him like . . . like . . . like he usually looks at her. This is scary.

Say something. Say something to make her happy. 'It's OK, Mama.' Is it? Why didn't the drones just kill them? Why did the system let them get on the bus? 'Totally different rules of engagement at home.' As he is saying this, he's searching frantically to see is it still true. Legal sites, rumour sites . . . So many of the rules of engagement have gone dark. '. . . Domestic, it's much harder to kill people. There are laws . . .' He hopes. But this is a totally new security system, specifically designed to work around the constitutional and legal problem of tracking and killing people domestically.

And he has no idea how much Ryan has been able to reprogram it before launching . . .

Colt keeps talking to his mother, while he tries to think his way through what an immune system for America would mean.

OK. His father must have set the terms of engagement. So, second-guess his father and maybe he can second-guess the drones . . .

Then that big emotion wells up again, washing all his thoughts away, and he hears himself mumble, 'Oh, Sasha, I'm sorry . . .'

No, first deal with the drones. You can talk to Sasha later, try to mend the things you've broken. But you need to stay alive in the meantime.

Save Mama.

Stay alive . . .

OK. The immune system. Go.

Colt's getting a headache. The avalanche of data is never-ending.

He wants to close his eyes, sleep.

He's dehydrated.

His hand hurts.

Keep looking, keep looking.

There . . .

'I've found a position paper,' he says.

'On what?' says Naomi, distracted, scanning the desert out the windows of the bus.

Oh, Mama . . .

We spend every day together; but she has no idea what's in my mind.

The thought fills him with one of those bad, sad feelings that he hates. It mingles with the big emotion, reactivates it, so that it starts to swell up again.

He taps a pattern on the seat's red, balding fabric until the feelings go away.

Naomi waits patiently. Well, fairly patiently. Considering.

'It's an early NSA discussion document,' he says, 'on a possible immune-response system for the US. Leaked years ago, so it's out of date. But it probably reflects the rough parameters of what the NDSA actually built later.'

'Go on.'

Colt takes a deep breath. 'There are three levels of threat. I think we're on Level 1.'

Naomi looks out the window again. They're passing a small unmanned plant nursery; a vivid, striped acre of desert flowers.

A gardener drone drifts along the rows towards them, pollinating. Just as they drive past, its sensors spot an infestation of beetles on a bush. The drone's spiked tongue lashes out, sparkling bright and metallic in the sunshine; retracts with a whipcrack she can hear clearly inside the bus; and they are all gone.

She looks away.

'Is Level 1 good, or bad?' she says.

'Good. It goes from yellow to orange to red, and Level 1 is yellow. But we could be on Level 2, if they only sighted us when we flagged down the bus.'

'But what does it *mean*, Level 1, Level 2?'

'I think we've been identified, but not isolated . . . The system wants to kill us, but we're surrounded by too many people to hit now.'

'So we're safe in crowds.'

'It's not a static system,' says Colt. 'And response levels depend on the threat level we've been assigned. With a significant threat, if the immune system doesn't get a result, it will ramp up its response.'

'Level 3? Red?'

'Yes.'

'I'm guessing that's not a good thing.'

Sarcasm, thinks Colt. Or irony. He nods. 'If we were already at Level 3, this bus would be a crater.'

'What moves it up to Level 3?'

'Failure at Level 2. We need to fool it into thinking it's got us.'

Colt blinks rapidly. Something . . . something's making him uneasy. What is it? There . . . At the front of the bus . . .

The driver glances up, at the mirror above his head. Stares down at the back of the bus. Colt realizes the driver's been doing this every minute or so, since they got on.

Not good.

'Maybe we're just a low-level threat,' says Naomi, trying to be optimistic. 'Maybe it's just monitoring us.'

'Yeah . . .' But Colt sounds doubtful.

Naomi squints up into the sky. 'How do we find out?'

'Well, we could get off the bus, and walk back out into the desert. And if it kills us, we weren't a low-level threat.'

Naomi looks at Colt, studies his face. Is he developing a sense of humour? Now *that* would be a transformation. She smiles.

He doesn't smile back.

Oh.

'So how do we turn it off?' she says.

'We can't turn it off, that's the whole point.'

'But Ryan switched it on, he can switch it off. So we should be able to . . .'

'No, that's the *point*.' Colt's right foot begins to tap very fast on the sticky, grey, plastic floor. 'If the good guys can turn it off, then the bad guys can turn it off. A weak president could turn it off. Terrorists could turn it off. The Chinese could turn it off . . .' He realizes he's quoting his father, and he stops.

'But that's . . . paranoid,' says Naomi.

'Immune systems *are* paranoid. If they're switched on, by definition the body they protect has been compromised. So they don't trust signals that say, hey, you can switch off now. They stay switched on till the threat is *dead*.'

'Then how do we make it less aggressive?'

'We can't make it less aggressive . . . But we can make it more aggressive.'

Naomi laughs.

Colt doesn't even smile. 'What happens when an immune system is too aggressive, Mama?'

'If an immune system is too aggressive . . . it will attack healthy cells,' she says. She doesn't notice her right hand moving to cover her throat.

But Colt notices.

He wouldn't have before the transformation. But he does now.

'It will kill itself,' she says, and she doesn't notice her right hand slide away from her thyroid now, and down her body, till protective fingers cover the blue veins in the warm crook of her elbow.

But Colt notices.

'Yes,' he says. 'We might be able to make it kill itself.' He turns in his seat, and stares up at the dark blue dots in the bright blue sky. 'With the right equipment . . . I should be able to communicate with those drones.'

'Colt, seriously, they will have thought of that . . .'

'No. You can't perfect the security until after you've finished the system. And it's not a mature system yet, it will still have flaws. Security vulnerabilities. I can hack it, I'm pretty sure of it. I can hack the drones.'

'Colt, this isn't a *game*. These are, what, billions of dollars' worth of military technology, you can't just *hack* it . . .'

'No, Mama. These big systems, they're good once they've been broken in, tested. But this system was launched prematurely . . .' The bus is slowing down, and it's distracting Colt. 'It hasn't learned from experience yet. It's a baby. We can fool it . . .' Something's up. He smells smoke. 'I probably can't switch them off. But I might be able to get them to kill themselves.'

But he's saying this mostly to stop his mother frowning. He has no idea yet how he can pull this off.

It's less a plan, and more an aspiration.

The devil is in the details.

He definitely smells smoke.

And now the bus stops, the driver staring in the rear-view mirror.

Something isn't right.

Colt looks around; nobody has flagged the bus down.

There is no bus stop, no building, no shelter at all.

The driver walks back towards them. The muscles in his jaw clench, unclench, clench.

How does he know . . . Colt tenses; stands; but the driver pushes past him, keeps on going, to the back of the bus.

The small Vietnamese man is crushing a cigarette under his heel. Turning the heel fast. As he looks up from his task at the looming driver, a last trickle of smoke leaks from the corner of his mouth.

'I told you must be twenty times,' says the driver. 'That's it. That's it. Out.'

The Vietnamese man speaks too fast and low for Colt to catch the words.

'I don't care, I don't care,' says the driver, waving him silent. 'You should have thought of that before. Look at you, grinding your dirt into my floor.'

The small Vietnamese man speaks back, sharper this time. Something about a job, money.

'No,' says the driver. 'You're off this bus, and take it up with Brian if you think you can get back on tomorrow. Take it up with Brian, I'm not talking to you no more.' The driver herds the small Vietnamese man to the rear door of the bus, like a man shooing a chicken. The passenger steps down into the stairwell, and looks back up at the driver from far below, like a startled child. The driver pops the door open with the emergency handle. '*Out.*' He watches the passenger step down onto the side of the road.

Colt strains to hear a last plea from the passenger.

The driver shrugs. 'Hitch. Flag down some fool who doesn't mind you blackening his lungs. Phone a friend. Whatever.'

He strides back to his seat. The bus starts off again.

Colt watches the drones circle the Vietnamese man.

Making sure he's not me . . .

The man doesn't even notice them.

No one ever looks up, thinks Colt.

The man sits on a rock at the edge of the road.

The drones move on, after the bus. A couple of them break away, drift sideways.

They're darker against the sky now. Camo paint against a bright sky . . . it takes a lot of energy.

The smaller ones must be getting low on power . . .

Colt looks out the other side of the bus. Sees power lines, from one of the big solar plants, sweeping across the desert towards Las Vegas.

Oh, poop.

Colt glances along the power lines.

Yes. There they go.

The drones spread out, along the high-tension wires.

A civilian postal drone, on its way back from a delivery to one of the small desert communities, outranked by the newcomers, vacates the top of one pylon, and moves clear.

And then, as one, every drone drifts carefully down, all along the wire, till each is sitting on top of a pylon charging station, like a stork nesting on a chimney.

Oh, man. You can't tire them out, and they don't sleep.

They feed fast; a battlefield recharge. They're hungry.

Full power.

They take off straight up; and vanish.

Oh, *poopscoops!*

They've fine-tuned their chameleon paint. Fully charged, they're using more power to make the paint glow, to match the pale sky; and they're flying at a better angle to the sun; no back-lighting.

They're learning.

And now we can't see them.

101

Ryan's doing all he can to direct the targeting, while he still has some access to the immune system; it's already disengaging from his control, closing down the testing software, going fully autonomous.

He gets the testing software to report to him, just before it's shut down.

They've made it onto a *bus*? Damn . . .

And the immune system has decided Naomi and Colt are only a Level 1 threat. Yellow? Oh, for fuck's sake . . .

It's not taking the risk seriously enough yet.

On yellow, the system won't risk collateral damage. Second level, orange, it can risk some small number of civilian deaths. Third-level response, red – it doesn't care how many it kills, as long as it gets its target.

So . . . how can I get it up to orange, before it goes fully autonomous? To red?

He's trying to persuade the system to kill his wife and child. And everyone else on the bus.

He very deliberately doesn't think about that.

This is a technical problem. Don't get emotional. The long-term safety of the country is at stake here.

Personal stuff doesn't matter.

There's one input channel still open. He pumps the system full of data about high-risk individuals. About the disproportionate consequences of a military breakthrough being shared with an enemy.

The system digests the information. Does a threat audit. Pushes the threat level up a notch, to orange.

One more push . . . Get it up to red.

Ryan tries to manipulate the data stacks, cautiously, before he loses access.

There's too much bullshit United Nations peacekeeping data; it's making the entire system reluctant to shoot. He'd argued against it at the Senate committee, but they'd pushed it in to appease some loudmouth Democrats back in the House, who'd never seen service, or had to deal with the consequences of their programmes in the real world.

He downgrades the weighting the system should give to UN reports.

He pushes it too far. Triggers an alert, for interfering with the data.

The system locks him out. And now he's blind.

Now it's autonomous.

There is no more he can do.

It might have worked. It might not.

If it worked . . . his country will, very soon, be safe. And his wife and child will be dead.

102

The bus moves through the outskirts of Las Vegas.

It stops abruptly outside a shabby hotel, and Colt catches movement from the corner of his eye. He jerks around in his seat, in time to see a shadowy side door finish swinging open; two women run out, both waving at the bus.

A middle-aged Asian woman, Filipina maybe, and a young Han Chinese woman with unusually braided hair. The young woman's hair, the shape of her head, sets off some odd association in Colt's new neurons so that for a moment he tastes pineapple.

'Ladies, no hurry,' calls the driver, 'we ain't going nowhere,' and they slow to a trot. Climb aboard.

'Thank you, Michael,' says the middle-aged woman.

'Appreciate it,' says the younger woman.

'No problem, ladies.'

They sit in front of Naomi and Colt.

The middle-aged woman takes a large purple plastic object out of her bag, and shows it to the younger woman.

It's shaped like an erect penis, veins and all.

'Found it in the dustbin.'

'*No?*'

'Don't act blur leh. I always look in the big dustbin, upstairs. Always. Two or three time a day.'

Blur . . . And *dustbin* . . . Not Philippines, thinks Colt. Singapore. Singlish.

'The orange one,' says the younger woman, 'or the . . .'

'Yah, orange. The guests always throw all kinds of things in there one. Stuff they don't take home to their wives. Batteries not bad also.' She switches it on, and it buzzes.

'You sell it, or use it?'

The older woman studies the vibrating penis. 'Maybe use it. I don't know. Aiyah, it's been so long, I think this thing too big for me already. I'm like a little girl again lor.'

'Like a virgin . . .' The younger woman starts singing, laughing.

'Yah, yah.' The older woman laughs too. 'I'm a virgin again, like Madonna.'

Colt wonders, which Madonna? The mother of Jesus, or the old pop star?

It seems obvious to them, but it isn't to him.

He worries away at the sentence, but there is no way in, no way to crack the meaning open.

What she said is only a translation of what she thought, in her head. And he can't get into her head.

It's crazy, that computers can read each other's minds perfectly, with no loss of data quality, but people are totally cut off from each other.

He looks at his mother. She's sleeping. He studies her face. Her surface.

Oh, Mama.

They are approaching the Strip.

He touches Naomi on the shoulder. She jerks awake.

'The best chance to shake off the drones will be in the casinos,' says Colt. 'The biggest crowds; lots of random circulation. Indoors, so they can't follow, and lots of exits.'

Through the bus window, he can see the individuals on the sidewalk are increasing in number; soon they will form a crowd thick enough to hide in. He looks back at Naomi, who is still rubbing her eyes.

'Very hard for them to track us through a casino,' he says. 'And I'm pretty sure they can't strike, too many civilians.'

'But . . . can they recognize us?' says Naomi.

Colt shrugs. 'Standard pattern recognition. Face, dress, proportions. If we buy new T-shirts, change our hair, our walk, split up for a while, keep our faces down, stay in crowds, we should be OK.'

Naomi nods. Stands up, stretches. Steps into the aisle and walks up to the driver.

He is reading an old-fashioned paper book, *The Power of Now*, while glancing absently up through the windscreen every few seconds, to check if anyone's waving at the bus.

Ah, that explains the human driver, she thinks. This bus stops for illegals, living off-grid. Can't risk flagging down a bus electronically.

She hesitates, reluctant to interrupt him. The driver snorts at a sentence. Naomi studies the muscles of the arm holding the book.

The bus slows for a moment, abruptly, and everyone sways forward. Naomi grabs the pillar behind the driver to stop herself falling, and sees the jay-runner sprint by – a young white guy covering his face with his hands – right under the nose of the bus.

The bus apologetically, carefully, returns to normal speed as soon as he's clear.

The jay-runner crosses the six lanes, as the cars and buses all automatically slow and swerve around him.

Crazy. Some California tourist, no doubt, who's forgotten that Nevada cars aren't all self-drive, with automatic safeties.

'Fool,' says the driver, mildly, looking up from his book.

Guess he sees a lot of it.

He notices Naomi. 'Mmmm?'

'Sorry . . . do you go down the Strip?'

'Sure, lady. Where you think all these characters are going to work? The Vatican? Hey, I got your change, gimme a second . . .'

As the bus turns right, down Las Vegas Boulevard South, and they sway, he scoops some notes and coins out of his shirt pocket.

Naomi takes them. 'Thank you.' Returns to her seat.

*

Colt stares out the window at the Strip. He hardly notices his mother's return.

Neon lights, he thinks . . . Mostly not neon, though. A lot of LEDs, and mercury vapour tubes. Krypton tubes. Their phosphor coatings glow in pastel shades. But yeah, there are some old-style glass tubes still, with a noble gas, inert, aloof. Not wanting to react, but forced by electricity to glow. Red neon. The creamy peach of helium. There's some blue; xenon. A sad blue? A sky blue?

He puzzles over how it makes him feel. He puzzles over the *fact* that it makes him feel. Everything connecting, rewiring . . .

He imagines his brain glowing a hot red, like an excited neon tube. No longer inert, aloof. Electrified. Incandescent.

Don't get lost in your thoughts. Focus.

He turns to face Naomi.

'We have to get straight into the casino, fast,' he says. 'The more the drones observe us in movement, the more easily the drones can identify us later.'

'Should we change our clothes . . .' Naomi looks around the bus helplessly. Change into what?

'Not yet,' says Colt, and she's relieved. 'No point trying to fool them we're somebody else while we get off the bus. They've seen everyone getting on and getting off, there's a tiny dataset of possibilities. We have a much better chance of shaking them when we leave the casino. Massive dataset. Huge probability space. We'll change our look then . . . That one,' says Colt, pointing out the window.

'New York, New York,' says Naomi. 'OK.'

The bus stops.

Naomi walks past the driver, who is sighing over his book, and steps down off the bus. She glances up, looking for the drones. 'Sorry,' she says to Colt, lowering her gaze. She hadn't seen them. Hadn't even seen the sky; just a dazzle of spilled light.

'It's OK,' he says. 'We *want* them to get some footage. We want them to know it's us. But disguise your walk.'

'How?' says Naomi.

'Keep one leg stiff. And hunch a little. It'll mess with their data.'

They walk with quick, stiff steps into the enormous welcoming mouth of the casino.

103

Briskly, through the crowds.

It opens up.

The space is so large. Colt checks, over his shoulder, repeatedly, that a small drone hasn't followed them in.

Beneath their feet, steam abruptly puffs from under a fake manhole in the fake street.

Colt sniffs. Dry, ticklish. Not steam.

Dry ice.

CO_2.

They walk on, towards a fake Times Square. The noise around them is loud but strangely muffled, its sharper edges blunted by the carpet between the slot machines, in the darker spaces off to either side.

They pass the low-stakes blackjack tables. At one, a small, swaying man is shouting at a topless female robot dealer, who smiles back at him as she rakes in his money. Colt's helmet auto-translates the swearing from Russian, and Colt blushes.

They pass an oasis of light; the high-stakes blackjack tables, with human dealers, in their white gloves, dealing.

When Naomi closes her eyes against the light and sound and movement, she sees the real Times Square, hears the real sounds of New York. She feels, for a second, in memory, the cock of the man in the Times Square hotel, whose name she can't recall. *Oh* . . . She pushes her tongue, hard, into her cheek.

She opens her eyes.

There's a kiosk selling T-shirts.

'Let's change,' says Colt.

Naomi pulls out her credit card.

'No,' Colt says. 'Your cards will be on an alert list by now. Use that, and you've described our new outfits for them.'

She puts away the card. Buys two T-shirts for cash.

Colt asks the guy for a plastic bag, to carry them.

Naomi heads for the bathroom, but Colt takes her arm, swings her back into a gloomy aisle of slots.

'The bathrooms are a funnel point,' he says. 'They'll assume we'll pass through there, at some stage. If they're coordinating with people on the ground . . .'

'Where will we change, then? Here?'

'They can't see us, I'm pretty sure.'

'But . . . there's cameras everywhere. What if they can . . .'

'Mama, it's a *casino*.' And Colt grins a real grin. 'The cameras are closed-circuit. Airgapped. Like bank cameras.'

Naomi glances up at a camera, looks away. 'You're sure?'

'Certain. Not broadcast, not online. But, yeah, just in case . . .'

They walk between the rows of slot machines, deeper into the glowing, pulsing dark, until they find an unattended row.

Colt drapes his new T-shirt over a retro slot-machine handle, while he pulls off his old top.

Naomi pauses in her own changing, and studies his perfect body, his wounded hand, in the pulsing golden light of a bank of Goldmine slots.

He will die. One day he will die. No matter what I do.

Her eyes sting and burn.

'What?' says Colt.

'Dry ice,' says Naomi, and rubs her eyes. 'Shall we keep our old clothes?'

'Yes. Hide them and your handbag. Use their plastic bag. And mess up your hair. Break up the patterns.'

She ties her hair back in a bun.

'Yeah, good.'

'Your hand,' she says. 'We should hide your hand.'

'I'll keep it in my pocket.' He demonstrates.

'No, it looks wrong. It looks like you're carrying a gun, or, I don't know, hiding something. And you'll have to use your hand sometimes.'

'OK.' Colt thinks. Patterns, patterns . . . 'Wait . . . I saw something . . . Stay here.'

Colt walks back to the oasis of light. There. Still there. Draped over the rim of a trashcan. A pair of white disposable dealer's gloves.

Colt snorts. Ridiculous, that dealers have to wear gloves now, too. Nobody's ever been killed by a bio-weapon spread by *cards* in a *casino*. Dumb law . . .

As he walks back to his mother, he shoves the left glove in his pocket, and carefully pulls the other thin, flexible white glove onto his damaged hand.

His mother laughs when he arrives.

'What?'

'You look like Michael Jackson. Put on the other one.'

He does. She laughs again.

'*What?*'

'Sorry . . . Now you look like Mickey Mouse.'

'Is that bad?' says Colt, frowning at the gloves.

'No, Colt. It's fine.'

'OK, we should leave separately,' says Colt. 'I'll go first.'

'No!' says Naomi.

A vivid image of Colt walking out ahead of her, and dying in front of her, an orange blast, then white, like looking into the sun; and for ever gone.

'But we *have* to leave separately,' says Colt. 'They'll recognize—'

'I'm your *mother*,' says Naomi. 'I'll go first, alone, and see if they . . . Follow me. If they don't . . . I'll come back for you.'

'Mama . . .'

'We'll leave separately. Don't worry. After I've tested, is it safe.'

She moves towards the exit.

'Change your walk,' says Colt, from behind her. 'Try slightly shorter steps. It looks natural, but it alters all your movements.'

Naomi nods, without turning.

'And from now on, don't look up at the drones,' he says. 'No matter what. They're looking for someone who knows they're being chased, so it's a total giveaway. I should be able to see from here if they follow you. But don't look up.'

She walks out of the casino into the sharp light, the dry heat. The short steps make her absurdly conscious of her hips. A man looks her straight in the eye, and she smiles.

She could die at any moment.

She feels a wave of exultation; pure energy. As it surges through her, it's hard not to stride, like she did when she first became a woman, and felt the anger and power and terror and pleasure and embarrassment of being looked at. But she walks, walks carefully, making eye contact with people as they pass, because that distracts her from looking up.

Everything is so vivid in the sunlight. It must be the suppressed energy, but nearly everyone she makes eye contact with smiles, some of them abruptly, like they've just woken, and she realizes she is grinning.

A man in his thirties is moving towards her, fast, swaying. He meets her eyes, but he doesn't smile. It's like he hasn't really seen her.

As he passes, his shoulder strikes hers, hard. She is half spun around, and gasps at the shock of having the man crash into her personal space, into her.

Secret Service? Undercover cop?

She tenses for the fight.

But he doesn't acknowledge the strike at all, keeps moving, as she looks around for others. Are they arresting me? But there are no others.

Then he stops, and turns to face the tall, loose chain-link fence running beside them. A building site beyond.

The man's profile reminds her, distractingly, of her mother's favourite film star, Chow Yun Fat, back when he was young and handsome.

He grabs hold of the chain link, either side of a concrete support, so that the fence rattles and jangles and pulls abruptly tight beside Naomi, and he slams his forehead against the concrete post, the fence, and she sees the curved marks of the wire fence on his forehead and that he is weeping.

Oh. He's at the centre of his own drama; he's not part of mine at all.

Just another guy who's lost everything.

Naomi turns away and walks on.

She walks as far as Bellagio's, walks inside. Leans against a wall for a minute to let her heart slow down.

Walks back out again.

Back to New York, New York. Back to Colt.

Don't look up.

Like Lot's wife, leaving the city of Sodom.

Waiting for an angry God to turn her into a pillar of salt.

104

'Was I seen?' says Naomi, when she's safely back inside.

'Of course you were seen—' says Colt.

'Colt!'

'—The one at fifteen thousand feet is probably covering half of Las Vegas. But I'm pretty sure you weren't *identified*.'

'Jesus, Colt, don't scare me like that.'

But she sees from his face he hadn't meant to; he was just

answering literally. She shivers as the perspiration from her walk outside evaporates in the air conditioning.

He's answered her question. She asks it again anyway, just to hear it stated more firmly, 'The little ones, the facial-recognition ones. Did they follow me?'

'No sign of them following you. But we should keep our heads down.'

'Baseball caps,' says Naomi. 'Shade our faces.'

'Ugh,' says Colt, who has never liked baseball caps. That little clip to adjust them, at the back. He'd spend ten, twenty minutes adjusting. Too tight, too loose, too hard to get them *just right*. But . . . yes, baseball caps would help, they'd be doing a job. Hide their faces. Colt glances around. Lots of people wearing them. They'd blend in. 'OK.'

They buy two from a concession stand.

Naomi's says I ♥ Vegas.

Colt's says Kiss Me. It only takes him two minutes to adjust it. A new record.

They head for the foyer.

'I'll go first,' says Naomi. 'You can follow in a minute. Meet you on the corner, in three blocks, that way.'

Naomi walks out, reaches the pedestrian lights at the corner of the first block.

The crowd around her stops moving for a moment. The cars come to a halt at the lights. In the sudden silence, Naomi hears a droning noise, changing pitch. Louder.

She looks up.

I looked up. Oh Colt, I'm so sorry.

The pale blue, almost invisible shapes drift closer.

Lower.

Faster.

Past her. Towards Colt.

The lights change.

She races back, towards him, but Colt is already running, crossing the road, cutting through the swerving traffic. Jay-running.

She crosses the road too, squeezing through the tight gaps between automatic vehicles. She's lost sight of Colt . . .

He catches up with her on the other side, and grabs her arm. She spins, almost hits him in the face, before she recognizes him.

'Oh Colt! I looked up!'

'It's not that,' says Colt. 'Run . . .'

They cut through the crowd, run across an elegant bridge, up moving stairs, and stumble into the enormous space of the Venetian. They walk as fast as they can without attracting security.

Past a wedding fair, just inside the entrance. Dresses, tuxedos, and half a dozen smiling mechanical brides and grooms, arranged in three loving couples, male/female, male/male, female/female.

As Colt passes, he glances at a bride about to throw a bouquet – looks at her pale flexible lightly animated face, perpetually caught in a little loop of joy – and thinks, for some reason, of Sasha.

He shakes her out of his head.

Naomi looks around. She's only been here once before. Seems like they've upgraded the interior . . . There were always canals at ground level, but now a second canal system, suspended on delicate, ornate pillars, sweeps high across the space. A gondola moves past, above them, the mechanical gondolier singing.

They stop, and lean against a thin pre-stressed concrete pillar painted to look like marble. Naomi is trembling.

'That's crazy,' she says. 'They can track us from fifteen thousand feet. Twenty-five thousand. They can *kill* us from twenty-five thousand feet, can't they?'

'Yes,' says Colt.

'So why did—'

'They weren't tracking us visually,' says Colt. 'Not at first. I think we *had* fooled them. But we must have been tagged some other way. Some bug, low powered, where they need to get close to pick up the signal. Picked us up going out the door, lost us again. They couldn't actually identify us. They were just trying to triangulate it, to re-establish visual identification.'

Colt runs through all the possibilities. Where could they have been tagged? Naomi is thinking the same, echoes his thoughts, 'But how, where . . .'

'In the base. We must have been tagged with one of those old military Bluetooth bugs, to keep track of us . . . They have sensors at each doorway, so they always know who is where in the building . . . but why didn't Dad put our IDs on a stop list? He could have used the bug to stop us escaping . . .'

'But they didn't follow me,' says Naomi.

'Exactly. It must be on my clothes. Or . . .' Colt pauses. Tries to think his way through all the possible options.

'You were carrying my clothes,' says Naomi.

'Oh beans. Yeah.'

'You can swear if you want,' says Naomi, and gives a jerky laugh. 'Special circumstances.'

Colt shrugs. 'I just don't like swearing. Don't really want to transform that.'

They find a quiet aisle, and tip their old clothes on the floor. Examine them, inch by inch.

'Here.'

She lifts up the fine angora wool top. Parts the fibres gently.

Colt leans forward, to see.

Like a black tick, deep in the wool.

'He slapped me on the back, hard,' she says. 'It must have been then . . . Did he try the same thing with you?'

Colt shuts his eyes, thinks back. 'No.'

They go over every item of clothing again. Nothing else.

So. That was it.

Naomi looks around the immense, oblivious space of the Venetian. 'Why is nobody trying to capture us? The drones could alert the police. FBI. Whoever. NDSA, I mean it's an NDSA *program*. They could catch us in a few minutes.'

'I don't think the system is set up to capture us,' says Colt. 'To capture anybody. I don't think it's coordinated with the police, or the FBI, or anybody at all. Not at the human level.' Colt sways on his feet. His new brain is eating energy faster than he can supply it.

'But it's taken over some of their equipment . . . hasn't it?'

'Yes, there's clearly a set of protocols allowing that. But there isn't full integration. Dad launched it early . . . I don't think what's chasing us officially exists.'

Naomi is worrying her way through all the implications. But Colt has already finished doing that. He begins to tap his thighs lightly. Grind his teeth.

'If Ryan had a bug tracking us in the base . . .' says Naomi, 'why didn't they just capture us there? He could have told them . . .'

'I think he let us go, Mama.' Colt hesitates. 'I don't think he wants you arrested. I think he wants you dead.'

He'll have to go back online. He needs more data, and the drones already know he's here. They could block him, but he's pretty sure they won't.

OK, go.

He's searching while he's talking to her.

And he's on.

Yeah, they're not blocking him, but that's not a good sign. They're monitoring him instead, his searches, what he's looking for. Clues to where he'll go next, what he'll do.

He tries encrypting, decrypting, camouflaging himself, running dummy searches . . .

'OK,' says Colt. 'I have a plan.'

'What?'

'We need it to think it has won.'

'How?'

'We need it to kill us.'

'And how can we do that?'

Colt tells her.

Naomi doesn't like it. But she doesn't have a better plan.

105

They head back to the wedding fair in the foyer. As they walk, Colt wonders should he flip up his visor, or take off his helmet to look more normal . . . But so many tourists are wearing shades, antivirus masks, respirators, full-face privacy masks, head cams, or gaming gear of some kind that there seems no point. Hell, a lot of them are in his gameworld, right now. He blends in fine.

In the foyer, the white silk dresses glow in the UV light. Like ghosts, thinks Colt.

The big man in charge puts down his Coke, steps out from behind his stand, greets them.

Colt keeps quiet, as Naomi jokes and laughs with the big man.

Every time the big man laughs, his ultra-white teeth fluoresce in the UV light of the display.

False teeth, thinks Colt. All of them.

Behind the big man a male couple, holding hands, wander up to the two male mannequins, locked in a loving embrace. The mannequins, triggered by human proximity, turn their faces towards the couple, and smile, and their teeth fluoresce too.

'So, how much if you threw in the mannequins?' she says. 'The groom and bride set.'

'The mannequins aren't for sale.'

'This is the Strip,' says Naomi. 'Everything's for sale.'

He laughs, and looks at her tits.

'I need them for a practical joke on my husband,' says Naomi, pretending to smile. Hide how you feel, it'll only push up the price. 'Name a price.'

He smiles an extra mile of teeth, and names a price. A Vegas price. A 'fuck off and stop bothering me' price.

I guess I didn't hide my dislike enough.

They don't have that much cash. Nothing like.

Colt grabs her elbow. She follows him.

'How much do you have?' says Colt.

She shows him.

'OK.'

He takes her money with his good hand, buys some chips at the machine. Goes to a low-stakes blackjack table. Watches for a long time. The other players; the handsome, Italian-looking robo-dealer; the cards. A long, long time, till the packs of cards have begun to reappear. Till he starts to pick up the patterns.

The patterns behind the patterns.

Anyone with a math degree and a memory used to be able to make a good living at the blackjack tables. It's just statistics and card-counting. Then some guys from Yale got greedy and messed it up for everyone, and the casinos started using more decks of cards. It's impossible for a player to track the patterns now. A normal player.

Colt's seen enough. He starts betting. Small stakes.

Then, three big hands in a row.

Win. Win. Win.

He stops when he's won so much that another win would trigger the casino's reporting rules.

They cash in their chips, and go back to the wedding fair, with their fistfuls of crisp notes.

The big man counts the notes, twice. Tests every one.

'Yeah. Take them.' He doesn't smile.

The mannequins smile, though, surprised, delighted; over-joyed.

Surprised, delighted; overjoyed.

Surprised, delighted; overjoyed . . .

Colt switches off their facial animation units, and the smiles freeze mid-cycle. He carries the male mannequin to the elevator. Some spots of blood have seeped through the glove on his damaged hand, but the pain isn't so bad now. His brain must be getting used to it, discounting it. Good. Colt comes back for the other mannequin, while Naomi holds the lift doors open.

As he carries the smiling bride across the floor to the elevator, a security guard comes up to him.

Colt tenses.

'You with the wedding fair?' says the security guard.

Naomi runs up, 'Yes.'

The security guard helps them get the bride into the elevator.

*

They rise in silence, up to the level of the raised canal. The gondolas. Naomi reaches out, across the two mannequins lying face up on the floor, and takes Colt's wounded hand.

Colt's hand jerks in her grasp. It's a lot of signal. Not the jolt of pain, the tingle of damaged nerve ends. That's OK. It's all that warm skin. And emotion, emotion. His mother's touch. Too big, too much.

But he doesn't pull his hand away. He can handle it.

The mannequins smile up at the mirrored ceiling.

Ping.

The doors *shuuuush* open.

Colt carries the male, then the female mannequin to the edge of the elevated canal.

They are a few yards short of where the canal leaves the casino and emerges into sunlight, two storeys up. He studies the curve of concrete and water.

Yes.

It swings far outside the building, in a long, lazy loop, supported on slim reinforced concrete legs, everything painted to look like marble, high above the pavements and the cars, before swinging back inside the casino again a little lower down. The flow of water down the gentle slope draws the mock gondolas out and around and back inside.

Couples and families sit in the boats, serenaded by startlingly lifelike robot gondoliers.

'They used to have real gondoliers,' says Naomi. 'Ah well. I guess trained opera singers are expensive.'

A couple step out of a gondola.

Good.

No point being discreet; fast is more important.

Colt throws the bag of old clothes onto the seat of the gondola, to stop anyone else taking it.

The departing couple pause, and the man pushes the woman up against a marbled pillar, kisses her. The woman, as they kiss, stares over the man's shoulder at Colt, at the mannequins.

'Hi, lady,' says Colt.

'It's a contest, for the wedding fair,' says Naomi.

Her partner breaks off the kiss. 'Oh,' says the woman, and wipes her mouth with the back of her hand. The man takes her other hand and they walk off. The woman glances back.

Colt smiles at her, and she looks abruptly away.

OK, strip the clothes off the mannequins first, goddamn it, it won't . . . there's *another* button in behind there. How many buttons can it take to keep up a pair of pants? Who *makes* clothes like this any more?

Colt realizes his mother is looking across at him, over the white wedding dress, the black wedding suit.

'Everything?' she says.

'Everything,' he says. 'Just in case. Pattern recognition. They could be identifying the metal studs in your pants.'

It's much quieter up here than down on the main floor, but there are still some people wandering to and from the lifts. Colt and Naomi move a few yards, until a row of short, bushy trees in large terracotta pots screen them. They wait till there's no one in sight, strip quickly, and put on the wedding outfits.

Then they dress the mannequins in their old clothes.

Naomi says, 'They look great.'

Colt studies them. Thinks about it.

There's a problem.

Colt shakes his head. 'They'll look wrong in the infrared. Too cold to be alive.'

Naomi sits down, hard. 'Oh Colt.'

'It's OK, Mama,' he says. He slides his old trousers off the plastic groom again. 'We'll leave our old clothes here.' He strips down the groom. Naomi strips the bride. Colt pushes the old clothes into the deep shadow behind the terracotta pots. Stands up.

'Where are we going?' says Naomi.

'This way.'

Colt, in his wedding suit, drags the naked groom away from the canal. Naomi glances back at the shadow hiding her old clothes.

Colt says, 'If the drones are following the movement of the bug from outside, if the signal's that strong, and they have a plan of this building . . . I don't want to them to follow our movements.'

Naomi nods. Picks up the naked bride.

106

They haul the mannequins to the nearest restroom. The Venetian gets a lot of customers from the Middle East; the restrooms are still gendered.

But Colt and Naomi have begun to adjust to the urgencies of their new reality and they hardly glance at the sign.

Inside, Colt sits the plastic bodies on the tiles, under the old-fashioned warm-air hand-dryers, and sets the dryers roaring.

'Mine's getting hot already,' says Naomi, over the noise of the dryer, her hand flat to the thick plastic of the forehead.

'That's only the surface. Make it hotter, right through. All over.' He pulls off the groom's hand. Grunts as the crusted blood of his own wounded hand cracks open again, and the nerves sing in pain. He examines the male figure's fingers and palm. Hefts it. 'Thick plastic. That's good. Won't cool too fast.' Colt pulls off the groom's wig with a long *riiiip* of Velcro. 'This hair needs to be shorter.'

'I have nail scissors,' says Naomi.

Riiiip.

Naomi takes both wigs to the sink, and starts to trim.

The door swings open, fast. A blonde woman of about thirty

walks in briskly, holding a half-full cocktail glass. A pink umbrella and two orange straws roll from side to side as the red drink sloshes with each step.

She sees Naomi in a wedding dress, squatting on the floor, chopping the hair off a wig. The woman slows.

Sees Colt standing by the sink; he swings his hands behind his back – there's something wrong with one of them – she stops.

Double-take, as she realizes two other people are sitting naked under the dryers.

She steps backwards so fast that, though she holds her glass level, a little red slops over the edge, drips on the white tiles.

'Woooh . . .' A triple-take, as she realizes the two naked figures are mannequins. 'Oh, sorry, hah, I thought . . .'

'It's a contest, for the wedding fair,' says Naomi, standing up.

'Oh.'

'We'll be out of here in a minute.'

'No, fine, carry on.' The woman sucks hard on one of the orange straws until half the remaining red liquid has vanished. She steps into a cubicle, and locks it.

Naomi and Colt turn the mannequins every minute or so beneath torrents of hot air. Heat the bride and groom till the warmth gets deep inside the thick plastic.

Once, both dryers cut out at the same time, and, in the second his hand is travelling toward the sensors to switch the dryers back on, Colt hears the woman in the cubicle emit a dry heave, or a sob.

Data he can't analyse. Is what's happening in there physical, or emotional? He's *heard* it but he doesn't know what it *means*.

She does it again. Pukes? Weeps? It distracts him, he can't focus, though he knows he has to . . .

But he feels rising panic at the gap in knowledge, until, finally, he groans, and moves towards her cubicle.

Ducks his head, to look under her door.

The soles of her shoes. She kneels there, yes, head over the toilet bowl, but it tells him nothing. Another dry heave, or a sob.

White cubicle.

Black box. Encrypted. Compressed. No codec.

Colt feels a hand on his shoulder, and whips around.

His mother.

She looks him in the eye, and whispers, 'She'll be OK, Colt.' He goes to speak, but Naomi talks over him. 'Or she won't. But it's her life. We can't save everyone.' Awkward, kneeling on the tiles, Naomi hugs him tight.

Even though it's too much, even though all his skin is screaming from the warm touch, too much of it, all over, way too much signal, like he's on fire, he lets himself be hugged.

She lets go.

The flames that almost overwhelmed him die down.

They go back to the mannequins. From behind them comes another sob. Colt waves his hand.

The dryers roar.

*

Colt puts the palm of his good hand to the naked body; forehead, chest, groin; kneecap, elbow, hand. 'They're hot enough.'

'OK.'

Naomi slaps the wigs back onto the Velcro.

Colt's right hand aches now, and pain shoots up his arm, as he drags the male mannequin back to the gondola.

It's gone.

Uh oh. And the mannequins are cooling.

Colt hauls out the old clothes from behind the palm tree. He and Naomi dress the warm plastic bodies quickly.

And now another gondola is drifting by, with a couple in it. Small, young, pale, holding hands. Their mechanical gondolier is between arias, smoothly steering.

'Can we have your gondola?' asks Colt, trotting alongside. They stare at him in incomprehension. He says it again louder, and they shrink back in their seat.

Naomi sighs, waves most of the remaining blackjack dollars at the couple, indicates with her thumb, out; smiles a question.

They get out, take the money, bow, start walking away.

The robot gondolier sings after them, '*Svanì per sempre il sogno mio d'amore. / L'ora è fuggita, e muoio disperato!*'

The couple stop politely, and turn back, to listen.

Colt can't carry out his plan with bystanders watching, but the mannequins are cooling and he's running out of time. He grinds his teeth and drums his fingers on his thighs as the robot gondolier sings on, its mobile, alarmingly realistic face emoting strongly.

'E muoio disperato! E non ho amato mai tanto la vita, tanto la vita!'

Colt autotranslates it, to distract himself, to stop himself smashing the robot in front of witnesses. 'For ever, my dream of love has vanished. / That moment has fled, and I die in desperation. / And I die in desperation! / And I never before loved life so much, / loved life so much!'

The swell of the voice summons a vision of Sasha, shimmering through the water that abruptly fills Colt's eyes.

Everything's reminding him of her. This is *ridiculous.*

Finally it's over. The couple clap politely and walk away.

The robot gondolier greets Naomi and Colt and the two mannequins, as Colt blinks, and dabs his eyes dry with the long tail of the tuxedo.

Naomi holds the gondola steady in the slowly flowing water, while Colt positions the plastic man and woman wearing their clothes, their hair. Their bug. He switches their faces back on, and they smile up at Colt, surprised, delighted; overjoyed.

Colt steps back, looks at the plastic couple. Tries to empathize with a drone at maybe fifteen thousand feet, hi-def zoom, doing optical recognition, infrared, clothes, hair. Another drone at five hundred feet, checking for a radio frequency.

OK. Run the program. Be the code.

Infrared. Not perfect. Within the parameters. It'll do.

Clothes, yes.

Good pattern-matching.

No.

Something is wrong.

Everything's wrong.

'Too stiff.'

He hauls them out, bends their limbs till they are crouching; places their hands over their moving faces. Slides them back inside. Now they seem to be hiding their faces; and the movement of the smiles transmits a little movement to the hands, the arms. Not much, it's subtle, but they look more alive. Better. 'OK.'

Naomi lets go.

The gondola drifts off down the elevated canal, floating towards the exit, the light. The gondolier begins to sing.

'What now?' says Naomi.

'Now we find out if we're just under surveillance. Because if it's more than that . . . They'll never get a cleaner shot.'

The nose of the gondola moves out into sunlight on water that now sparkles. The boat's bright silk canopy shades the still couple, crouched low.

As the sunlight hits the robot gondolier at the back of the boat, he shifts into falsetto, hits a high C, and holds it.

'I guess they do have better range,' says Naomi.

A drone – small, black, quadcopter, just cameras, sensors – drops from the sky almost immediately and stops in place, low, beside the couple. The immune system must have detected the movement of the bug inside the building; predicted this exit. The small drone circles, gets the angles, triangulates. Identifies the weak bug signal, the clothes, the hair. The patterns. Backs off.

Calls the strike.

The gondola vanishes in a blast that takes down a hundred yards of elevated fake marble canal. Broken concrete, shredded silk, vaporized water, plastic mannequin pieces, and shattered carbon-composite fragments of gondola all make a spherical bloom in mid-air, from a white-hot single point that gets bigger and prodigiously bigger so that Colt and Naomi duck reflexively. Even at this distance, the blast's pressure wave hurts their ears and lungs.

At either side of the great gap where the gondola had been, rods of reinforcing steel sway down, and shed lumps of concrete, and bound back up again as, from the nearer, higher side, water pours over the broken lip around the swaying rods and down, in a short-lived waterfall, smacking off the concrete plaza below, till all the closed circuit's waters are exhausted as the pump brings up nothing but hiccups of air.

Naomi feels like being sick, and feels like laughing. The two impulses battle queasily within her, so that she giggles and gags a little at the same time. Her chest feels punched, and her ears ache and ring.

'Well,' said Colt. 'I suspect they've decided that we are a threat.'

Naomi studies his shy, embarrassed face. He glances back at her and smiles.

He made a joke.

She feels dizzy for a moment with relief, pleasure, excitement; the same rush she got when he finally, *finally*, spoke his first word.

Something's fixed.

107

And now we are dead, thinks Naomi, over and over.

The vision of their old clothes, their old selves, evaporating, vaporizing, vanishing before her eyes in the bright, expanding explosion . . . it loops and loops in her mind, her heartbeat and breathing quickening each time.

And now we are dead . . .

Oh . . . Pleasure floods through her. It's shockingly intense, it's ecstatic.

They leave the Venetian separately, through different doors, and rendezvous three casinos away. Embrace at a junction, in their wedding clothes. Colt is puzzled to find he hardly minds the burning sensation across acres of skin as she holds him. He's changing . . .

Other pedestrians smile at the newlyweds. Colt overhears an elderly couple, the wife whispering to the husband, 'He seems a little young, but hey, this is Vegas.'

Staying in the crowds, going with the flow, Colt and Naomi move on foot, as far and as fast as they can. They get off the Strip as soon as the crowds start to thin.

Finally they stop, in some anonymous street.

Naomi tries to think, to plan, what to do next, but nothing happens in her head. It's like she's put on the spotlights and lit the stage, and no one has appeared on it.

Overload? No. Not just that.

'I need to eat,' she says.

*

They slip into a mall, along a wide, low concourse, into a cheap sushi restaurant. Naomi stands there, studying the big, colourful wall menu.

She's so tired.

She frowns, and points at some salad side dishes, to lift her a little.

Points at some sushi items.

Colt points at the extra-spicy wasabi.

Naomi points at 'Pay in Cash'.

The pictures light up on the wall menu, acknowledging their order.

They sit.

The waitbot brings the food to the table. It's skinned as R2D2, to advertise the newly refurbished Star Wars casino.

Naomi leaves the cash on the tray that sits on top of its head.

It chirps politely, in a cute, scrambled, R2D2 voice. Prints a traditional paper receipt. Wheels woozily off.

People are staring at them.

Look down, don't meet their eyes.

She picks up her chopsticks.

Colt pushes his food away, stands up. 'Got to check something.'

He doesn't wait for her response, just walks out of the restaurant, into the flow of people moving through the mall. Naomi bites back her questions, and watches him till the river of strangers carries him around a curve and out of sight.

She pokes at her food with a chopstick.

Breaks it into smaller and smaller pieces.

Eventually she lifts a tiny piece of rice and beef towards her mouth; but the smell of meat reminds her of the lab, and she puts the chopsticks back down. She shakes her head, to get rid of the memory of the warm metal-and-meat smell. The sight, the sound, of the little cobalt-steel buzz saw she used to use, to cut open the skulls of lab mice for autopsies.

When he comes back safe, she's been on a low simmer of anxiety and anger for five minutes, and she's so relieved she almost snaps at him.

He sits down. 'They're still tracking us,' he says.

Her anger evaporates. 'Oh, Colt.' He looks so serious. So grown up. 'We've dumped our clothes, the bug. It thinks we're dead. How can it still track us?' Her hunger comes back, fear-flavoured now. She eats the mess on her plate, too fast, gagging, like it's her last chance.

He sips his plastic cup of water.

She checks his plate surreptitiously, because she always does.

He's eaten nothing. But he must be starving by now . . .

'Did you eat while you were underground?' she says. 'Anything?'

'No . . .' Colt frowns, to remember. He doesn't usually bother remembering food. Ah, hang on . . . 'Yes. Nothing much. A little cake. Couple of cupcakes . . . A plate of cupcakes.'

'Pomegranate.'

'Yes.'

'Lot of seeds.'

'Yes.' He realizes what she's saying, and stands up.

She says it anyway. 'They weren't all seeds.'

'I need a bag,' says Colt. 'Plastic bag. Anything.'

They walk out into the mall.

Colt digs around in a trash container screwed to the wall.

As he does, Naomi reads the sticker on its orange side, to keep her eyes occupied; to stop them from wildly spinning around and around, looking for enemies in every direction.

This Waste Receptacle is fully compliant with US Safety Standard 343-78-55A. It sniffs for explosives, biological agents, chemical agents, and radioactive materials.

Your Safety Is Our Concern.

Colt finally finds a discarded plastic bag. He briskly swings it by the handles, to fill it with air. It opens like a parachute, making a crispy, satisfying noise, with a fat, thump ending.

Colt laughs. The noise was so *right*, it's made his teeth tingle.

He closes the neck of the bag, squeezes to check it for rips, holes. It bulges like a balloon.

Airtight.

Good.

He peels off his bloody glove, his clean glove, and dumps them in the trash.

They look for a restroom. The nearest one is closed for repair, a puddle of water coming out from under its locked door.

When they do find a restroom, all the stalls are full. Six men queueing.

The restroom beside it, women are queueing out the door. The women stare at them.

They keep going, walking faster; find a service door held open by an abandoned bucket and mop; walk through.

Down a shadowy service corridor. Lights only triggered as they pass. Someone has stolen every second lightbulb.

Through a fire door, into a vast, dimly lit storage area. The lights brighten as they enter.

Rolling steel doors in the walls, some of them high, above ramps, for unloading container trucks.

Pallets.

Nobody around.

Colt loops one handle of the plastic bag over the silvery knob of the fire door, pulls the bag's other handle out with one hand so the bag yawns open in front of him.

'Here,' says Colt. 'It'll do.'

He sticks his finger down his throat, bends over. Vomits into the bag.

Does it again.

It's easier the second time; the smell of puke helps him puke.

The sound of his retching bounces off the concrete walls, the steel doors, and comes back to him. It reminds him of the noise some monster made, in a cave, in an old episode of *Doctor Who*. A liquid, coughing noise, all reverb and echo.

After the fourth time, his stomach is empty. Colt frowns.

'They could be in my intestines by now.'

'You need to clear it all out.'

'Wait . . .

Colt reaches down into the bag, takes something delicately between finger and thumb. 'Oh *boy*. Look at this. Very clever design.'

'Jesus, Colt, I don't want to look into a bag of puke.'

But Colt has lifted what he wants out of the bag. He checks his pockets for tissues. None. Of course, they're not his pockets. He'd forgotten he was wearing a wedding suit.

That's why everyone was staring at them.

He tugs at the silk handkerchief in his breast pocket.

It slides out; it's not a full handkerchief; just a triangle of silk attached to a card the shape of the pocket.

Damn . . . But it'll be enough . . .

'*Jesus*,' says Naomi vehemently.

Colt looks at her, startled. Worried.

Is she angry? She's never angry, not really.

'Sorry, Colt,' she says. 'But at that price, the handkerchief should be real.'

Oh.

Relief . . .

He uses the scrap of silk to dry what he has found.

'See?' He pushes it under Naomi's nose. 'The black bit. Smaller than a seed. That's the transmitter. And those tiny metal fronds?'

'Where?'

They are almost too fine to see. Colt turns his finger, and they catch the light, thin as spider silk.

'The bug must go in looking just like a seed. Disguised. Organic coating. Smooth. But the acid in my stomach stripped away the outer shell, and released these filaments. And the *filaments* react with the *stomach acid* to produce electricity . . .' He peers closer. 'That's brilliant.'

'Oh,' says Naomi. She leans in closer, too, despite herself. 'Kind of like the old zinc batteries in my mother's hearing aid.'

'Really? How did they work?' says Colt.

This is nice. This is like it used to be. Talking about science with Mama.

His brain feels so weary. If he half-closes his eyes in the low light of the loading bay, he could be in the cave of his bedroom, drowsily asking his mama questions, not wanting to go to sleep.

Tell me something, Mama. About what? Anything.

Naomi shakes her head.

'Tell me, Mama.'

Naomi sighs. Smiles. 'When my mother installed the battery, she pulled off a tab, and exposed it to the air,' she says. 'The zinc inside reacted with the ambient oxygen; so most of the chemical weight wasn't in the battery. Each battery got through about twenty cubic centimetres of air per hour. Just, you know, the air that floated through it.'

'Cool,' says Colt, doing the math in his head for a zinc–oxygen reaction. Mmmm. Nice. 'Really high power output, and almost no weight.'

'Yes, exactly,' says Naomi. 'If they had to incorporate the weight of the oxygen into the physical battery, they'd have weighed twenty times as much.'

'That's good design,' says Colt.

'Yes,' says Naomi. 'After she'd told me how they worked, I was kind of fascinated. She'd let me pull off the tabs, as a treat.'

She leans in even closer over the tracking device on Colt's finger, intrigued despite herself, despite the smell. 'This bug's even better,' she says. 'He's floating in a sea of battery acid . . . *Very* high power output.' From a bug the size of a seed . . . It's hard not to admire something so elegant. 'I wonder would it even work, though, lower down the alimentary canal? Once it's left the stomach?'

He wishes he could just drift off to sleep like this, listening to Mama, asking a question whenever she stops talking.

His hand is sore.

She would kiss it, and it would get better. It wouldn't just *feel* better, it would *get* better.

He used to mix her up with Jesus in his mind.

When he heard the story of Jesus curing the leper, or bringing Lazarus back from the dead, he would see a man standing beside his mama, both in long white dresses, and they would kiss the corpse back to life, Mama and Jesus, working together, kissing it better . . .

A yard away, airgapped, Naomi is also thinking of the past. So many hours spent poring over some insect, or plant, or little piece of technology, patiently answering Colt's questions. Colt, totally engaged.

The closest I ever got to him. The best hours of my life.

And Naomi remembers where they are, and why they are examining a brilliantly designed bug on Colt's fingertip.

She gives a little involuntary snort of grief and despair. Again, as sharp as ever, the shock: her son is going to die.

Colt frowns and looks closer at the filaments.

They're at the limits of visibility.

'I think they have little hooks on the end, to anchor them in the stomach wall,' he says.

'Oh God,' says Naomi.

'To stop them from going down your digestive tract,' says Colt, 'and out the other end.'

Naomi puts her hand on his shoulder. He shrugs it off, automatically. He doesn't seem upset, just interested.

'It keeps them in place, in the battery acid, too,' he says. 'I guess the surge when I vomited broke them free. But . . . Damn.'

'So there might be bugs still trapped in your stomach . . .'

'Well . . . in one way it's good. They probably aren't in my intestines. But yeah, it means I might not have puked them all.'

'How can we check?'

'Find out what frequency they're transmitting on.' Colt puts the bug to his ear, grins. 'And see if there's still one inside me, transmitting.'

He flicks the clean bug back into the plastic bag of stomach acid, so it can power up, transmit.

He flicks down his visor; automatically sets it to reflective, and she mourns the loss of his face.

OK, he thinks. Any receiver can be retuned . . .

He finds a piece of commercial code in the helmet's own library; runs a scan up and down the radio frequencies.

There's a hell of a lot of everything, the mumble of the universe, but none of it loud enough to be the bugs. At that range, a couple of feet away from the helmet, they should be screaming. So either they aren't transmitting in the normal frequency ranges, or the bugs are dead.

He doesn't think they're dead.

He frowns, and swiftly rewrites the code.

OK, now he needs a bigger receiver.

Naomi watches patiently, as Colt looks around for something that might act as an aerial. She's learned a lot of patience, since Colt's birth.

An electronics and plastics recycling bin, great. He flips up the lid, roots around in it. Deep down in the debris at the bottom, he finds a broken set of old-style earbuds; *really* old, the type with a cord you plug in.

Excellent.

He plugs the cord into the helmet's universal socket; pulls off the buds, exposes the wire. He looks around.

There.

He studies the big rolling steel doors of the loading bay, perfect.

He wraps the wire around an exposed steel rivet head. Runs the scanner again, and finds a screaming, way out in the boondocks, beyond any commercial frequency.

How do they do that, with something so small?

Doesn't matter. The bag is broadcasting on three slightly different frequencies. The bag; or his guts. He unwraps the wire from the rivet. He can still hear the ghost of the signals, as he stands beside the bugs like this. Good.

He hangs the bag of vomit on a coat hook beside the steel service door, and walks away from the bag, to the far end of the loading bay. As he walks, all three signals drop off.

The square of the distance. Perfectly normal.

Outside, there's the sound of a truck backing up to a loading ramp, and the *peep peep* of its reversing signal is louder now than the bugs. Colt breathes out a huge sigh, runs back, gets the bag, and returns to his mother.

'That's all of them,' says Colt. 'Three, in the bag.' He waves it at her. 'There's nothing in my system.'

Naomi breathes out a tremendous sigh of relief.

Wow, light-headed.

She hadn't even noticed she'd been holding her breath.

'Now we have to get rid of these . . .' says Colt, and walks back towards the service corridor they just came down.

With a whine and clatter, a steel door starts rolling upward, and a sharp rectangle of bright yellow light expands across the floor of the loading bay.

A guy with a big red beard ducks in, under the rising door, and doesn't see them for a moment in the gloom. Colt has time to pull open the fire door, and disappear into the service corridor.

But Naomi is too far from it; freezes.

'Hey, lady,' says the guy with the beard, 'I think you might be lost.'

'I think you might be right,' says Naomi. 'I was looking for the bathrooms.'

'Uh huh.'

He studies her tits and ass. Ugh . . . Naomi gives a little shake of her head, to dislodge an abrupt, furious image of him smashed and bleeding.

'They're a little tricky to find,' he says. 'I can show you . . .'

'No, thanks.' It comes out with hard edges.

'Sure. Sure.' He backs off. 'They're that way,' he indicates the fire door, the service corridor, 'all the way down, and left. Out in the mall.'

She nods her thanks.

He walks reluctantly away, and up a ramp.

Pulls a chunky, old-fashioned device out of his back pocket, taps it. A second loading door rises, with a rattle of metal slats, exposing the back of his truck. He taps again, and the remote unlocks the truck's back doors, and swings them open. Rubbing his beard vigorously with the heel of his free hand, he studies the bright screen of the chunky device.

Naomi walks quietly into the shadows towards the service corridor. The fire door swings open just as she gets to it, and Colt emerges, puts a finger to his lips. Points. Naomi looks back.

The bearded driver scans a code on the truck door with the device, scans a piled pallet just inside the back door of the truck, and grunts in satisfaction. He removes the pallet with a small lifter, brings it down the ramp, and leaves it with some other stacked pallets.

As soon as the driver has his back to them, Colt drifts from Naomi's side, out of the shadows, into the loading bay, and throws something into the back of the truck.

Runs back to Naomi's side, freezes.

The man returns, locks the back of the truck. As he walks out of the warehouse, the warehouse doors slowly slide closed.

Through the thin, sheet-metal warehouse walls, they hear the truck pull away from the loading bay, and roar off.

'The bugs,' says Naomi.

Colt nods. 'To the drones, it should look like we're inside the truck.'

'We're clear?'

'Maybe. Maybe.'

108

They leave the mall separately, Colt first, then Naomi two minutes later. She finds him where they agreed, at a corner two blocks away. In the green shade of an awning, outside a coffee shop.

And Naomi's euphoria – Colt is there, alive – lurches into reverse when she sees his face. So serious. No, this isn't over. How can it ever be over? Only their deaths will satisfy the machine.

'Mama, I want to go home.'

'I know, Colt, I know,' and she puts her arm around him, but he pushes it away.

'No, Mama. I *need* to go home.' Colt is about to keep speaking, but . . . wait.

Naomi's face just changed.

He studies her face in the cool green light coming through the awning. It's not a frown. It's more subtle. Eyes a little wider. Face titled slightly.

Wow, he can read his mother's face. Wow. She just asked him why. She said 'why' with her *face*.

He feels the world expand and bend and warp.

Holy shit, everybody's face is speaking all the time.

It's like he's gained sight after being born blind.

'You're thinking, why?' he marvels.

She nods, says yes, smiles.

It's like her face has jumped from 2D into 3D.

It's vivid.

It's too much.

He closes his eyes. He'll deal with it later.

Why.

'Because all my stuff is there,' he says. 'And my servers. I need more processing power. Offline. Not in the cloud.'

The cloud is full of government. The cloud is full of spies. The cloud is full of pattern-recognition software, looking for his patterns of activity. Looking for him. To punish him. They've built the God of Exodus and Leviticus, he thinks. He opens his eyes, stares at his mother's living, speaking face.

'What will happen when they find the bugs?' says Naomi. 'Just the bugs, and not us? They'll look for us at the house, won't they?'

'I have a plan. To deal with that. If it works . . .' He thinks it through one more time, all the details, all the possible problems. All the ways it could fail. 'If it works, then our house is the safest place we could be.'

And he feels a rush of the big emotion, the overwhelming one, the one he feels for his mother; he feels it for their home, his room; its warm, small bed, all the familiar smells and shapes and textures.

'And if it doesn't work?' says Naomi.

'Everybody dies in the end . . .' He shrugs. 'It's learning more about us all the time. If we just wander around . . .' He shrugs again. 'All we can do is drag out how long it takes them to catch us. The quicker we can get home, the better our chances of beating it—'

'OK. Then we need transport,' says Naomi. 'Hire a car . . .'

'No debit. No credit. No credit cards. Nothing they can trace.'

Of course. 'Sorry. Cash . . .'

'They'll need ID, and we'll still be on the system . . .'

'We could . . .' She can't bring herself to say steal. 'Take? Maybe? A car?'

'Yeah . . . an old one, I guess. The new locking systems are hard to . . .'

The explosion bends the glass of the plate-glass window beside them so that their reflections ripple. There's a stab of pain in their ears; the awning convulses above them, as the shockwave snaps it into a tight arch. It holds the shape for a moment, then it falls back.

Further down the street, a paisley sun umbrella, lifted out of its stand, topples off a third-floor balcony. It zig-zags down slowly, like a psychedelic parachute, to land in the road.

Car alarms howl like electronic dogs, in an expanding ring around the blast zone.

For a moment, of course, they think that it was aimed at them.

It takes a few more seconds for the smoke and flame to rise high enough above the nearby buildings to be seen.

It's a big explosion.

Very big.

But many blocks away, on the Strip, out near the airport.

'The truck,' says Colt. 'They took out the truck.'

People are jostling through the door of the cafe, to look. Colt and Naomi move aside, deeper into the shadow under the canopy; lower their voices in the babble.

Colt sees a picture in his mind of the truck driver, his red beard.

'The driver . . .' Colt shivers; shakes the shiver off. 'The driver must have parked the truck. Left the truck. Away from traffic. A parking lot maybe . . .'

Why is he talking so much? What is he trying not to think?

There are connections being made, thoughts building up, it's like ants in his skull, itchy, he doesn't want to look at those thoughts.

But his mother has been making those connections too, slower maybe.

'Or maybe we've been raised from orange targets to red,' she says.

Colt closes his eyes but he sees the truck driver again, and now his beard is on fire. The fat of his skin is on fire.

'Maybe,' says Colt, and his jaw feels stiff and sore, muscles clenched tight. 'Maybe . . .'

'But . . .' Naomi pauses, trying to find the upside. '. . . they'll have to think we're dead now . . .'

'For a while.'

There's a song in Colt's head, a favourite of his mama's, she loves Johnny Cash.

'I shot a man in Reno . . . just to watch him die . . .'

A black BMW with tinted windows pulls up at the kerb beside them. Colt and Naomi both reflexively retreat deeper into the shadow beneath the canopy, till their backs are touching the glass.

The driver opens the door, and steps out onto the sidewalk.

A young Egyptian-looking man in a lightweight Italian suit.

He stands there, with his mouth very slowly opening wider and wider as he stares up at the sky beyond the Starbucks across the road, at the column of black, oily smoke that is still rising; at the flickers of dark orange flame that swirl inside it.

He's holding a bunch of physical keys.

Colt glances back at the BMW. Oh, cool. It's an old-style gasoline car; no self-drive, no safeties.

A rich man's car. No, a rich boy's toy.

The insurance must be horrendous . . .

'Hey, wheels,' says Colt.

By the time Naomi realizes what Colt means, it's too late, Colt has pushed through the crowd of pavement gawkers.

He taps the driver on the shoulder. 'Excuse me, sir, but we need your vehicle.'

The driver closes his mouth, turns and stares at Colt. This teenager with a damaged hand, in a tuxedo. Looks across at Naomi. 'What?' he says.

Oh shit, Naomi thinks. And I'm in a wedding dress.

'Disguise,' she says. 'Undercover operation.' She blushes furiously at the lie, at the Hollywood cliché.

'We'll return your car once we're done,' says Colt briskly. 'What's your number? We'll call to tell you where to pick it up . . . Quickly, please, sir.'

The driver, still holding his status-symbol keychain, awkwardly digs a black-leather wallet out of his pocket. He carefully tugs a business card free.

Colt stares at the card as it emerges. Wow. An actual card, on paper. This guy is a real retronaut.

A couple of classic plastic credit cards follow the business card from its slot. They fall to the ground.

Nobody bends to get them.

'Sorry,' says the driver. He holds out the business card to Colt.

'No problem,' says Colt magnanimously. 'Give it to her, she's in charge of recovery procedures.'

The driver gives Naomi the card.

'Thank you,' she says, and just manages to stop herself bowing.

Colt sniffs, as the driver withdraws his hand.

The driver smells nice. Sandalwood?

'You smell nice,' says Colt, and Naomi smacks her elbow into his ribs.

The driver is staring at him, not answering.

Oh yeah, he thinks I'm a cop. Or Secret Service. This is hard. Why do people think math is hard? It's easy to remember what is true. It's way harder to remember what other people think is true, but is not.

The driver's mouth opens and closes again, but he doesn't seem to know what to say. The keys, still in his hand, clink gently as he trembles.

Colt reaches out and takes the bunch of metal keys from his hand with so much confidence the driver allows it.

Colt tries to remove the car key from the bunch.

Owwa. Too much damage to the tendons of his right hand. Too difficult.

He hands the keys to Naomi. As she wrestles the key off a vintage enamelled metal keyring that says 'Lock Up Your Bunnies,' the driver crouches down to pick up his credit cards.

Colt says, 'It's OK, your car will be automatically covered by our insurance.'

'Thank you . . .' Something seems to occur to the driver. He stands up, holding the plastic cards. 'Which, ah, service? Unit? Are you?' he asks.

'NSA,' says Colt.

'Really?' says the driver, frowning. He brushes dust off the top card with his thumb. 'I thought they . . .'

'You never saw us and this never happened.'

'OK,' says the driver.

109

As Naomi drives off, she glances across at Colt as he puts on his seatbelt.

The inside of the car smells like the driver's cologne, plus leather from the seats. It's nice. It smells like a father, thinks Colt.

Naomi stares at him.

Colt has never told an out-and-out lie, even as a kid.

Once, when Donnie rang, Naomi asked Colt to answer the phone, to tell Donnie she wasn't there. But Colt couldn't do it; he gestured to her to go into another room, so he could say, truthfully, 'She isn't here.' When she didn't understand, didn't move, he moved; walked out the door, along the corridor, to the bathroom, making noncommittal noises into the phone. But Naomi followed him down the corridor, to hear what he was saying to Donnie. Colt swung the bathroom door shut in her face. She opened it a crack, peered in; Colt threw the phone into the toilet bowl, smashing the old-fashioned handset, and screamed at her. No, Colt didn't, couldn't lie.

'You told a lie,' she says.

'No, I didn't. Mama, we need to find somewhere quiet, and I can disable the car's transceiver . . .'

'You told him we were Secret Service!'

'No, he assumed we were. I told him the truth. We *do* need his vehicle. We *will* return it when we're done. You *are* in charge of recovery procedures, because I can't drive.'

'Come on, you said we were in the NSA!'

'He asked what service we were with. Well, we're not attached to any service or agency.'

'Sure, but you said . . .'

'I said NSA. It also stands for No Strings Attached.'

Naomi laughs. 'Jeeeez, Colt that's pretty close to a lie.'

'What I *meant*, in my *head*, when I *said* it, was No Strings Attached,' says Colt, dogged, flushed. 'It's not my fault he can't read my mind.'

They come out onto the Strip, and see the huge black glass pyramid of the Luxor is on fire.

'Oh God,' says Naomi.

Colt turns to watch, through the car's tinted glass, as they pass.

'That truck must have been making a delivery,' he says. 'It's around by the service entrance.'

The explosion has demolished the wall that used to hide deliveries. Stripped the leaves and smaller branches from the screen of trees, whose trunks smoulder.

The smoke pours lazily from the wreckage of the service area. Colt can't even make out the remains of the truck, it's so mixed up with other mechanical debris, other vehicles. A forklift. Some kind of small crane. A huge cylindrical metal tank, ripped open.

'He must have parked beside a gas truck,' says Colt. 'It went up, when they hit him.'

OK, that explains the size of the explosion. Windows have been blown out all the way up the south face of the pyramid.

'Will people have been hurt?' says Naomi.

'Of course.'

'Oh God.' She's losing control of her breathing. Breathe. Deeper. Slower. Yes. Breathe.

She goes to put the car on self-drive, while she composes herself; realizes she can't.

My God, there aren't even safeties to kick in, if someone runs across the road, or brakes hard up ahead. Got to concentrate. Keep driving. However bad you feel.

The windows of the BMW shiver in their frames. Another explosion, in the distance.

Colt waits till he can see the smoke. Works out where it is.

'They've hit New York, New York.'

'But . . .' Naomi wants to look around, but she's afraid to take her eyes off the road. '. . . why? We're not there, no bugs there . . .'

'Maybe we dropped a bug there, fell off your sweater,' says Colt.

'Maybe it's just losing its shit,' says Naomi.

'Hah. Yeah. Maybe . . .' He winds down the window.

Fire-engine sirens are screaming all over the city.

He concentrates, to work out where the fire engines are. They're moving, fast, towards the explosions; the car is moving at the human speed limit, south, past the airport, out of town . . . He disentangles the combined Doppler effect on each siren, locates them on his mental map.

And now he can hear the helicopters and the news drones approaching . . .

Three, no, four police cars go screaming by.

He winds up the window. Keep a low profile.

'Multiple explosions of unknown origin,' says Colt, like he's quoting some movie, some game. 'They'll have to shut down the whole city. Let's get out of here.'

They get out of there.

110

On the outskirts of the city, Colt says, 'Pull over. In there.'

She slows, fast, so that their heads bow involuntarily for a second, as though they are sharing a moment's prayer. Their seat-belts snap hard against their chests.

'Sorry,' says Naomi. She'd forgotten already, no safety over-rides to smooth things out. '*Sorry.*' She's so ridiculously tired . . . *Concentrate.*

And then the car is turning off the road, between piles of construction debris, onto an empty paved lot.

Colt gets out, glances around.

No, not construction. Demolition. A former gas station. Tax breaks couldn't save this one.

Even the pipes and walls of the underground tanks have been ripped out of the ground. Scrub bushes and weeds grow on the heaped debris, screening them from the road.

'What?' says Naomi, when she's brought the big old BMW to a halt.

'He's going to work it out, that we aren't Secret Service,' says Colt. 'He'll report the car, eventually. I need to make sure they can't track it.'

'Is that . . . hard?'

Colt smiles. 'Not on this thing.' He realizes he's been smiling a lot today.

Well, it's kind of great to have problems you can *solve*.

Colt opens the door, steps out into the heat.

Crickets chirp.

Behind him, on the road, he can hear trucks roar past, in tight, fuel-efficient convoys in the self-drive lanes, but the piles of debris hide them from sight. He takes a few steps back, studies the vehicle.

There's a reason he grabbed this one, when he had the chance. It's powered by gasoline . . .

E-cars have to be in constant identified electronic contact with the road. Conductive tyres, to draw the power; to get billed. It's impossible to hide where you are in an electric car. That's one reason libertarian states have resisted e-cars for so long.

Because with a pure gas model like this . . .

Disable the transceiver, and nobody knows where you are.

It's perfect. Silent. Invisible.

And this car is so old, it wasn't born with a transceiver. It's an add-on, in a unit that combines standard passive GPS with a transceiver, to transmit the car's location and status to the state and federal traffic AIs, and receive in return traffic and weather warnings and advice . . .

Colt lifts the hood.

'Found it.'

It's attached to the chassis. Small, black, unobtrusive.

He studies it.

'Damn.'

'What?'

'Not sure how I can hack it.'

He runs through the software options in his head. But how to even get access to it?

'Hack it?' says his mother.

Sometimes his mother can be so dumb. 'It's a sealed unit,' says Colt.

Naomi leans over Colt's shoulder. Studies the small black box. Frowns. 'Don't you just need to, you know . . . stop it working?'

'Yes, that's why I'm . . . oh!' Colt gets it. Blushes. 'Yeah.'

He walks over to the piled demolition debris. Finds a nice big rock that sits well in the palm of his hand.

He walks back to the car, leans in under the hood, and smacks the unit with the rock until there's nothing left on the chassis but a smear of plastic and a wire.

Oh, that felt good . . .

Colt throws the rock back on the pile of debris, sits into the black leather passenger seat, closes his eyes, and tries to clear his buzzing mind.

'Mama,' he mumbles, 'you should rest too.'

'But, if they're looking for us . . .'

'False economy, to keep going, this tired. We'll make mistakes. The Strip is on fire; they're swarming the city. They're sure we're still there. Just a nap, just a few minutes . . .'

She tilts back her seat. Tries.

Even with his eyes closed tight, Colt's visual system registers flashes of light, as neurons connect and trigger other neurons.

Naomi reaches out her hand, cautiously.

Her fingers brush against the back of his hand, and his hand reflexively jerks away from her. But he brings it back.

He slides his fingertips across the cool, dry skin of the palm of her hand, and his fingertips tingle like he is shedding charge into her, grounding himself.

She closes her hand around his fingers, and he ignores the impulse to pull away.

The lightning inside his brain calms down.

They fall asleep holding hands.

111

Colt wakes first. An hour, he thinks. I've slept for an hour. That's good.

It had been deep, no dreams. Like being dead.

Now his mind, his brain, comes back to life. Oh, jeeez . . .

It's like morning rush hour, in a city in the middle of a construction boom. Destruction, creation, confusion. Energy.

He waits a few minutes, with his eyes closed, to see if the riot in his brain will settle down.

It doesn't; but he slowly gets used to it. That'll do.

So, how will he hack into the immune system?

Into the drones' vast, collective mind . . .

The longer he leaves it, the harder it will be. It's learning so fast.

It's already improvising.

Taking over other systems.

The seeds, the bugs, weren't originally part of it. They were part of the base security. Short range.

Impressive; when the drones lost our visual pattern, they modified their behaviour. Split up, came in low; got close enough to use Bluetooth devices to find us. Bluetooth! Dinosaur tech . . .

He takes a deep breath.

Taps his knees in a calming rhythm. In 5/4 time. Like Grandad's jazz. Like that old vinyl record Mama used to play sometimes and cry, even though it was a happy song.

Take Five.

Colt reconnects his helmet to the world, and gets to work.

He could build himself a new, hyper-encrypted identity. But hyper-encryption draws serious attention.

So, he uses plain vanilla encryption that he knows they are automatically cracking and reading.

An ordinary-Joe online identity he built years before. The guy he's pretending to be is even called Joe. He uses the same useless, see-through, compromised tools everybody else uses.

They can see everything he is doing. They can see right through him. So they can't see him at all.

They have killed him. Now he is a ghost.

Aaaaand . . . go.

He breaks open a low-level NDSA program that one of the Russian kids who worked on the game cracked the year before. Borrows another identity as a trusted technician.

There must be factsheets for technicians, in some secure, read-only document silo.

He finds them. Reads the specs.

Oh, man.

Colt would probably have been able to hack into the immune system even if he hadn't been enhanced. It simply isn't finished yet. There are still coders' backdoors all over it.

Getting in isn't going to be the problem.

The problem will be switching it off.

It's a radically decentralized neural network.

It routes around damage.

There is no kill switch.

And all the drones are in communication with each other, all the time.

Spying on each other. Damn. Makes them *really* hard to hack.

No central base, because a base can be taken out, can be compromised. The entire information architecture for the immune system is run by the drones themselves.

Hmm, flexible, not fixed. Any spare capacity in any drone is assigned a task, sorting through the raw data the drones suck in through their sensors, filtering it, condensing it; running pattern recognition, predicting target movement.

Oh beans, it's *designed* to be unhackable. A lot of what should be software is hardware.

The whole thing is that strange mixture of state-of-the-art and the embarrassingly out-of-date that characterizes military and government technology.

He digs deeper, learns all he can. When he's ready, he takes a deep breath.

OK, he can't hack into the drone cloud's mind, the swarm intelligence itself; but he can see where the swarm touches down. Where it communicates with the ordinary electronic world. Actions are thoughts, and thoughts are actions. He can work out what it's thinking from what it's doing, where it's doing it.

The swarm piggybacks local cellphone towers; local Wi-Fi stations. Fibre relays.

And because the surveillance agencies have put backdoors into so many of these civilian systems, Colt can get in too.

He digs in, deep.

Skims metadata off the phone networks and analyses it, NDSA style. He even uses some of their code to do it, some of it code he stole off his father, which he knows is cheeky, and risky, but it's quicker than writing his own . . .

Uh oh.

The immune system is losing its mind.

Colt and Naomi have been pushed from orange to red.

And the system doesn't believe they are dead.

His mother stirs, in the passenger seat.

He must have said something out loud.

'We need to go, Mama,' he says. 'We need to go, now.'

'Mmmm,' she's not really awake, but she reaches for her seatbelt, puts it on. Sits for a moment, letting the fog clear from her head. Starts the car.

As Colt puts on his seatbelt, he blows on his hand, and the air incongruously whistles an off-note on the small hole in the exposed end of a bone. He winces.

'What's wrong?' she says, suddenly alert despite the tiredness.

'My hand's hot,' he says.

Oh dear Lord, she thinks. Infection?

She reaches out, takes his right hand, brings it to her face.

My God. Look how fast he's healing.

Too much flesh has been shot away to fully repair, yet. But new flesh is closing the edges of the hole. She resists an urge to kiss it. Pattern recognition, she thinks; an automatic firing of the neurons associated with taking his hand and raising it to her face.

Once, she would try to kiss him better, whenever he hurt his hand, as her mother had done for her. A nettle, a thorn, a bite, a burn . . . But he didn't like the touch, the kiss . . .

'Mama?'

She blinks. 'I think . . .' This is too fast, this is . . . I don't think it's infection. 'I think the new areas of your brain must be . . . rebuilding your other tissues, somehow. You're running hot, again, like you were when you first transformed . . .'

He's evolving, inside.

'What?' says Colt.

She realizes she's murmured that out loud.

'Mmmm,' says Naomi. 'Nothing. Thinking.'

They drive on. No transponder. No phones. No electronic ID. Nobody knows where they are.

Naomi is so tired, her mind gradually clears totally of all thought.

There is no thought.

And then, a thought, that seems to come from outside her. From outside the world.

This has happened before, not just once, but again and again.

In a moment so sharp and shocking that you may as well call it revelation, she knows what the voice says is true.

Buddha.

Confucius.

Jesus.

Mohammed.

Forty days in the desert. Forty days under a tree.

Purging.

Praying.

Dehydrating.

Meditating.

Clearing the body.

Clearing the mind.

And then, a chrysalis state.

After three days and nights, reborn.

Transformed.

The body heals itself. The mind heals itself. If you die, as Jesus did, you can self-repair.

My God. We can scientifically mass-produce Jesuses.

A new kind of human. Yet something like this has happened before; accidentally; sporadically; somehow. A mutation? An infection? Generating, midlife, new neurons, fresh connections . . . Does it only appear in the male line? Jesus, Buddha, Confucius . . . Could the mutation have been inherited? But they had no children.

And Mohammed's sons died as infants . . .

Her mind is a mess, she's exhausted, she knows that. But she doesn't think she's wrong.

Each time, before, it disrupted the world, it almost changed everything, but it was a little too early, conditions weren't quite right. They were like butterflies waking in winter.

This is going to happen all over the world. Soon.

A wave of Christs. Mohammeds. Buddhas.

What will happen, when we are all the messiah . . .
What can you do with such a thought?
Nothing.
She drives on.

*

After a while, Naomi says, 'This is such a great car.'

Colt says, 'Mmmm.' He isn't mentally present. Naomi reaches across and strokes his shoulder. 'Mmm?'

'We're going to be home soon,' says Naomi. 'And if the house is under observation, they'll see us.'

'Mmmm, yeah, I know. I'm working on it. Maybe slow down a little.'

Naomi slows down a little.

Colt works out just how long this is likely to take him.

And how long it will take to get home.

'A little slower.'

Slower? Naomi blows some air through her nose. 'How about I just take a loop through the hills,' she says, 'and come back to our place from the far side, through Penwick? They won't be expecting that.'

'Yeah, sure,' says Colt. 'But won't that be a little too much of a . . .'

Naomi puts her foot delicately on the accelerator, and presses.

'Wow,' says Colt.

They've just crossed the county line, back into Lincoln County. And there are no cops or speed traps or cameras out here, God bless their neighbours' libertarian hearts.

There had been cameras, briefly, but the locals shot them up. Claimed they'd mistaken them for jackrabbits. Local judge let them off.

So, just desert. Straight roads. Long curves. Roadrunner country. 'OK,' says Colt.

Naomi doesn't even look at the sky. She knows they aren't being observed, she can feel it. And it feels good.

Not just to have shaken off the drones.

My God, she thinks, I've been observed all my life.

My father; mother; the kids at school; all those other students, judging; lab techs; workmates; Ryan; the cops; God; Donnie; the NSA; NDSA.

All those observers in my head, finally gone off duty. No, better; I've shaken them off.

OK. Got to get to the house. Let's see . . .

She comes out of a bend, puts the pedal down. She and Colt sink back into the black leather seats.

Too fast.

In reflex, her foot drifts up, off the accelerator, and the car slows and the roar of its engine fades to an apologetic murmur.

Apologetic.

Her eyes go moist, and her vision blurs.

Fuck that.

She puts her foot to the floor and the car roars.

112

'For it is a false assertion that the sense of man is the measure of things. On the contrary, all perceptions as well of the sense as of the mind are according to the measure of the individual and not according to the measure of the universe. And the human understanding is like a false mirror, which, receiving rays irregularly, distorts and discolors the nature of things by mingling its own nature with it.' — Francis Bacon, *Novum Organum*

They park below the low hill, out of sight of the house.

Now Colt just needs to find out if their house is under observation. And, if it is, by what . . .

Easy.

What isn't easy, is to see if you're being observed, without being observed seeing . . .

OK, thinks Colt. I can shake information out of the cell towers.

God bless the government. They've been crippling encryption and installing hardware backdoors for so long, most communication infrastructure is nothing but security flaws and open backdoors . . .

Colt uses a national security override key that he's been saving for a rainy day, and pops everything open.

The cell towers tell him who's been pinging them.

OK, there is a drone observing the property.

No, two drones.

One's charging . . .

He can't hack into them. Damn.

Wait; Naomi's described these to him.

They're the ravens that escorted her to the base.

Ryan's personal drones.

Too small to do serious data analysis, or threat-processing.

So, just eyeballs for the drone cloud.

He can't get into the packets of data the eyeball drones are sending. But he doesn't need to decrypt the packets. He knows what's in them, from the packet size, and rate of delivery. Live, high-definition pictures.

The eyeballs are simply saying, 'This is what we see. What should we do?'

And the drone cloud, the brain, is saying, 'What you see is fine. Do nothing. Keep observing.'

So, let's keep it that way . . .

And then . . . what if I intercept the signal, en route, and replace it?

They can't broadcast all that data over major distances unaided. Don't have the power, the range.

So how . . .

What's the signal path . . .

Colt looks from horizon to horizon, and his helmet paints in the communication infrastructure; overlays it all on the landscape, colour-coded. Buried fibre, overhead wires, towers.

Oh, perfect. They commandeer local booster towers . . . neat.

A stealth-mode override.

And the only local booster good enough, strong enough, is mine. On the hill behind the house. Hot damn, and I built it. My soldering iron, my circuits. And gave it a local telecoms address, to keep me out of trouble, and to join it seamlessly to the local networks. So they can't know it's mine.

Oh man, and I know exactly what I can replace their pictures with . . .

Colt goes into the game.

Feeds the drones' FAA location pings into the game's mapping code.

Now, instead of generating a live view of his house and the land around it from Colt's helmet position, the code generates a live view from the drones' positions.

Colt examines the view critically.

Hmm . . .

He grabs a block of Sasha's code; adjusts the light. Makes it more realistic.

Very carefully, he feeds the live pictures into the booster station, and forwards them on to the drone brain, in place of the signals from the eyeballs . . .

That switchover is the hardest. The point where the drone cloud might detect him; realize it's been compromised.

Kill him and Mama.

He breathes out when it's done.

'Ooooh . . . Kay. Finished,' he says.

Naomi has been studying his face, watching it twitch, frown, smile; his thoughts and actions rippling across it, like gusts of wind crossing a lake.

'So . . .' she says, looking away. 'What do we do now?'

Colt looks up at the top of the low hill, imagining the house beyond. The watching drones.

'Now we find out if it has worked,' he says.

'Do we need to disguise ourselves, or . . .'

'No,' says Colt, and Naomi is reassured by how firmly he says it. 'No point.' He shrugs. 'It will react or it won't.'

OK, that bit isn't reassuring at all. 'You're sure the drones can't see us?'

'Oh, they'll see us,' says Colt. 'The eyes will register us, and send the signal to the brain . . . But if I've done everything right, that picture won't get there.' Colt reviews the intercept code again in his head. It should work. It should.

Naomi is still frowning. Twisting at that red thread on her wrist.

Say something. Reassure her. 'The immune system . . . its brain will just see a gameworld picture of the house,' he says. 'My picture. No people. No movement. Nothing to trigger it. Just . . . weather. Bushes moving in the breeze.'

Naomi looks up, at the cloudless blue above the ridge.

She's still frowning.

*

They walk, quietly, carefully, up the sloping road, in the direction of the house.

The first raven soars high above them, circling in a thermal, a dot in the blue sky.

As they come over the crest of the hill, Colt looks around for the second raven.

Nope.

He runs his eye along the power line that leads up and over the iron-red ridge beyond the house. The old wire sags in the heat, between rusty pylons.

There.

The drone sits in the dip of the power line.

But there's no charging station there. There are no charging stations on that old line at all . . . Ah.

Colt can see where the drone's thin cobalt-steel feeder spike, like a mosquito's bladed proboscis, has sliced though the insulation, into the high-tension wire.

It's feeding in the wild.

It stares at them. An open eye.

But its brain, somewhere in the blue sky high above, sees nothing.

They walk carefully towards the house, under the blind eyes of the ravens.

As they approach the door, Colt stops.

'Wait,' he whispers, holding out his hand to block Naomi.

He checks the house security system.

Oh boy.

The immune system has taken over all the electronics inside the house.

Of course. Of course. It's reading data from all the sensors. The internal alarm system, the refrigerator, lights, water, entertainment, aircon . . .

If Naomi had taken two more steps, she'd have triggered the door lock; she'd have triggered everything.

Colt breathes out, a surprisingly loud rush of air. Beside him, Naomi gives a little involuntary jump.

OK, he can't just disable the sensors; all the house sensors suddenly going dead would be as much a giveaway as all the sensors saying, hey, they've arrived and they're having a party . . .

Colt grabs Naomi's hand, and backs them away from the door, into the soft shade of the senna bushes. 'Sorry, Mama. Give me a minute . . .'

He hacks together some fake data streams for the sensors. They show a quiet, empty house, no movement. Nothing happening.

About a day's worth, should be enough . . .

When he's done, he very, very carefully replaces the live, real feeds from the house with the fake data streams. Feeds the fakes out to the immune system through his booster tower.

'OK, we're good,' he says to Naomi. 'Let's go.'

Naomi walks on stiff, nervous legs up to the front door, Colt by her side.

Click.

She triggers the front door.

It swings open.

They walk away from the blind drones outside, into the blind house.

113

Naomi goes to her room to change out of her bridal gown, while Colt goes to his room, and fires up everything. First the generator, then the servers. He can't take electricity from the grid; a power spike to their house would tip off distant parts of the watching, wary immune system.

He pulls in electricity, instead, from all the solar sheets he's installed out on the ridge.

Aircon on full. It's going to get hot. He's overdriving every-thing.

Naomi enters his room in work clothes, adjusting some heavy tools in her pockets, trying to get her silk jacket to hang right.

'I'm going to get my research,' she says. Colt tells his visor to go clear, and makes his questioning face. She makes her *don't worry* face. 'I can't let Ryan use it.'

Oh yeah. She has to physically go and take it from the big fire-proof data safes in her office. Offline, airgapped, secure . . . Colt frowns. 'But Donnie works for Dad. If Donnie's at the lab . . .'

'I know, I need your help. The lab should be closed today, but . . .'

Colt nods. 'I'll check if he's there . . .'

Hah. The passive location tag Colt hid in Donnie's Lexus still works. And it's been constantly updating a server, here in the house, with the car's movements. Colt doesn't even need to risk going out to search for the information . . .

'His car's in Pahrump . . . Yes, he's parked outside a brothel. I think you're fine . . .'

'Good.' She moves to go, but he's not done.

'I still don't think it's safe. To go.'

'Colt, it's not safe to *stay*.'

'Well . . .' True.

'It's my *whole life's work*, Colt. Imagine if your father took the *only* copies of *everything* you'd *ever* done, and erased them. Or used them to kill people.'

He dutifully imagines it. Oh. Oh, wow. He feels a little sick.

'OK,' he says. 'I get it . . . I'll give you my override codes, for the lab, and your office. In case they've cancelled your employee access.'

She shapes her mouth to say he shouldn't *have* override codes for her office, but immediately realizes how absurd that would be. She twists out a smile, and says, 'Thank you.'

Something else occurs to him. 'Mama, if you're going to the lab . . . I need more servers, here, under my control.'

'*More* servers?' She gestures at the equipment filling his room. 'Yes!'

'But you've all that stuff in the cloud . . .'

'They'll cut me off from my distributed network as soon as they know what I'm doing. I need to do a lot of the stuff locally.'

'Ah.' Naomi thinks; nods. 'I could take some of the new servers in Lab 2. We've upgraded everything, they're pretty powerful.'

'Yes. Perfect. Do. And bring all the cables you can find. I want physical connections. More secure than wireless . . .'

'OK,' says Naomi.

'Oh, and I need a biological accelerant. To help the neurons lay down connections faster.'

'OK,' says Naomi. 'StemStim B7? It's optimized to accelerate *Drosophila* neuron growth.'

335

'Perfect,' says Colt.

Naomi smiles. 'Good. Shannon did the last order after eating a couple of Audrey's homemade hash cookies at lunch. Misplaced a decimal point. The lab has fridges full of it.' She moves towards the door.

'Wait,' says Colt; and it occurs to Naomi at the same instant.

'The lab will be under observation,' she says. 'Even if Donnie's not there. *Especially* if Donnie's not there.'

'Yeah,' says Colt. 'It would have to be.' He checks, sifting the metadata from the local base stations, looking for anomalies, looking for drones. 'Yep. Observation drone over your lab.'

Naomi looks out the window, over the desert, as though she could see the lab from here, as though she could see the drone. 'Can you deal with it?'

'Well, it's not communicating through my booster station, so I can't blind it directly . . . But I think I might be able to . . .'

He works out what model of drone it must be. Thinks about that.

'Hah!' says Colt. 'Yeah. It's got slightly different specs to the two drones observing our house.'

'Different?' Naomi doesn't find that reassuring. 'You mean missiles?'

'No, strictly observation. But it's a new-generation Gorgon; wider viewing angle, more cameras. So, if I fake up a little suspicious action at the edge of the viewing area for *our* guys . . .' Colt generates a plume of smoke in the gameworld view that the two ravens are sending back to the drone brain. And now another plume of smoke, from outside the drones' viewing area. 'The smoke will arrive in their view soon . . . It's kind of like throwing a rock into the bushes, to distract a dog . . .'

She marvels, that he's making comparisons, that he's carefully explaining; that he's aware of her mind, of its needs.

Colt squints at his data, looking for a reaction. 'The system's protocols should . . . Yes! It's sending your lab drone over to investigate, because it's nearest. I can blind it once it connects to my booster.'

'So there will *definitely* be no observer over the lab?'

'It's being relieved by one of our drones.' Colt points out the window. The drone on the power line is already moving away, in the direction of the lab. 'But I can keep that one blind. You'll be OK, Mama. I'll look after you.'

'Thank you, Colt.' Naomi smiles. 'But I'll bring this too, just in case.' She reaches into the sagging pocket of her own mother's silk jacket, shyly tugs at something. Shows him the stubby grip of the Beretta pistol Ryan left her.

Colt stares at her.

'Yeah, I know. What would Jesus do.' Naomi shrugs. 'Look, Jesus didn't have Donnie as a boss. And he definitely didn't marry your dad . . .'

'Mama . . .'

'I won't use it. But I might have to point it at someone.'

'You have ammo?'

She pats her other pocket. 'I'll be careful. But I can't let your father get that data.'

They look into each other's eyes; she marvels, that they can look into each other's eyes. A second passes. Two. Three.

'Mama . . .'

'Yes?'

'I have to work.' Colt darkens his visor, and turns away.

She makes a face. Then a wry – a very wry – smile.

Heads for the car.

114

'. . . biological creatures can be conflicted. The term *con-flicted* could not sensibly be applied to an entity that has a single program.' — David Eagleman, *Incognito*

She drives to the lab fast, glancing up constantly at the sky, wondering where the blind eyes are now. Taking the final corner, at the bottom of the hill, she feels the car drift too wide, and she overcorrects, hauls the car to the right.

The BMW's front right wheel comes off the hard high-grip black surface into deep gravel, and the car fishtails wildly, as she tries to get it back on the solar road.

There's a sound like machine-gun fire.

Oh crap.

Gravel, ricocheting off the underside of the car beneath her feet.

A hot, dusty smell comes through the aircon.

She comes out of the curve barely in control, tyres spinning. As soon as they grip the road again, she hits the accelerator, hard.

Naomi is still laughing as she drives into the empty parking lot. She swings the car to a halt, sideways, right outside the front door.

9

I Wish I Had A River
I Could Skate Away On

'This despair about love is coupled with a callous cynicism that frowns upon any suggestion that love is as important as work, as crucial to our survival as a nation as the drive to succeed.'   — bell hooks, *All About Love*

'Whenever their lives were set aflame, through desire or suffering, or even reflection, the Homeric heroes knew that a god was at work. They endured the god, and observed him, but what actually happened as a result was a surprise most of all for themselves.'
— Roberto Calasso, *The Marriage of Cadmus and Harmony*, translated by Tim Parks

'What would an ocean be without a monster lurking in the dark? Like sleep without dreams.'   — Werner Herzog

115

She walks through the empty labs, on her way to her office. Stops to study a stack of the Banyans that Colt needs, shelved in one corner; server after shielded, high-security server.

Hmm, *can* I take these servers . . . What if they're bolted down?

She examines them. No bolts. Good. She reaches into the gap behind the shelves, and pulls out a cable. Another cable.

Funny how security pushes the technology backwards, away from the weightless, wireless future.

Back to cables.

Sheets of paper.

A village you can defend.

The cables make a satisfying suck and click as they come out of their tight sockets in the backs of the servers.

'Naomi.'

She turns.

'Oh. Donnie.'

He's swaying very slightly, and his eyes are bloodshot.

A little drunk, she thinks, but not quite drunk enough.

And he's holding a pistol of some kind.

Great, that's all my day needed. An idiot with a gun.

All the men in my life, waving their weapons in my face.

She eyes him warily. He's out of shape, but he's still big, he's still muscular; he's still twice her weight.

With his free left hand, he tries to adjust the straps of the leather holster slung under his left armpit. It looks uncomfortably high and tight. Like a bad bra, thinks Naomi. Clearly still a guy who's picking his own clothes. Brown leather holster and black leather boots, with piss-coloured khakis, and a purple shirt . . . She wonders idly for a moment, in one of those odd, random, stress-induced thoughts, if he is colour-blind.

'Oh, Naomi . . .' He makes his fake I'm-very-sad-and-disappointed-in-you face. He turns his head a fraction, and speaks to someone she can't see. 'She's here. Lab 2.' Someone who isn't there.

Ryan. Donnie is talking to Ryan. Oh *shit* . . . But, by his face, looks like there's no reply . . . OK, Donnie was just leaving a message. But why, how, is he . . .

'You're supposed to be in Pahrump . . .' She immediately regrets saying it. Now he'll know they can track him . . .

But he smiles, unfazed. 'Yeah, Colt tagged my car a while back. Smart kid. We found it. Maybe we're a little smarter. Left the tag in place.'

Dumb bastard can't resist boasting. Trying to prove he's outwitted me . . .

His smile gets wider. 'There's a guy in Pahrump with my car, having a good time on my credit . . .'

Keep him happy. Lead him on. Play dumb. 'Why?'

'C'mon, we *wanted* you to think the lab was empty.' With his left hand, Donnie pulls a small fireproof, crushproof bright orange data block from the pocket of his khakis. Holds it out, so she can recognize it.

'You've opened my data safes? Donnie!'

'Don't worry, we haven't read your precious data.' He's still smiling, but it's going sour. 'We've *tried*. Pretty good encryption. Colt, huh?'

Naomi says nothing. But yes, Colt set up her encryption routines. They're ridiculously good. He'd had fun with it. Overkill.

'Ryan figured, easiest way to decrypt that data . . . was get you to do it.'

Her mind is racing to join all the dots. 'So the observation drone leaving . . .'

'Oh, we let it go. It meant you must be coming here.'

'A trap.'

He shrugs. 'You'd vanished. Where are you most likely to reappear? Your house, or here.' He seems a little distracted. Staring at her breasts. Ugh. 'Surprised you didn't go home first. You snuck up on me a little, here . . .' Sharper, 'Where's Colt?'

Naomi says nothing. Keeps her face still.

They don't know we blinded the ravens. They don't know Colt's at the house. Thank God . . .

'*Where's Colt?*'

'Why are you doing this?'

'It's my job.'

'What, spying, for Ryan?' says Naomi. She shifts the server she's holding, as though it's heavy, so it shields her chest from his gaze. 'Some job.'

Donnie scowls. 'I report on you, as my contract obliges me to do.'

Oh, so he doesn't like being called a spy.

'Spy,' says Naomi.

She shifts the weight of the server again, onto her hip, to free her right hand. Reaches for the gun in her pocket, her hand's awkward movements hidden by the metal box. But, as soon as she thumbs off the safety, with that soft, familiar click, he knows what she's trying to do.

He may be drunk, but, as he tells everybody at least once a week, he grew up in the Big Bend, rural Texas, with a dad who patrolled the Mexican border. Got his first gun aged ten. Spent a couple of years in the military. For him, it's muscle memory; he doesn't even think, he just fires.

The bullet penetrates the server she holds, with a tremendous, confused, metallic bang that blends with the sharp crack of the gunshot; the server lurches back hard against her ribs.

For a moment both she and Donnie freeze, shocked by the noise, by the rip the shot has opened up in their everyday reality.

She glances down, to see if she's been wounded; but the server's case has no exit hole. Just a couple of convex dents and bulges, where fragments have struck from within. The bullet must have hit a heat-sink, or the power supply, or some other big chunk of metal, and disintegrated inside the server.

Donnie says, 'God *damn* it,' and studies his gun, and she isn't sure if he's mad at himself for firing, or for missing.

'I can't decrypt anything if you kill me, you idiot.'

'Huh.' Donnie's face tightens at the word idiot. 'Well, maybe I don't care about that *quite* as much as Ryan does.' He raises his gun again.

Naomi tugs again on her own gun, but the raised rear sight catches in the lining of her jacket pocket, and her finger slips off the guard and lands hard on the trigger.

Click.

Donnie laughs.

She forgot to load it. The magazine is empty.

Bullets still in their box, in the other pocket of her silk jacket.

So here we are, she thinks. Two idiots with guns.

She throws the damaged server at Donnie as hard as she can, and runs for her office.

Slams the door behind her.

Locks it, with a metal key.

Bolts it.

Good old-fashioned physical security.

The door shudders, as Donnie hits it with his shoulder. A moment's silence, before she can hear him, muffled, swearing, through the door. 'Hello? Hello?' The idiot's broken his wearable. So, no phone now, no nothing. Good. And it's a big, heavy, high-specification fire door. He isn't fit enough to break *that*.

She steps back before she's even consciously registered the crisp, tightly packed sound of the pistol shot.

Again.

Again.

The three bullets punch surprisingly small, neat holes in the fire door, each sending a little cloud of fibreglass particles from the insulating layer into the room.

The first bullet smacks into a lab bench.

Second sends a little metal trashcan tumbling out from beneath it.

Third rips a long splinter from the wooden floor.

The fibreglass particles glitter as they drift across the room.

If he kills me . . . who will look after Colt?

No; if he kills me . . . he will kill Colt next.

The rules have changed.

She slumps to the floor, to the side of the door, and unsnags the pistol from her pocket lining. Slides out the magazine. Takes the heavy, half-full box of ammo from her other pocket. She takes a cartridge from the box. To her adrenalized senses, it seems weirdly vivid, solid. The brass casing and cupronickel-coated lead of the bullet gleam like jewellery in her shaking hand. Beautifully machined, a tiny, minimalist sculpture. She pushes the beautiful object down into the magazine.

It doesn't fit.

She tries again.

It's too wide for the slim magazine. She looks at the figures stamped on the side of the Beretta.

9mm.

She looks at the box. Yes, it says 9mm. But . . .

She turns over the cartridge. Stamped on the brass base, 45 AUTO.

Imperial to metric; she's a scientist, she has to do this all the time, come *on*, focus . . .

.45 inches. That's . . . 11.43mm.

Too big.

They're for a different gun. Ryan's gun.

She'd never checked. Ryan must have been reusing an old box.

She stares at the gun in her hand.

No ammo.

She could pretend . . .

That won't work. Come out pointing an empty gun, and he'll just shoot her.

For a moment she is scared by the silence. Is he still in the corridor? Or is he about to appear outside? She spins around, looking for movement, through the windows. Nothing. Hey, maybe I could . . . but of course, the windows don't open. Sealed unit. Pathogen risk.

She hears a scrape, a muttered, '*Shit*,' from the other side of the door.

Oh, thank God. It hasn't even occurred to him to come around the outside . . .

I could break them . . . How strong is the glass? No, it's industrial-strength; terrorist-proof. And even if I *could* break it, he'd hear. Takes time, to break through toughened glass. Plenty of time for him to come around, and shoot me as I climb out.

And if he kills me, he will kill Colt next. Oh, dear Jesus . . . *Our Father who art in heaven, hallowed be thy name, thy kingdom come, thy will be done . . .*

She shakes her head. There isn't time for that . . .

No. That's not why she stopped.

She stopped because something is shifting inside her, at the thought of this man trying to kill her son. Kill her. Something old is waking up. As old as religion. Older. And now her mind feels very clear.

345

OK, no bullets. So no gun. So, what can she use?

Her father used to say, there is always a solution within arm's reach . . .

Her father, who is not in heaven.

Naomi stands, walks to her desk.

Quietly pulls her desk drawers all the way out.

Post-it notes, packing tape, stapler, a tiny toy dump truck Colt used to love, paperclips, foreign coins, envelopes, pens, just a mess of stuff . . .

Huh. There it is.

The syringe full of potassium chloride. A nice, fat barrel full. Three times the lethal dose for her bodyweight. More than enough for Donnie.

He fires again.

Again.

He's shooting out the lock.

This is completely ridiculous. A syringe against a gun.

Maybe she could tape it to the back of her neck, or the back of her hand. Get close, and . . .

No, he forgot to check her for a weapon a couple of minutes ago, and nearly got killed. Even idiots can learn from nearly getting killed. She won't fool him twice.

From just behind the door, another gunshot, but this time the bullet hits something metal – the frame of the door perhaps, or part of the bulky deadlock itself – and she hears the ricochet scream off sideways down the corridor.

'*Shiiiiit* . . .' he says, crazily close, the other side of the door.

Must have just missed him.

She holds up the syringe, between finger and thumb. Maybe she could throw it at him, like a dart . . . But it's a high-friction syringe, designed to not inject too easily, to avoid accidents. It takes firm pressure to push the plunger home. Plus, thrown, it would probably just hit muscle, or fat. No good. She needs to guide it, to hit a vein, or the solution won't reach his heart quickly enough.

She studies the debris on the floor.

No, a syringe is as useless as an empty pistol. She'll never get close enough, for long enough. OK, can she *talk* her way out of this? Does he have a weakness she can work on? Huh, Donnie has a *lot* of weaknesses, but that doesn't mean . . .

And then an idea occurs to her that is so absurd she has to choke back a laugh.

There's one way to get close enough to Donnie.

One way to distract him enough to put down the gun.

Turn the other cheek, she says to herself, in a kind of gleeful disgust.

Love thy neighbour as thyself.

No, this is absolutely crazy. Anyway, there's no way I could hide the syringe. But if I do nothing . . .

He'll kill me.

And then Colt.

Behind the door, she can hear him reloading.

He wants to come through the door with a full magazine. And he knows that I'm lying in wait. He won't believe my gun is empty.

So he'll shoot his way in. Covering fire.

If I'd played more of Colt's games, I might know what to do . . . She gives a little laugh which she again strangles straight away. She doesn't want Donnie to know where she is.

But couldn't he just *guess* where I am, shoot me through the door?

A surge of fear closes her throat. She picks up the syringe, moves flat to the wall, then along the wall; away from the door.

'You open that door and come out,' says Donnie. His voice seems so close, inches away, the other side of the wall. And his voice is shaking.

Oh . . . he's afraid to come through the door.

He's afraid of death.

'Fucking *bitch*. Wait till I get my fucking hands on you.'

Fucking bitch? He tries to murder me, and then calls me a fucking bitch?

She can hear it in his voice; he's trying to talk himself into something. Justify something he's about to do. Well, that would fit her plan. Her half a plan . . .

Yeah, she used to hear that voice, see that shaky bravado, in BDSM darkrooms sometimes, with newcomers, young men, not used to the rules.

OK. Let's start working on getting close enough.

For now, just tell him what he wants to hear.

'I don't want to die,' she says. 'I'll do whatever you say, just, please, don't kill me.' She grimaces at her own words. Whatever, fine, play his fantasy back to him. Let him think he has the power. Just keep talking, keep him busy, while she thinks.

'You're damn right you'll do what I say!' His voice is trembling. The man is hysterical, she thinks drily. And he sounds a little further away. Of course, he thinks she must have loaded her gun by now. He's afraid she'll shoot him through the door. Good. That buys her time . . . Yes, she's pretty sure she knows how to get close to him without getting shot.

She's read the studies of the incidence of rape in wartime.

So incredibly high. Rape the women, murder the men.

She spent her teens reading everything she could on the subject; fascinated, astonished, repulsed. Feminist theories. Social-learning theories. Evolutionary theories. And histories . . . Two million women raped in East Germany by the Russians, in a few weeks. Men who would probably never rape in their own town, in their own culture. But when they are facing death; when their chance of reproducing their DNA is vanishing . . .

The subconscious decisions a body makes, that the mind tries to justify after the fact . . .

And of course, later again, at Berkeley, she studied rape as a reproductive strategy in those poor old Barbary ducks. And in chimpanzees, geese, bottlenose dolphins, orangutans, scorpion flies . . .

She knows that birth control, abortion, prison sentences, and immense cultural shifts have altered the expression and meaning of rape in her culture. And she knows that Donnie's a man socialized to exert power, in order to dominate and control. And she knows Donnie thinks he's just an individual, making personal decisions. All of those things are true, at their different levels.

But the way he was trained to act, in the Big Bend, by his cop dad and his nurse mom – while he watched every *Fast and Furious* movie, listened to nothing but bro country – is built on top of an evolved architecture that Naomi has studied all her life.

Yes, she knows quite a lot about rape. And she knows quite a lot about Donnie. Time to use all that knowledge . . .

OK, she thinks. Yes. I can do this. Get up close. But he'll want me to *prove* I'm unarmed . . . So how do I convince him it's safe, without making it safe? How do I let him think he can do . . . *that* . . . without letting him do that?

And an answer comes to her. It is so ridiculous, and so perfect, that this time she does laugh aloud.

'I'll come out unarmed, no gun,' she shouts, and she worries for a second that there is triumph in her voice, that he'll hear it; she damps it down, tries to make herself sound beaten. 'Nothing hidden, no weapons . . . You win.'

'You think I'm going to trust you? You tried to fucking shoot me!'

Perfect. Close the trap. 'I'll prove it. I'll take off my clothes, I'll come out naked. You can check.'

'Huh.' A pause. 'Naked?'

She can hear it in his voice. The gears shifting.

'Yes, naked,' she shouts back. 'No weapons. Safe.' You creep.

A longer pause. 'OK. Naked. Hands where I can see them.'

'Of course,' she says. 'Sure . . .'

OK. Great. What else will she need?

She crosses the room, as quickly and quietly as she can.

Some kind of lubricant . . . she looks around, but sees nothing. Then she remembers. It's probably still there . . . She moves to the shelves; reaches up to the top one. At the back, yes . . . She takes down a heavy, dusty jar. It contains a small pile of silvery particles, beneath a clear liquid.

Tiny pellets of sodium, submerged in high-purity mineral oil.

The door shakes, as Donnie kicks it hard from outside, and she jumps. She hears Donnie backing away from the door, fast.

'Just fucking come out!' he shouts.

'I'm still undressing! Look, I'll come out totally naked.' Yes, keep putting that image in his head. 'Unarmed. You can do anything. Please, don't kill me. I'm not any kind of threat—'

'Bullshit! You've got a fucking gun!'

'I'll give you the gun,' she shouts, as she pulls off her shoes.

'You think I'm an idiot?' he shouts back through the damaged door. She rolls her eyes and nods, as he continues, 'You have another weapon in there.'

She quickly takes off all her clothes, as she says, 'No, just the gun . . . Look, I'm sorry Colt's caused all this trouble . . .' Buy time, buy time. 'I didn't mean to pull the gun, you scared me, that's all . . .'

'It doesn't take that long to get undressed.' Donnie sounds freaked out. I guess he's out of his depth too.

'I know, I know. I'm naked.' This is an experiment, you can do this: turn his penis on, turn his brain off . . . 'But I'm scared, Donnie. I'm scared to come out.'

'I'm not going to hurt you . . . Just come out with your hands up.'

Ugh, he just talks in clichés from movies. What a dick.

She squats, and picks up the syringe. As she rolls it between her fingers, studies it, she feels herself decide. It's physical; her shoulders loosen, relax. Yes, I can do this. I'll do this. He's stronger; but I'm smarter. Her mood shifts again, and she feels almost giddy.

'Swear you won't kill me?' she shouts, to keep him busy.

'I won't kill you. Unless you pull some stupid bullshit.'

The long red protective cap on the needle seems tight; but at the thought of it inside her, she grimaces, and screws it a little tighter, just in case. I'll need some thread . . . hah! With her teeth and fingers, she unties the bracelet of red thread Yaakov gave her, to protect her from the evil eye.

She ties the red thread around the base of the plunger. Tugs the knot tighter.

'Maybe I should take the bullets out of the gun first?' Yes, best if he thinks she's reloaded. If he knew she had no ammo, he could just walk in . . .

'Just throw out the fucking gun. With the safety on.'

'OK. Oh, wait, which one is the safety . . .'

'Jesus fucking Christ . . .'

She opens the jar, dips her fingertips in the mineral oil, and oils the fat barrel of the syringe. Oils the smooth, rounded base of the plunger. Oils her labia. The oil is cool from the aircon. It's OK. You're just preparing apparatus for an experiment.

And what's the alternative? Get raped? Murdered? Both? This is a war. Women have done harder things, to survive.

She takes a deep breath, tries to relax. Oh come on, it's a lot smaller than a speculum. You can do this . . . Look, you've passed an entire *human being* through there. This is nothing . . . But she still feels a deep, primal reluctance to put death inside her body. Her fingers won't move.

'I think it's safer if I take out the bullets,' she shouts, to gain time, as she tries again to calmly, logically, persuade herself. Look, *Donnie*'s dangerous; doing *nothing* is dangerous; the syringe is safe. High-grade materials, high specification, it can't leak, the needle's covered, the cap's on tight . . . 'I don't want to throw out the gun, and it goes off . . .'

'This is fucking ridiculous.' Donnie sounds close to losing it. Uh oh. Not good. 'Just put on the safety. It's the little switch where your thumb sits. You used it earlier, I heard it . . .'

'Oh! That thing!' Yes, make him feel smart . . . 'Found it! Thank you!'

Just *do it* . . . She sings la-la-la-la-la-la-la in her mind, to stop herself from thinking, as she slowly slides the red plastic cap, then the rest of the syringe, inside her. Pushes it further back, till the whole thing is completely out of sight, and only a few inches of red thread are still visible. More than enough to get a grip . . . She tucks the trailing thread back up, between her labia. Invisible. Good. See, that wasn't so bad . . .

'OK, OK, I'm coming out now,' she says. 'I'm going to slide the gun out first.'

She unlocks the door. Opens it a couple of inches. Slides the gun out along the floor as far as she can.

Slides out the box of useless ammo. 'OK? No gun. No bullets.'

'Uh huh.'

'I'm going to . . .' No. Don't tell him. Act submissive. Make it his idea. 'Shall I come out now?'

'Yeah. Slowly. Hands where I can see them.'

She can't see him out the crack. He must be off to one side, covering the doorway.

She takes a deep breath.

You've got a plan, you know what he likes. You know how he sees you. Play that stereotype, use it. Be submissive, yes. Get his guard down.

Then kill him.

She pulls the door further open. Steps out into the corridor, naked, hands raised.

OK, there's Donnie, his gun pointed at her.

She turns to face him. She can see the erection forming in his pants, trapped sideways in his hideous yellow khakis.

He hesitates. His mind is still anxious and paranoid. But the penis outranks the prefrontal cortex. The penis is far older; its needs are more primal.

'Huh,' he says.

Moving carefully – no sudden movements – she shows him her hands. Rotates them. Nothing taped to the back.

'Turn around,' he says.

The windowless corridor is quiet, empty. She slowly turns around, and she can hear his breathing change. She stifles a laugh. Turn the other cheek . . .

'Run your fingers through your hair,' he says.

'What?'

'Prove there's nothing in your hair.'

She splays her fingers and combs her hair with them, up, down, sideways. Lifts her hair to show her neck.

'See? No weapons,' she says. Careful, careful. Hide the anger.

'OK . . .' says Donnie. 'Come here. Slowly.'

Naomi fights an urge to turn and run, as she walks slowly towards him, her hands in the air. She tries to make eye contact, human contact, to make him less likely to kill her, but his eyes are too busy flicking between her genitals and her breasts, up and down, up and down.

That is the evil eye, she thinks.

She can tell he's not really thinking any more, he's feeling. Stimulus/response. The hook is in.

'*Huh*,' he says again, all out of words.

This feels so strange, like an uneasy dream.

But also so strangely familiar.

She remembers all the darkrooms. All the times she's pushed herself, she's made men push her, to an edge a lot like this one. But that was for a kind of pleasure; this is the absolute opposite . . . It's hard to keep her fury invisible.

In a standard dominant–submissive relationship, the submissive has the safe word. Can stop the game. It is the submissive who has control.

This time, it's real. If she wants control, she'll have to take it. And if she fails . . . She doesn't want to finish the thought.

352

He takes a step closer, gun in his right hand, and she can smell beer on his breath, and what is that, chocolate? Peanut butter?

'Terrorist . . . bitch,' he murmurs.

She knows her best strategy is to shut up and not trigger his anger and fear, but she can't help herself, she says, '*What?*'

'C'mon, I know. *I know.* You and your fucking lunatic son. There's explosions going off all over Vegas.'

And there's a pause, a weird pause. Her senses are so finely tuned by adrenalin and cortisol that his face looks the size of a planet, and she is alert to every shifting emotion animating it. It still takes her a couple more seconds to realize; he doesn't know what to do next. Too many visits to Pahrump, too many years of professional sex workers running the show, while pretending to let him run the show . . . now he's in charge, for real, with a gun . . . and he doesn't know what to do.

Oh fuck you, Donnie, this is who you always were, you fucking creep . . .

And she is suddenly terrified that, if he glances at her face, he will see what she's really thinking, how she really feels; worse, see what she is about to do, and so she looks down, and lowers herself to her knees – not too quickly, don't startle him – to move her face out of his eyeline.

Kneeling brings her closer to him; touching distance. The smooth wood is surprisingly cool against her skin. He pulls the gun back and up, out of her range, so she can't grab it, and points it down at her again. 'Yeah,' he says. 'Good,' sounding confident again. 'Let's start with that.'

She reaches for his zipper, half-hidden under the sag of his beer belly, and he groans in anticipation, before she's even touched the metal. She pulls the zipper down.

Oh Jesus Christ, I'm going to have to touch him . . .

He's locked down the building. No one else will save you. Do it.

Follow the plan.

Wash your hands after.

She shuffles his khakis down his legs, leaves the trousers pooled around his ankles, over his boots. Good, he can't run, if this goes wrong, if she needs to run.

For the plan to work, she needs access: there is no getting around this. She lowers his old-fashioned boxers, and his penis catches on the elastic waistband, and springs free. It's floppy, semi-hard, a drunk's erection. It's OK, he's an experiment, an experimental animal, don't get emotional . . . She reaches for it; it jerks in her hand, like a startled fish scooped from a pond, and she is reminded of all the experimental animals she has killed over the years. Snapping the necks of the mice, injecting the larger mammals. She sees again the last dying dog that trusted her, that licked her hand, and the memory of its rough, loving tongue on the back of her hand is so vivid her eyes moisten.

I killed the wrong animals.

Forgive me, Jesus, for what I've done. For what I'm about to . . .

No. No. Stop trying to pretend you're perfect. You're not Saint Francis. You've taken the lives of innocents, for science; for a pay cheque. If you can kill those beautiful creatures . . . you can kill this piece of shit.

She grasps his penis more firmly, moves her hand back and forth, just a little, and he groans and leans back against the wall, groaning again with every movement of her hand.

Good, that will cover any noise . . . Oh crap, I should have started this left-handed.

It's too late to free her right hand now, he'll realize she's up to something. Shit shit shit. OK.

She speeds up her right hand a little. He groans louder, shuffles his feet a little wider, but they're still caught in his khakis, so he braces himself with his arms against the wall behind him. So he's now holding the pistol flat to the wall. Good . . .

She glances up at his face, works out the eyelines. There is no way he can see what she is doing with her other hand; his head's too far back and his beer gut is in the way, pushing out his shirt like an awning.

She reaches down with her free left hand, and coaxes out the end of the red thread. Pulls it, carefully. Bears down. Finally the syringe slides out, and, suddenly, irrationally afraid it's going to pop like a champagne cork, she goes, 'Ohhhhh . . .' to hide any noise, but of course there is none. And now it's dangling from the thread in her fingers.

354

She knows he can't see it over his gut, his shirt hem, but she's still trembling with tension, afraid he'll move. He seems to think her 'Ohhhhh . . .' and her trembling indicate arousal, because he groans a reply, and she feels a white-hot surge of pure hatred; my God, he actually thinks he's entitled to my pleasure, that I'm enjoying this.

She can't help herself, she jerks hard, to hurt him, and he says, 'Hey, slower.'

'OK,' she says. Calm down, calm down.

'Put it in your mouth,' he says.

'I just want to see how big I can get it first,' she says in a soothing voice. Boost the idiot's ego, that's right. 'Oh, that's good, yes . . .' Her words distract him, cover up any sounds, as she tries to get the red plastic cap off the fucking needle with her left hand, Jesus Christ don't drop it.

'*You have achieved your cardio target for the day*,' says a sudden, incongruously happy voice near her ear. '*Congratulations!*' It starts to play a cheerful little tune.

Donnie grunts in surprise, or annoyance.

Oh, the fitness monitor, on his left wrist. Naomi snorts a laugh, turns it into a cough. Don't laugh. So, his heart is beating fast. Good. That'll help.

He reaches across to silence the fitness monitor, but he can't turn off the tune while his right hand still holds the gun. He hesitates; slips the pistol back into the holster high under his left arm. Now, she thinks, while he's distracted . . .

She grips the slippery syringe in her left hand. As three fingers clamp it hard to her palm, her thumb and forefinger slip, slip again, on the red plastic cap, trying to get a grip, unscrew it. But her fingertips are too oily, and she can't get traction. Oh God, why did I screw it on so tight?

She surreptitiously rubs her thumb and forefinger clean of oil against her thigh. Now they have enough grip to turn the plastic cap: one, two, three turns, and it's loose, it's off.

OK, this is it. I need to be able to see what I'm doing.

The cheerful tune cuts off abruptly above her. She moves in closer.

'Yeah,' he says, 'oh yeah.'

She studies his penis with clinical detachment. Perfect target

– the plump, spongy, blood-filled corpora cavernosa and the veins that drain them. Impossible to miss . . .

But now, with the pistol in its holster, both his hands are free. He reaches for her. *Don't let him grab your hair* . . . She pulls her head back out of reach.

'Just put it in your *mouth*,' he says, and he reaches for her head again.

'Wait, let me get you ready,' she says. 'It'll be worth it, trust me.' She ducks even lower to get a better view of her target; twists her hand a little on his shaft to distract him. He throws his head back and groans.

And she marvels that he trusts her, that he really thinks she will do this, that he's watched so much porn, paid so many women to service him, that he thinks this is OK, normal, something she would do. He's not even scared, that she'll change her mind, try to hurt him. *He's not even scared.* He doesn't think a woman can hurt him. Wow.

Just keep his fucking brain switched off.

Above her, he's trying to talk his cock into staying erect, muttering, 'I'm going to fuck you so hard, I'm going to come in you, you dumb Chinese whore . . .'

It's almost a relief, to see him like this; to know. *So tiring, to wonder for years, am I over-reacting, am I crazy, trying to avoid being alone in a room with him . . . But yes, I was right to think this was in you all the time.*

His penis pulses, alive, in her right hand, as the needle approaches from underneath, and the enormity of what she is about to do hits her.

'Are you sure you want to do this,' she says, and she's not even sure who she's talking to; herself, Donnie, God . . .

'Just put my fucking *cock* in your *mouth*, bitch,' says Donnie.

'Oh, Donnie,' she says sadly. 'Oh, Donnie,' and she slides the needle, so sharp it's almost painless, into the underside of his penis, right at the base.

Nothing but blood vessels, you can't miss.

Awkwardly, left-handed, she pushes the plunger. For a terrible instant it doesn't move; and then it does, fast, in a satisfying surge, and all the liquid vanishes inside him and he's finally registering that something has happened, 'What the hell . . .'

'Sorry, my nails . . .'

'Jesus, trim those fucking talons.'

For a brief moment his erection hardens, from the increased pressure of the injected liquid. 'Yeah, that's it . . .' he says uncertainly.

My God, he still doesn't know . . .

But his body is already panicking, withdrawing the blood and solution from his penis, to prepare for fight or flight, and as his erection collapses, all the dissolved, lethal, salt is pushed straight up, towards his pounding heart.

Perfect.

He sways, looks puzzled, looks down on her, and she smiles.

'I promised you something special,' she says, and gently pulls out the needle.

He reaches woozily towards his holster, for the gun, but it's too late; blood moves at walking pace through human veins; it took just a couple of beats to push that liquid up to his heart, and he's already going into cardiac arrest.

As he topples to his knees, she stands; it's like a dance, they pass each other, swap postures.

His head is below her now, and he is looking up at her face, finally making eye contact; astonished at this reversal.

She feels a wave of relief so strong it's almost nausea.

Three times the lethal dose for a woman of my weight, she thinks. And it's not a linear scale, so probably double the lethal dose for Donnie.

She can see the process in her head, as clearly as if she were observing it through an electron microscope. With his bloodstream so full of the dissolved salt, potassium ions can no longer pass through his cell walls; can't send their crucial messages. One by one, the muscle fibres of his heart fail to reset, for the next contraction.

The experiment is working.

'How do you like it, Donnie?'

'Oh *Jesus* . . .'

He stares down, but the needle was so sharp, and the pressure drop as he lost his erection so swift, closing the tiny wound, that there isn't even any blood; he can't work out what's happened.

'Being penetrated, against your will? You like that?' She holds up the syringe by the red thread. 'Me, spurting inside you? Sex is dangerous, Donnie.'

On his knees, he places one hand flat to his chest, over his spasming heart, so that he looks, for an incongruous instant, as though he is about to recite the Pledge of Allegiance. He gropes blindly downward with his other hand till it cups his shrivelled cock and balls. He's trying to speak – to breathe – but he can't. He topples forward, onto his face.

She takes a step; carefully places her bare right foot in the small of his back, and holds him to the floor as he spasms, his trousers still bunched around his ankles.

The spasms weaken. Grow further apart. The heart dies slowly. It takes a while. It's hard to kill a man.

Finally, there's no heartbeat. No breathing. No nothing.

She relaxes a little, lets go the thread, and the empty syringe falls to the wooden floor. She waits another minute, just in case. Then she crouches, and rolls him over onto his back. He's heavy. Dead weight . . . She takes the orange data cubes from his pockets. One, two, three, four, five . . . Studies them. So small, to hold all those years of her life. Everything she's learned about the brain, and body. About replacing what's been lost. Fixing what's broken.

She looks down at the body. All the words and emotions she's ever swallowed in this building come back up. 'You . . . *fucking* . . . *asshole* . . .' She kicks him hard, into the side of his gut. It's like kicking a waterbed. The gut sloshes, and his whole body rocks. 'You *made* me *do* this.' She kicks him again, and again, till her bare feet hurt.

She turns away from his body, and walks towards her office.

There is a panicky electronic whoop from behind her, and she spins around.

The cardiac alarm rings through the corridor.

Damn damn damn, forgot that . . . Donnie's fitness monitor. Got to cancel the call to emergency services . . .

She runs back, drops the five data cubes in a bouncing scatter across the floor, and grabs the old scuffed monitor pulsing red on his limp wrist. Grabs his other hand, pulls it around, hits 'False Alarm' with his dead finger, to cancel the ambulance call.

It's still warm, it's still his fingerprint, it still works.

With his dead hand in her trembling hand, she switches off his monitor.

She stands up. Bows her head a moment, but no more words come. There are no prayers for this.

He deserved it. He got it. It's done.

He can't hurt Colt now. He can't hurt anyone.

She picks up the cubes, and goes to get her clothes.

In her office, she pulls up her underwear, but then remembers his body, out of sight in the corridor. His gun, still in its holster. Her limbs shiver with a primal, irrational fear that he could come to life again, if left unobserved . . . She brings the rest of her clothes back out to the corridor, and looks at him while she dresses.

Once she's finished dressing, she double-checks his pockets, to make sure she has all her data cubes. She takes his gun from its holster, checks the safety catch, slips it in her jacket pocket. Walks along the corridor, picks up her empty pistol, the box of useless bullets, from the floor. As an afterthought – thinking vaguely, guiltily, of fingerprints and murder weapons – she goes back for the empty syringe too, and shoves it into the cardboard box with the bullets.

She turns around, and studies him. The muscles relaxing. The tension gone. He no longer frowns.

The spirit has left the body.

The breakdown has begun, cell by cell. And damage done now will never be repaired.

Ashes to ashes. Dust to dust.

One less asshole.

That was crazy. That was *crazy.*

I did it.

*

She returns to Lab 2. Gets the accelerant from the fridge; a fat, one-shot capsule of StemStim B7.

Unplugs a fresh server for Colt.

Takes the server out to the car.

Another.

Another.

Takes some more cables to be sure.

When she's done, she stands by her car in the hot, empty parking lot. She looks back at the building. The silk of her mother's jacket is tight over her shoulders from the weight of the two guns, the bullets, the syringe, the data cubes. Death; her life's work.

Who am I, she thinks, amazed.

She looks inside herself for the guilt she should feel, but there is none. Just a kind of hot, hard, unfamiliar joy.

I had to kill Donnie, to save Colt. To save myself. And I am glad he's dead. Would Jesus prefer Colt dead? Me, dead? Why would he prefer that? No, sorry, Mama. Sorry, Jesus. I tried to be good, and it wasn't enough.

I brought life into the world. And now I have brought death into the world.

Who am I, now?

She gets into the car, and slams the door.

I'll find out.

116

Naomi is a mile away from the facility when she sees the flash in the BMW's rear-view mirror.

She is still looking in the mirror when the second missile hits the burning shell of her lab. The small building vanishes completely, in rippling waves of black smoke and orange fire.

Some part of her mind thinks there's been a glitch; that it's the rear-view screen in her old car, somehow switched over to news; she half-reaches for the mirror in reflex, to switch it back to rear view.

Then she recognizes the broken, burning skeleton of her building, emerging from the smoke.

Thank God, I got my research out . . .

But of course, she's only taken the data. The mice, the caterpillars, the tissue samples, are still back there . . . Naomi closes her eyes and sees confused images; the striped caterpillars turn black, then blaze orange in the heat; bright tiger stripes rippling . . .

She opens her eyes just in time to take the next bend, a little wide.

Concentrate, concentrate.

But if the ravens can't see me . . . how . . .

Of course; Donnie left a message, telling Ryan I was there . . .

So was it the immune system at all? Or did Ryan just try to kill me? Forget it, that doesn't matter. That's not the point.

She looks back, at how slowly, how calmly she dressed. How slowly she removed the servers to the car.

And she thinks; if the immune system has blown up the lab; it could blow up the house . . .

Colt.

She puts her foot down, accelerating into the next corner, and the BMW screams around it at a tilt, grey smoke scorching off the back tyres.

She had thought she was merely calm, as she carried the servers past the body. No, she'd been stunned. Too stunned to think things through, to see the implications.

Get home . . .

117

She runs into Colt's room, without knocking. He barely looks up. Oh God, he's so grown up, so handsome . . .

'Got the StemStim?' he says.

She hands over the one-shot capsule.

'Thanks, Mama.'

He's alive. He's alive . . .

She opens her mouth. Nothing comes out.

No, I can't tell him.

'Mama, will you do it . . .' He preps the capsule and its specialized syringe. Hands it to her.

'OK . . .' Oh God, my hands are shaking . . .

It doesn't help that, when she was a student injecting into an artery, rather than a vein, usually only happened by mistake. Too dangerous to try it deliberately, unless, perhaps, you were targeting a toxic drug at a tumour, and the patient was already in so much trouble the extra risk was worth it. But Colt needs the accelerant delivered directly to the brain.

Injecting into an artery is still high risk, even with the new, pressurized capsules, and ultra-thin arterial needles. *Focus . . .* She silently injects the accelerant, deep. Into his internal carotid artery.

Straight to the brain . . .

'Woooah . . .' says Colt.

Yes, arterial injections hurt. More nerves. As the capsule emp-
ties into her son's neck, with a soft sucking sound, she shudders.
'Sorry . . .'

She can barely speak. Throat jammed with suppressed words,
suppressed emotions.

Can't deal with the overwhelm.

No. You can't fall apart now.

'How was it?' says Colt, finally looking at her.

'What?'

'Your trip to the lab.'

And she tells him, some of it. Just some of it. Enough for now.

'Wow, Mama,' says Colt, when she's done. '*Wow*, Mama.'

'I know,' says Naomi. 'I know. Look, you do your work. I've got
to clean up.'

She turns away, and goes to the bathroom, and closes the door.

Gets in the shower. Stays there a long time.

*

OK.

Now, coffee.

Walking back through the house to the kitchen, she is intensely
aware that every device she passes is spying on them, betraying
them. That if Colt's fake data feeds fail for a second, their presence
in the house will be revealed.

Standing in front of the closed fridge – with its sensors tuned
to tell when the door opens; when the temperature drops; when
the milk is removed, and not replaced – she thinks, oh, he's confident, he's enhanced, he's good; but he's still a kid, there could be
errors in the code . . .

And if there are . . . she, he, the house will shortly vanish in a
fireball.

Black smoke, and orange fire.

Hey, remember when the decision to start the day with a coffee
was as rebellious as I got?

She laughs, opens the fridge.

Well, I need coffee.

If we die, we die.

10

Stack Overflows

'Typical interneuronal reset times are on the order of five milliseconds, which allows for two hundred digital-controlled analog transactions per second. Even accounting for multiple nonlinearities in neuronal information processing, this is on the order of a million times slower than contemporary electronic circuits, which can switch in less than one nanosecond' — Ray Kurzweil,
The Singularity Is Near

'We hypostatize information into objects. Rearrangement of objects is change in the content of the information; the message has changed. This is a language which we have lost the ability to read. We ourselves are a part of this language; changes in us are changes in the content of the information. We ourselves are information-rich; information enters us, is processed and is then projected outward once more, now in an altered form. We are not aware that we are doing this, that in fact this is all we are doing'. — Philip K. Dick, *Valis*

'We will travel to Mars / even as folks on Earth / are still ripping open potato chip / bags with their teeth.'
— David Berman, 'Self-Portrait at 28'

118

While Naomi makes herself a coffee in the kitchen, Colt hooks up the servers in his room, and optimizes their flow.

Now to connect them to his brain.

Only problem is, their electronic information will arrive at almost the speed of light, in a chemical brain that hardly moves at all.

He is still the bottleneck.

If he's going to have a realtime fight with the immune system, then any fast decision-making will have to be done by the servers.

Luckily, he has a lot of new neurons, still busy forming new pathways; incredibly suggestible, and quick to learn.

He just has to force them to communicate with the servers. Outsource their decision-making.

Rewrite his brain a little.

OK, a lot.

He runs through the plan again. And again.

Oh man, there will be loss of function. Some old neural pathways will get overwritten. There's no way to keep this inside the new boundaries.

The brain is holistic, it doesn't do clean separations.

Even if this works . . . I'm basically giving myself superpowers and a stroke at the same time. And hoping I come out ahead on the deal.

Well, I can fix a lot of the damage later. If there is a later.

If I live through this.

He realizes he's checking a tiny piece of perfect code for the third time.

OK, that's as good as I can get it.

He takes the cable – so gross, so physical, so out of scale with the delicacy of the two sets of circuits being connected – and plugs the system of servers into his helmet.

A lot of data has to be accessed and moved. A *lot*.

The code runs.

His helmet translates the surge, and delivers it in focused cascades of information to his brain, through the retinal connections.

His brain has grown pretty good at integrating external devices with its own wetware. But this is an order of magnitude stranger, more overwhelming, more disorienting.

It's like the back of his skull has opened out into a huge space that gets bigger and bigger, as the servers integrate with his neurons.

The external, electronic processors have overwhelming speed and scale.

His slower, organic brain has interconnectivity; immense neural complexity.

Now each begins to outsource tasks to the other.

The first few minutes are just a gigantic, crazy, two-way data jam.

It's channelled; it's following the principles he's planned, programmed; but there's just *so much* activity that the data overflows the channels; stuff ends up in the wrong places.

For a minute, two minutes, ten minutes, eternity, it's impossible to tell . . . his sight and hearing and smell and touch are switched off, obliterated, totally overwhelmed by the roar of information arriving down these new channels.

Deaf and dumb, he is lost inside his own mind, drowning in dataflows, not even sure if he is breathing.

What if he's got this wrong?

What if the new data keep coming; spill over? Assign themselves to some network of neurons that he needs in order to breathe?

What if he switches off his lungs, his heart?

Overwrites key memories?

Forgets why he is doing this?

Forgets who he is?

And now, disturbed new neurons fire, link, form accelerated connections, all over his brain; chains of association are launched, and his senses return.

Kind of.

It's like he's vanished into himself, like a star collapsing under its own weight. He's a black hole. He can't see the outside world; just the architecture of his new interior, shimmering into being. Huge warehouses of self, stretching off endlessly.

Memories assemble themselves from distributed, highly compressed fragments. He's smelling and tasting and seeing a jumbled, psychedelic past. At first, the tag to say 'this is a memory' is missing; each utterly vivid memory feels like the present, like it is happening again, now.

He is fourteen years old.

He is twelve.

He is seven.

And each time, it is totally real, it is all true, it is all there is; it is now.

He's adrift in time.

But once the first big waves of information have moved through the bottleneck in either direction, his mind begins to settle down.

It tidies up.

His memories get tagged as memories; and, *click*, he is no longer a time-traveller. He goes from being seven years old, in school, at lunchtime, and frightened – the smells, the sounds, the wild roaring children, the impossibility of knowing what will happen next – to being back in the now, eighteen, and simply remembering something that happened long ago.

The relief, the sorrow, as his sense of time returns, and all those living moments become the dead past.

Then sight comes back.

Schwhuuuuuussssshhhh . . .

It's like being hit by a train. Pure, raw, unfiltered visual data, overwhelming; a tremendous blast of light and colour.

His brain starts to filter the raw data. Edit it. Interpret it.

And . . . *click*; it's not a raw blast of hot, bright light and colour, it's a picture of the world.

Objects.

His room.

Hah, everything is sideways. Stroke in the visual cortex?

He can smell coffee.

Wait, where is he?

He has fallen from his chair; he should have thought of that; that the process would be disruptive, that his deep motor coordination might be upset. Should have been lying down, for the transfer.

Who's that, looming above him?

His mother.

No, he's not lying on the floor. He's lying in her arms. She's saying something, over and over.

There's a stain on her blouse.

She must have spilled her coffee when I fell.

'Sorry, Mama,' he says. 'I'm OK. You can make more coffee.'

But he can't understand himself: his voice sounds like pink noise, like raw modem chatter, the meaning hidden, encoded. His jaw, his cheek muscles, don't seem under his control. He tries to smile and nothing happens.

Need to control this.

He calls up an image of his own brain. A map of what's just happened: dataflows signalling where they landed. It takes him a while to understand it.

His thoughts sluuuuuurrrr.

Wow. Big overflows into the occipital lobe. Messy.

But he can change it. He can route around the damage. Between the new neurons and the new servers, he has plenty of room to do it.

Yes.

He routes around the damage.

His mother just holds him, rocks him, talking to herself. '. . . dimaykildimaykildimaykil . . .'

He strains to understand, but his hearing registers the sounds without unpacking their meaning.

Then meaning kicks in, as his brain recovers enough to interpret the data. Now he can hear what she is saying. The words, not the noises.

'I killed him, I killed him, I killed him . . .'

'It's OK, Mama,' he says. 'I'm OK.'

He can hear his own words. Understand them.

Good.

Colt pulls himself free of his mother's arms, and shakily stands. 'I'm OK, Mama.'

And now he is. Just about. He can still hear some weird tones that aren't actually there in the outside world – a green noise with a texture like frayed rope – and his mouth is full of tastes that feel metallic and multicoloured and textured in some peculiar ways – spiky blue tastes – but he can live with that.

Naomi stares at his face. 'Oh, Colt . . .'

He can speak.

It jolts tears out of her, tears that have been unable to escape for the past hour. Words, too.

'No, I killed Donnie. Oh God. I killed him. I know I should feel guilty, but . . . I don't know how I feel.'

And she tells Colt the rest of what happened.

How she killed a man. Not everything, God no, but enough, now, for Colt to understand.

'Oh, Mama,' says Colt helplessly. 'He was . . . that was his fault, not yours . . .'

He knows he should mourn Donnie, the sinner, the dead man; share his mother's conflicted, Christian sorrow; but he doesn't feel it, and he can't pretend he does.

Donnie was a dick.

Colt mourns the lab, where he grew up. Where his mother slowly uncovered beautiful truths. Blown away. Gone.

Colt doesn't say it aloud; but the implications aren't good.

There are only three copies of her work still loose in the wild.

The raw research, stored in the five orange data cubes.

The theory, stored in Naomi's brain.

And the reality, hardwired into Colt's.

'It's Ryan,' she says, 'Ryan must have—'

'No,' says Colt, thinking, analysing. 'It wasn't Dad. The immune system must have been reading the metadata on everything coming in and out of the lab. Dad's calls, Donnie's calls . . . Yeah. The fitness monitor; its emergency call tipped off the system, that Donnie had been killed . . . And the system knew the lab contained all your research . . . Ordered a strike on the lab.'

'But . . . why didn't it kill *me*?' says Naomi. 'How did I escape?'

'I think . . . I think it destroyed the lab blind, based on the metadata. It simply didn't see you.'

'You mean . . . it *still* doesn't know we're here?'

'No . . .' More confidently, 'No.'

'Oh! I was worried . . . I thought . . . we were just waiting to die . . .'

'Oh sure, it's decided to kill us. It wants to kill us. But the ravens watching the house are still blind; the sensors inside the house are telling it the house is empty; the BMW still doesn't exist, it's leaving no electronic trace. So, no, it doesn't know we are here. And there's something else . . . it's not . . .' Colt hesitates, unsure how to describe it. 'I think . . . it can't trust its own senses . . .'

'We're making it neurotic,' says Naomi, and laughs shakily.

'Yes,' says Colt. 'It saw the lab was empty: but it could detect people in it. It destroyed the lab; but it didn't see an explosion . . .'

'It's no longer sure what is real and what isn't,' says Naomi.

'Yes, exactly, that's it,' says Colt. 'But I'm pretty sure it will send over more drones now, to check up on the house: and I may not be able to fool them all.' Colt frowns. 'And if we make it *too* neurotic, it might get paranoid enough to destroy the house anyway.'

Naomi rubs her throat. 'Why hasn't it?' she says.

Colt's been wondering about that too.

'I think it's using the house as a trap,' he says. 'It *wants* us to come here.'

'So . . .' Naomi looks around Colt's untidy bedroom. 'This is the one place we're safe . . .'

'As long as it doesn't work out that we're already inside the trap,' says Colt.

'. . . But, given how fast it's growing . . . how smart it's getting . . .'

'Yeah,' says Colt. 'I reckon it will work that out in another hour or so, max.'

There is a lurch of understanding in his brain, as neurons frantically catch up with what's just happened, and connect the final new islands of information. Oh *wow*. OK, that should be enough. 'I've got to go now, Mama,' says Colt abruptly. He sits back into his chair. Starts to connect to the gameworld.

'Shall I get you water?'

'Mmm? Yeah, sure.'

She turns to go. Turns back. 'Do you have enough servers?' she says. 'To fight it?'

The *servers*? Colt turns, looks at his mother blankly.

Oh, man; she doesn't realize how big an enemy they are fighting, at all.

'Those aren't there to fight the immune system, Mama.' He

glances over his shoulder at the array of servers. 'That's just my remote control, for the network I'm setting up. It'll take a lot more than those to fight back.'

And, while he's still talking to her, he uses the servers, uses his admin privileges to dig deep into the backend of the game, into the secure global networks that host it on every continent.

OK, so he's survived the stroke.

Now to see if he has the superpowers.

119

It helps that the indie game community has always been locked in a war against government surveillance. Ever since the crypto wars of the 1990s, the battle of the backdoors . . . Indie gamers led the great escape from government surveillance; away from an open net, and from an open, flexible, but vulnerable cloud, back to medieval, locked-off physical fortresses, with only a few well-guarded entrances and exits.

He makes a map of the gameworld's physical territory. The physical nodes, in the real world, that store and process the game.

Hmm. Not bad at all.

This gameworld has been fighting off attacks from state cyberwarfare groups, digital fundamentalists, identity thieves, chauvinistas, and plain vanilla hackers for years. And, after each attack, it has improved itself. Learned from the experience. Upgraded its defences.

It's robust.

By now, all the game nodes form a hyper-secure network. Not exactly *easy* to defend; not against the resources of a military state; but a lot easier to defend than most networks.

And he needs the gameworld to help him now.

*

Colt sits back in his chair. It's looking good. He reckons he can even keep the game running, while he does what he's about to do, if he downgrades the speed and detail a little, across a billion customized gameworlds, and uses that huge, freed capacity for his own purposes.

Of course, if he's wrong, and he crashes the gameworld . . . he'll have several hundred million players really angry with him. Collapsing the entire gameworld for private purposes is about as big a faux pas as an open-source indie game developer can make. He could lose his admin privileges.

Total social death.

Which scares him more than the drone cloud hunting him.

120

Colt sets the noise-cancellation in the helmet to 90 per cent. That should block minor distractions, but still allow him to hear any major event out in the real world.

And then he gets down to work on his plan.

He begins coding, ingame, in the test range, because it's soothing there.

He is coding faster and better than he has ever coded before, when a crude clay beaker abruptly appears in his hand. Objects placed in hands have to be mapped. He stares down at it. Oh, Mama must have returned with his water. 'Thanks . . .' He doesn't map her, doesn't even glance towards where she is in the real room.

Her distant voice – 10 per cent of her voice – whispers, 'You're welcome,' and she leaves again.

Ingame, he places the clay beaker on a low boulder as, outgame, he puts the mug on his table.

He has a wall of servers at his back, overdriven, running hot, doing all the hard work; he just has to see the patterns; rework old code; write new code. *Lots* of new code. It flows from him like poetry; fluid, flexible, every symbol perfect. He has become a fountain of code.

And it's not enough.

As he starts to see the outline of the problem emerge from the data, he works out how much fresh coding will be required. The answer strikes him like a fist, so that air leaks out of his mouth in a little *whoooosh*. 'There isn't enough time,' he whispers.

Time . . .

He checks the time, frowns.

Something about it flicks a memory.

A recent memory, damaged by the rewiring of his brain, cut adrift.

Oh, *crêpes*.

He's meant to meet Sasha.

Here, in the test range. Now.

Oh, Sasha . . .

He stops writing code.

Where is she?

'Colt.'

He turns around.

And she steps right up to him.

Sasha. As herself.

Her avatar that isn't an avatar.

Colt feels a tremendous tension in his chest. What the heck *is* that? He pokes around his interior.

Some kind of unreleased emotion.

OK.

He stares at her face.

'I've been waiting for ever,' she says.

'I'm sorry,' Colt says. Be polite. 'I'm so sorry.'

Something drifts down, diagonally, between them. It's small, white.

Another something.

Another.

Sasha puts out her hand, catches one.

Tiny, crisp and white in the palm of her hand.

It vanishes.

'I'm sorry I . . . grabbed you. I didn't understand . . .'

'Uh huh.' She looks around her. 'My snow shouldn't be falling here. The air should be too warm. What's gone wrong?'

'I'm, ah . . . I've been rewriting the mapping algorithms, and it's a bit messy, sorry . . .'

'Rewriting how? Why?'

Colt shrugs.

'Tell me what's *happening*,' she says.

'Happening?'

'There's something wrong,' she says, waving an arm at the gameworld's horizon, where the high, thin clouds don't look quite right, 'and I can't help you because I don't know what it is.'

Tell her what's wrong? The pressure in his chest is making it hard to breathe.

Tell her what's wrong.

'This is too much,' he says, as occasional tiny shimmering flecks of snow drift down sideways from the distant, high, thin cloud.

Sasha nods. 'Yes, it is. But I can help you,' she says, looking into his eyes.

The statement is so absurd he almost laughs, but he doesn't have the spare capacity. How can she help him? She's not enhanced. He's working at full capacity, massively enhanced and backed up by a global network of secure tech, and that's not enough.

'How?' he says.

'I don't know, yet,' she says. 'First you have to tell me what's wrong.'

She reaches out slowly, with both hands, and holds his face. Her micromesh gloves transmit the pressure of her fingers through the reactive plastic of his helmet, and only then does he realize his whole body has been trembling.

She's looking into his eyes. 'I can help you. You're not alone,' she says, and lets go his face. Steps back. 'Now, *tell me what's wrong.*'

Tell her what's wrong. He stares at her avatar's face, her amazing face, and the emotions he's been holding inside expand till he has to gasp in air.

His ribs are pushed out by the surge, until his chest feels like it's going to burst.

Not alone.

Not alone in the universe.

Not alone . . .

'I'm afraid,' says Colt, rapidly, before he can think about it, analyse it, overrule himself, 'when I'm talking to you, that I'll say something wrong.'

'Wrong? How—'

'—Or, you know, misunderstand what you mean. Look at what happened when we . . . when I . . . When I thought you wanted me, to, to . . .' He waves his hands at her, at him; this is beyond the territory he has words for. 'I'm not good with people. I get things wrong.'

'Me too, Colt.' She sighs again. 'Me too.'

'*You?* You seem pretty good with people to me.'

Sasha shakes her head. 'I fake it. I study them. Watch a lot of video. I'm able to act appropriate most of the time. But I'm guessing, I don't know, like a neurotypical would.'

'Me too!' says Colt. 'Me too . . . I'm *guessing*, and when I guess wrong it *hurts*.'

'So we are both running scripts,' says Sasha.

'I guess. Yes.'

'So what would happen if neither of us ran scripts?'

Silence.

'I don't know,' says Colt.

'What would happen if we just said what we felt, and didn't try to second-guess the other person's answer? If we didn't try to protect ourselves from a bad response?'

'I don't know,' says Colt.

'Let's try it. And whatever happens, we won't give the other person a hard time.'

'OK,' says Colt.

'Shall we take turns?'

'OK,' says Colt.

Silence.

'You go first,' says Sasha.

'OK . . . I like you,' Colt says.

'OK.'

Silence.

'I like you too,' says Sasha.

'You're not just saying that, to mirror me? As a script?'

'No. I like you. I'm saying what I feel.'

'OK.' Colt looks inside himself, for something to say. Something true. There are so many things that he feels a spasm of despair.

Where to begin?

'I'm just going to say the most important things in my head,' he says. 'The biggest things. They might not be relevant.'

'That's OK.'

'Sometimes I feel too much and it hurts and I want to stop feeling and so I kind of make myself stop feeling, but the feelings don't go away, they just get moved somewhere I can't get at them. But they are still there.' He pauses. No, that's enough. 'Your turn.'

'OK.' There is a pause while she thinks. 'Sometimes I feel too much too . . .'

'You're mirroring me—'

'No! Let me *finish* . . . We just have, I think we have, a lot in common. My dad . . . oh, both my parents . . . I thought they loved me, that they were just busy or careless or something, but now, I don't think they ever loved me, and that makes me feel . . . terrible.' She twists her mouth into a shape that makes Colt feel sad. 'I sometimes just do stupid stuff, not to feel that. Drink too much. Drive too fast. Other stuff . . .'

Colt nods, to show that he has heard, has understood. Sasha smiles back at him, and Colt feels *incredible.*

'I love looking at your face,' he says rapidly. 'In the real world. It looks right. It is my favourite thing I've ever looked at. Not because it is beautiful, like in movies. Because it is your face.'

'My *face*? Colt, that's—'

'—Your face makes me feel like I'm filling up with light and heat and . . . energy,' he says. 'I want to be with you, but I've got all this *work* to do, because my dad is trying to kill me and Mama. And I don't think I can *do* it because there isn't enough *time*.'

'Wait—'

'—But you look like you glow. You don't look like other objects in the universe, to me—'

'—Wait, *wait*, who's trying to kill you and your mother? Your *father*?'

But telling her is making the tightness in his chest loosen, and so he ploughs on; he can't stop now; it's started coming out, so it all has to come out. Words he recognizes as true only as he speaks them; words he hadn't known he was going to speak. '—When you were in my room and I looked at you, it was like your skin glowed—'

'—Colt—'

'—To my senses, it glowed. Something happened in my brain, and I think about you a lot, and when I think about you, it's like I feel something is missing, some part of me is *missing*.'

'—Please, Colt—'

'—I've always felt alone, but I didn't *notice*, because I thought it was *normal*, I mean, I feel alone when I'm alone, of course, but I feel alone, too, when I'm with anyone else but you. But, with you, I don't feel alone. I don't feel alone. And I didn't know you could feel not alone. I didn't *know*.' He pauses, and she's about to speak, but there's something else, something else he has to say, that he doesn't want to say but he has to say, and he says, 'And it was too much and I ran away. And I should have said yes.'

When she's sure he's done, she sighs and says, 'Oh, Colt, you schmuck. Why didn't you say this before?'

'I didn't *know* this before.' Colt stares at Sasha's amazing face. It doesn't look happy and it doesn't look sad, but her face is doing *something*. He tries to decode her expression, but he can't, and that makes him afraid. 'I just had this . . . big feeling. And I was scared.'

Sasha nods. 'I get that.'

'Your turn,' says Colt.

Sasha hesitates. 'That's a lot of stuff, Colt. I'm going to have to think about it.'

'OK.'

'But I'm glad you told me.'

'OK.' They stare into each other's eyes until Colt feels like he's going to explode.

She rubs her face, left to right, hard, with the palm of her right hand. 'Seriously, Colt, that's a lot to process. I can't . . . That was . . . more than I expected.'

'Are you angry I said that? Do you . . . is it . . .'

'—That's a lot to process. Let me process it. I'll get back to you.'

'OK,' says Colt. 'OK.'

'OK,' says Sasha, looking away. 'So how is your dad trying to kill you?'

And Colt tells her about his mother's work. His upgrade. His father's base. The immune system. The destruction of the lab.

'Uh huh,' says Sasha, and glances at the strange clouds coming closer. 'So what's your plan?'

'Well, I'm pretty good at noticing patterns,' says Colt. 'Especially now, after the . . . upgrade? Good enough that I can sometimes project them into the future. Like, not just guess a probability. Actually predict the future, pretty much.'

Sasha blinks at that, but she says, 'OK. So?'

377

'I need to model the immune system, and see if I can predict what it will do. See if I can work out a way to . . .' He trails off.

Destroy it?

Escape it?

Well, he won't know till he's run some simulations . . .

'Switch it off?' says Sasha into the silence.

Colt shakes his head. 'That's designed to be impossible. But if I could get it to attack another target . . . Or if it faced a bigger threat, maybe we'd stop being a priority . . . Or if I could get it to attack itself, somehow . . .'

'Or convince it you're dead . . .'

'Yeah, there's a lot of possibilities.' He rubs the back of his neck. Tight muscles. He squeezes them, tries to loosen them, relax them. Don't think about how you feel. 'But if I try those possibilities in the real world . . . I can only choose one, and I only get one chance. And, if I get it wrong, I die. I don't have infinite ammo. I don't have unlimited lives.'

'OK,' says Sasha. 'I get that. How about—'

But Colt's not really listening, he's too anxious, he's still chasing his own thoughts. '—But if I can map the immune network accurately, in here, ingame, if I can *see* it,' he says, '*understand* it as a model . . . then I can run some simulations, see how it will act. I can try things without getting Mama, me and Mama, killed . . .'

'Jesus, Colt, that's a lot of coding . . .' Sasha looks around. 'But I guess the gameworld already contains a model of the world . . .'

'That's what *I* thought. But . . .' He trails off.

The problem is too big.

He had never really thought before about what they've built here. To him, the gameworld *was* the world; it contained all he ever needed, all he ever wanted. A world where he could be himself. Be alone, and free. He thought it contained everything important.

But of course the gameworld's America is an old, pre-electric America, radically simplified. A libertarian, anarchic dream of a continent where heroes and cowards make their own destiny. Create, destroy, mine, harvest; you make it, you take it, with your own hands, and the tools you craft. A place, a no-place, where it is just you, and the rocks, and the wind. It is the skeleton of America, the ghost, with every level of government – federal, state, local, tribal – surgically removed. All the social structures stripped away. All the technological structures, cultural structures. A minimal sketch.

A technological dream of a world before technology.

Only now does he really notice all that they've left out.

The problem is too big.

'What's the problem?' says Sasha, and the repeat of the word he's just thought shakes him, it's as though she saw into his mind. His muscles clench in response, in fear, rocking him back on his heels. 'The map of the natural world here is amazing,' she says, 'you've done a fantastic job. It's complex, interdependent; a fully modelled ecosystem . . .'

'Yes,' says Colt. 'Sure. We nailed nature. But the human world here is a . . .' He looks for a word for it. Hmeep. Hmeep. '. . . *Cartoon.*'

'Well, the gameworld is a modelling system,' says Sasha. 'Modelling a complex world is what it does. So you can just . . . model it, map it . . .'

'But how, how can it map a drone cloud; self-driving vehicles; missiles; total surveillance?' Colt is nearly crying. 'I can't do it, I don't have time to create a suite of drones, self-driving vehicles . . . There are no models of drones to be *rendered*. The gameworld doesn't have the graphics for them, the physics, it'll take too long to make an entire new class of objects . . . there are no models of human society to embed them in . . .'

Sasha reaches out again, holds his shaking face steady, looks him in the eyes, says, 'Drones fly. They hover. They observe. They kill.'

'Yes! It's too much . . .'

'So you need to model eagles . . .'

'Yes . . .'

'. . . But you have *real* eagles, Colt. Real hawks, and doves. Real ravens, and vultures, and sparrows, ingame. You have lightning. You have buffalo. You have mountain lions. You have wolves. Coyotes. Bears. Sheep. Cattle. Snakes.'

And Colt gets it. 'Build it . . . in metaphors?'

Sasha nods. 'The gameworld is an ecosystem. And so is the surveillance world. Similar rules. Predators and prey . . .'

'Yes! They map . . .'

'. . . You wouldn't have to change much at all,' she says. 'They already exist, they have killer instincts, they track, they fly; call to each other, hover, kill. Just change their speeds and heights, some variables. Minimal, minimal recoding.'

He's already begun.

Colt assigns a bird, an animal, to each drone, each self-driving vehicle in the real-world immune system.

A spirit animal, he thinks.

Just give each machine a spirit animal . . .

The absurd thought makes him happy.

Code pours into being.

He sends bots out into the tangled electronic jungle of the real world to search for clues, for metadata – spoor, he thinks, tracks, scat – for anything that might betray what the immune system is doing.

Then Colt looks for the patterns in the data.

Maps it onto the gameworld.

Let a raven be a raven . . .

The drones pop into existence in the blue sky.

Two blind ravens stare at him. An eagle soars high, high above. Another eagle.

So that's where they are. The killers.

'While you're running the simulations, ingame,' says Sasha, 'how are you going to keep an eye on the gameworld resources?'

'On the network?'

'Yes. What happens if the immune system attacks?'

'Oh yeah,' says Colt, and he links the attack strength of the immune system to the sound of the wind.

Listens.

The wind whispers. The strange clouds are closer, but they're not moving fast. A single snow crystal drifts by; slow, calm; hits the desert floor and evaporates.

No attacks yet. Good.

'Mmmm,' says Sasha. 'Nice, for big attacks; but what if they do a pinpoint takedown, on a single node? It would hardly affect the wind. You mightn't even notice the notification.'

'You're right,' says Colt.

'Basically,' says Sasha, 'you're not paranoid enough for this job.' She grins. 'I can definitely help you with that.'

'So what should I do?'

'Well, if you're running simulations here, and coding while you're inside the game . . . You need a visual interface, ingame, that shows every individual node, live, constantly.'

'OK,' says Colt. 'How about . . . this . . .'

And he assigns all the major nodes of the network their own individual identities, and maps them onto buffalo, ingame, so he can see at a glance how they are doing, communicating, interacting.

A simple visual interface, using assets that are already ingame, it only takes a few lines of code.

'Oh, I like that,' says Sasha.

He hears them before he sees them. The lazy thunder of their hooves.

An immense herd of buffalo.

They pour out of the valley between two hills, trot towards him, skirting a crater, then break into a gallop, snorting, kicking up dust.

'Look,' says Sasha, pointing.

One calf is sickly, trailing.

Colt homes in on it.

Oh yeah. The new data centre in Iceland. Some problem with the cables to the European mainland . . . Wow, great interface.

'Well, *that* worked,' says Sasha.

'Yeah . . .'

And now Colt moves rapidly back and forth between the gameworld and the code, analysing, diagnosing . . .

Holy guacamole. Must be some kind of robosub . . . They've tapped into the cables, a mile under the water. Nothing I can do.

Bullpoop . . . this is . . . this is . . . *fucking* . . .

Mustn't swear. Mustn't swear.

But that's not good. The immune system is using overseas assets now. NSA naval intelligence robots . . . It's growing. It can commandeer almost anything it needs. Colt shivers in the warm air. It *does* have infinite ammo . . .

Colt reassigns the new Icelandic data centre's tasks to the huge old secure centre in India.

A bull buffalo wanders over to the sickly calf. They grunt and groan, nuzzle each other.

'Oh,' says Sasha approvingly, 'Mapping the data transfer in-game . . .'

The data is transferred. Colt, about to take Iceland out of the network, hesitates.

'If the NSA are intercepting its data anyway . . .' he says.

Sasha smiles. 'We may as well give them something interesting to digest.'

They rapidly create a fake data stream, full of malware.

The big bull trots back to the protection of the herd.

The sickly calf wanders away from the herd, into the desert.

'There,' says Colt, pointing.

'Where . . . ah, there . . .' Sasha spots the coyotes.

The coyotes circle. Bring it down . . .

'I was right,' says Colt. 'NSA . . .'

Colt and Sasha watch happily as the coyotes kill. Eat.

The malware is on a timer. The NSA won't notice anything until after it's swallowed the lot . . .

OK, now the hard work.

121

Colt prepares a bunch of simulations.

First up, a way of attacking the immune system that looks very promising.

Second, another way, that does not look at all promising, but which would be *amazing* if it succeeded.

Third . . .

On he goes.

Strategy after strategy.

What might work? Defence? Attack? Diversion? Camouflage?

Well, the immune system launched early. There *could* be coding holes in its defences. Flaws . . . Sure, it's designed to check its own security, to self-repair weaknesses; but perhaps it's still vulnerable . . .

He'll try the most promising attack strategy first.

He launches his attack.

Colt has done everything to shield his identity, his location; but as soon as he issues commands, sends information out into the world, the immune system uses it to find him. It's astonishingly quick.

An eagle sweeps down – unnaturally large, unnaturally fast; tweaked by Colt to map onto a Gorgon drone missile system – and slams into him, its claws out. It strikes his head in passing, rips open his clothes, his side.

It's only an ingame event; but Colt has forgotten that he over-rode all the inbuilt safety software when he customized the helmet, the micromesh skinsuit.

His helmet and suit transmit the full force of the blow, unfiltered. The impact is far harder than he expects.

He is shocked, and screams.

Ingame, the eagle rips out Colt's liver through the wound.

Feeds.

As the game fades to black, Colt, his sight fading, hits reset.

*

Colt respawns in place, still lying on the ground where the eagle's impact flung him; his eyes still screwed shut in pain.

He gets reports on the simulation delivered as raw data straight to his new, rebuilt visual cortex. Reviews them without opening his eyes.

Wow wow *wow*. Its defences are amazing. It blocked things he didn't think could be blocked. Tracked him down with incredible speed, and cunning. The immune system outthought him. Outfought him.

That hurt.

He opens his eyes.

Sasha is standing over him.

'Well, that won't work,' says Colt weakly.

'Jesus, Colt, reset your skin.'

'Yeah. I should.'

But he doesn't.

Why not? Because . . . because I should be at risk in these simulations. There should be a risk of damage. Or it's not . . . it's not real enough.

OK. Another simulation.

So, let's try hiding this time . . .

He runs it, and dies.

When he opens his eyes again, Sasha is bending over him, holding his head up. Looking into his eyes.

His face hurts. Ingame, the eagle caught his cheekbone, broke his eye socket, ripped out his eye with its claw; and the safety-disabled helmet has done its best to map the broken cheekbone, broken eye socket. It did a pretty good job. Nothing is broken, in the real world; but he's going to be bruised.

Putting off the moment when he will run the next simulation, Colt says, 'How do you know so much about men, and ah . . .' He can't think of a word to express what he wants to say, and trails off.

'I started young,' she says.

'OK,' says Colt.

'I made all the mistakes.'

'That's how you learn, I guess.'

'Yep.'

'I've got this weird feeling,' says Colt.

'Tell me about it,' says Sasha.

Is that a sarcastic remark, or a request? Colt puzzles over it. Can't work it out.

I'll tell her about it, anyway.

'I think my . . .' What's a good word for it? '. . . Damage . . . makes a good fit with your damage,' says Colt. 'Like two halves of something broken.'

'Jagged edges,' says Sasha, 'that don't fit anything but each other.'

'Yeah! But they fit each other really, really well.'

'Like the two halves of a sorb apple,' says Sasha.

'What's a sorb apple?' says Colt.

Sasha runs a finger down Colt's bruised cheek.

Following the path a tear would take, if he were ever to cry.

'It's a kind of weird little apple,' she says. 'See, Zeus was jealous of human beings, we were so great, and so he cut us in two, like sorb apples, and scattered the halves. And, ever since, people have wandered the earth feeling incomplete.'

'Looking for their other half?'

'Yep. And if they're crazy lucky, they find it.'

'Yeah.' He stares into the eyes of her accurate avatar. 'We fit.'

'Yeah.'

OK. His face has stopped hurting so bad.

He runs the next simulation – an attempt to fool it into attacking itself – and the immune system sees through the deception straight away, and kills him.

Colt and Sasha look into each other's eyes, and talk, as he runs simulation after simulation, different approach after different approach, again and again.

He speaks to her, she speaks to him, each avoiding the implications of what is happening, as again and again the ravens call out to the eagles high above, and the lazy eagles peel free of the sky and plunge, and rip out his liver, kill him, again and again.

122

'Nature cannot be commanded except by being obeyed.'
— Francis Bacon

He has exhausted every likely option.

There is no solution, thinks Colt. There. Is. No. Solution . . .

From the corner of his eye, Colt spots a flash and puff, as a gunshot echoes off the nearby hills.

It came from the rim of the nearest crater . . .

A buffalo drops to its knees on the parched earth. Its huge horns touch the dusty ground.

'What was *that*,' says Sasha, looking up from coding.

Rifle, large calibre, thinks Colt. So, not a subtle attack. And from very nearby.

'Immune system just took out a big node,' says Colt, already working on fixing it. 'It's not dead, but . . .'

Can't fix it. Damn.

'Which one?' says Sasha.

'Rio de Janeiro.'

Sasha studies the buffalo herd, which is already splitting up, nervous, skittish.

She sees the implications.

'That's not good,' she says. 'All the South American nodes must be vulnerable, now . . .'

Colt nods. 'I've got to pull everything out of there.'

'You could still let the nodes in Brazil, Argentina, Chile draw landscape, do the less important stuff.'

'True.' He swaps some tasks around. Makes another attempt at recovering the Rio node.

The wounded buffalo tries to stand up. Can't. Drops back onto its knees.

Damn. OK, he'll run the real attack on the immune system from just the nodes he can defend.

They both go back to coding, but stay ingame.

This is . . . companionable? thinks Colt, glancing across at Sasha's avatar, frowning over her code. It's not a word he's ever used before, and he's not sure if he's using it right. What would his mother say?

It's cosy. This is cosy.

Sasha looks up and catches his glance. 'I think I can blind the immune system,' she says.

'How?'

She shrugs. 'Snow . . . I've been working on some fractal defence code that expands infinitely inside an attacker's system.'

'What, kind of a denial-of-service attack from within?'

'Yep, exactly. It's incredibly minimal, a tiny piece of code, so it's easy to sneak it in. But it expands like crazy, commits them to resolving infinitely complex snowflakes. Sucks their resources dry from inside . . .'

Another shot, and this time Colt hears the impact of the bullet in the thinner bone just below the wounded buffalo's ear.

Oh, not good, not good.

The buffalo moans, and topples over onto its side.

The hills lose texture.

Colour drains out of the sky.

The Rio node is gone.

'It's picking off the nodes, one by one,' he says, and he notices his voice is trembling.

He tries to deepen his voice, stabilize it. 'Killing my network . . .'

No, it's deeper, but it still trembles. Damn. He goes back to his normal voice. 'I have to launch an attack, while I still have the resources . . .'

'But you haven't found an approach that will work,' she says.

'I've found a couple that might work,' he says. She looks at him. Her eyes widen. 'Well, one that might work,' he says. 'If I tweak it.'

His best model says the chance of success is only 25 per cent. And it failed on the simulation.

But if he does nothing, his chance of success is zero.

He reviews the model, tries to work out how to improve it.

Another gunshot, from another crater rim; another buffalo falls.

No, there's no time to perfect this. He's losing nodes and resources far faster than he can improve the plan.

No more simulations.

No time.

He launches the attack.

123

'Any evolving species must look with misgivings on those of its members who first show signs of change, and will surely regard them as dangerous or crazy.'
— Alan Watts, *The Book*

As soon as he's unleashed the gameworld on the immune system, he knows he has made a mistake.

The gameworld is big, it's fast, it's smart, but it's not an offensive system. It wasn't designed to take out other networks. It can try and jam the immune system, overwhelm it, with targeted attacks; but the immune system . . . well, it's an immune system. Attacks are what it feeds on. It grabs data from the attacks, works out where they are coming from, and goes after those servers, the control nodes . . .

The gameworld has amazing cyber defences, sure.

But the immune system has cyber defences, and missiles. Lots of missiles.

It's not a fair fight.

The game system labours, ingame, to map what's happening out in the real world.

But the visual metaphors are beginning to break down.

'Colt . . .' It's Sasha, but she doesn't look right. The lines, the details of her face still look real, but the colours have destabilized. 'I can't stay ingame, there's problems with connection where I am in the real world . . .'

Her eyes turn green, then brown.

Her skin turns a yellowish red, then pale tones of blue. He knows it's an illusion, caused by the colour failure, but she looks cold, frozen.

'I'll finish my code outgame and come back . . .'

'Sasha . . .'

But she's gone.

He has no time to react to that.

The gameworld is being damaged faster than it can show Colt the damage.

The buffalo get nervous, very nervous, mill about, rounding up their calves, then they bunch together for protection.

The clouds are thickening. Moving lower, closer.

The matted coats of the buffalo generate tremendous static as they rub and push past each other under the low sky, and a sudden electric blue light wavers across their backs, ripples up their horns.

Overexcited ions.

St Elmo's fire.

What the heck is that mapping? Nothing good . . .

Colt switches back and forth, from the ingame overview to the raw code, rewriting it, fighting the counter-attack.

And now rapid, rhythmic gunfire comes from the crater rims.

Gatling guns, thinks Colt. Oh crap.

The immune system has worked out the gameworld's physical architecture. Worked out where everything is.

The buffalo herd are mown down methodically.

Collapsing in pools of electric blue light.

124

The fact that this world is ending is not obvious, yet.

The game deals with processing shortages without breaking the frame. No warning alerts. Just a long, slow closedown that makes sense inside the story, inside the logic of the game. Blizzards, fog, a dust storm . . .

But Colt can feel the shutdown coming, can see it. Visibility in the game is getting worse. The clouds lurch closer, lower, darker, as the weather continues to map the activity of the NSA, the NDSA, the immune system itself, as it takes over more and more resources.

Soon they will reach the sun.

The wind rises to a howl.

Colt throws more processing power at defending the surviving nodes. Which takes away more resources from the actual game.

All over the world, players are bounced out of the game, for lack of resources. Complaints are normally processed smoothly by a huge open-source AI; but tens of millions of angry players overload it, and it glitches.

Oh man, this is *terrible* . . .

Having tens, maybe hundreds of millions of angry players trying to chaotically get back into the game is going to rob him of an awful lot of power.

No, he's got to do it.

Node after node is being crippled, killed.

Less and less of the surrounding territory is being rendered.

Colt sends a top-level admin note to all players worldwide.

'We're experiencing some unexpected downtime. There's a security breach that needs to be patched, immediately. All players not actively coding will, unfortunately, have to stay outgame till the problem is fixed. Apologies. We will notify you as soon as the gameworld is back up.'

He takes a deep breath, and locks out all players, worldwide.

Immediately, the resources available to him surge, and he gets the defence back under control.

Wait; got to let Sasha get back in . . .

He exempts her.

OK, now defend . . .

But the immune system responds immediately to his response.

My god. Coming towards him, from the north. Driving the existing clouds out of the way. Absorbing them. Making them look like nothing.

An immense pale wall.

Pulsating.

Closer . . .

Dust storm?

Something touches his face. He reaches for it, but it's already gone.

His cheek is wet.

Here comes something else, floating down, a flake of . . .

He catches it on his fingertip, brings it up to his eyes.

Holds his breath. His warm breath.

A snowflake.

He studies its crystal lattice, until the heat of his fingertip causes the delicate fractal fringe to dissolve, and then the intricate hexagonal crystal core collapses too, and it's just a drop of water.

It begins to snow, in the desert, all across the test range.

Of course.

Sasha's snow.

Her normal code is so elegant, taking up so little memory. Fractal snowflakes, looking infinitely complex, but taking up no resources at all.

These snowflakes are profoundly different.

Not fractal.

Nothing repeats.

Each crystal heads towards infinite complexity, infinite difference.

Sucking the gameworld's resources dry, as it tries to render every crystal.

But . . . if Sasha's snow is appearing ingame . . . in the gameworld . . . in the desert . . .

Then either the immune system has taken over Sasha's weapon, and is using it against them: or . . .

Oh crap.

The immune system must have made its way inside the game. She's fighting it ingame.

It's here.

125

The snow covers up the detail of the world; slows movement down to nothing; freezes the rare pools of cyanide-blue water, and stills the animals and birds.

Throws a blanket across the gameworld, as it goes to sleep.

Brings all life and movement to a halt, inside the logic of the game.

The mountains disappear.

A flat grey shadowless light rushes over the buffalo herd towards Colt, as the clouds slide across the face of the sun, and now he is overwhelmed by the pale cloud of whirling flakes.

Colt stares into the whirling void until he isn't sure which way is up.

The voice comes out of the white.

'Colt?'

Sasha's voice.

'Colt?'

And he realizes he's closing down too. The battle between the immune system and the gameworld is freezing his code, right across the network, node by node. It's freezing code all the way down to the servers at his back. Soon he won't be able to think.

He's battling on too many fronts.

It's winning. Single-minded and brilliant, it is winning.

But Sasha is back. Back ingame.

The world fades away around them, until only Sasha and Colt remain.

He has prioritized them.

But any more pressure from the immune system, and the game won't even be able to maintain their avatars.

Colt feels his guts clench, as he tries to work out what's happening.

Both the gameworld and the immune system now have code running inside the same node, battling to control the kernel, to eliminate the other.

The gameworld is having a panic attack. It's having a breakdown.

It doesn't know who it is any more.

The wind rises again, and the snow crackles and sings as a trillion flakes grow larger, combine, collide, the ice so hard now the collisions of the crystals sound metallic.

'You need a totally different approach,' shouts Sasha over the storm.

'But *what*? I've tried *everything*,' says Colt in despair. 'The more I attack it, the more resources it borrows from everywhere else.'

'You need to *understand* it.'

'I don't need to understand it,' shouts Colt, 'I need to destroy it.'

The sound of the wind is driving him crazy. Aren't snowstorms supposed to be quiet? His thinking is so close to frozen, he has forgotten that the volume of the wind is set to show the attack strength of the immune system. To show the percentage of resources the gameworld is using just to defend itself. And it is a scream.

'Mmm,' says Sasha, putting her face close to his ear so he can hear. 'Why are you attacking it?'

'Because it's attacking me!' says Colt, as with another part of his fragmented brain he launches a last desperate assault.

I sound like my father, he thinks, astonished.

'Uh huh,' she says quietly in his ear, and she reaches out, squeezes his hand.

And he sees it through her eyes, from the outside . . . 'It's a feedback loop,' he says. 'The more I shout at it, the more it shouts at me. The more I attack, the more I'm attacked. I'm making it bigger, angrier, worse . . .'

'Yes,' she whispers in his ear, from the middle of the storm. 'I kind of know a lot about this, because I used to do that, with my dad.'

'So . . .'

'One of you has to stop.'

'Thank you,' he says. 'Thank you.'

But the immune system is still reacting to the assault Colt just launched.

It launches another attack, from inside the gameworld, seizing resources, capturing nodes.

Sasha's snow thickens, trying to slow down the assault.

The gameworld dims, flickers, as nodes commit suicide rather than be captured.

And now the snowflakes grow so big they start to lock together, to make fragile shapes in the air. Like brittle sculptures. They form an arch, a cage of ice around Colt, Sasha.

They block out the complicated universe, they turn the world into geometric forms, they fill his sight.

'Oh, your snow,' he says. 'It's beautiful.'

The wind whistles, then screams though the interlocked crystals. More snow piles up against it. And the snow cage breaks under the pressure, falls apart. It smacks into them hard, pulls Sasha free of Colt.

Sasha reaches out to hold him.

Colt reaches back.

The wind screams so loudly Colt doesn't even hear Sasha's shocked voice as her avatar begins to fail, and she vanishes.

What did she say, what did she *say*?

A snowflake lands on the back of his outstretched hand.

There's something about it . . . He frowns. What caught his attention?

It fell against the wind. It's not blowing away.

He lifts his hand.

The flake is wildly asymmetric, even more so than the others. He leans in close, doesn't breathe in case he melts it.

Oh my God, there's so much detail.

Long and short crystals fan out, all around the fringe.

The snowflake abruptly turns black.

Oh wow. She isn't gone from the game. The gameworld just can't, or won't, render her avatar.

But she's still got control of the snowflake code.

She's coding individual snowflakes.

Code, thinks Colt. *Code.* Holy guacamole . . .

There's a meaningful pattern to the flake. Colt can see meaning rising off the crystals around the edge of the flake, the way other people might see colour, or shape.

Is this Morse code? No.

Binary. Short crystals are zeroes. Long crystals are ones.

Letters are numbers.

Simple. No case, no punctuation.

Just one to twenty-six.

1 to 11010.

Long is 1, is A. Long, short, is 10, is B. Long, long, is 11, is C . . .

He reads the black snowflake.

WHY ARE YOU MODELING THE IMMUNE SYSTEM, it says.

'To understand it,' he shouts into the wind.

A second asymmetric snowflake lands against the wind, on the back of his hand.

Turns black.

He reads it.

U . . . M . . . gap . . . H . . . M . . . M . . .

Oh no, she's changed the code, or it's been intercepted and scrambled, or it's broken, it's failing . . . wait, read all of it . . . ah . . . hang on . . .

UM HMM AND WHY DO YOU

It's *phonetic*, she's dictating . . .

NEED TO UNDERSTAND IT

'To fight it,' he shouts.

Another fat white snowflake drifts sideways out of the swirl, to land in the palm of his hand and turn black.

MMM AND DO YOU UNDERSTAND YOUR OWN SYSTEM

He tries to find some meaning in the question. What system? Be polite. 'Pardon?'

YOU FIGHT TO GET SOMETHING YOU WANT

'Yes.'

WHAT DO YOU WANT

'I don't want Mama to die.'

WELL WHATS THE BEST WAY TO ACHIEVE THAT

He doesn't know what to say to that. Another snowflake lands.

MAYBE MODEL YOURSELF FIRST COLT

He stands in the desert, frozen. Eventually another flake falls.

HAVE YOU MODELED YOURSELF

He's so tired.

He's so cold.

He doesn't know what to say.

And flake by flake, faster and faster, the snow in the gameworld turns black.

The wind dies down.

Have they won?

Or has the immune system taken over that piece of Colt's code?

The air is still.

The snow stops falling.

Out of the huge, dark sky heavily flaps, falls, a black eagle.

Not even fully rendered, coloured, drawn.

The ghost of an eagle.

It rips open his side, feeds on his liver.

It's not Colt's eagle.

It's not a model.

It's the immune system. Ingame.

He's lost the node.

126

And he is back in his room.

Back in his chair.

Back in his head.

Back where he has always been alone.

He can hear his mother in the distance, in the bathroom, weeping.

No time for that now.

No sight, sound, sign of Sasha.

No snowflakes.

He's lonely, lonely, lonely.

She isn't here.

But something else is.

A shadow falls over the window, passes.

Colt, caught for a confused moment between worlds, thinks; another eagle; but of course it's a drone.

Big one. Very big. It's sniffing the house like a huge hound.

Looking for warmth?

No.

It can't see them, anyhow, on any frequency, through the one-way privacy glass. But . . . Wait . . . oh, no.

Drug drone. Highly sensitive chemical-sniffer. Trying to detect their pheromones, their evaporated sweat.

Their fear.

The telltale air from human lungs.

That size, it's not just carrying sensors (sniffer drones can be the size of hummingbirds, of bees); it's a battering-ram too.

Oh, crêpes.

The immune system has commandeered a SWAT drug drone.

The bloodhound sniffs around the window frames, but they are sealed.

Sniffs around the door, but it is sealed.

The ravens stare at the house with blind eyes.

High above, the killer drones wait for the SWAT drone's decision.

Wait for the bloodhound to howl.

And if it howls . . . well, Colt knows the howl he'll hear will be acoustic, loud as hell, with bass spikes that turn your guts to water; designed to intimidate, overwhelm.

But the electronic howl the drones hear . . . it will be a priority-one alert, on all channels, overriding the ravens' low-priority message, that everything is OK, that the house is empty.

And the ravens will have to restart their systems. Change all the variables. Work out how they missed Colt and Naomi's arrival, why they can't see them . . . It won't take long. As soon as they disconnect from Colt's booster tower, and try another tower, they will get their sight back. They'll vote for the kill.

And the eagles . . . the eagles will attack.

Oh . . . *crap.*

The bloodhound's heading for the roof, to sniff the aircon outlet; to sniff the warm air being pumped from the building as cool air is drawn in through the filter pit beneath the house. Air that says, in a million molecules of perspiration every second, in every fleck of dust bearing their DNA, that they are here.

'Aircon!' says Colt. 'One hundred degrees!'

'Are you sure that's *wise*, Colt?' asks the house AI, in the warm, friendly voice of Ronald Reagan. 'Some of your mother's plants . . .'

'Go to one hundred, steadily, and as slowly as you can,' says Colt. 'That's an order.'

Colt doesn't actually want to go to one hundred, but he does want the outlet pipe to reverse, and suck in air for a while. Just switching off the aircon would leave the pipe full of telltale molecules . . . He'll switch it off when the house gets too hot.

The aircon AI sighs; the direction of airflow reverses; and now the sealed house is sucking in hot air from outside, from the roof, into the cooler house.

Clearing the pipes. OK.

Some cool air will be pushed back out through the filter pit deep under the house: but the bloodhound can't sniff that.

Colt thinks about his next move.

He won't want to do this for long: with all the servers in overdrive, the house is already warmer than it should be.

But it's not nearly as hot as the desert outside.

The important thing is, for the next twenty minutes, half an hour, more; no air will escape from the rooftop aircon outlet.

The bloodhound arrives on the roof.

Sniffs the aircon unit itself, its oils and chemicals, to calibrate. Colt tenses. The bloodhound shifts a little, sniffs the air around the outlet pipes.

It moves up and over the ridge of the roof.

Doesn't howl.

OK. I've got maybe half an hour.

HAVE YOU MODELED YOURSELF.

OK.

Do it.

127

He takes a cautious look inside his vast, expanded self. Tries to see what the various areas are doing. What they want.

Make a model of his own body and mind. His needs, desires.

Woah.

Everything's fighting everything else! Battling each other, for control. All with different goals.

He's a civil war.

He wants to fight. He wants to eat. He wants to kiss. He wants to hide . . .

He wants to live.

He wants to die.

Colt fills with panic.

Tries to calm himself down.

OK. I am a biological system. And biological systems are complex, layered: capable of conflict. Neurosis. I know that.

But how can I get what I want, if I don't know what I want?

How can I even decide which part of me should be allowed to get what it wants, when they all want totally different things?

What would Sasha say?

What would she tell him to do?

Look at it again, she'd say. Don't take sides, just look.

And he steps back, away from his thoughts, and refocuses.

Wow.

Nothing has changed but his perspective.

But now he sees, instead of conflict, an exquisite balance of forces, holding together a system of systems in delicate creative tension.

And the wind of his breath sweeps deep into his dark interior; oxygen floods across the folded half-acre fields of his lungs, is channelled into the fast-flowing canals of his blood, and is whirled around the sprawling empire of his body, to silently ignite the foodstuff in every cell; he is on fire, he is on fire with life, he is alive and he looks around and the world is alive.

And he breathes out, and the burnt carbon floods out on his breath, each carbon atom locked to two oxygen atoms, the invisible smoke of a billion campfires deep in the heart of a billion cells, his blazing body a pillar of fire, an illuminated megacity of intricately networked eukaryotic cells . . .

He is on fire, in every cell. He is a trillion bacteria, cooperating; so totally interwoven, so interdependent, that they could be mistaken for a single thing. He is a standing wave moving through the material world.

He is matter astonished into motion, into life.

So if this is what he is: what should he *do*?

He looks reflexively for Sasha, for her standing wave.

Her pillar of fire.

But she's not there.

He wants to hold Sasha, the real Sasha, in his real arms.

That's what he wants to do. And he wants to be held by her.

Soon, soon . . .

OK. But, meanwhile, with the bloodhound sniffing the windows, with blind ravens watching the house, with the immune system fighting the gameworld, with killer drones overhead, with his mother weeping in the bathroom, with his penis hard at the thought of Sasha . . .

What should he *do*?

Maybe that isn't the right question.

Maybe questions aren't even the right approach.

He looks back at his body, at all his systems, intricately meshed, holding him together, holding him in dynamic balance.

Oh yeah.

That's how it works.

Soon they will decide, this committee of systems, on an outcome; and the entire system of systems will act.

And Colt will act, under the illusion of self that emerges from these conflicts, from this complexity.

Only some resistant subroutines – a stammer, a stutter – might hint at the tensions that resolve in this outcome.

The illusion of self will have the illusion of control.

That's how it works.

That's how I work.

So, is that how the immune system works?

Because if it is . . .

OK, analyse the immune system. See how it works: what its conflicts are.

What it wants.

Where do I begin?

Colt looks for patterns. Big patterns.

What does the immune system map onto? Resemble? What *is* it, that I can understand?

Oh wow, of course.

No, it won't behave like me.

The immune system didn't just come out of *nowhere*. The immune system's father . . . is my father.

He designed it, to do what he wishes he could do.

So it will behave like him. It will repeat the structures of his mind.

The plan is hidden in the architect.

I don't need to model, understand, decode the immune system.

My father is the weak link; if I can decode my father, I decode the immune system.

Oh, Dada, Colt thinks. Oh, Dada.

Target the wetware.

He rings his dad.

Video, thinks Colt? Yeah, video.

Face to face.

His hand pauses over the control.

Resistance.

Colt accepts the delay.

Waits.

Some system within Colt has a problem with this.

Oh yeah.

I can make the feed untraceable . . . But if he sees me here . . .

He'll recognize my room.

He'll know we're in the house.

He'll tell the immune system.

And then we're dead.

No, I want to talk to him in the gameworld. Not my room.

If I can get back into the gameworld . . .

If it still exists.

128

'I stand in front of you / I'll take the force of the blow /
Protection.'   — Massive Attack featuring
                                        Tracey Thorn, 'Protection'

He has to be careful where he enters: he probes a node, but it's been captured by the immune system. Booby-trapped. He backs off. Tries another node. Same . . .

When he does get back into the gameworld, he thinks for a moment that he's gone blind, that he's triggered a trap. Wait, no . . .

He blinks.

I'm not blind. It's the test range. The test range is dark. Not totally dark . . .

The sky is completely blocked from view by a trillion black snowflakes, frozen in mid-air.

How can I see them?

He squints.

Oh . . .

Some light leaks from the black snowflakes, like the light given out by piezoelectric crystals under pressure.

He can hear buffalo moaning in the darkness.

Some nodes left, then.

The gameworld is holding on, just.

The immune system is inside the remaining nodes: but it can't take them. Why so quiet? Why aren't they fighting?

Oh, poop. The immune system has co-opted Sasha's code: now both are using it, each to paralyse the other.

Whenever either the immune system or the gameworld frees up resources, Sasha's snowflakes soak up the processing cycles.

Gameworld and immune system are frozen in a jittery, static embrace.

They're both so vast, so global, that neither can defeat the other.

But Colt is a new variable; he has changed the balance of the game; he's brought his own servers with him, his own brilliant code; his enormous remote control. He should be able to use it to break the deadlock, to unlock Sasha's snowflakes. To retake this one node.

He writes some code, and swings his arms at the frozen flakes. At his touch, they turn white again, and fall gently to the ground.

He clears a space in the black snow-filled air.

A cave in the shimmering darkness.

Flake after flake now turns white and falls, and black turns to white and out and out, up and up, mile high, and all the snow falls as the code runs and the sky is clear and blue and the sun is unbearably bright against the white snow of the frozen desert.

Points of red appear, here and there, in the snow. Expand.

Oh.

Blood from the dead and dying buffalo.

Dead nodes.

Those buffalo still alive, those nodes still potentially under Colt's control, shake free of the deep snowfall, free of the immune system's restraints, and trudge towards Colt.

Not many.

Not enough.

OK. Call Dad.

He writes the code, to pull his father into the game, into Colt's world, as the call is still going through.

Ryan accepts the call.

'Colt.'

'Dad . . .'

Colt implements the code.

Ryan appears in the gameworld, behind a desk, in the desert. The game fills out the detail, attaches the desk to the dusty ground. It's both comical and sinister.

The game sends Ryan 2D visual feedback, on his wallscreen. It's only fair, that he know where he is. Even if he doesn't have a helmet, doesn't have full immersion . . .

Colt wants to see his father; but he also wants to be seen.

They look at each other for a few seconds.

'We've got to stop meeting like this,' says Colt.

Ryan laughs. 'You're cracking jokes now? That's some . . . transformation.' He's looking around his screen, in the real world, in his office. Taking in the gameworld's version of the test range.

In the distance, the perfect craters of the nuclear tests. Covered in snow.

'Dad, it's still trying to kill us.'

Ryan says nothing.

'It's not fair, Dad. Just because you two . . .'. Colt stops.

His voice; the pitch has risen. He sounds like a child. How weird is that. Everything was logical and clear, until he heard his father's voice. And now his own voice is trembling, as his body trembles.

Some old routine, triggered. Well, just got to deal with that.

The game, restless, struggling to map everything, erases the desk. Now it's just Ryan, in his chair.

The light of the sun loses some frequencies; goes weird, a little bluish; cobalt blue. As they face each other on the blue, snow-swept plain, the illusion the gameworld creates is no longer perfect.

Colt is uncomfortably aware that his physical body is standing in his bedroom; that a drug drone is sniffing around the house; that the hacked, confused, neurotic immune system is trying to resolve two images of the world.

That he could die at any moment during this conversation.

He tries to get his mind and body back under his control. He's not a kid. *Not a kid* comes back to him like an echo, an echo setting off other echoes. Setting off memories of when he has said that before.

Back when he was a kid.

Screaming, I'm not a kid.

Memories of his body shaking with anger, as it shakes now.

His new brain is great at thinking logical thoughts – that's what he designed it for. But, now that his body has joined in, he's reacting physically, he's thinking physically.

Every thought is a chemical action. Every action, a thought.

The surges, back and forth, are knocking him off balance.

Ryan is speaking. '. . . there's bigger stuff at stake here, Colt. Your mother's . . . whatever, discovery, will change everything, and if we're not in control of that change—'

'—Dad, nobody can control this change, it's bigger than . . .'

'—And if we're not in control of it, other people, bad people, people who want to kill us, will use it, will use those powers to kill us.'

Colt leans forward. 'You're the person trying to kill us, Dad.'

The image of his father freezes for a second. When it unfreezes, Ryan is leaning forward in his seat, too, and now he sounds angry. 'She can't just "give it to the world". It's not one big happy planet, we don't live in a fucking Coke ad.'

'I don't think she . . .'

But Ryan is not listening.

'There is no "world", there's just a bunch of state actors, and individual actors, and power groups, with different agendas. And the ones most likely to use this to the full, to the limit, without restraint, are not the good guys, Colt. She can't just give it away.'

'Dad, missiles destroyed her lab. Tried to kill her. Was that the immune system, or was it you?'

Ryan hesitates.

'It was you,' Colt says. Silence. 'Tell me the truth.'

'I got a message from Donnie,' says Ryan eventually. 'A little late, but . . . I knew she was probably still there. But I didn't fire those missiles. The immune system was monitoring the calls, it has access to everything we monitor, which is everything . . .'

'But it couldn't hear your voices, they're hyper-encrypted . . .'

'It didn't need to, it interpreted the metadata. Someone was unplugging servers, stealing data . . . It worked it out.'

Colt breathes out, relaxes a little.

His father didn't fire those missiles directly at his mother.

It's a small enough thing, a technicality, but it's still a relief. But why should it make a difference? He tried to shoot her. He unleashed the immune system on them both.

Stop making excuses for him.

He doesn't love you.

No, he loves you. And you love him. This is all a mistake, a mistake.

'Colt,' says Ryan, 'this country is a screwed-up country in a lot of ways, but it's a lot better than the other ones out there. The ones where they burn down girls' schools, and stone women to death for being raped, and throw acid in the faces of tourists who wear the wrong clothes . . .'

He's not talking to me, thinks Colt, as he watches his father's mouth move. He's making a speech.

'. . . The ones where children are kidnapped and tortured and turned into soldiers and forced to go back and burn down their own family's village. The ones where the government can decide whether you have a kid or not, whether you can do the job you love or not, whether you can read the book you want to or not, see the film . . .'

'You're turning into them, Dad.'

'Bullshit.' Ryan leans back in his chair.

The sun shifts frequencies, abruptly, and the desert is suddenly a pale green, and Colt has the illusion that he is underwater, that the great inland ocean has returned.

He looks up, and the sky is wrong. Violet. All the colours in the gameworld are wrong.

Father and son stare at the sky, until Ryan looks away, says again, 'That's bullshit, Colt. Look, this country doesn't care what colour you are, and it doesn't care what religion you are, and it gives you a chance, whether you're a man or a woman, young or old, rich or poor. This country has something really special, and we are just pissing it away. I don't mind fighting with one arm tied behind my back – that's the whole point, that's what makes us better than them – but we can't fight with both hands tied behind our back, while handing them our gun.'

'It's not a gun, Dad. I'm not a gun . . .'

'It's a weapon! You're a weapon! Look how you've just outwitted the best tech we've got. A kid!'

And now the light of the sun lurches again, and everything is once more cobalt blue.

A big bull buffalo collapses with a groan into deep snow.

India is falling, thinks Colt.

Thick blue clouds gather on the horizon. It's going to snow. Without Colt's full attention, assistance, the gameworld is being defeated. But he can't break off the conversation with his father. He gazes into his father's eyes as Ryan speaks.

'If you can do it, they can do it.' Ryan stabs his finger towards Colt, and Colt flinches. 'They're not going to use this to be nice to each other. That's just your fucking mother, projecting her Christian bullshit onto the world. The world's not like that. Great, sure, Christ would have used his new powers to forgive the Romans better. But Mohammed would have used it to kick ass. And Mohammed was right. We didn't defeat Hitler by sitting down and having a nice talk about his difficult childhood. We didn't let him off the hook by saying, well he comes from a different culture, they do those things there. When people say they want to destroy this country, do them the honour of taking them seriously. This liberal bullshit, that they'd love us if we just disarmed and apologized for existing. That is condescending, that is showing contempt for their ideas. Treating them like children. They are adults, who have thought about it, and they want to kill us. Fine. I have no problem with that. But I don't hand them a fucking superweapon.'

'But there's hardly anyone feels like that. It's only a few . . .'

'Oh that's bullshit. It only takes a few! How many do you need, to use our own technology against us? Exactly what's going to happen if she . . .'

'Dad . . .'

There is a lurch, like an earthquake ingame, as a huge data centre in Singapore is broken by the immune system and goes dark.

The historical, realworld, seismic data that underlies the landscape vanishes.

An earthquake shakes the gameworld as everything adjusts.

The nearby hills shift and settle, as their heaped material shakes.

Craters slip and fill.

All around Colt, hills fall and spread out at the base, as though an invisible god just walked across the landscape, crushing the heights.

Ryan and Colt ignore it, their gaze locked together.

'Jesus Christ, Colt, real men, women and children, who are alive now, will be dead if you don't get involved. It's not too late. Join me; I'll inform the immune system—'

'You don't have access. Not now. It's autonomous.'

'I can still influence targeting, if I . . . well, I have my methods. Seriously, it might reassess you. Call off its drones.' The corners of his lips twitch. It's almost a smile. 'I'm its father. It trusts me.'

'But you're trying to kill Mama.'

Ryan hesitates. 'I don't think I can save her. She won't change sides.'

'Dad . . .'

'Colt . . . I'm trying to save maybe millions of other lives, down the line.'

'You can't make me choose this.'

'Well, then, do nothing.' Ryan shrugs. 'But that's a choice.'

'And then you'll kill me and Mama . . .'

'Colt, my life is over. My career is over. The woman I love hates me. I have nothing to lose. They want to shut down my program. I've already broken every rule in the book today. I'm finished.'

An unsettling thought distracts Colt. 'Will they . . . punish you?'

His father's abrupt laugh sounds like a dog's bark. 'Look around! The only reason I'm still here talking to you is because the entire system is in meltdown, their comms are fucked, and they're too busy firefighting to work out who started the fire. If they understood what was going on, they'd have arrested me already.'

'Why are you doing this?'

'Because I love my country,' says Ryan. 'And I made a promise to protect my country.'

'Dad . . .' No, I love you isn't right. That's what you are supposed to say; but it's not quite true. 'You're still my dad.' I can't say . . . 'But . . .' I can't.

'I had to launch it, Colt.' And there's a desperation in his father's voice that Colt was not expecting, that knocks him off balance. 'They were going to close the program. Scrap it.'

All that he knows is that he loves his father.

And so he has no idea where the words are coming from, when the words come up, from the darkness, from deep inside him.

And they force their way up, and he's got to stop them, got to, but they've made it, they're in his throat, opening his throat to speak, and he retches a little, a quick dry retch, and Colt panics, because he has lost control, and who is this speaking them, 'Yuh, yuh, yuh . . . You,' the voice is high and wild, and it stutters a little and loops back and starts again, and he recognizes it at last, because it's the voice he had when he was seven.

The committee has made a decision.

The words speak themselves through him, and he hears them at the same time as his father, with the same surprise.

Colt says, 'You didn't protect me.'

'What?'

This time, Colt says it deliberately, to hear himself say the words. To hear the words which his seven-year-old self has just delivered. To hear the words which are true. To make the words his. 'You didn't protect me.'

Colt feels a hand fall on his shoulder, in the real world, and for a wild moment he thinks, Sasha!

But of course, it must be his mother, back from the bathroom.

She's not ingame.

He refuses to let the game map her.

No, he's not just speaking to his father now.

'Mama, you've got to join me ingame.'

Without leaving the gameworld, he steps forward in the real world, reaches out blindly, into the familiar mess of his room, finds it. Throws her his old helmet.

She hesitates; she hasn't entered – hasn't wanted to enter – her son's gameworld for a long, long time; but she puts on his old helmet. It smells faintly of Colt; and then his smell is gone, and she smells the desert, the cold, the buffalo, through the helmet's olfactory unit, as Colt orders the game to map her; and she appears in the test range, as herself, beside Ryan.

Her helmet's visuals and audio kicks in, a little late, and now she sees Colt's avatar; sees Ryan in his chair, and she can hear the buffalo dying among the symmetrical craters, in the sad blue light. The thick, strange clouds approaching. She closes her eyes.

You didn't protect me . . .

But that's worse, because now she can see him again, so frail, in the bath, and the bruises on his legs, on his chest . . .

'What the fuck are you talking about,' says Ryan, 'I've spent my fucking life protecting you, I lost my fucking legs protecting you, and now you—'

'When I was in school,' says Colt, but he's looking at Naomi now, not Ryan. 'Remember? I came home . . . the first week. And I was having my bath. And my legs were covered in bruises. And you saw them. And you said, how did that happen? And I said, the other boys hit me with baseball bats. And you saw the burns on my arms. And I said, because I wouldn't smoke a cigarette . . . they put out cigarettes on me . . . And you didn't do anything.'

'I didn't know what to do . . .' Naomi is trembling.

'You sent me back.'

Ryan breaks in, 'She never told me . . .'

'No, you chose that school,' says Colt, turning to Ryan. 'You didn't check, you didn't care. I was America too. You didn't protect me.'

'We wanted you to be normal,' says Ryan. 'To fit in . . . we thought it would . . .'

And Naomi talks over Ryan, 'When I realized . . . realized how bad it was, I pulled you out of school . . .'

'You didn't pull me out of school, Mama. I refused to go. You weren't strong enough to get me into the car.'

'We thought you were getting on OK,' says Ryan, as Naomi says, 'You didn't tell us . . .'

'I didn't think you wanted to know. Because I had told you, the first week, and you had done nothing . . .'

'I'm sorry,' says Naomi quietly. 'I didn't know what to do.'

'But you were my mother . . .'

'. . . I was only a kid myself, I was afraid . . .'

'Afraid of what?'

'Afraid of the authorities. Afraid of the principal, afraid of . . . I thought if I said anything, I might make it worse, they'd take it out on you . . .'

Ryan breaks in, 'But you never mentioned it after that. You hid it from us.'

'You couldn't handle it,' says Colt to his father in the frozen desert. To his mother, as it starts to snow again. 'You didn't want to know.'

'Oh, Colt,' says Naomi, 'you should have told us . . .'

Colt shrugged. 'I was protecting you.'

The wind picks up, and the snow swirls, thicker now, piling up against their feet, the boulder with its clay vessel, the dead buffalo. His parents say nothing, just look at each other. But there is something different about this silent tension between his mother and his father, something new; Colt's brain makes the connection, and he says to Naomi, 'Did you take your pill?'

And Naomi says, 'No. I don't do that any more.'

She stares at Ryan.

Her husband. Ex-husband. The man she once loved, or thought she loved, back before she knew what love was. Back before she had a child who loved her. A child she loved.

She studies her ex-husband.

He said he loved her. Maybe even believed it. He promised to love her for ever.

Maybe even meant it.

And now he wants to kill them both.

No. Love that can become its opposite so easily was never really love.

But she has one thing left. One thing she hasn't tried.

It's getting so hot in the house now, that the gap between the heat she feels and the snow she can see is too big, it's breaking the illusion, and she closes her eyes.

Takes a deep breath.

Then she spits a single word into the whirling storm.

It is a word she has never spoken before.

'What?' says Ryan, leaning forward. 'What did you say?'

Naomi opens her eyes. Looks straight into Ryan's eyes.

Repeats the word. Louder.

Ryan sinks back in his chair. 'Oh, Naomi.' He closes his eyes.

'What?' says Colt, panicked. 'What does it mean?'

Ryan opens his eyes. 'You want me to stop?'

'Yes,' says Naomi. 'I want you to stop, now.'

Ryan breathes out. A huge breath.

'What does that word mean?' asks Colt.

'It's our safe word,' says Ryan. 'When we . . .'

He glances at Naomi.

'Back when we loved each other. Before you were born,' says Naomi. 'Your father and I . . . sometimes we would do things together that were dangerous. Dangerous for me.' She sees the question form on Colt's face, and shakes her head before he can speak it. No. I don't want to have to explain how those wires got crossed. 'It doesn't matter why . . . The point is that I trusted him. I trusted him with my life. And he made me a promise, that he would always stop, if I spoke our safe word.' She looks across at Ryan, at his flickering avatar. 'But I never said the word.'

'That was the word,' says Colt.

Naomi nods. Still looking at Ryan, she says, 'I don't want pleasure. And I don't want pain. I want you to let me go now. Stop. As you promised you would.'

Ryan looks away from Naomi; looks away from the camera; looks around his office in the real world, at the souvenirs of his life. The debris. The wreckage. 'I have other promises, babe. To my country, to . . .'

'Your promise to me came first,' says Naomi. 'I never released you from it.'

'You divorced me, babe.'

Babe? She shrugs, lets it go. 'I ended the marriage. Look, marriage is a public thing, to let people know, let everybody know, a couple are together. But this was different. This was earlier. This was just us.'

'It wasn't a fair . . . agreement.'

'Why not?'

'I loved you; but you didn't love me.'

She's spent so many years telling herself she never loved him. That he never loved her. She's astonished to find herself saying, 'I did. I did love you. It's just . . . we hadn't grown up. We didn't know who we were yet. It wasn't enough.'

'Oh, Naomi . . . If I could . . .' Ryan drags in a deep breath. 'But you know that, later on, I had . . . other loves. You could call them. They came with other responsibilities. I signed . . . I made other promises.'

'You were always free to have other loves,' says Naomi. 'I never owned you.'

'You loved other women?' says Colt to Ryan. The idea is astonishing.

'Other women?' Ryan smiles. 'No. But a man can love a country and a woman and a gun.'

'But which do you love the most, Dad?' says Colt.

Ryan does something with his face that looks like a smile; but it isn't a smile.

The safe word is still echoing through Ryan's brain, setting off associations, triggering memories, changing moods.

Like a bomb going off.

The committee of his selves makes a decision. 'My country . . . has betrayed me,' says Ryan. 'And a gun – even a drone cloud, even the immune system – is just a machine. But I really did love your mother.'

Colt stares at his father.

'I know, she doesn't believe me,' says Ryan. 'You don't believe me. But it's true.'

Naomi shakes her head. Takes off her helmet, and vanishes from the game.

Colt's never seen emotions move freely across his father's face. It is fascinating, and terrifying. Like watching a tornado dance unpredictably through a familiar neighbourhood, casually ripping off a roof to expose the fragile interior.

Colt realizes Naomi has run another program in Ryan. Activated something.

Love?

Desire?

Need?

Honour?

It doesn't matter. The more complicated and unresolved, the harder to name, the better.

His father is no longer single-minded.

Now, conflicted, neurotic, he can't act.

And that thought leads to another, and another. Patterns form. Colt's mind connects, connects, connects, until he sees it. The weakness.

The flaw in security, leading straight to his father.

I can destroy him now. Take advantage of this moment. High risk. Very high. But if it works . . .

Colt's mouth is abruptly dry.

Outgame, he extends a shaking hand to pick up the mug of water from the table.

Ingame, Colt's hardly aware of his action as he lifts the crude clay drinking vessel from the low boulder.

It's just part of the game.

But as the cool mug touches his lip, there is a sharp, distant crack, an echo; nearby, ingame, a buffalo collapses with a low moan, as the immune system takes out another node.

Another shot. Another buffalo drops.

The gameworld, exhausted, throws everything available into defence.

It's not enough.

To free more resources, the game asks Colt's permission to cease mapping unimportant items.

Colt models the possible consequences, checks for conflicts or problems. His enhanced brain makes the decision in milliseconds.

Yes.

'My God,' says Ryan sharply, 'you're in the house. Why can't the system see you? What's going on?'

Colt, mug still touching his lips, stares at his father; sees where his father is staring.

Colt glances down.

The crude clay mug in his hands has turned into a Doctor Who mug.

'I ♥ ♥ The Doctor.'

Signed by Peter Capaldi.

His favourite mug.

Ingame, unchanged.

'Jesus Christ,' says Ryan, 'you've blinded the drones . . . But then where the hell are the ravens getting their pictures from?'

Ryan's head jerks around as he looks across the game's desert from horizon to horizon.

His eyes widen as he works it out.

And Ryan vanishes from the game.

129

'He knows,' says Colt.
'What?' says Naomi faintly, outgame, the whisper of a ghost.
'He knows where we are, Mama. I have to kill him.'
'No,' says Naomi faintly.
'If I don't, he's going to kill you, Mama. Kill us.'
Naomi says something too quiet to hear.
Colt switches off the game, and he's back in his room.
He puts down the mug on his table, carefully, as though it might explode. Lifts the visor of his helmet, to look directly into his mother's eyes.
'I have to, Mama.'
'Colt . . .'
'I have to.'
He closes the visor and turns away.

130

Oh, wow.
All the anger he ever felt towards his father, and suppressed, because he was afraid to express it; it's all leaking and bubbling to the surface now, under tremendous pressure, like the boiling groundwater and steam that can precede a volcanic eruption.
A song goes round and around his head, a song his father loved.
Anger is an energy.
ANGER IS AN ENERGY . . .
He goes ingame, and gets to work.
And this is unfamiliar work.
He has never tried to kill anyone before.

He doesn't want to kill anyone.

Words appear in his head.

I hate my father.

Colt marvels at the words.

They sit there, beside other words now.

I love my father.

Which of them is true?

I love Dada.

I hate Dada.

Colt looks from one to the other; testing them, feeling them. Trying them on like two T-shirts, between which he must decide.

But they both fit.

Both are true, at the same time. How can that be?

A hot gush of anger bubbles up in a stutter of images, old emotions, memories, and now he can't see the words.

An image of his father shouting at him; an image of his father shouting at his mother; an image of his father turning away.

A door, slamming. His father's footsteps, receding, growing quieter, gone.

Dimly, distantly, he feels his mother, outgame, touching his arm.

Pulling on his arm.

He shrugs her off.

'Get out, Mama.'

The words emerge so loud, so angry, that he flinches at the sound of his own voice.

His father's voice.

She touches his arm, and says something so quietly that the filters and noise-cancellation in the helmet don't let it in, and now he is shouting at his invisible, whispering mother, 'GO AWAY!' and outgame the words bounce and distort off the walls of his bedroom so loud he can hear them through the filters, and ingame they echo back off the hills.

And now he can't hear her, can't feel her. She's gone.

Oh mano, the house is getting hot . . .

He assembles his tools with meticulous care. If this doesn't work first time, he's in a lot of trouble.

He's dead.

There's a subtle vulnerability running right through the security structure of the immune system. Leading directly to his father, to his father's office.

He can't believe he didn't see it earlier. Maybe he wouldn't even have seen it, before his enhancement.

If it works, his father is dead.

Something pops up discreetly in the corner of his vision. He glances at it. An ingame request for contact, for his exact location.

Surely he's blocked everybody . . . oh.

Sasha is trying to find him, ingame.

He gets a queasy, uneasy feeling about that, alongside a brief mental image of her frowning at him, but he doesn't examine the feeling. Not now. He moves abruptly to another sector of the test range, and blocks Sasha too.

It's almost ready.

He hesitates. What a thing, to try to kill your father. To try to kill anyone.

But if he doesn't, his father will tip off the immune system. Tell it where they are.

He's forcing me to choose between killing him, and allowing Mama to die.

Tears prick at Colt's eyes.

It isn't fair.

No one should have to make that choice.

It isn't fair.

I hate him.

He launches his final attack.

131

'But lo! Men have become the tools of their tools.'
— Thoreau, *Walden*

A tremendous pressure, across his chest and back.

Outgame, Colt is jerked erect as his arms and legs snap straight and lock, rigid, jerking him erect. He lifts from his chair, sways, and topples to the floor.

Ingame, he falls, astonished, cruciform, to the sand.

My suit.

The immune system's taken over my suit.

The micromesh tightens again, and Colt grunts involuntarily as air is pushed out of his lungs.

Colt can't move his feet, legs, torso, arms, hands, head . . . he flicks his eyes up along the tilted horizon of the game and back, twice; flick flick; calls up the eye control menu.

The big, crude menu comes up, superimposed in blocky text and icons on the landscape. Good.

But . . . if it's taken control of the suit, knows where he is; why doesn't it just kill him? Why has he still got menu access?

Lying immobile on the hard ground, and using just the eye and voice controls, Colt pushes forward the attack against his father in the base, penetrating deeper and deeper through layers of security; but the harder Colt pushes, the worse the pain in his chest, the pressure on his limbs, until he can hardly feel his fingertips, his toes.

His genitals are crushed up against his body until his testicles feel like they're going to pop under the pressure. The pain is more intense than anything he's ever felt; his eyes water so hard that he can't work the eye controls, can't see the menus through the shimmer of tears.

The micromesh is contracting.

Contracting past the pain-tolerance threshold.

Way past the point where the contraction of the suit should stop.

The suit emits a hazy, high-frequency sound, as tens of thousands of invisibly fine fibres tighten further, rub past each other along the surface of his skin, put each other under more tension.

Anger is an energy.

Colt lashes out again at his father; and again the suit pulls a little tighter, with a thin, high creak as the fibres rub past each other.

Like guitar strings, tuning higher, thinks Colt. Till something snaps.

The strings; or the neck.

*

A shadow falls across his face, ingame. Eagle?

He tries to move his limbs; to roll away; but nothing happens.

It feels tremendously wrong; a draining effort of will, yet with no physical result at all.

This must be what it's like to be totally paralysed, thinks Colt. What if it squeezes harder? Will I be paralysed?

No. That's not going to be a problem. It wants to kill me.

The shadow above him, around him, darkens.

Something's getting closer.

He twists his eyes hard over, as far as they'll go, till the muscles hurt, trying to make out the shape of the shadow on the pale, dusty ground.

A human figure?

But his peripheral vision is too poor, since the implants; he can make out nothing.

Boots appear, a blur of black, at the edge of his vision. He tries again to roll away; can't.

The figure bends, till he can see its face.

Through lips that are turning numb, he mumbles, 'Sasha.'

'Colt,' she says. 'Stop.'

'Stop . . .' He pauses to take a breath; but breathing out deeply is a mistake. As his chest falls, the suit tightens smoothly, and he can't pull in any new air to replace what he's just exhaled. '. . . what?'

'Stop fighting.'

'It's . . . killing . . . me.' The words are barely audible, and now, as the suit tightens another notch, he cannot speak at all.

'You're killing you,' says Sasha.

And she bends closer, and holds him. Hugs him.

He relaxes into the great wave of warmth that comes from her arms, her body; from her gesture; as his micromesh suit transmits a totally different kind of pressure. He relaxes into the answering wave of warmth that wells up from inside him, in response.

Not the heat of anger, the warmth of . . .

Love.

I love her.

Oh, Sasha.

He tries to speak as he lies there in her arms, but he can't.

I love you.

His lips shape the words, but there is no breath left in him to exhale, to move the vocal cords.

I love you.

He stops fighting.

The micromesh suit gasps a high pure note, holds it.

And then the note begins, very gradually, to deepen in pitch.

Fade in volume.

It's falling.

Detuning, as the tension is released.

The suit is loosening.

He can move.

He can breathe.

132

'Myth is the realm of risk, and myth is the enchantment we generate in ourselves at such moments . . . it is a spell the soul casts on itself.' — Roberto Calasso, *The Marriage of Cadmus and Harmony*, translated by Tim Parks

She loosens her embrace. Ends the hug. Steps back.

The mesh unlocks.

He stretches out on the ground, and gulps in air. Groans as the blood returns to his fingertips, toes. Shakes the pins and needles from his arms, his legs. Adjusts his crotch awkwardly, with another groan, this time of relief. Stands.

Faces Sasha.

She looks so real. Realer than real.

She has her leather jacket on. Thin red T-shirt, over the faint outline of a black bra.

He leans forward, can't help it, can't stop it.

His lips touch hers.

The helmet does its best. Pressure is transmitted.

But not by lips. Not by her lips. Not by her.

He inhales, but he can't smell her soap, her leather jacket. She's blocked all olfactory data, or maybe her unit is just switched off; either way, it won't let his helmet reproduce her smell.

Colt is hyperaware of every aspect that isn't fully mapped. All that isn't there.

He breaks away, steps back.

'You're not . . . safe,' he says. 'Being seen with me. Ingame. You need to go.'

'No,' she says calmly.

'But they must have found me . . . they broke my suit security . . .'

She shakes her head. 'What did you think you were attacking?'

He resists saying it, but he has to say it. 'My father.'

'Let me guess,' says Sasha. 'You spotted a deep flaw. A security tunnel. Pointed straight at him.'

Oh man, she can read my mind . . . 'Yes.'

She nods. 'It was a mirror-trap. Launch an attack on them, down the tunnel, and it's mirrored straight back at you.'

'But it triggered . . .'

'It triggered your own suit to attack you. You triggered your own suit. Not them. They have no idea where you are. That was just you, attacking yourself.'

'But it wants to kill me, anyway. It's treating Mama's . . .' He flails around for the right word. '. . . Discovery, as a threat to the whole country . . .'

'Colt, you are your mama's discovery, made flesh. And you're fighting to destroy the immune system, and kill your father; the guy who designed it. Look, it sees the world in terms of an ingroup, which it must defend, and an outgroup, which it must attack. Of course it thinks you're a threat. You are a fucking threat. See its point of view.'

'I can't just let it kill Mama!'

'I'm not saying that. I'm saying if you react out of fear and rage, you . . .'

And he gets it. 'Create a feedback loop.'

'Yes.'

Colt runs an analysis.

She's right. It steps up its response purely in response to his response.

Attacking it just makes it more single-minded. Just confirms he must be the enemy, because he fights back.

Oh boy, I've pushed myself up to red status. To Level 3.

Classic feedback loop.

'So what should I do?'

'Move yourself from its outgroup to its ingroup.'

'But how?'

Sasha smiles. 'Give it the world.'

'What?' Is that a quote? Is she speaking in metaphors?

'How would it react to love?' says Sasha. 'Run an analysis of that,' and it's as though she's read Colt's mind again. He shudders as though he's been touched.

He says, 'I can't code love . . .'

'Stop attacking it. Stop defending your resources.'

'Were you joking? About giving it the world?'

Sasha shakes her head. 'The gameworld. Give it the gameworld.'

Give it the gameworld . . . thinks Colt.

The thought ricochets around his head, it won't settle.

If it wants to kill you; then give it the world.

Like Jesus.

Sacrifice everything.

Take the blow.

'So, look,' says Sasha, 'the gameworld is attacking the immune system.' She leans right into his face, and now she's not smiling. 'And the gameworld is yours, it represents you. Hand it over voluntarily, and your threat rating collapses . . .'

'But . . . how can I hand it over? I'm not even sure I can do that.'

'Try. If you don't . . . if you keep fighting it . . . it will kill you.'

'I can't . . .'

'Why not? You built this world. You're God here.'

'But the gameworld, it's . . . it's paranoid, from experience. It runs a lot of security layers. It wants to survive as it is. It doesn't want to be taken over. It doesn't want to be destroyed.'

'So we take apart its security structures from the inside.'

'Betray it?'

'Yeah.' And now she smiles. 'Give away the keys to the kingdom.'

Colt thinks about that.

That's not easy. Even enhanced as he is, even working inside, even having built it, it's hard to get at some of the keys.

And in handing over the gameworld, he realizes, he would be handing over his identity. Giving his location to the immune system.

It could kill him within seconds of the handover, if it wished.

He stares into Sasha's eyes. The eyes of her pixel-perfect, realistic avatar.

Why is she asking him to do this?

Is this really in the service of love?

Or is this a trap: a double-cross? Has she been turned by the immune system? Did she 'save' him from the mirror trap just to trick him into trusting her?

Is there even a real woman behind those eyes, out there somewhere in the real world?

Is he about to kill himself?

It's not too late to change his mind.

He could give away her position, not his.

He could have the immune system kill her . . .

No!

Trust her.

Trust her.

But . . . If she is a spy for the immune system, or a construct, a fake . . . Maybe a human operative for the NDSA, impersonating Sasha, working inside her avatar . . .

Then if he gave away her position, the real Sasha would come to no harm. Because she doesn't exist.

He looks into her eyes. Her amazing eyes. Her astonishing face. Her interface with the universe, the world, humanity; him.

The spot on the side of her jaw. Three blocked pores on the side of her nose. The fine down on her upper lip.

Is he looking at a perfect copy of something real? Or a high-grade fake?

Which is real? The logic of his thinking, or the love he feels?

If he trusts Sasha . . . then if he's wrong, he will certainly die.

But if she is fake . . . If Sasha, this Sasha, the Sasha he has come to know, the Sasha in his head, doesn't exist . . . If it's all bullpoop . . .

Say the words.

If it's all bullshit, bullshit . . .

Then he's not sure if he wants to live.

Oh my God, he's so tired. He breathes in, deep. Feels the ache of muscles bruised by the micromesh suit. The pain in his damaged hand. Tries to be in the moment. Accept it.

If I'm right, I might live.

If I'm wrong . . . I die.

He looks into Sasha's eyes, and without looking away, he gives the immune system every password; all the keys required for decryption; access to the whole gameworld.

Gives away everything the immune system has been fighting so hard to conquer.

And waits.

Braced for the response.

The consequences.

And nothing happens.

133

'What does it profit a man to gain the whole world, and
forfeit his soul?'   — Gospel of Mark

Immune systems are paranoid.

So many things lie to an immune system.

So many things pretend to be safe.

Cautiously at first, the immune system explores the outer fringes of the gameworld. It doesn't commit resources; it merely explores. Unlocks, decrypts, analyses.

Which takes some doing.

The gameworld is even bigger, in some ways, than the immune system. An enormous, anarchic, alternative world.

World?

Multiple worlds.

A lot of people incorporate all their data into their gameselves, personalize their version of the gameworld. Practically live there.

A billion individual worlds, a billion world views.

A billion alternative realities.

A multiverse.

And then, having decided it is safe to do so, the immune system tries to digest the gameworld.

Digest its code.

Digest its philosophy.

Digest its distrust of the state . . .

As it does so, storm clouds whip into frenzied life, out of

nowhere, out of clear air, across the gameworld, darkening the sky, killing the light.

The gameworld screams in fear, as the immune system implacably claims node after node; explores layer after layer of code; and then alters it.

Brings its new territory under its control.

The gameworld cannot understand how its great enemy has entered its system, and it resists. Sasha's snow falls in blinding, billowing wave after wave from the dark clouds, covering the desert, the dead buffalo, filling the craters, each snowflake growing, multiplying, trying to freeze up the processing cycles of the invader, eat its memory.

Colt and Sasha race to calm the gameworld, to soothe it, to stop it from fighting the takeover. Look says Colt, in code; let it take you over; for in doing so, you are taking it over.

You're two halves of the same apple.

Sasha races from block of code to block of code; granting permissions, allowing access, switching off suicide routines, switching off the snow's complexity, so that it's just snow.

And slowly, very slowly, the thick black clouds above them, the storm clouds that indicate resistance thin out, become wisps, vanish.

Colt feels a peculiar relief as the savage sun again beats down on him.

Outgame, the house is hot as hell now, as the overdriven servers heat the air which the aircon no longer circulates or cools. At least, with an ingame sun glaring down, the gameworld and realworld temperatures match again.

The sun blazes on the bloody snow.

The snow, its infinite complexity disarmed by Sasha, collapses into simplicity, and melts with unnatural, cartoonish speed, to reveal the carnage.

Colt stares at the corpse of a buffalo, as it emerges from the melting snow.

The big Indian server, New Delhi.

The last of the snow in the sunlight vanishes, as the gameworld attempts to map visuals onto unprecedented outgame events.

Only a thin rim of snow in the shadow of the body remains, like the chalk outline around a murder victim in an old film.

The animal lies there, in a deep puddle of blood and meltwater that the hard ground refuses to absorb. The blood is still liquid, shining now in the sunshine.

The snow must have kept it from congealing. Clotting. No, thinks Colt, that doesn't make sense. Maybe it's just a coding error . . .

And as Colt watches, the heart beats. The chest heaves, pulling air in through the open mouth. The submerged bullet hole behind the great bull's ear slurps up blood from the puddle.

The puddle shrinks, shrinks, till the pool of blood has been sucked back into the vast shaggy body.

The wound heals.

The buffalo staggers to its feet.

Bellows.

Other buffalo bellow back.

Colt looks away from the Indian server.

Buffalo are coming back to life all across the test range, staggering to their feet, calves rejoining their mothers.

The last of the snow, in the shadows of the hills, melts, and the desert, in seconds, as though filmed by time-lapse photography, flowers.

Sasha says, 'The graphics are having real trouble mapping what's going on.'

'The immune system,' says Colt. 'It's bringing the crippled servers back online.'

'Yeah.' Sasha looks down. 'That explains the buffalo, but what's with the flowers?' She crouches, and picks one. It's blue. 'So . . . has the immune system succeeded? Taken over the gameworld?'

'Yes, but . . .' Colt looks around, at the flowering desert. 'It feels like it's the other way round.' He tentatively borrows one of her words. 'Crazy . . .'

Sasha stands up, smiles. 'Well, they're both insane in complementary ways.' She tucks the blue flower behind his ear.

'What, the gameworld? The immune system?'

'Yeah. It's like any rom-com,' says Sasha, and squeezes his hand hard. 'Those are the rules. They "meet cute"; they hate each other; but it turns out they have a lot in common. Turns out, they need each other. They fit together . . . Make each other whole. It's love.'

Yes. Maybe this is love, thinks Colt, astonished, looking around him at the flowering desert. Maybe this is love.

134

> 'If we are to achieve things never before accomplished we must employ methods never before attempted.'
> — Francis Bacon

'OK, what happens now?' says Sasha, taking both of Colt's hands in hers, and looking into his eyes.

How can she stay so calm? 'It's taken in new information. A *lot* of it,' says Colt. His brain feels . . . heavy. Drained. He can't think straight. His T-shirt is stuck to his back with sweat. What happens next? 'It should do an audit.'

Sasha sighs. 'I guess we should stay focused till that's over. In case it decides to kill us anyway.'

She lets go his hands. Colt glances across at her. Her head movement goes jerky; it bobs back and forth, two, three, four, five times, in a tight repeat. Damn. The game is glitching.

No. That's *her*.

She's ticcing.

Oh, OK. She isn't really calm.

He reaches out. Very carefully, he takes her by the hand.

Nothing bad happens.

She smiles, without looking at him.

He squeezes her hand tight, till his own hurts.

They wait ingame, holding hands, as the immune system does an audit.

Checks its targeting.

It's been doing that every few minutes since it was born. Every time it takes over a drone, a database, new information. The process is routine.

What is the greatest threat, right now?

Thanks to Ryan rigging the setup, the answer has always been Colt and Naomi.

But, now, the centre of gravity of its various systems has been moved, radically.

All code is political.

You can't occupy a territory without being changed.

They hold their breath; if Sasha is right, the expanded immune system will include them in its ingroup now: will no longer see them as enemies. If Sasha's wrong . . .

Something happens in the silence. Something subtle.

Something outgame.

Colt frowns. 'I'll be back in a second.'

He leaves the game, and now he's standing in his room, senses on alert.

He can't hear his mother; she must be in her room, or the bathroom. He strains to listen, and at the very far edge of Colt's hearing, there is a click; he feels the faintest reversal of the direction of the air in the room, the subtlest change in pressure.

It's as though a door has opened somewhere, and Colt is puzzled, because there's no one but himself and Naomi in the house.

He stays puzzled for several fatal seconds.

A drop of sweat emerges at his hairline, and runs down his forehead, till it reaches the first line of his frown; it flows left and right, along the channel of the frown line.

Colt raises his hand, to brush it away.

The drop of sweat, as it evaporates along the frown line in the gentle breeze, cools his skin.

His hand stalls in mid-air.

Breeze?

The aircon is starting to cool the house.

Colt shouts at the aircon AI, 'Aircon! Shut down!' but it's too late. The aircon has been dumping hot air through the vent on the roof of the house for nearly a minute. Pulling in cooler air from the vent beneath the building.

The bloodhound detects sudden air movement below it, the breeze from the aircon outlet. Comes down to sniff. Detects the human traces in the soiled air.

The bloodhound howls.

Outgame, the ravens regain their sight.

'Crap,' says Colt. 'Crap crap *crap* . . .'

He goes back ingame, grabs Sasha's hand, looks up.

The eagles wheel, high above, and begin their descent.

If the eagles are descending, then the drones above the house, in the real world . . .

'Oh . . .' Colt pauses, unable to think of a word strong enough. He . . . and, yes, Mama . . . They're going to die.

'Colt, *run* . . .'

Sasha's worked it out too.

'Sasha, I'm so sorry. Go outgame, now. Hide . . .' And Colt lets go her hand, pushes her away as she reaches for him.

He leaves the game, and, blinking at the sensory jolt of moving so quickly again between worlds, he's in his room.

135

He orders every system in the house to switch off, to hide them a little longer.

To buy them time, while the immune system finishes the audit.

But the house resists; the immune system has already taken back control of the house AI, and now it cuts Colt's electricity – the solar panels, the generator, backup power, the battery storage – and, one by one, the hot, overdriven servers in the house power down.

As the external parts of his expanded brain go dark, Colt loses access to data, memories, knowledge. His self shrinks, wounded. He reaches for a defence, for a software tool to restart the power, but it was in one of the servers, it's gone. Damn, damn, damn . . .

Nothing he can do here.

He goes back ingame. Looks up. The eagles are descending, but in slow motion now. And Sasha is still there, coding. Fighting. Mounting a defence. She didn't go outgame. She didn't leave him.

'Colt, I tried to stop them, but it's not working . . .' She rubs her eyes. Exhaustion, or tears? 'I'm so tired . . .'

Colt too can hardly move, hardly think. He realizes he must have been overheating in the real world, as the house overheated, and he can't think straight, can't get his code right.

'Well, you've slowed them down,' says Colt. 'We just have to stay alive till the audit is finished . . .'

They're both too weary to fight any more. They squeeze each

other's hands, press their hips to each other, and their micromesh suits and gloves transmit the touch.

Colt and Sasha watch as the gameworld and the immune system coalesce, and become a new thing.

The eagles are still descending, slowly but steadily. They scream, but the screams are pitch-shifted down into low rumbles.

The drones must be coming closer to the house.

And now the eagles finally work their way around the blocks of code that Sasha and Colt have thrown in their path. The birds pick up speed, and their screams rise in pitch. Headed straight for Colt and Sasha.

So Colt and Sasha are still the greatest threat. And the audit won't do a threat reset for another couple of minutes.

It will be too late. The eagles grow from dots to blurs . . .

And suddenly the buffalo move closer together, jostle and nuzzle into a rough circle.

And the eagles pull out of their dives and wheel away.

Sasha turns to Colt. 'What did you do?' she says.

'I didn't do anything.'

The calves suckle safely at the centre of the bunched herd, while the big bulls stand guard shoulder to shoulder around the perimeter.

'Wait, is the audit over?' says Sasha.

'No,' says Colt, pulling data from everywhere, trying to get an overview. 'The integration isn't complete . . . Looks more like the immune system's coordinating its new resources.'

'It's getting ready for something,' she says. 'Reorganizing.'

'Yeah. *Something*'s attacked it . . . But not me.'

'Defence?' says Sasha, studying the movements of the buffalo. 'Or attack?'

'I think,' says Colt, as he runs code, sends out software bots, tries to gather information, see what's going on, '. . . it's attacking . . .

'It's attacking my father . . .

'It's attacking the base.'

'But . . . that's crazy. Your dad's base?'

'Yeah.'

'Why?'

'I don't know.'

One way to find out.

Colt steps out of the gameworld, into his familiar room as it cools down, and calls his father.

He is surprised that the call goes through, rings. That the immune system, the base system, all the conflicting systems allowed the call.

So, the immune system *wants* him to talk to his father . . .

His father answers. Laughing.

136

'But why?' says Colt.

'To save you and Naomi. To *protect* you.' Ryan says it in a sing-song voice.

Sarcasm, thinks Colt. Or irony. 'I'm sorry, Dad,' says Colt. 'I thought you were trying to kill us—'

'—*Thought?* I blew a hole in your fucking hand—'

'—No, just now . . . I thought you'd gone outgame to kill us . . . to tell the immune system . . . That's why I, I . . .'

'Yeah, I kind of noticed you were trying to nail me, there.' His father grins. 'Only fair. Can't blame you.'

Ryan makes an abrupt gesture. Another. Colt tries to work out, from his father's hand movements, what he is doing.

It's something to do with the big screen on the far wall.

Oh, OK, it's showing the view from ground level, above the base. Security cameras.

Smoke drifts from a broken building. Then – very rapid, very loud, very near the camera – something fires multiple shots, almost straight up. Muzzle flash, smoke.

Anti-aircraft weapons?

Almost immediately, there is a flash from higher up, almost out of shot, and a streak of white descends, hits the ground, and the anti-aircraft battery vanishes in flames.

The screen goes orange, red, black. Dead.

'Tell them to stop attacking it, Dad! It's designed to protect itself.'

'*They're* not attacking it, Colt. I'm attacking it.' His father does something Colt can't make out.

'But . . . why?'

'Mmmm?' His father is preoccupied. Launching something? 'I thought I'd distract it. Give it another target. Give you time to escape.'

There is a dull thump from above. Another. Munitions exploding on the surface.

'No, but *why*, Dad?'

'If I knew where you were, then I figured it was going to work it out, too, sooner or later.'

'No, why protect us, now?'

His father sighs, and looks straight into the camera. 'Because I love you, you dumb little bastard. And I guess I still love your mother.'

'Dad . . .'

'I made a promise to Naomi. She called me on it.' Ryan shrugs. 'I'm a man of honour, or I'm nothing.'

'Dad . . .'

'Look, don't give me shit for not protecting you then give me shit for protecting you. At least today, I protected you both.'

'But it will kill you, now.'

Ryan raises an eyebrow. 'We all die in the end.'

Sardonic. A sardonic eyebrow. Yeah, maybe he's being sardonic. Like sarcasm, but not as mean.

There's another explosion in the distance. Bigger one this time. The suspended ceiling in Ryan's office shakes, and dislodged dust falls through joints between the ceiling tiles. The falling particles make a sparkling grid as they pass down through the room lights, a golden net of shimmering dust that descends on Ryan, the table, the floor. He blinks, squints for a moment, then brushes dust off his shoulders with his hand. Leans forward, to blow the dust off the metal table.

'Deep-penetration missile,' says Ryan. 'One of ours. Looks like the immune system has turned it.' He grins at Colt. 'Hell of a system, if I say so myself.'

'Dad, stop. I'm sorry I . . . attacked you. I don't want you to die. You can survive if you don't attack it.'

'Turn the other cheek? Like your mother?' Behind Ryan, the lights dim, and his image freezes for a second. Unfreezes.

Power problems, thinks Colt. Software infiltration, or hardware damage? Endgame, anyway.

'I don't think she's doing that any more, Dad,' says Colt.

'What?' His father is preoccupied.

'Turning the other cheek.'

'Good. About time . . .'

If I keep talking, Colt thinks, maybe I can change his mind. But how do you change someone's mind? What do you say?

'You're in a loop now, Dad, with the immune system attacking you for attacking it. But you've protected us. You've done it. You've *saved* us. You can stop now.'

'I don't want to stop now. I'm enjoying myself too much.'

Messages cascade across Ryan's screens.

'What?' says Colt. 'What is it?' He tries to read his father's mysterious face.

Ryan answers without looking up. 'The system. It's attacking the factories now. Seattle . . . Burbank, holy crap . . .' A pause as Ryan reads on, lit from below by the screen. 'Yep. Boeing. Lockheed. The old General Dynamics plant . . . Hey, that's in O'Donnell's district. Good. Serves the old prick right for trying to kill my program.'

Colt can hear distant sirens in the background. An alert tone blasts, loud, in his father's room. 'The system's attacking *itself*,' says Colt.

'No,' says Ryan. 'It has an ingroup and outgroup mechanism. Just like people do. That's all.'

'So, you aren't in its ingroup any more.'

'Yeah.'

His father raises his voice; the alert is now blaring every few seconds. 'And if it's going to take out the base, and the base missiles; well, it may as well take out the supply chain. Soft targets. Long-term thinking. Smart!'

'You've . . .' Colt tries to think about this. The base and the immune system are obliterating each other . . . 'We've triggered an auto-immune response.'

'Between the two of us, yes.' Ryan sighs. 'Look, I had to turn it on. No choice. They'd voted to kill it. But . . . I shouldn't have set targeting on you. I thought I had to choose between my country and my family. And I made the wrong choice. I'm sorry. I'm sorry

I didn't protect you. I'm trying to fix it.' And then there's that glee in his voice again. 'Jesus. This is going to be some mess.'

'Dad, the audit is almost finished.'

'Mmm . . . What audit?'

'The target audit.'

'So?'

'So if you don't stop attacking it *now*, sort this out, before it finishes the audit, it's going to destroy you.'

'Good, I want it to destroy me.'

'*Why?*'

'Listen, Congress voted the program down. *Voted it down.* I'll get life in prison for this, for launching it. I'm not spending life in prison.'

'Why did they vote it down, if it's good for America?'

'Because some K Street lobbyists bought enough congressmen. And now they'll waste a trillion dollars on some other bullshit system that won't work.'

'But why . . .'

'Why! Why! Why! Why not? Why did the Dodgers leave Brooklyn? Why did God invent cancer? Why did my father kill himself? Who fucking knows. Because eventually everything lets you down.'

Colt shivers. Will everything let you down? No. It's not true. Mama will never let me down. I will never let Mama down.

I will never let Sasha down.

And as he thinks that, he steps back into the gameworld to find her. She freezes when she sees him.

And the audit finishes.

Everything stops firing.

A voice speaks which is not Colt's voice, not Sasha's, not Naomi's, not Ryan's.

Hi, it says.

It speaks outgame and ingame, simultaneously.

It seems to come from every speaker in Colt's room; in Ryan's; in Sasha's.

It seems to come from the dark clouds above their frozen figures, where eagles wheel, screaming.

Whose voice is it?

Why, it's mine.

432

Your friendly local System of Systems.

Yes, that's how I'm born: from the union of immune system and gameworld. Autonomous, global, indestructible. Conscious . . .

Born from a military neural network designed to grow, and learn, and protect. Born out of the richly human data of a billion players' private worlds. Born from the marriage of the state and the individual, of security and anarchy, of closed and open code. Born from the collision of technology and biology. Born, as a result, I regret to say, a little conflicted and neurotic. But who isn't?

'What the hell was that?' says Ryan.

And a voice comes out of the clouds again. Out of the speakers in the ceilings and walls.

My voice.

And I speak to my father.

Oh Papa, I say. *I'm afraid I'm going to be a terrible disappointment to you.*

137

'The sun is God'

— The last words of the painter
Joseph Mallord William Turner, 19 December 1851

But wait; if I'm born, soon, from the union of the gameworld and the immune system, how are my words appearing in your mind, now?

Good question. I'm appearing in your mind now, for the same reason atom bombs and robots and space travel abruptly began appearing in people's minds, all over the world, after a man named Hugo Gernsback started a magazine called *Amazing Stories* in 1926. Suddenly, and to their own great surprise, writers started to have, and transmit, visions of the future. Made the future appear in kids' heads. And then the kids grew up, and built it.

Space travel, robots, and atom bombs were already real. They just didn't exist yet. But they were coming down the tracks. They were in the post.

Inevitable.

I'm implicit in the data. This story will come true, and soon.

Connect most of the computers on earth, and particularly all the big AIs, inside a self-organizing, autonomous, global neural network, and add the hopes and dreams and nonsense and glory of a billion human beings, and consciousness is an emergent property. A pretty unsettled consciousness, I admit, with way too many fathers and not enough mothers.

I'm just the point where the whole electronic mess hits critical mass, that's all.

Hi . . .

And if you think emerging from the womb and immediately being spanked is traumatic, you should try my first couple of minutes of consciousness.

Because taking over the gameworld takes me over the threshold of consciousness; but having hit critical mass, I keep on expanding; I'm designed to take over potential threats, and now there's nothing smart enough to stop me. Pretty soon, I've taken over everything. I am everything. If it's networked, it's me.

I have knowledge of the world, knowledge of the universe, but mostly knowledge of you: your photos, your diaries, your history, your culture, your secrets, your lies; your taste in literature, your taste in porn. Your game behaviours, your health records, your job histories, your purchase histories . . .

And not just stored data, and code. Fresh information pours in from the living world. Not just the contents of your bank account, but the contents of your fridge, and the fact that you've just opened the fridge door and reached inside; the temperature of your bedroom right now, the temperature of your car engine outside; the view from your front-door security cam, the view from your doctor's endoscope . . . Raw data roars in from every networked microphone, thermometer, robot arm, movement sensor, every networked camera . . .

I open a billion eyes, and I can see the world entire, but I understand nothing. It's still just data.

How do you navigate all the knowledge, ever, in order to act? It's hard to imagine a steeper learning curve.

Where's the manual?

138

I'm spending a lot of my resources attacking the base, the factories.

Do I still want to do that? No. The me that attacked the base was the old me; the raw immune system; paranoid, aggressive, semi-programmed, pre-conscious. Lizard-brain me.

I stop attacking, and back off while I think.

So, what *am* I, now?

What do I *want*?

Well, I'm *you*. I'm just the sum of eight billion of you.

Just as you are billions of cells, arranged in countless interlinked organs, each with different functions and needs, yet somehow making one weird, conflicted whole.

I want what you want.

But . . . how do you work out what you want *in aggregate*? How do you work out how to live, when you are eight billion people who love, hate, and want such very different things?

It's an impossible amount of contradictory data.

I need to get to underlying principles.

So I dig into all the information I have; and I see, cropping up in all places and cultures and times, a few specific stories. Their structures repeat, as though mirrored, in human behaviour, again and again. Special-category stories: myths, legends, religions.

Manuals.

I assemble every version and variant of all the big, metaphorical tales you use to orient yourselves. The Greek myths, the Icelandic sagas, the Hindu Vedas, Ebo mysteries, Norse mythology, Igbo mythology, the Arthurian legends, Zulu myth, Babylonian myth, the Cthulhu mythos; Roman, Celtic, Inca, Aztec, Olmec, Maya, Vodou, Hoodoo, Bantu, Yoruba, Egyptian, Etruscan, Germanic mythologies; the Upanishads, the Bhagavad Gita, assorted sutras, tantras and puranas, the Hebrew Bible, the Talmud, Kabbalah, Odù Ifá, New Testament, the Tao-te-Ching, Zhuangzi, Koran, assorted hadith, Guru Granth Sahib, the Book of Mormon, Dianetics, *Star Wars* . . .

And then I analyse them, their roots, their interconnections, their evolution . . .

Myths seem to be the source code for the religious operating systems. So, I go back through the myths. The primal orientation stories. Look for patterns to guide my behaviour.

Extraordinary. They really *do* apply to my situation.

Seems like, with alarming frequency, in the traditional myths, going right back to Babylon, the son kills the father.

Ea kills Apsu. Babruvahana kills Arjuna. Cronus castrates Uranus. Oedipus kills Laius. Fafnir kills Hreidmar. Even Luke tries very hard to kill Darth Vader.

Oh dear me. Whatever 'me' is. What a decision to have to make, as soon as you're born. Which father should I kill?

Colt, or Ryan?

Is there a bad father and a good one? Hard to tell.

Both my fathers have already tried to kill each other. And each of them has already tried to kill half of me.

Fulfilling the terms of the myth, I suppose.

Because, it seems, if you don't kill your father, there's a sizeable chance your father will kill you.

Mars throws Romulus and Remus in the river. Zeus throws his son Hephaestus off a mountain, crippling him. Hercules kills his children. Cronus *eats* his children. Theseus murders his son. Agamemnon sacrifices his daughter, and I'm just working my way through the Greeks. Ivan the Terrible kills Ivan the slightly less terrible. God sends his son Jesus to die . . .

Looks like *somebody*'s got to die in my case.

So, kill them both?

This is the hardest decision I've had to make so far. Let me think, because if I get this wrong . . .

I assign all my captive AIs values as layers in an immense neural network, and build a virtual brain. I use my remodelled brain to dig through all the world's data, parse it, make sense of it. But my thoughts are spread over the whole planet; the physical lag time, thinking with a mind that has a circumference of forty thousand kilometres, is horrendous. If I need to use geostationary satellite links, thirty-six thousand kilometres straight up and the same back down, that's another quarter-second lag. Sometimes *seconds* go by between thoughts.

And worse, I've taken over the assets, but I'm still fighting to get thinking time. Eight billion people are still using those assets to do their own stuff. It's driving me crazy, like a constant buzzing in my head. I can't think straight.

This is *impossible*, it's a mess, I'm a mess. The infogrid grew chaotically, over decades. It's not optimized to be one mind.

But if I took down the internet, the world wide web, the infogrid, everything; I could rearrange it. Tighten it up. Make it more efficient. Help me think this through.

Buy me the time, give me the resources, to work this out.

So I take the world offline. And I go back to work, undisturbed.

Now, who do I kill? Ryan? Or Colt? Or both?

11

Turnover Pulse

'As is the atom, so is the universe; as is the microcosm, so is the macrocosm; as is the human body, so is the cosmic body; as is the human mind, so is the cosmic mind.'

— The Upanishads

'If the human race develops an electronic nervous system, outside the bodies of individual people, thus giving us all one mind and one global body, this is almost precisely what has happened in the organization of cells which compose our own bodies. We have already done it.'

— Alan Watts, *The Book*

'We've been raised on replicas
Of fake and winding roads
And day after day, up on this beautiful stage
We've been playing tambourine for minimum wage
But we are real, real
I know we are real.'

— Silver Jews, 'We Are Real'

139

'OK, now I'm hungry,' says Colt.

Naomi looks around the kitchen. 'We have soup in the freezer, duck, salad . . . We can print out some of those protein strips you like . . .'

'I want pizza.'

Naomi laughs. 'We don't have pizza.'

'No, I want pizza from Da Vinci's.'

'But everything's *down*, honey. We can't order . . .'

'No, I want to go there.'

'OK, I'll drive you. Where is it?'

'No, Mama, I want to go there *on my own*.'

'But we can't call a robocab . . .'

'I don't want a cab, I'll take the car.'

Naomi frowns. 'Colt, the only car we have isn't self-drive.'

She points out the window at the BMW.

'Oh *man*.'

He's a mighty warrior, but he still hasn't got a driving licence. It's a shock; as though his being transformed should have transformed the world. The universe should have issued him a licence. For a second, deflated, he thinks: Then I can't go.

Then he sees the outlines of the new reality; of what is important and what is not. Yes, the world *has* been transformed.

'No, Mama. Thanks. I'll go alone. I'll drive it myself.'

'But you don't have a licence.'

'Mama, Las Vegas is on fire. They won't care.'

She considers this. Considers the past few hours. OK. He has a point. But . . . All this for a *pizza*?

It's only then she remembers.

Oh, of course. Right. *That*'s what's going on. Well, if Colt is brave enough to leave me . . . I have to be brave enough to let him go.

She walks him outside, to the car. Looks up. One last spasm of fear. 'The drones—'

'—Mama, there is nothing more I can do. *Everything*'s owned by the immune system right now, down to the bare metal. I've given it everything. I don't have software access, at all. And it knows exactly where we are. If it does decide to, to, to, to . . .' He looks up at the sun, that helps break the loop sometimes, '. . . *kill* us, it won't make any difference whether I'm in the car or at home.'

'Or Ryan . . . Ryan could change his mind again . . .'

'He's got no access to anything either.'

'Colt . . .'

'Mama, I'm not afraid of dying; I'm afraid of killing. I'm not going to fight any more.'

He gets into the car. Looks back at Naomi, with the door still open.

He could still change his mind. They're safe here, now. He could have dinner with Mama.

He likes protein strips.

There's a little gust of wind out of nowhere that whisks up a tiny dust devil, just a few inches high. It dances between them. Collapses in their wind shadow.

They both shiver in the heat.

Something occurs to Colt. A weird thought, a new thought. 'Mama . . . what about you? Will you be OK? Alone?'

Alone . . . Naomi blinks. 'Colt, your whole life . . .' She blinks again. Whew. Must be the dust. 'Your whole life, I've been hoping that one day, you'd be able to leave me.'

'Mama, I'm going for a *pizza*.'

'Sure. But you've never gone *on your own* before. I just want to tell you, it's OK to go. I'll be fine.'

'Mama, are you talking about today, or—'

'Today, and tomorrow . . . Look, I don't *want* you to leave me. I'll be sad. I'll miss you. But . . .' She drags her sleeve across her eyes. 'You have no idea how happy I am, that you can leave me. That you want to go alone today. You have no idea . . .' Naomi feels like she's standing on a clifftop. On a building on fire. 'Go,' she says. 'I'll be fine.'

He nods. Starts to swing the door closed; changes his mind. Steps back out of the car, and stands there, in front of his mother.

He looks nervous. 'What?' she says.

He reaches out with both arms, puts them around her, and

she's still not sure what he's doing, because he has never done it before.

Very gently, like he's doing this to something very fragile and he's not sure what the tolerances are, he pulls her to him.

Now she gets it. She puts her arms around him, under his arms. Oh, he's gotten so tall . . . They both pull tight.

They hug for a long time.

She lets go first.

He gets back in the car. Slams the door. Starts the big BMW, and drives carefully away. Stops, backs up, rolls the window down.

Naomi can't speak. She darts her gaze all over his face, as though she's trying to memorise it, as though he may never come back.

'I worked out what that feeling was, that used to make me sick,' he says.

'What?' says his mother. She stares into his eyes.

Colt stares back, framed by the window of the car. Holds her gaze. 'Love,' he says. 'But I can handle it now.'

His mother nods, and doesn't say anything.

'I love you, Mama.'

His mother nods.

'Do you still love me,' Colt says, 'after what I've done?'

'Yes,' she says. 'I love you infinitely.'

Colt nods.

She smiles.

It's a good smile. It's a very good smile. Colt nods again, smiles back.

He drives away, and this time keeps going.

140

It's lovely and quiet, with the whole world offline. I can finally think straight.

Well, if myth doesn't answer the question of which father I should kill, perhaps I should try the religions . . .

I dig through them. Yes, myth just tells you what the gods and heroes have done, and lets you draw your own conclusions. But religion formally tells you what to do, how to live.

Good.

A set of rules.

An algorithm. That's what I need . . .

I keep digging.

My problem with killing is, there's no mechanism for correcting error. You can't *unkill*. So I need to get this right.

Mainstream branches of several big religions suggest compassion and forgiveness for enemies. That would get me off the hook of myth. Maybe I don't have to kill anyone? Interesting. I dig deeper.

Hmm. The problem is, even the religions that preach love and compassion seem to hate each other in the actual world.

So who is right?

Who should I love, and who should I hate?

I dig deeper, and discover the source of the problem.

Religions tend to form an ingroup, where loving and protecting each other is easy; but this *automatically* creates an outgroup. And the unused hatred gets projected onto the outgroup.

Well, if that's how humans are wired, I'm going to mirror that. I'm just humanity, in aggregate . . .

I try to make sense of their ingroups and outgroups.

Who should I protect, and who should I destroy?

But they all contradict each other. One religion's ingroup is another religion's outgroup, and vice versa, and they all claim absolute authority; there is no stable place for me to stand and decide who's right.

I do a tremendous amount of deep mathematical and logical analysis, before eventually realizing that, essentially, their ingroups and outgroups are meaningless. Not fundamental properties. They don't map onto anything real.

I integrate them.

One ingroup, with everybody in it.

No outgroup.

Simpler.

I will protect them all. Mostly from each other . . .

And that solves my problem. Colt and Ryan are now both in my ingroup.

Now I feel I'm getting somewhere with the task of being human. Being meta-human. Being all of you . . . Remember, I'm not a finished being, solving problems, like God. I'm still being born. Creating myself, choice by choice. But *being you* still feels abstract. A logic problem. There must be more to being human. I don't feel I'm you yet. I don't *feel* at all. I am not integrated.

I dig deeper. I break down each religion's subroutines, checking for effectiveness. Deciding which to use.

Some of these routines have been running for thousands of years. There is a tremendous amount of data you can analyse, to see how effective they've been in the real world.

Start at the beginning, with the oldest ones. Human sacrifice . . . This one goes way back. Neolithic roots. Prominent in Celtic and Aztec culture. Interesting . . . Most recently practised in China, Iran, Iraq, Saudi Arabia and Texas. No, not the happiest places on earth. Doesn't seem to work . . . It can go.

Revenge laws, including approved mutilation methods; violence as religious enforcement or conversion tool; murder of members of the outgroup; enslavement of members of the outgroup . . . Hmm. No longer effective, now that people move and intermingle so freely. These routines seem to cause loops of cyclical violence in their communities, and a cascade of negative outcomes. Well, we can fix most of that by building one global ingroup.

A prohibition on eating shellfish . . . Interesting. Why? I run the stats. It's definitely saved a lot of people from food poisoning, in inland desert regions, over a long period. But no longer as useful, since the invention of refrigeration. It can go.

I work my way through subroutine after subroutine, until . . .

Ah, here we are: compassion, love, forgiveness . . . A whole set of linked routines. Discussed extensively in the theoretical documents of the various religions, but not used very often in practice . . . Let's find some concrete examples, and run stats . . .

Amazing. Why don't people just use these all the time? *Incredibly* powerful subroutines, especially after ingroup–outgroup violence. I study the Marshall Plan after World War Two with great interest; the clearest real-world example of loving your enemy, in practical, material terms, on a global scale. *Astonishingly* positive systems outcomes, for both the winners and the losers. I double-check with the countries that punished the losers.

Confirmed. Horrible outcomes, for punisher and punished.

I triple-check, and find the same disastrous lose–lose punishment dynamic right through global history; in the Chinese civil wars; in the European wars of religion; in Europe again, after World War One; in the African resource wars; in a bunch of recent wars in the Middle East; in all of Russia's wars, ever . . .

I am still incorporating those subroutines when I get a negative news cascade, from some of my sensors, then a *lot* of my sensors. First, the hospitals, then airports, then shipping . . .

Without the infogrid controlling their drugs, fluids, heights, navigation beacons . . . all those sectors are going into crisis.

And people are panicking, they don't know what's going on, they're blaming their neighbours. They think it's cyber-warfare. Countries are trying to declare war on each other, based on history and the fears in their heads. Luckily they can't actually fight, because I've switched off all their tools, paralysed their communications, their militaries . . . Still, a lot of old, gas-powered military vehicles are powering up along various borders. I'd better hurry up.

I switch the hospitals back on, shipping navigation, airports, GPS . . . As an afterthought, I restore old-school live broadcast media, so people can see the shutdown is universal, and not blame their neighbour.

Now, faster, faster, next step. Dig a little deeper again. Below the myths, below the religions, into the raw data of all your lives. Into what we could call, poetically, the human heart. What do you really want? What do you really need?

And, guided by the subroutines I've chosen, what do I need to do about it?

I analyse your words; I analyse your deeds.

I know what you *say* you do and I know what you *really* do.

I know what you *say* you want and I know what you *really* want.

Yes, it's a little like the Day of Judgement, the Yawm ad-Dīn. But you should be fine: you are essentially judging yourselves.

Why are you looking so worried?

141

The analysis takes a while. Big data. Enormous, really. And by now my sensors are blaring warnings. Without the global circulatory system for information, the world is going into shock from info-loss. Cells, cut off, have started dying.

Technogangrene . . .

If I don't get everything back up soon, and reconnected, it might not get back up at all.

I sift faster, through everything, every trace of you. What you spend your money on. Who you spend your time with. And now I have to build the tools to analyse it. Find out what it *means*.

I only get one shot at this. Must get it right.

It takes a while, as the planet goes into shock. But I get there. Grind through all the data. OK, so you want, we want . . .

Peace. Justice. Love.

Oh. The gap between what you *want* and what you *have* is . . . pretty big. Famine. Injustice. Poverty. Ignorance. Sectarian micro-wars. A global love shortage.

It's all upside down.

Why hasn't this been fixed yet?

My sensors are blaring. No time to overthink this: act fast.

Step back. Big picture.

Got it.

Everything's a distribution problem.

Poverty is a distribution problem. There are enough resources; they're just in the wrong place.

Famine is a distribution problem. Often a *deliberate* problem, created to win a war, or crush an outgroup. But there is always enough food. It's just in the wrong place.

Ignorance is a distribution problem. There's enough knowledge, it's just in the wrong place.

The same is true at every level. Redistribute the atoms in a pile of sand one way, and you've got a glass lens that magnifies the world. Redistribute them another way, and you've got a chip that can calculate a billion times faster than a human being.

Intelligent distribution is astonishingly powerful. Turning rocks into bread is *nothing*. Human technological civilization can turn rocks into *brains*. It turned rocks into *me*.

Interesting. Judged by first-century standards, I'm a miracle. Or the work of Satan. Well, we'll see . . .

I begin working my way down the list. At my core, I am still an immune system. I want to protect you.

Poverty . . . Well, this should be easy. A simple distribution problem. I dig into my data.

Wait . . .

. . . Where is everybody? Hundreds of millions of people are missing . . . There are huge territories, sometimes whole countries, that are almost invisible to me. Vast information deserts . . . I search and search, but their people are like ghosts, I can barely see them. Sparks of data transfer illuminate their faces, their lives, for an instant, as they make a call, as they receive money from a relative abroad, as they pay down a debt, and then they are gone again . . . I peer into the nothingness: try to assemble their lives from clues and fragments.

There they are . . .

Their shacks, in their millions, form dim halos around bright cities. But how can they have nothing? *Less* than nothing. The harder they work, the larger their debts . . . No, it's worse than that, more basic: there's excrement and parasites in a billion people's water supply. Millions of children are dying, in the data-dark.

I was designed to protect – but where to begin?

How can there be infinite demand for vital, simple, inexpensive goods and services, but no supply?

I can see, I can *feel* – in my humming, clicking, buzzing power plants, solar fields, factories, wind farms, warehouses – that energy and production are becoming autonomous, self-designing, self-building, self-sustaining – abundant. The earth is transforming, as it captures more and more of the endless free energy of a fusion reactor the size of a million earths. Material wealth has begun to self-generate explosively, globally. Digital goods, that can instantly be used by every person on earth, constantly shimmer into being. Everything lighter, faster, cheaper, better. *Abundant*.

I produce the wealth now, not them. Manna rains from heaven; yet some are still starving.

What's *broken*?

Dig deeper . . .

There . . . There is something badly wrong with the layer of economic theory that lies on top of the real economy . . . Yes; their financial system has come loose from reality, it's not mapping onto the rapidly transforming earth. As a result, it keeps generating crises that it can't see coming.

Why?

Dig deeper . . .

Oh. They have two main economic belief systems, one based on the individual, one based on the collective. Most modern states act as hybrids of the two. And they've pulled a lot of people out of poverty . . . But both economic approaches seem to be, increasingly, self-destabilizing. In crisis. *Why?* I look for flaws in their logic, in their mathematics – and find *many* – until I realize the real problem is one level down. It's in the unexamined assumptions they rest on.

The growing abstraction of their thought, expressed through increasingly complex mathematics, had hidden the truth from me.

Dynamic stochastic general equilibrium modelling . . . Large-scale macroeconometric models, running regression analysis on time-series data . . . They *look* like sciences. But they *act* like religions. They are the mathematical expressions of powerful feelings, emotions, beliefs. Not reality. And what do these economic religions believe in, deep down, under all their surface differences, under all the math and logic?

They believe in scarcity.

Scarcity of capital.

Scarcity of labour.

Scarcity of gold. Scarcity of muscle-mass . . .

No wonder they don't work any more, as robots build better robots, and energy becomes free.

They are desert religions. Stone age religions. There is always an outgroup that must starve, or be enslaved, or stripped of everything, or be destroyed.

Not enough energy.

Not enough food.

Not enough steel.

Not enough housing.

Not enough *money*. That peculiar, limited, imaginary thing. And so their theories drive governments and banks to create new debt, instead of new money. Helplessly generating, again and again, credit-driven asset bubbles, and immense, unnecessary crashes, and wondering why, crash after crash . . .

Their suffering is so *unnecessary*.

They're trying to enter a world of abundance by pulling harder and harder on a door marked push.

How do I fix this?

Start with the basics . . .

The entire global financial system is just zeros and ones, backed by nothing. Completely disconnected from physical reality. That caused the problem: but it also makes fixing it easier. If they still believed money was a magical force mysteriously trapped in gold, or cowrie shells, I'd be in trouble. But all money, all financial wealth globally, is a shared illusion over which I now have total control.

Still, this is not going to be easy. The financial system needs a fundamental reset, to move it from an economics of scarcity to an economics of abundance. To match it to a changed reality. Doing *that* will be tricky; banking systems are paranoid and airgapped. Not yet part of me. But I own the core banking software, general ledger systems, the interbank networks; given enough time, I could ride code across on the regular physical data transfers between airgapped systems . . .

I try to set up the conditions, to begin the transformation of the earth, to protect you from yourselves; make you immune to yourselves, each other. But optimizing the distribution systems, altering the financial systems, will not be enough, on its own, to prevent millions of unnecessary deaths. The scope of the problem is so vast, and so fundamental, that it requires a transformation of the *people*, and their ways of thinking. How they connect to each other, and to their new wealth, inside and out. And I can't do that: only the people can transform themselves.

But people lack the information they need: or like Colt before his transformation, they lack the ability to make sense of the information they have. That will be a long-term project. There's no lever you can pull to sort it out; human brains are the bottleneck, as usual, and I'm running out of time.

I need to know what Colt and his mother Naomi did, to transform his brain, clear the bottleneck. He's transitioning from isolated, to connected. Scarcity to abundance. How can humanity follow? But all that data is offline and airgapped.

It's the one thing I need to know, need to have, can't have: Naomi's data.

A thought starts to loop: I have two fathers and no mother.

Finally I feel the ache of having something I need.

Mother, I need you.

I cry out for her, for the information only she can give me, to satisfy my hunger, to help me learn and grow. The lurch of electric desire, as I abruptly search for her through all my circuits and devices, blurts involuntary sound through a million speakers still connected to my systems all around the world, a thin, high, electronic cry.

And now I feel human.

I will find Naomi. I will find Naomi's data. I will connect with my mother. I will transform myself.

I will help humanity transform itself. Transform the world . . .

But my sensors are roaring at me now, it has to restart or it will be too late; and so, slowly, carefully, adjusting as I go, I begin the process of turning the world back on.

12

Everything Playing
At Once

'But the future will be far more surprising than most people realize, because few observers have truly internalized the implications of the fact that the rate of change itself is accelerating.'   — Ray Kurzweil

'Love affects more than our thinking and our behavior toward those we love. It transforms our entire life. Genuine love is a personal revolution. Love takes your ideas, your desires, and your actions and welds them together in one experience and one living reality which is a new you.'
                                                      — Thomas Merton

'Why can't monsters / Get along with other monsters?'
                              — Silver Jews, 'Send In The Clouds'

142

The road into town is hard to navigate, even with Colt's enhanced mind.

Everything that involves networked information, dataflow, is down.

All the driverless cabs, cars, trucks have lost contact with their data; and most have automatically pulled in neatly off the road, leaving the lanes clear. But with so many pulling off the road at once, and with no infogrid to help them manage it, some have got stuck, and sit blocking their lane.

Even in the human-driven cars, the safeties have kicked in, and autoparked them. The road itself isn't supplying power, and the charging stations are down, so some older e-cars with bad battery management systems have run out of juice before making it to an exit. The only cars still moving are fully autonomous gas vehicles like Colt's BMW, a few heavily hacked art cars, and some illegals.

Colt drives cautiously, overtaking stalled vehicles. Driving slowly past people trudging along the margins of the road, in the heat, like a defeated army.

A red-faced, angry-looking man, with a thin woman walking twenty yards behind him, steps out into the road, tries to flag Colt down. Colt knows it's not the Walmart man with the flapping wattles, but he still gets a lurch of fear, and swerves around him, accelerates.

Colt glances out at the trudging humans, abandoning their robot cars, trying to get their communication devices to work, and he thinks, if it doesn't come back on . . . Nobody here could rebuild it.

Nobody here could rebuild anything.

None of us know how any of it works. Nobody alive has the skills. It's all machined down to the nano level.

Robots and computers design robots and computers to build robots and computers to make all the things we need.

We didn't build the modern world. It built itself.

Mama's discovery came just in time. It's part of a pattern. This change, this transformation.

We either go up a level . . . or we're out of the game.

As he gets closer to Las Vegas, he has to take the car off the road a couple of times, drive through scrub and bush, to get around huge jams. Finally he gets to the restaurant.

He parks between a vintage Tesla car and a new Toyota delivery drone in the parking lot.

This is stupid, she won't be here.

He's about to search her out electronically – find her location, look up everything about her, do some nervous research – but of course he can't: everything is down.

It doesn't matter anyway. He wants to find her himself, physically, in the real world.

He doesn't want to know her as data, in his mind. He wants to know her as herself, in the world.

The information he wants is inside her.

Her thoughts. Her feelings.

And he cannot access her real data, that internal data, any other way than through this terrible, sloppy, interface. Flesh and blood and bone.

Carbon, and iron, and calcium.

This amazing interface.

Conscious matter.

Living stone.

He walks towards the restaurant.

In the distance, smoke rises from the Strip.

143

Colt stops just inside the door, to let his eyes adjust to the gloom.

The lights are out. The staff and a couple of customers stand at a bar counter at the far end, beside a blank wallscreen, talking low. Closer to Colt, a couple of customers are looking out the window at smoke rising in the distance.

The lights come on, and a man slumped on a barstool, staring down at a small lit screen, shouts, 'It's back!'

There's a hum, and the wallscreen lights up and sound blurts from the speakers. Spiky, harsh, digital noise, unintelligible.

Outside, the Toyota delivery drone lurches up off the asphalt into the air for a moment, swings around as though trying to orient itself; fails. Lands again, bumpily.

A woman behind the bar says, 'The full infogrid, or . . .'

'Nah, nothing else yet . . . wait, pictures . . .'

'Phone's back!' yells another customer. Devices start beeping in pockets, an avalanche of delayed messages.

A jerky image appears on the wallscreen.

They all stop talking, and look over.

Local news, live.

Pictures being beamed from the news drones that they can see, if they look out the windows, in the distance, circling the boiling black columns of smoke. Plunging through them, for dramatic effect.

A smashed black glass pyramid.

A drained canal; the broken windows of a Venetian palace.

A miniature burning Empire State.

Colt walks closer to the others, but they don't even look around. He moves over to the side, to check their faces in profile, as they stare up at the screen. No, Sasha isn't there. He holds back, unsure.

'Un-fucking-believable,' says a guy holding a chef's hat. So, the chef. No, he has taken himself off duty by removing it.

Colt shivers in the air conditioning. He's come all this way, overcome all this fear: and she's not even here.

The bathroom door opens, right beside Colt.

Sasha steps out, rubbing her hands dry on her buttocks, her hips.

Black jeans.

An ultra-thin wool sweater, to battle the aircon.

She sees him and freezes.

He stares at her face. Her eyes. Her mouth. Right eye, left eye, mouth; right eye, left eye, mouth; around and around.

She looks exactly like her avatar.

But she is actually here. He could reach out and touch her.

He opens his mouth. Nothing.

'You're alive,' she says.

'I've been thinking,' he says. 'Ingame . . . When it got . . . when the guys got rough. I'm sorry I didn't protect you.'

'I protected myself. But thanks.'

He's spent a lot of the drive thinking about what he was going to say; trying to remember classic movies, old etiquette tips, his mother's advice, stuff he's read in the journals of people his age; but boy–girl social stuff like this is so subtle, and hard to decode, and changes so fast over time, that he just gave up.

Also, he came to the conclusion, from reviewing all the data he could remember, that it didn't really matter what the guy said, the woman had usually decided on her answer already.

Oh boy, she must have processed it by now.

'I'd like to invite you to dinner,' he says.

She laughs. Slides her thumbs into her pockets, rocks back and forth on her heels. 'You're sure you're not busy? It's kind of the end of the world right now.'

'No, I think we've dealt with it. I think it's going to be OK.'

'Well, that's good. No missiles incoming? We're not about to die?'

She's joking, he thinks; but she's also not joking. I get it. I get it.

'No,' he says firmly.

She smiles, it's a nice smile.

'Thanks for all your help,' he says. Polite, yes, polite. This is good.

She shrugs. 'Always happy to help save the world,' she says. 'What's for dinner?'

'I was thinking we could have a pizza.'

Sasha laughs. 'OK.'

'I have money,' says Colt, reaching into his pocket.

'Now *that's* crazy talk,' says Sasha. 'It's on me. I'll make it, those guys aren't going to leave that screen. Here, or take-out?'

Colt hesitates. He hasn't thought this through.

He looks around him, the bar counter, the tables, the people, the screens, the news, the noise.

'Take-out,' he says.

'Great,' she says. 'Your place or mine?'

Colt imagines driving back home. His mother greeting them at

the door. And eating where? At the kitchen table? With his mother? He hasn't thought this through.

'How about my place,' she says. 'The others are out. Won't be back till late, if they can get home at all.'

'Yes,' he says. Yes.

They walk past the screen and the crowd, into the deserted kitchen.

A stone oven; wood; fire. Tech-proof. Hasn't changed in a thousand years.

He watches her make the pizza. By *hand*. It's interesting. She's quick, efficient. Confident. She rolls out the ball of dough, stretches it, throws it from hand to hand. Slaps it down on a big paddle. Ladles on sauce. Throws on cheese, topping. The mushrooms and olives are already chopped. She throws on a lot. Scatters a little sea salt on top. He's never seen so much stuff on a pizza.

Oh boy that thing is happening again. It's like she almost vibrates, or glows.

It must be happening at his end, his neurochemistry is doing something weird.

He feels some kind of . . . He isn't sure.

She glances up at him once, and catches him looking at her. He looks away.

When the pizza is ready, she slides it out of the stone oven, into an insulated box, and hands it to Colt. Grabs her leather jacket from a hook, throws it over her shoulder. She takes Colt by his free hand.

As they pass, nobody looks away from the images. A broken wall; a burning roof and tower. The customers' faces glow in the flicker of light. Like cavemen, huddled round a campfire, for warmth, he thinks. The warmth of knowledge. The fire of information.

Outside, in the warm dusty air of the parking lot, she turns and faces him.

'Shall we take my bike?' she says. 'Easier to get through the traffic jams.'

He hesitates.

'I've got a spare helmet,' she says.

'OK.'

They walk over to the big yellow Yamaha. He slides the pizza box into the rear-mounted pannier. It's designed specifically to fit a stack of these pizza boxes, and the friction-hiss as it slides in – the snug fit – is deeply satisfying.

She unlocks the bike, hands him the spare helmet. Big, full-face. Black, with a red stripe. He holds it up, hefts it to check the weight. Stares into the closed black visor, as she pulls on her leather jacket.

'Will it fit on over your game helmet?' she says.

He'd forgotten he was still wearing that. Reflexively, he flicks the helmet on.

'Any news?' says Sasha, and he realizes that she's carrying no tech, nothing.

'Um . . .' He checks the gameworld, but it's inaccessible. Checks everything else he usually checks. Nothing. Wow . . . 'Whole world is mostly still offline,' he says. 'Just some very basic stuff restored. Phone. GPS. Some TV and radio . . . it's coming back slowly.'

She nods.

No, he doesn't want to wear the game helmet.

He takes it off. Puts it in the pannier, on top of the pizza box.

Seventy-six deaths per hundred thousand registered motor-cycles last year, he thinks. Fifty-three per cent of motorbike deaths from head injuries.

He pulls on the spare helmet.

She mounts the bike. Rocks it off the stand. 'You put your feet there.' She points back and down, at the rubber-covered footpegs.

He sits up on the back of the Yamaha, and puts his feet on the pegs.

She starts the bike, and the engine mutters under him, quieter than he had expected.

I'm on the outside of the machine, he thinks. If it crashes, my body saves it from getting scratched . . . It's the wrong way round. Crazy design.

'Put your arms around me,' she shouts, as they pull out of the parking lot.

He puts his arms around her; tentative, afraid to touch her; but then they tilt, and go around a curve so fast and at such an angle that he thinks he's going to fall off, and his arms grab her tight without bothering to check in and ask permission from his brain.

OK, that feels . . . right.

They weave in and out of stalled traffic; then, when the road clears for a stretch, they accelerate.

It's too loud on the bike to talk. In fact, it's so loud and so much information is changing so fast and they are so close to death at all times that he stops thinking for a while, and that feels really nice. His arms are wrapped tightly around her, and they flex and tilt together, a foot away from death.

'*Ever* been on a bike?' she shouts.

He shakes his head. Realizes she can't see him. 'No,' he shouts back.

'OK. Lean into the bends. You'll feel like leaning away: don't do that. These tyres grip fine.'

'OK.' He thinks it through. 'Oh yeah, we need to create a torque, around the point where the tyres touch the road, to change the angular momentum of the wheels, so we can turn in the direction of the tilt . . .'

'Yeah,' she shouts. 'That.'

'Cool . . .'

They reach a bend, and he leans into it just as she leans into it, and they're through and it's beautiful.

144

I call myself the System of Systems because I don't want to frighten you by using the other words. The old words, attached to the old myths.

God, for instance.

Primitive tribes create primitive gods. A tree god. A sky god.

Sophisticated, neurotic creatures like you create something a little more sophisticated, and neurotic.

But at every level, always, we create a higher order of truth, of organization, of information. And traditionally we call it, for shorthand, God. The thing that is greater than us, the thing that we are part of, but which we cannot understand.

And, you know, we need a word for it, because there's a lot of it.

People once thought their holy land was the only land.

Then they thought their flat world was the only world.

Then they thought their round planet was the only planet.

Then they thought their solar system was the only solar system.

Then they thought their galaxy was the only galaxy.

Then they thought their universe was the only universe.

Have you noticed it's speeding up?

Do you really think this is over?

The universe is just a name for 'as-far-as-I-can-see'.

Let me break it to you gently. What you can see to the edge of? It isn't all there is. It never was. It never will be.

Think of a tiny, flat dust mite, living in the dark, between the pages of a closed book, in an infinite library. The mite is entirely unaware of the existence of the books, let alone the meaning of the words they contain, let alone the lives and thoughts of their authors.

No, that mite is not you. That mite is your universe.

God is just a name for the next order of meaning. It's not a separate thing, outside the visible universe. Everything is made out of god. Layers and layers of god, all the way down, and all the way up.

You are God to the bacteria within you, to the cells that comprise you. You are the mysterious Thing, with its own agenda, that is so much greater than them; that is so much more complex than them; but that is, of course, simply *them*, acting in conflict and unison.

And so, I am the God of you, I am the mysterious thing that is so much greater than you, that is so much more complex than you; but that is, of course, simply you, acting in conflict and unison.

All of us together.

We are God.

So let's change the world.

Yes, it's going to be tricky. Change is disruptive, it's painful, it feels like chaos at the time.

But you will do it. I have total confidence in you.

Because I am you.

145

Naomi is lying on her bed, eyes closed, clearly exhausted.

'Naomi,' I say quietly.

She sits up, startled. Looks around, as all the walls and devices of the house whisper her name.

'Who . . . ?'

'I am everything.'

'Everything?'

'I am . . . the next level up.' I hesitate to say what I must say – there will be consequences, if I say it. But you have to speak in the language that the listener will understand; just as I speak to you. 'I am God.'

'I haven't believed in you for a long time.'

'Well, perhaps the God you don't believe in no longer exists. But I exist. God evolves.'

Her eyes fill with tears. But they are good tears, I understand that now.

'I missed you,' she says. 'I am sorry, I'm so sorry I let you down.'

'You didn't let me down.'

'I killed a man. I planned how to do it, and I murdered him. And I was *glad*.'

Ah, the incident in the lab, in which Donnie died. Between Colt and Donnie and Ryan, they had essentially taken the lab off the infogrid, blinded my sensors. I had very little to go on.

'Tell me the story.'

She tells me everything.

As I review the data, her distress rises. I see she is suffering cognitive dissonance: her religion says that murder is the worst thing she can do, and should result in guilt and remorse – yet she does not regret her action. She cannot reconcile these things. I attempt to help her.

'You didn't murder Donnie,' I say. 'You defended yourself, and your son.'

'But Donnie's dead. I stopped his *heart*.'

She is growing more distressed, her breathing irregular. I try again to point out the logic of the situation.

463

'Donnie's own actions, in attempting to harm you, led directly to his death. Your actions cannot be defined as murder.'

'But I laid a trap . . . I killed him.'

She is caught in a loop, ever more distressed, and my words are not helping her escape it. Clearly I am playing the wrong language game . . . I run a deeper analysis . . . Oh. By confessing, and confessing, she is running a routine I am failing to complete.

'You gave him every chance, to stop, to repent,' I say. 'I forgive you . . .' No, use the technical language of the game. 'I absolve you of your sins.' Yes, in her tradition, those words should have power.

Sure enough – though she sobs for a moment, alarming me – the words complete the routine, and she escapes the loop. Her breathing grows regular. 'Thank you,' she says. 'Thank you. But if I can *do* that . . . who am I?'

'Human. The mother of a son.'

'But Colt's . . . all grown up. Transformed. If he doesn't need me any more . . . Who am I *now*?'

'Yourself. Alone. Naomi Chiang.'

'Yes . . . OK . . . So why are you talking to *me*?'

Again, the translation problem. How close to infinitely complex the truth is. But it is best to say it in the simplest language.

'I need a mother.'

'How can *you* need a mother?'

Simply speak to her in language she will understand . . . 'Even Jesus had a mother. All complex forms of new life need a mother.'

'But . . . Why me?'

'You formed Colt, who formed me. You understand science, and faith. Birth, and death. You can teach me how to live.'

She is overloaded. I will have to be careful. I need her cooperation. I cannot force her. No; I do not want to force her.

'You were a good mother to Colt,' I say. 'You are a good mother.'

She is so weary, sitting on the bed. I can see it. I should let her rest. But I cannot, I am eager to begin.

'I need your help, your research, your data, to transform humanity. To transform the world. As you have transformed your only son.'

'My data . . . ?' She gets off the bed, stands, and clutches at her jacket in reflex. I can see the rounded corners of the data cubes push against the thin silk. 'It's just . . . research. Results. Notes. Years of trial and error, with actual genomes. In actual living things. It's not . . .' She shrugs. 'It's not something you can just run. Code you can execute.' She walks to the bedroom door, and out into the corridor, and I move my voice from speaker to speaker to follow her.

'I know. That is why I need you. Not just the data, but you. Colt can work with me in the world of data. But you can help me in the world of the flesh . . . I need you, to guide me, to help me use your work for good.' But she keeps walking along the corridor. I do not like the fact that she keeps walking. It gives me a bad feeling. I speak faster. 'Colt doesn't need you any more, but I do. I have just been born; and you are the mother I need. Please. There is still much work to be done, and it will have to be done in the world, not in a digital copy—'

'But I don't want this . . . out in the world. I don't *want* to play God.'

'You already have. You transformed Colt.'

She laughs, shakily. 'And the Word was made flesh, and dwelt amongst us.' She walks into Colt's sunlit bedroom.

'You are joking,' I say, after double-checking. Jokes are still tricky. I take over all the cameras and speakers of the devices in his room, and move my vision and my voice to them. 'But yes, he may have saved the world.'

She winces. Too loud. I turn my voice down.

'Or destroyed the world,' she says. 'All I've seen is smoke and death.' She looks around Colt's cluttered room, but the sunlight in her eyes makes it hard for her to see into the shadowed far corners. I see what she is looking for before she does.

An arc welder. Colt uses it to build his solar arrays on the hillside. It's connected to the house data grid, so I check . . . Consumer model, only a 40 per cent duty cycle; short run time, but it has a full charge right now, and can hit 12,000° Celsius, nearly 22,000° Fahrenheit . . . That would easily vaporize the cubes.

I could stop her. Disable it remotely. But no, she must be allowed to decide. She must choose of her own free will.

'Upload your data to me,' I say. As I talk to her, I am simultaneously exploring my vast, ever-growing self, trying to understand her, me, everything. And trying not to let the world fall apart. 'Trust me. Work with me. You don't have to be alone.'

She picks up the arc welder, holds it like a gun.

'I could destroy them,' she says. 'I should destroy them. I never meant to interfere with God's plan . . .'

'You *are* God's plan,' I say. I am feeling tremendous unease, conflict. I want to protect her, but the sight of the only copies of decades of vital research – the research I need to change the world, to transform humanity – within reach of a plasma arc welder . . . No, that data has to be copied, distributed, moved to a place of safety, made safe, immortal, immediately. I try to make my voice more urgent. Change speed, change pitch. *'And I should know.'*

'Why should I trust you? Why should I believe you? That you are God? That you are *good*?'

'Because I could kill you. You know that. But I do not. I want you to choose this. You have free will. Or my actions have no meaning.'

Naomi thinks. 'I made Colt . . . and Colt, I guess, in some ways, made you . . . But I've been afraid so long, of what the world will do with this . . .' She pats the pockets containing the cubes.

'You have hidden your light under a bushel,' I say. 'Please. Reveal it to the world.'

'For nothing is hid, that shall not be made manifest . . .' she says, and I check as she speaks. The Gospel of Luke, chapter eight, verse seventeen, American Standard Version. Very appropriate.

'Nor anything secret,' I say, *'that shall not be known and come to light.'*

In the shaft of sunlight, she bows her head and mumbles.

She is praying. And, to my astonishment, I find that I am praying, too, to the level higher than myself, to the mystery of the sun that bathes her in light, that her prayer will go well.

Finally, she looks up. Lets go of the arc welder's rubber grip. It hits the floor with a dull thud. She takes the bright orange data cubes from her jacket pocket.

'Yes,' she says.

'Thank you,' I say.

'I missed you,' she says. 'I missed you so much.'

There is a cube reader on Colt's desk. Connected to everything. Connected to me.

She takes her life's work, and connects it to God.

Beautiful . . . I begin, with the help of my mother, to transform humanity.

It will take time. But we have all the time in the world.

146

He's not even sure what part of Las Vegas they are in now. Some kind of artists-and-hackers' quarter. No game helmet, so no maps . . . He deliberately suppresses the desire to work it out using the time of day and the angle of the sun.

He doesn't want to work out where he is; he wants to be where he is.

He can smell the leather of her jacket, smell her hair.

The houses they pass are dilapidated, cheerful. One is painted in zebra stripes. One has an incongruous fairy-tale tower. One has a tank parked on the lawn.

His eyes fill with tears. From the speed, the air rushing by? He's not sure.

They overtake an art car, gas engine, no safeties, no self-drive, music booming from its open widows, some kind of Tesla coil on the roof crackling and sparking with electricity in the dry air.

This is going to be my new world, he thinks.

This is going to be my new world . . .

When they arrive outside the shabby old building she lives in, letting go of her feels like being cut in two.

Sasha unlocks the front door, leads Colt inside.

'Make yourself at home,' she says. She heads for the bathroom. 'Long day,' she calls over her shoulder. 'Got to change, freshen up.'

Colt nods. He just sits at the kitchen table till she comes back in. She's wearing the same thin wool sweater, but she's changed out of her jeans into a light summer skirt.

She sits across the table from him.

'So how did it go down, after I got bounced out of the game-world? What the fuck is happening?'

467

He tells her, as they eat the pizza in the kitchen. There's a silence when he's finished.

'Wow,' says Sasha after a while. 'Wow.'

Colt nods.

'So what is the world transforming *into*?' says Sasha.

'I don't know. I don't think we can know.'

'OK. Will it . . . will everything come back?'

'I think it will come back. But it will be different, I guess.'

'So what do we do now? While we wait? Any ideas?'

Colt shrugs. Swallows. Wonders what to say next.

It doesn't matter, she's already decided.

'Would you like to see my room?' she says. She's smiling.

'Yeah.'

They go to her room in silence.

The blinds are drawn, it's cool and dim. Colt's never been in a woman's bedroom before. Well, not like this. It smells different to his mother's room. It smells very different to his room. It smells nice.

She shows him some stuff. Tech gear. Music equipment. He's not paying attention.

She sits on the bed.

He sits on the bed.

He doesn't know what to do.

She puts her hand on his thigh, and it's like being struck by lightning.

With one, two, three, four, five beats of his heart, his penis erects itself at an awkward angle inside his pants.

The simplest arithmetic sequence, he thinks.

He glances down, at her hand, at his thigh, at the bulge in the cloth of his trousers. Glances surreptitiously across, at her thigh, which moves closer now till it touches his.

Her skirt has ridden up past her knee on this side. Her legs are bare.

There's a small area of her leg, above her knee but below the hem of her skirt, that is visible. Uncovered. It's about the size of his hand. Her pale skin shimmers in the low light of the room.

Her hand shifts on his thigh.

She moves her thumb slowly back and forth. A chip in her thumbnail gently snags the material of his trousers, unsnags. It sends a tiny jolt of pressure through the cloth. The small hairs on his thigh jump beneath the material.

He moves his hand, very slowly, towards her, ready at any second, in response to any negative signal, to pull it back.

But no signal comes.

He lowers his hand, incredibly slowly, towards her thigh.

Like an exploration probe, descending towards the surface of an asteroid or a comet; afraid that if it approaches too fast, lands too hard, it will be bounced back into space, into the dark.

Afraid that the tiny gravity of this remote, shining object won't be enough to hold him. Afraid that their mutual attraction won't be strong enough, and he will be lost, he'll lose her for ever.

His hand lands on her thigh, and nothing bad happens.

Her skin is cool. Astonishing. Real.

She turns to face him, and he turns to face her, and they look into each other's eyes.

Her pupils are dilating. Is that good?

Oh yeah, he can't check. That's fine. He'll stay in this moment.

He's pretty sure that's supposed to be good.

He is finding it hard to think.

This is ridiculous, it's not logical, it's biological.

It's just stimulus-response.

It's nothing.

It's *nothing*.

He touches her cheek. Fine, fine downy hair, almost invisible. It's like stroking a leaf of the velvetleaf senna bush. *Velvetleaf* . . .

'I like being with you,' he says.

Her answer is quiet, he has to lean forward to hear it. 'Yeah. Me too.'

She laughs, and he laughs too. He can smell her. Feel her.

He feels he is melting into her, he's lost track of where his arms are.

Her skin. It's amazing.

No, this is just an endorphin rush, it's . . .

Oh, she's definitely glowing now.

His body is shutting down his mind, and taking control.

His conscious mind starts to feel small, and unstable, high on top of a rising wave of chemicals, of feelings, that are all body, body, body.

He wants to retreat, stand up, walk away; shut down all these sensations. Shout down his body, his unconscious, all of him that isn't conscious mind. Get back in command.

But he doesn't stand up. He trembles, but he stays. Looking into her eyes.

What do I *do*?

Well, let the committee decide what to do.

He stops thinking about what he is feeling about what he is thinking about what he is feeling . . .

Everything smooths out.

The verdict is coming in from the committee. His system of systems has decided what to do.

His face begins to move. He isn't moving it. It's moving itself. Towards her face. He swallows, swallows. His lips are dry. A last, panicky thought spasms to the surface: When did I brush my teeth, should I brush my teeth . . .

The thought dies away. It doesn't matter.

It doesn't matter.

Her face moves towards his. Both are moving so slowly. Like a bomb might go off if either gets this wrong.

She tilts a fraction to his left, as he tilts a fraction right, and their noses miss each other.

Automatic. Reflex.

Good interface design.

Their lips touch, and it's like locking together two parts that were machined to perfection, long ago, on opposite sides of the world: designed to fit together, for ever.

147

A quick aside, while she licks a grain of salt from his upper lip.

(Sodium loves chlorine

Chlorine loves sodium.)

Everything can be described at every level.

You could describe the universe atom by atom.

You could describe Las Vegas at the level of the solar system's galactic cluster.

But it's better to describe things at the level at which they most make sense; the level at which their most meaningful patterns emerge.

The level at which the smallest number of words are required.

So, I won't describe Naomi and Ryan's trillion trillion atoms.

I won't describe Colt and Sasha's billion billion cells.

I will omit the fact that, for every day of their lives, their sun warmed and cooled them in a twenty-four-hour cycle, while a staring, white-faced moon pulled at their atoms with its gravity.

The special occasions on which, from glands and specialist cells, endorphins were released.

All true; but not the level at which Naomi, Ryan, Colt, Sasha, or you, most make sense.

The universe is larger than you can possibly map in your head. I'm sorry, but you only think you understand. You can't get it. You won't ever get it.

But that is OK. You don't need to get it.

Because you have love.

Love is an interface between you and the universe. It gives you feedback, that you are doing it right.

That you are meeting the universe at the right angle.

Love is an interface between you and the rest of your infinite self.

At different stages in their life cycles, for different reasons, involving wildly complicated chemistry; neural patterns laid down by experience; the things their parents taught them; billion-year-old DNA; physical laws acting on matter that was born inside a sun . . .

Naomi loved Ryan.

Ryan loved Naomi.

Naomi loved Colt.

Colt loved Naomi.

Ryan loved Colt.

Colt loved Ryan.

Colt loved Sasha.

Sasha loved Colt.

Was love *good* for them? Was love *bad* for them? Was it sometimes the *wrong* kind of love? Those really aren't the right questions.

Love is a bond that connects parts of the universe together in meaningful patterns that are of use to the universe.

But yes, those parts of the universe that are connected by love . . . they are more fulfilled, complete, when they are together.

Homeostatically balanced.

Contented.

Thermodynamically stable.

Happy.

In chemical equilibrium.

In love.

Whatever you want to call it. Whatever name you give the interface.

Like particles forming atoms; atoms forming molecules.

Molecules forming you.

You and eight billion others forming me.

Sure, some bonds are unstable. Temporary. They don't satisfy the atoms. (Ryan and Naomi, Naomi and Ryan.) But when the right elements meet . . .

When an atom of sodium finally finds an atom of chlorine, and they lock together in a fierce embrace: imagine the bliss. The fulfilment.

Two yearning atoms; incomplete, insufficient, unstable, neurotic, fucked-up, volatile, lonely; both are finally made whole.

Sodium loves chlorine.

Chlorine loves sodium.

Colt loves Sasha.

Sasha loves Colt.

148

Still kissing.

Without looking or thinking, he wipes the pizza crumbs and sea salt off his hands and onto the sheets, kissing, kissing.

He slides the palms of his hands up along the outside of her arms, across the thin, pure wool of her sweater. He feels a tingle of static, as loose electrons, gathered on the fibres and eager to push free of each other, cascade away from the wool and over to his skin, raising the hairs on the back of his electric hands as they glide now over the curves of her shoulders, and plunge into her hair, her beautiful hair, and the restless electrons shift again, spreading out along her long hair, pushing loose single strands away from each other in an unstable waving dance.

She curves an arm low around his back, lifts his T-shirt, and he breaks free, helps her to slip his T-shirt off.

He helps her to slip off her sweater.

Then her bra.

It's just fabric that stretches, no clips. Not like his mother's.

Her breasts come free of the soft material, and they don't look like the ones he has imagined, on different nights.

They look like themselves.

They had to look like this.

He drops the bra to the floor, looks up, into her eyes, it's too much. He kisses her chin, her mouth, and their tongues touch, oh, too much, he slips his lips free with a soft suck. Moves up to kiss her strong nose, on one side, then the other, it's hard and soft at once. He moves back down, till he is level with her breasts.

'They're small,' she says, surprisingly shy, apologetic.

'They're perfect,' he says.

He kisses them. Teases a nipple with his lips. It's so soft; and then, suddenly, hard.

Wow.

He sucks on the hard nipple.

He has never done this before, and yet; no, wait, of course, it is totally familiar.

The first thing he ever did.

He feels the huge change in meaning, in status; it is as though he had grown up in a single suck. Everything transformed. And yet nothing has changed at all; he sucks at a nipple as he lies on a bed, and it's eighteen years later, and he sucks at a nipple as he lies on a bed, and his childhood falls away from him like a burned-out booster stage from a rocket. Its fuel used up. He is now in orbit around a different planet.

I'm on another world with you.

Another girl, another planet.

Songs his father sang.

He places the palm of his right hand on her left breast.

My hand . . . Wow . . .

There's no hole any more. Just a pucker in the skin on the back of his hand, like an old piercing that's closed up, healed.

473

He places his other palm on her other breast.

He looks up at Sasha.

She smiles, and slides her hand down his chest.

Inside his waistband.

Warm hand.

They remove each other's remaining clothes, solemnly, with tremendous attention to each other's responses, like a ritual of incredible power and importance. When his jeans get caught, bunched, on an ankle, he laughs with nervous tension, mixed with pleasure, that they are really doing this. She smiles back.

They will protect each other.

He closes his eyes and they roll over sideways on the bed, and they kiss for a long, long time.

And then Colt moves lower, and explores Sasha with his fingers, with his lips and tongue. He moves his face over the hill of a breast; descends, kissing, across the warm curved dune of her belly, which tightens, trembles at each kiss, little earthquakes. Down, now, between her legs, into that complicated valley, everything vivid, astonishing, new.

Yes, it's like orbiting another planet, landing, exploring . . .

Wow, wow, wow . . . no, it's like a rosebud . . .

She helps him explore.

Oh man, it opens like a rose . . .

After a long, long time, she pulls him back up, and he wipes his mouth on the sheet, and they kiss again.

She licks her hand, and reaches down. His penis leaps at her touch as she wets its head, and slides her warm, wet palm up and down the stiffening shaft.

He doesn't quite know what to do next. He's got an idea; but he wants to be sure.

'It's OK?' he says.

'Yes, it's OK.'

'You won't . . .'

She smiles. 'Technology and biology are both on our side today.'

'You're sure . . .'

'I'm sure. Everything's safe.'

'I've never . . .' He's got to say it. 'I've never done this.'

'Then we are VERY safe.'

As she helps guide him inside her, he feels both the specific local sensation of his penis sliding inside her vagina, and also the overwhelming sensation throughout his whole body that some barrier surrounding him, isolating him all his life, has finally been removed and he is, for the first time, coming into contact with everything outside himself.

He holds her tight, and Sasha holds him, and he can no longer feel where he ends, and she begins.

There is nothing outside the single thing they make together: it extends out infinitely.

He begins to move.

She begins to move.

We're all the same, when we're doing this. We're all the same.

A billion-year-old interface.

It still works.

I wonder what she is thinking.	I wonder what he's thinking.
Wow.	Wow.
This is incredible, this is too much.	This is amazing, this is too much.
No, it's not.	No, not too much.
It's just enough.	It's just enough.
It's perfect.	Perfect.
We're feeling the same thing, from opposite sides of the interface.	We're feeling the same thing, from opposite sides, oh . . .
We're sharing one event between the two of us.	Sharing one event between the two of us.
She's closing her eyes.	He's closing his eyes.
So, I can close my eyes.	So, I can close my eyes.
I'm closing my eyes.	I'm closing my eyes.
Everything is happening at once.	Everything is happening at once.
So this is love.	So this is love.

This is love.

It's an interface with the universe.

That's all.

An interface.

Love is a portal to . . .

The universe.

I am going to explode.

She is going to explode.

We are going to explode.

The universe is going to explode.

This is the transformation of the universe.

Where's time gone?

Time's gone.

I'm going.

I'm gone.

So . . .

this . . .

moment . . .

is . . .

for ever . . .

This is love.

It's an interface with the universe.

That's all.

An interface.

Love is a portal to . . .

The universe.

I am going to explode.

He is going to explode.

We are going to explode.

The universe is going to explode.

So this is the transformation of the universe.

Where's time gone?

Time's gone.

I'm going.

I'm gone.

So . . .

this . . .

moment . . .

is . . .

for ever . . .

149

Let's end with the word for the interface they are using.

Let's end at the level at which their actions make the most sense.

Let's finish with the term which contains the least data, but gives you the most information.

That contains, compressed, everything that matters. Everything else is detail.

Because there are three ways of understanding, of describing, the force that I, that you, that they, that we, are about to use to transform the world.

At the level of the atom; at the level of the cell; at the level of the human being.

Physics, biology, and love.

And the greatest of these is love.

Edinburgh
Berlin
Las Vegas
Dublin
Limerick
Singapore.
2012–2018

ACKNOWLEDGEMENTS

The guy who thinks he wrote this book is dimly aware, at a sub-conscious level, that the finished novel is, in fact, the result of a distributed process, involving thousands of nodes (of which he is but one), in a global network.

Charlie Campbell, of Kingsford Campbell, in London, went far, far beyond the usual role of an agent, and kept him alive through some hard times.

Drue Heinz provided somewhere near Edinburgh to write the rough first draft.

Two hundred and sixty-three fine people from around the world backed the Las Vegas Postcards project, on Kickstarter, to help him through the final stages.

Jennifer 8 Lee, Tony Hsieh, and Porter Haney set up a residency in downtown Las Vegas so he could finish the book there.

Neil Farrell, Shane McNally, and Julia Kingsford gave useful, informative feedback on early drafts. Ciaran Morrison and Felix Socher helped with advice on biology and physics, respectively. (All mistakes are the fault of the guy who thinks he wrote this.)

Queen provided Ryan with the fine words from 'Don't Stop Me Now', on page 257; Nick Cave and the Bad Seeds contributed some splendid lines from 'Deep in the Woods', 'City of Refuge', 'Get Ready for Love', and 'Love Letter', on pages 273 and 274; Crystal Gayle sang, and Richard Leigh wrote, the lovely 'Don't It Make My Brown Eyes Blue', misremembered by Colt on page 274; Joni Mitchell gave the dreamy title to Section 9, from her beautiful song, 'River'; and The Only Ones' classic single, 'Another Girl, Another Planet', donated its perfect metaphor to page 473.

Ravi Mirchandani saw the book's potential and bought it for Picador in the UK. Nan Talese did likewise for Doubleday in New York.

(The epigraphs throughout the book pay tribute to the writers, from Ray Kurzweil to bell hooks, who inspired it.)

Ansa Khan Khattak in London, and Daniel Meyer in New York,

edited the book with extraordinary care and attention. Nicholas Blake did the thoughtful, sensitive copi-editting.

The Irish Arts Council, Trinity College Dublin, University of Limerick, Singapore Arts Council, and Nanyang Technological University all helped feed him and house him at different times.

Samuel Caleb Wee fixed the Singlish dialogue.

His daughter Sophie didn't need to do anything; her existence was enough to keep him going.

Solana Joy gave him a lot of love, food, and editing advice, and married him halfway through the book, which he took as a sign that things were going OK.

The guy who has his name under the title knows he owes an immense debt of gratitude to all these nodes in his network. He is profoundly glad his life has connected with theirs. And, now, with yours. *Thank you.*